THE AUTUMN EFFECT

CASSANDRA MORTIMER

To Tim, who spent hours in a car
helping me wrangle this idea into a story.
You are my home.

PROLOGUE

I tried tilting my head to see who had grabbed me, so I would know what I was up against, but it was dark, and my body wouldn't cooperate. My limbs were too busy twisting and churning in my captor's hold, trying to get free. Now it was the inside of their elbow around my mouth as they yanked me against them. Mud streaked across my face, blurring my glasses.

I couldn't tell if it was a man or a woman. All I could discern was they were wet and cold, like they'd been waiting for me outside in the woods, and that they were so, so strong. I bit down on the flesh at my mouth, the skin damp and bitter on my tongue, and they jerked my head to the side so hard I heard something pop. My glasses flew off my face and clattered somewhere to the side.

Breath hitching with terror, I watched the car get farther and farther away from my kicking boots. The concrete scraped their soles, and then it was dirt.

Fighting and thrashing against my captor, I was able to turn my body like a crocodile in a death roll, finally surprising them enough to drop me. My knees hit the ground and my palms scraped along rocks and brambles as I attempted to crawl away.

A hand pulled at my shirt, but the cloth simply ripped under their strength. There was another sharp sting against my ribs, and my already frantic heartbeat stuttered with terror. Had that been their nails? Or a knife?

"Help!" I screamed, managing to clamber to my feet.

Not that anyone would hear me.

CHAPTER ONE

Days Earlier

If not for the old-fashioned wooden signs along this path, I was certain I would have gotten lost. The campus for Spindle River University was a sprawling mess of buildings, full of crisscrossing walkways, dense tree lines, and groupings of statues and benches tucked into peculiar alcoves. I would have used my phone to direct me to Artemio Hall, which I knew was nestled somewhere between the Old Campus Library and one of those odd statue parks, but since moving here my cell reception had been spotty at best. I reasoned it was better to get my lay of the land the natural way: by following signs and second-guessing every turn I made.

A light drizzle pricked my shoulders and a damp wind tugged at the tendrils of my hair, caressing my neck with chilled fingers. Shivering, I tugged my raincoat tighter around my middle and ducked my head, picking up speed as the mammoth brick building that was Artemio Hall came into view.

It was eerily quiet inside. My wet boots squeaking on the wooden floors was the only sound beyond a sporadic laugh from down the hall. There must have been a lounge nearby where people were having coffee or avoiding the rain, and I tried not to feel envious of their on-campus lifestyle.

This part of the building, where Professor Lewis held his office hours, was thankfully deserted. Blissfully, I was going to be the first one in line.

I shook out my coat and draped it over my arm, pulling my damp hair over one shoulder and adjusting my glasses. I put on my friendliest smile as I knocked on his door.

"Come in," said a deep male voice.

The professor in charge of the *Weekly Prowl*, the campus newspaper, was a wiry man, taller than he had any right to be, even sitting. His thinning hair was pulled into a low ponytail, and he looked vaguely sharp from all angles: pointed nose, serious eyes, and knobby elbows resting on the dark wood of his desk—which was littered with five different mugs, two of which were still full.

"Good morning!" I beamed as I shook his hand, and he humored me with a weak, preoccupied smile in return. "I'm Sadie Shaw. I'd like to join your writing staff."

"You an incoming freshman?"

He looked a bit overwhelmed at my enthusiasm, so I turned it down a notch as I replied, "No, I just transferred here after a year at the University of South Carolina."

At that, he tilted his head. "And did you work on the *Gamecock*?"

"I did." I hurried to pull my portfolio from the messenger bag hanging over my shoulder and handed it to him. "I had quite a few articles published, two of which made it to the front page."

"And as a first year..." he mused, thumbing through the pages. I could tell he was impressed, which was good. I just needed to get through this interview without him asking why I had left my last school.

"This is a smaller publication than you're used to, Ms. Shaw," he said, looking up at me.

"Please, call me Sadie. And even though you don't put out as many issues, I've looked through your catalog and I can tell you favor strong voices and a focus on local activism. I hope you'll find I excel in both."

I blinked, as charming and sweet as could be, as he raised one eyebrow. People always underestimated me, with my wavy blonde hair, square glasses, and my petite frame. I seemed more like a kindergarten teacher in the making than a hard-hitting journalist, but I'd found that a bright smile and friendly demeanor could get secrets spilled just as well as any harsh interrogation.

"Good to know." He shut my portfolio, handing it back to me. "We'll start you off with some proofreading, just so you can get a handle on the conventions we use here, though I don't think you'll need long to adjust. As a warm-up, interview an upperclassman of your choice and find me a story by the end of next week. Email it to me, and once Kim—the editor in chief—and I review it, we'll get to work on finding you a beat."

"That sounds great." I tucked the portfolio away, my hands almost shaking with excitement. "I'll get that to you right away."

"I look forward to it, Sadie," he said, nodding. Just then, there was a dim flash outside from far-off lightning that made his grin look just as sharp as his nose. I hoped that wasn't a bad omen.

Despite the dread I felt about going back out into the worsening storm, I rushed from the room and shoved my arms back into my damp coat, searching my pockets for my schedule to triple-check where I'd find my first class. I turned the corner to head back outside.

And that's when I hit him.

My shoulder collided with something firm and distractingly warm. I held out my hands without thinking, as if to stop the person from falling.

Beneath my palms I found the well-worn fabric of a blue hoodie, and the very solid chest of the guy beneath it. And he didn't feel in danger of tilting, let alone dropping to the ground.

"I'm so sorry!" I yelped, pulling my hands back from where they were—accidentally groping his chest. The hoodie was damp at the shoulders, the design on the center some mess of jagged letters I assumed was a band name.

"No worries," he said.

My heart gave an uneven thump as I looked up and met his eyes, which were a vibrant mix of green and brown—hazel, I corrected myself—and alight with humor as I stepped back. The friendliness in his expression and the heat under my hands had nearly erased the morning chill from my body.

I'd always had an innate sense that helped me make friends and romantic...*acquaintances* as I'd moved from place to place, and right now that sense was screaming. This guy and I had a spark. He was worth getting to know.

I studied his impish expression, his eyebrows angled a bit sharply at the edge, his brown hair mussed and damp from the rain as it hung slightly over his forehead. I wanted to run my fingers through that wavy hair. He was built like a wide-shouldered football player, and he had a cocky smile that turned a pair of bow-shaped lips into a curling masterpiece, with dimples appearing at both edges. His skin was tanned from the sun or some heritage I couldn't yet discern, and the strength in his arms was obvious as he easily adjusted the strap of the full backpack hanging over one shoulder. He nodded as he moved to pass me, heading down the hall, clearly uninjured from our collision. No harm, no foul.

Except, I felt like I'd been stunned.

I watched him as he walked away and clocked a *Prowlers* badge on his backpack and a metal water bottle in the side pocket. Definitely an athlete. From my research on the school, I recalled there were two sports teams that carried the same name as the newspaper: hockey and lacrosse, though I couldn't be sure which team he belonged to. When he reached the end of the hall he turned his head, looking back at me.

And then he winked.

I almost laughed. That brash bastard—he knew just how hot he was. But still, I didn't mind the view while watching him go.

Blinking myself out of whatever out-of-body experience had been brought on by one of the most attractive guys I'd ever seen in person, I shoved my schedule back in my pocket, pulled my hood up over my hair, and headed back out into the rain to make the long trek across campus to my Psychology class.

The trouble with transferring as a sophomore was that only some of my Gen Ed credits had successfully carried over. Spindle River University required a whole host of mandatory classes before I could even declare my major, which meant I'd have to suffer through Statistics to cover my math credits, Linguistics for fine arts, and Psychology for the humanities. History of American Media was the only relevant course I was able to squeeze into, and that only met one day per week, on Thursdays.

I shuffled through the damp, windy quad, wondering why I still seemed to be one of the only living souls out and about this Monday morning. There were a couple of solo cups rolling along the ground by a trash can and I took a second to throw them away, figuring there must have been a last-taste-of-freedom bash on campus this weekend. That would be the first of many parties I would miss by living off campus. I'd transferred so late that there'd been no dorm rooms left.

My dad had been generous enough to rent me a small place at the edge of town, and though it meant an almost thirty-minute drive to school, which would definitely dampen my chances of making close friendships for a while—and vis-à-vis, enjoy some frivolous parties—beggars couldn't be choosers.

After making my way across the grounds, I was surprised to find my Psychology course oddly fascinating, for a Gen Ed. The professor was a young woman who asked us all to call her Nina. Her brown hair flowed down her back, and she wore a long skirt under a drapey blouse, with bangles on her wrists. Her whole body jingled with bells as she wrote on the white board various "pleasure types" that the students in class were yelling out. She used profanity and everything. The girl sitting beside me screamed, "Role-playing the entire script of Shrek!" which had most of the room in hysterics, and when the girl turned my way, I felt a second small, subtle spark. Another person I'd get along with. I made a note to keep sitting next to her.

For homework, Nina assigned us each to pick one of the kinks she'd written on the board and explore the psychological and evolutionary reasons behind each pleasure. I decided on bondage, as it seemed like it would be an entertaining study topic. Besides, as an intrepid reporter, I did love doing research.

Despite the sodden start, this day was going impeccably well, and after I scarfed down a sandwich at the campus café, I was off to Linguistics.

Where my Psych class had only a few dozen students, my Linguistics class was huge. It was held in a stadium room with over a hundred seats, and, though I was early, already a dozen were filled. I made my way to the middle of the room, settling into one of the theatre-like chairs, and pulled out my laptop to start a new notes file. There were four words already written on one of the blackboards at the front of the room: "syntax, semantics, morphology, phonology." I typed them out into the doc before googling each one.

"Isn't it a bit early to be showing up the rest of us?" asked a voice to my right.

I looked up to find the guy from this morning carefully lowering himself into the seat beside me—as if he was sore, or maybe worried he'd break the chair. His damp hair had dried and now sat in soft, textured waves pushed back from his face.

He smelled like dark coffee and some kind of spicy cologne I immediately wanted to buy bottles of, but before I let the sight and scent of him derail my thoughts, I shrugged my shoulders and answered, "Who said I was going to use the knowledge to show off? Maybe I just hoard information quietly, like a dragon of dialectology."

"Dialectology?" he asked, smirking.

"The study of dialects."

"I gathered that much." His smile crinkled his eyes a bit, his big frame already heating the space beside me. "Well, either way, I'm glad that body check earlier didn't rile you."

"I'm not easily riled," I teased back.

"No, you're not, are you?"

He twisted his body toward me, pulling out a laptop that had seen better days. It was scratched all over and littered with a bunch of stickers I felt were probably covering even more scuffs. He turned on his computer and then held out his hand. "I'm Jamie, by the way."

"Sadie," I replied, as I took his hand.

His palm was hot in mine, and there was the strangest tingling sensation where we touched, like my hand was on the verge of falling asleep. I had bad circulation already, and this shift to a cooler climate on a rainy day was already messing with me, but the tingling in my hand made me want to snuggle in closer to Jamie's side.

I was a sucker for a warm, athletic body, and I wouldn't be ashamed of it.

"So, are you hoarding linguistic info to major in English?" he asked. "Or just here for the easy A like me?"

"Is it an easy A? I just picked it to fill a hole." I paused. "A credit's hole, I mean."

Jamie's smile got wider, flashing me those dimples again and showing off his straight, white teeth. His shoulders had stiffened as he worked to hold in a laugh. I had a feeling it would have been one of those rowdy, larger than life laughs, and I was a little disappointed I didn't get to hear it.

"Words do fill holes," he said eventually, still sounding a bit strained. He pulled the metal water bottle from his bag and took a swig, the Adam's apple at his throat catching my attention as it bobbed with each swallow.

"So do other things," I replied.

Jamie choked on his water and coughed into his fist, trying to keep quiet as the room grew more crowded. He turned his head my way, incredulous and seemingly impressed by my daring, but before he could give me what I was sure would have been a very saucy response, the professor walked in, and our flirtatious exchange was put to an end.

Spark *confirmed*.

The lecture was a long, in-depth outline of everything we would cover during the semester, and apparently the topics were going to stay very basic. It seemed Jamie was right, and this class actually would be an easy A, which was a relief since it meant I could spend more time working on my pieces for the *Weekly Prowl* and less time studying. Trading barbs with Jamie while he peeked over at my notes and bumped my knee with his also didn't hurt.

Even though it was just to fulfill some credits, there was a very real chance Linguistics might become my favorite class.

Despite my fun and successful first day on campus, my mood instantly darkened on my drive home. The trek to my new apartment was a nightmare.

It took twenty minutes to get out of the student garage, and then I had to traverse unfamiliar roads in a heavy downpour. My wet hair was dripping down the inside of my jacket, giving me goosebumps, and my car—a black Buick my dad had bought for me as a sweet sixteen present to apologize for making us move, *again*—had lately developed some heating issues and couldn't compete with the unusually cold September weather. I missed South Carolina.

No, I admonished myself. This was a new start, a fresh page. I could make friends, impress my teachers, and start down the path to my dream career. I could survive a little New England dreariness for that. I'd just have to keep a blanket in the car.

As I pulled into the driveway of the little cottage that served as my temporary housing, my body tilted into full-on shivers. With the sky as dark as it was, and the forest creeping along the edges of the property, what had seemed a somewhat-charming chalet by a pond this morning now appeared to be a menacing haunted house. The occasional lightning that streaked between the clouds wasn't helping.

The cottage was two stories tall, with a sharply angled black roof and lots of windows. This morning the living room had been a sauna from all the sunlight, but I realized that in the dark it would put me on display to anyone driving by. Not that many people would, since this was the edge of Spindle River's city limits, and only the train tracks and a few run-down businesses were further south along the route. Still, I would have to buy some curtains. The place already gave me the willies at night, with all the strange sounds of the surrounding wildlife. The last thing I needed was anything to add to the potential creep-factor.

I pulled the hood of my coat back up, grabbed my bag, and ran to the stoop. My cold fingers fumbled with my keys as I struggled to remember which one was for the front door. The landlord had left me three—one for the front door, one for the kitchen's back patio doors, and one I wasn't entirely sure about yet.

Beyond the sheet of heavy rain and the sweeping light of passing cars, something off to the side caught my attention. I looked to the left of the Buick and saw a flicker of movement in the tree line. It was probably an owl or some other bird fluttering in the leaves, I reasoned, but then a twig snapped. It was too loud to be something as small as a bird, especially over the sound of the rain.

My pulse started racing and my hands trembled, but I managed to get the door open. Swinging it shut fast, I locked it behind me, the smell of damp earth subsiding into floor polish and vanilla-scented room spray. The relief was acute, as if I'd narrowly escaped death.

Putting my back against the door, I took a slow, deep breath. Obviously, I was still settling into this new house, and this new town. What was strange is that I'd lived in eight different states over the last thirteen years, ever since my mom had left and my dad needed to start taking me with him on his months-long consulting jobs. Usually, I had no problem adjusting to a new space. After all, Dad had always been at work, and I got used to taking care of myself. But something about the storm must have triggered a latent anxiety about being on my own. I never did like thunder, or the threat of a power outage.

Turning on the lights, I scanned the boxes strewn throughout the living room, still mostly yet to be unpacked, and made a mental note to finish setting up my things soon. Maybe then this house would feel more like a home and less like a spooky cabin.

My rock collection was neatly displayed on the built-in shelves along the small dining area, next to my desk and computer chair. There was a stone picked for every new place we'd lived, aligned from left to right by age. When I was fourteen, I'd found a particularly nice chunk of smoky quartz in a quarry by the house Dad and I had stayed in, but the rest were just normal rocks. However, to me, they all had their own special value. There was a jagged piece of calcite from Missouri and a square piece of sandstone from Nevada. I remembered finding each one in this life of musical chairs I seemed to be living.

I picked up the thin slice of striped mica I'd picked up in South Carolina. I had thought that would be my home for a solid four years, the longest I'd ever lived anywhere, but I had to go and screw that up.

With a sigh, I returned the mica back to its place on the shelf and headed into the kitchen. To escape the uneasy, maudlin turn my mind was taking, I played dance music from my phone while putting together some dinner. I figured my anxiety had to be caused by the way the wind was whistling along the windows, and how the gloomy pond looked like gray sludge in the dark. Weeping willows stooped along the edge of the water, swaying like hundreds of curling snakes.

But even with the music blaring, I couldn't ignore the feeling that somehow, something was...off. Almost like I was being watched.

CHAPTER TWO

I was thankful to find the next morning sunny and clear, so I opted to move my desk chair beside the glass patio doors to have my morning coffee. The backyard was spacious: a couple wicker chairs sitting near the house at the top of an expansive lawn that sloped slightly downhill to an oval-shaped pond marked by a small dock at one end. It would be a pretty quick boat ride to go from one end to the other, but perhaps the pond had been bigger once. Either way, in the morning light it was utterly charming. Cattails swayed in the gentle breeze along one end of the water, and a whole host of white and blue flowers bloomed along the other, their petals opening wide in the morning sun. I could hear the muffled croaks of frogs from my seat, as well as the chirps of some kind of summer insect. It was so peaceful—I felt silly for being unsettled the night before.

Today would be another rousing day of general education classes, but after that I planned to make it my mission to find an upperclassman to interview for my *Weekly Prowl* piece. If I saw Jamie again, I'd have to ask what year he was. Or even what major. I wouldn't hate the opportunity to spend more time with him.

With a pep in my step, I dressed with more attention than I had yesterday, pulling an army-green sweater from one of the boxes I *still* hadn't managed to unpack last night, and tucking the front into a pair of black skinny jeans. I matched them with black boots that gave my short frame another inch of height and told myself it wasn't just for Jamie. Since it wasn't raining today, I would have a better chance to make some new first impressions, either with sophomores I could befriend, or with any other attractive members of the male species who might happen to have hazel eyes and floppy hair.

The thing about moving so often growing up is that relationships for me had always been fast and fiery. I never knew how long my dad would be at whatever company had hired him for his operations consulting expertise, so I could be at a new school for a few weeks, a few months, or a whole year. It meant saying yes to dates—because why not enjoy a good meal, some good company, and some potentially great physical moments—and not being too concerned with how things might end. I'd be leaving soon enough that the consequences were never too prominent in my mind. Suffice it to say, I was fine with making my interest known, but also with keeping my options open. It wasn't always the most ful-filling, but it was making the best out of my situation. And who knows, if I managed to stay for longer than a year here, maybe my days of quick flings were over.

Checking out my reflection once more in the hall mirror before head-ing out to my car, I reminded myself the intention here was to *last* at Spindle River U. That was the goal. This wouldn't be a repeat of South Carolina.

After all, how many scandals could I uncover at a rural college town like this, anyway? Hopefully not too many. Or at least...none that made staying impossible. I breathed in the cooling scent of petrichor and felt my steps lighten.

As I climbed into the Buick, something dark caught my attention, and I realized my passenger-side rearview mirror was coated in mud. It was thick enough that I couldn't see anything on that side, so I rolled down the window, leaned over to my glove compartment, and pulled out a few leftover napkins to wipe it off.

The strange thing, though, was there was no mud anywhere else. As I scrubbed the dried muck from the mirror, I looked down at the door and my hood. Both were clean. I must have brushed up against something on the drive the night before, I reasoned. Either that, or I'd skated through a thick puddle. Maybe after class I'd drive through a car wash if I could find one, in case there was a bunch of mud on the undercarriage.

My only class of the day was Statistics, which was apparently housed in the Janus Building near the north campus entrance. I found it easily enough and spent some time on a bench outside enjoying the sunshine and using my phone to search for information on the professor I was about to meet. What could I say? I really liked research. It turned out Professor Kirillovich was originally from Novosibirsk, Russia, also taught Cryptography here, and—according to *Rate My Professor*—had a habit of telling jokes during class that no one understood. That would, at least, keep what I expected to be an insufferably dry Stats class partially entertaining.

I looked up as the trickle of students in the quad became a steady flow; there were groups of two or three meandering by, with the odd student pausing to look around and check their phone in a way that pegged them as a freshman. A pair of girls were handing out fliers for a campus book club, and there was a group of students in matching gray outfits practicing what looked like a jazz routine. Then my eyes found him in the crowd, zeroing in like it's what they'd been waiting for all along.

Those angled eyebrows were low over his hazel eyes as he walked with purpose down the path. He was in a black T-shirt today, with a pair of thick headphones pushing down that unruly hair. I could see the glint of a silver chain winking at me from the collar of his shirt.

He must have felt me staring, because at that moment, Jamie looked my way. I grinned at him, hoping he would come over. He returned a closed-mouth smile, the dimples bracketing his mouth making an appearance, but he continued forward, his hands tucked into his pockets and his long stride eating up the ground. Maybe he was running late.

Or maybe he simply wasn't interested, my inner critic whispered.

Shaking off the slight sting of disappointment, I started scanning the other students, looking for someone I'd have that uncanny spark with that signaled we'd have an engaging conversation. I searched the crowd for someone who seemed lost in thought, or carried a lot of books, or who had a familiar face. I'd been to enough high schools that, for all I knew, a student I'd met before now matriculated here. But no one stood out as a potential target for my interview piece, so after another handful of minutes I went inside.

The Statistics room was surprisingly small. There were about twenty desks in neat rows facing a white board that took up the entirety of the front wall, and most of the seats were already taken. Apparently, I had spent too long people-watching.

Jamie sat near the back of the room, shoulders a bit hunched.

The desks around him were all taken, with only a few spaces at the front and middle available, so I aimed one more quick smile his way—just to be friendly—and took a desk near the front.

My research had been correct in that Kirillovich definitely thought of himself as a comedian, but out of three different jokes he told while drawing equations and graphs on the board, I think I understood only one of them. Maybe. A few students chuckled half-heartedly, and he muttered about everything making more sense in Russian, but other than that the class was just as boring as I'd feared. I spent most of my time thinking about the interview I was supposed to conduct, and what kind of lean I'd want on the article. A profile could be interesting with the right subject, but unless they came from a unique background or were some sort of savant, an angle was usually necessary. Maybe I could dig into some past news stories about the school, see if there was any history of hazing or campus crime, and find a student who may be connected to the entities involved. See if things had changed, and if so, how.

However, when class ended and we all ambled from the classroom, my entire focus switched back to Jamie.

I didn't know why I was so invested in getting him to talk to me. He had been welcoming yesterday, sure, and there was an obvious attraction there, but I'd had that before and had always been able to move on without any trouble. It's just...every time I saw him, there was this pause in my heartbeat. A moment that made my entire body halt for half a second, like...*oh*.

So, did I follow him from Statistics to see where he was headed, like a complete stalker? Sort of. But to be fair, he was headed toward the campus café, which is where I'd be buying my lunch for the second day in a row anyway, so I wasn't exactly following him.

Watching his easy lope across the grounds, I decided to stop ignoring the voice in my head begging to talk to him. After all, my instincts about connecting with people were rarely wrong. *Only my proclivity for writing about them*, that same voice taunted. I waved it away.

"Hey," I said, catching up to Jamie. "Are you an upperclassman?"

He looked over to me and pulled his headphones off one ear, slowing his walk. "Sorry, what?"

"Are you an upperclassman?" I repeated. "I want to join the newspaper staff here—the *Weekly Prowl*? And I need to pick a random upperclassman to interview as my first assignment."

"And you want to pick me?" His shoulders tilted toward me; they were a bit leaner than they'd seemed under his sweatshirt yesterday. The definition in his arms was impressive, though, and I couldn't help but imagine how they'd feel wrapped around me. I bet he gave amazing hugs.

"Why not?" I shrugged, trying to get my thoughts in order. "We have class together, and it will give me a chance to get to know you better." Looking up at him sweetly, I could see that interest there again—that spark. I caught the hint of his charming smile, those straight white teeth flashing briefly.

"It will be quick, I promise," I added.

Jamie hesitated for a second, which only hurt my ego the tiniest bit, but then he nodded. "Okay, sure. I'm a junior, so I guess I qualify."

"Great. It would be such a big help to me, I really appreciate it."

"No problem," he said, lifting one shoulder.

"Are you free now? Or do you want to meet up later?" We had reached the café and I realized he was continuing through the campus, but I slowed down enough near the door that he stopped.

"I have to go to work now, but I can meet you Thursday after class?" he offered.

"That's perfect. We can do it here and I'll even buy you a coffee."

This time, he answered my smile in full, reminding me more of the playful banter we'd had yesterday. "Looking forward to it."

"Me too," I replied, and in a moment of daring I brushed my fingertips over his arm, the warmth of his bare skin sending a tingle through me. "It'll be fun. Besides, I'll take any excuse for a vanilla latte. Something sweet, you know?"

With a turn, I waved over my shoulder and walked into the café.

Always leave them wanting more.

My steps practically bounced with triumph and the possibility of a good flirtation in the works, but I managed to keep my cool. When I reached the counter to order, I peeked behind me to see him walking away, while also doing a quick check over his shoulder.

Now I was really looking forward to that interview.

***

After lunch I went home and finished unpacking to keep my productivity-high going. I set up my bedroom in the only room upstairs, put up actual curtains, tucked all my clothes neatly into the closet, and started shopping online for a cheap coffee table and chairs to fill the near-empty living room.

It would have been nice if this place had come furnished beyond the short, pleather couch and single side-table the previous tenants must have abandoned, since I didn't own much furniture myself, but nothing could beat the view. From every window it was either the colorful break of early fall foliage, the trees just beginning to fade into yellow or burst into orange, or the gently-rippling pond out back, so I couldn't complain—spooky wildlife sounds aside. And actually...I should've been doing some excessive thanking right about now.

Dialing my dad's number, I sat at my desk by the kitchen and stared out at the pond, waiting for him to answer, but it rang several times until his voicemail picked up.

"Hey Dad, it's me," I said, tone bright and cheery. "Just wanted to let you know I'm finally all settled into the apartment and it's absolutely gorgeous. Thanks again for finding it for me. I've been to a few classes now. The school seems nice, and I might have already made a friend! No scandals or drama to report so far. Hope Texas is sunny, and the job isn't too rough. Remember not to scowl too much and scare them! Okay, love you, talk to you later, bye."

I wasn't surprised he didn't pick up; he was always like that for the first few days at the start of a new position, though he did try to check in a couple times a week. He talked me through the process of his job once—cataloging all the different positions in a company, the supply chain, and the calendar of their high and low demands, and then reorganizing everything from the ground up for ultimate efficiency. It sounded stressful to me. And even though I imagined myself one day traveling to far-off lands and interviewing famous politicians or prominent figures, at least that sounded...fun. What I loved most was finding a good story where it was least expected, consequences be damned.

Dad's job did have one major benefit though, which was the money he made. I never wanted for anything growing up. I got the newest phones, could go shopping for new clothes whenever I wanted, and was given a generous allowance. On my sixteenth birthday, Dad gifted me the Buick, and when we stayed in one place long enough for me to make good friends, he was fine paying for any fun adventures we wanted to have: an indoor skydiving lesson when I was fourteen, and even a beach house for a week the summer I turned eighteen. He just...wasn't around a lot as a result. But, that's how I became so independent, which would serve me well as a reporter, I reasoned. At least it helped me stay sane in this empty house.

I put on my music, got to cleaning up all the now-empty boxes, and spent the night writing probing and analytical questions to surprise Jamie with on Thursday.

CHAPTER THREE

When Wednesday morning rolled around, I spent some time researching my Psychology pleasure topic, finding a surprising number of articles that outlined various configurations for intricate rope-play, and then got ready for class. Again, I found myself primping a bit more than usual, taking my time putting on a bit of makeup. I'd forgotten how much fun it could be dressing up for someone, even if it was just a flirt buddy.

In Psychology, Nina had us pair up with whoever was seated near us to explain our research topics and assist with delving into "emotionally mature questions regarding the subject," making our upcoming papers more well-rounded.

I was partnered with a girl named Lynne who had bob-length black hair and looked cozy in a baggy sweatshirt over galaxy-print yoga pants. She was the one who had shouted about role playing Shrek the class before.

"My topic is boring," she said as soon as she introduced herself. "I don't know what to write about it other than obviously people who like to be watched have some issues."

"You picked voyeurism, and you think that's *boring*?" I laughed.

She laid her head down on her crossed arms. "All the articles I could find were so clinical."

"Well...what if you did some comparisons? Like to performance art? Or showmanship for something like singers or actors? You could even use images to compare body language between different forms of expression like that," I suggested.

At this, she perked up, seemingly more awake. "Well, at least it would take up some page space if I threw in a few pictures. That's a good idea."

I lifted one shoulder. "I do what I can."

She smiled at me, and then started taking half-hearted notes on some loose notebook paper she kept in a folder.

"But still," I added, "I feel like you must live a pretty wild life on campus if you think writing a paper about voyeurism is dull. Maybe you should have stuck to Shrek after all."

She laughed and I felt that spark between us flash like a tiny firework. I liked to imagine it was the universe giving me a little push forward. Lynne was someone I knew I'd like, right off the bat. It had yet to steer me wrong.

"You live off campus?" she asked, after a minute of scribbling in her notebook pages.

"Yeah, in an apartment on the southern edge of the city."

"Wow, that's a sweet deal. I would kill for some privacy. My roommate is a Musical Theatre major who practices her scales in the most..." And that was all it took. Instead of working on my paper, I spent the next forty minutes learning all about Lynne. She grew up in Vermont with two younger brothers, had spent most of high school playing video games and dreaming about designing them, and found most things unrelated to said video games to be "tedious." She invited me to her dorm to play the game she was working on, and I took down her number to text her with dates later. Suddenly, my day didn't revolve entirely around the one guy I would be sitting next to in an hour; I had actually made good on what I'd told my dad about making a friend, and I was looking forward to seeing the fantasy puzzle game Lynne was so proud of.

But sure enough, as soon as class ended, my brain reverted right back to Jamie. Would he be reserved today? Or full of jokes and charm? Would he flash those dimples at me? Tap his knee against mine?

I sat in the same row of the Linguistics class' stadium-seating, waiting for him to walk into the room. And damn, did he not disappoint.

He was wearing a long-sleeve navy shirt with a shark face on it that read "I'm Jawesome." It was snug over his impressive arms—which somehow seemed even more defined than yesterday—and as soon as he saw me, he smiled, mouth wide and bracketed by those adorable dimples. His hair flounced a bit with each step as he headed up the stairs towards me.

"Hey Sadie, miss me?" he said as he sat beside me, pulling out his computer. Again that comforting warmth that radiated from him seemed to reach out to me, better than any space heater. It seeped into every inch of my right side, teasing me to come closer.

I smirked. "So much. I had all this linguistic knowledge burning a hole in my pocket and I honestly couldn't wait to share it."

"Ah, more pre-class research?" he asked.

"Yup. Did you know Papua New Guinea has over 800 unique languages?"

He stilled, looking over to me with one eyebrow raised. "You don't say? Man, I really hope there are some group projects in this class, because I know whose coattails I'm riding."

"If you're lucky."

"Speaking of lucky," he began. I looked up from my laptop to find him watching me, those hazel eyes locked on mine and making my cheeks turn a rosy hue. "I'd consider myself lucky if I could get your number. Maybe...take you out sometime?"

Instead of immediately shouting yes like I wanted to, I let the moment drag on, enjoying every second of his attention.

"Any place in particular?" I finally asked. We still had our interview planned for tomorrow, but I guessed he wanted something a bit more defined.

"I've lived in Spindle River all my life; I know all the best places," he said with confidence.

"Well, I *am* new here."

"See? I could be your tour guide. Take you to see the sights. There's a park that overlooks the old riverbed, and downtown there's a historical section with lots of old shops and weird buildings. Something tells me you'd probably do some pre-date research on them, but I'd still tell you what I know."

At that point, the professor walked in and the people around us started to quiet. I pulled open my notes and whispered from the corner of my mouth, "Sure, sounds fun. It's a date."

Halfway through the lecture Jamie slid his phone over to me and I put my number in, only for him to immediately text me.

Jamie: *how about tonight?*

Wow, I guess he really didn't want to wait until tomorrow.

Me: *I could do that.*

Jamie: *I have hockey practice after this but come to the rink at 6?*

Ah, a hockey player. His build and swagger made more sense now, and I could easily picture him as a bruiser. I didn't know too much about the sport, but I had seen a couple of games in high school with my friend Amy. She'd been crushing on one of the players, and I didn't blame her—it was a fun, violent sport, and the guys playing it all had this intense aura around them like no one could get in their way once they were flying over the ice. They were fit, disciplined, and had goals—what wasn't to like? Except maybe the tendency to get hit in the face with pucks and potentially lose a tooth or two.

Jamie appeared to have all his teeth.

Me: *I can make that work ;)*

The rest of class was a blur as I fought the desire to do a deep dive into Spindle River U's hockey team: its roster, stats, history, and any information I could glean on one of its junior-year players.

Jamie winked at me as we separated after class. "See you later."

The words were full of promise and a hint of heat; more than a simple goodbye, his words were an invitation, and I was happy to RSVP.

Since I had no real plans for the next couple hours, I headed to the Old Campus Library. It was pretty empty, but maybe students weren't yet driven to abandon their rooms for a more serious study space this early in the semester. And this place *was* serious. And beautiful. The stacks were too tall for me to reach the top shelf, and most of the windows on the west side were covered in stained glass depicting fractal patterns that muted the sunset while painting warm designs on the dark wooden floors. The light just peaked through the stacks, making their shadows stretch into slender lines.

Other than a librarian at a circular desk ahead, and one or two other students wandering through the shelves, the place was as quiet as a graveyard.

Which made it a perfect place to give in to my covert desires and research the shit out of Jamie.

The hockey team roster and stats were easy enough to find. The Spindle River Prowlers were a surprisingly good team. They were Division II, whatever that meant, and they had a history of winning, according to last year's ranking. Jamie's full name was listed as Jameson "Jamie" Barreto. He was a defenseman, 6'1", 202 lbs., Major: Undeclared. Not much else was listed for each player, but his photo did him justice. While his face was solemn—no hint of a smile or those dimples present—there was still somehow a glint of mischief in his expression. Maybe it was the tilt of his eyebrows or a glimmer in his eyes, but he looked seconds away from laughing.

Trying to remember the money this education was costing my father; I spent the remainder of my time working on class assignments. I drafted an outline for my bondage paper and started the bibliography, and then worked on the Statistics homework that was due tomorrow.

When I ran out of motivation for homework, I pulled up the campus map on my phone—thankful to have connected to the library Wi-Fi so I didn't have to deal with spotty reception—and made my way to the rink.

The sun was close to setting and a brisk wind followed me through a tree-lined lane, but my beloved wooden signs made it easy enough to head toward the Silenos Arena. My hair tangled around my face as an unruly gust pushed at my back. Just as I brushed the strands away, the light posts along the lane all clicked on at once, startling me. They hummed with old electricity, their orange light turning the gray concrete path into a gold-tinted road. It would have been picturesque if the sound of them buzzing wasn't so disturbing. They were loud enough that I couldn't hear my own steps, let alone anyone who might be behind me.

The thought had me checking over my shoulder, and then feeling foolish. There was just something about this town that had my nerves frazzled.

The massive circular arena rose up in front of me, the facade nothing but frosted glass. It was obviously one of the newer constructions on campus, compared to all the old brick buildings where classes were held. The arena had lit, digital billboards on either side of the entrance listing upcoming games and events on the right, and an image of the mascot—a black cat with royal-blue stripes that reminded me of a saber-toothed tiger—snarling aggressively on the left.

I walked inside to the scent of stale popcorn and the sounds of blades slashing over the ice echoing in the chilly entry. There was no one behind the ticket counter and the concession stands were closed, so I walked through the lobby and made my way to one of the open double doors, light pouring onto the linoleum from within.

Practice was still going on. A group of over a dozen players—geared up in dark-blue-and-white uniforms, their names embossed in midnight black—were running some kind of drill where they sprinted from one side of the rink to the other. A few of them moved in sync, the leaders of the group, and the rest were struggling to keep up. I could hear some of them panting from the top of the stands, and I wondered how long they'd been at it.

Pulling out my phone, I took a couple quick pictures, thinking I might need one for the feature on Jamie, and made my way down the steps to sit closer to the plastic partition between the stands and the ice.

My gaze caught on the name Barreto above the number 26, one of the leaders, and it was a wonder I hadn't picked him out of the group immediately. He moved like a beast, his legs darting in sharp angles, eating up the ground beneath him, arms pumping.

A whistle blew and the group halted, some of the guys leaning on bent knees, and the whistle blew two more times.

As one, half the players left the ice and the remaining ten were handed sticks from a member of uniformed staff at the bench. With barely a break to recover from the sprints, the players skated out to one of the circles painted on the ice, and the game was on.

Jamie stayed back at first, watching two players fighting for the puck, and then without warning, he struck. Slamming one of the guys into the boards, the reverberation of which rattled the partition the entire length of the rink, he used his skate to block their stick and battered at the puck until it was freed. Shooting it to the teammate who waited behind him, he spun, racing ahead to back them up as they skated toward the opposite goal.

He was an absolute menace.

I watched him smash four other players into the boards as practice went on. He was clearly an enforcer. I would bet my entire future career that he was one of the main fighters of the team, considering the way he whipped his powerful body around the arena. Like he was the team's fist, swinging on their behalf.

The coach, a young man with a mustache that didn't fit his round face, shouted some encouragement here and there, but mostly critiques I didn't understand. Things like, "go for the backcheck," and "play high to slow down breakaways." That shrill whistle sounded one last time and the players immediately relaxed. The ones still at the bench tapped their sticks against the boards as a form of applause to end the practice, which I thought was adorable.

I watched as Jamie made his way to the bench and took off his helmet, his hair a damp mess along his forehead. He chugged from a water bottle, spraying a bit of it over his face, and then pulled off a glove to run his hand over his hair. The sight was...arresting.

I struggled to keep my mouth from dropping open.

That's when he saw me. His grin was a mile wide as he skated over to me, the rest of his teammates heading down into the locker rooms.

"Couldn't wait to see me, huh?" he teased. "Like what you saw?"

I had to say, with the way those pads fit over his muscles, and the added inch or two of height from his skates, he could have been a Viking. Some powerful warrior, larger than life. And I sure as *hell* liked it.

"You were brutal," I said approvingly, and I meant it.

"Barreto!" Called the coach, and Jamie turned his head. "A word."

Jamie sighed, looking back at me. "Wait here for me?" he asked. "I have to go deal with something and take a quick shower. Then we just gotta drop off my brother and you'll have me all to yourself."

"Sounds good." I said, leaning forward in my seat and trying my best to memorize how he looked now versus the cleaned-up version I'd see shortly. Would there still be that pink tint to his cheeks and nose? Would the energy in his expression be just as playful? "I can't wait to interview you about this."

"Kinky." He winked, then skated off.

I watched the coach pull him into some private discussion, both of their faces turning sour. Was he getting scolded for being too physical? For talking to me? Either way, after a moment Jamie nodded, lowering his big shoulders on a forced exhale, and meandered past him to the changing rooms.

I quickly googled "backcheck, college hockey" on my phone while I waited, and read up on some of the rules for hitting other players against the boards, wondering if this exposé was about to become an indictment of violence in the sport.

Someone entered the door behind me, their shoes making a quiet *shuff* sound against the stone steps, and I looked up to find...

Jamie?

"How did you..." I started, looking from the bench on the ice to the door at the top of the steps. He'd only been gone for five minutes.

Jamie's hair was dry, headphones hanging around his neck. A silver chain rested over a black button-up shirt he wore with dark jeans. There was no way he had showered, changed, dried, and made it around the arena so fast.

We just gotta drop off my brother, he'd said.

Shit.

A brother. An identical brother.

And this is the one I'd spoken to yesterday about the interview. The one who's arm I'd touched. I struggled to recall all my interactions with Jamie, wondering if any of them weren't with the hockey player who'd just skated off, and were with this guy instead.

Our eyes met and I could see the minute he realized our encounter after Statistics and this meeting today were related. I was waiting in the arena—to meet Jamie. His hazel eyes dimmed with something like disenchantment as he halted on the concrete stairs.

Was he as stunned as I was?

"You're twins," I said aloud. I felt foolish, and yet also offended, like I'd been purposefully tricked.

"Unfortunately, yes," the guy who was *not* Jamie replied.

CHAPTER FOUR

After a pause, he continued down the steps, his movements jerky and slow. I got the distinct feeling he didn't want to talk to me, but didn't know what else to do, so he forced himself closer.

"You didn't mean to ask me about that interview...did you?" he asked.

I shook my head, struck silent as I continued to sort through what I thought I knew about Jamie, and separate those details into two mental columns.

He nodded. "That makes sense." Something in his tone was solemn, and despite the indifferent expression he wore, tinted with good-natured exasperation, I couldn't help but worry I'd hurt him.

"I mean, I would still interview you," I hurried to say, as if coming back to myself. "I *will* interview you. You're not Jamie, but it's not like I know him that well either, you know? I just have a class with him, and I thought he was you, or you were him, and I figured it would be a good chance to learn more about..."

"About him."

"Or about you!" I offered. "We *do* have statistics together, don't we?"

He nodded again.

"Then you're still an upperclassman, and I still need to interview a student for an assignment to get on the newspaper staff. Why can't it be you?"

The guy glanced across the rink, his grip on the backpack over his shoulder twisting as he deliberated. This was a strange apology—and I wasn't even sure I needed to *be* apologizing—but I felt bad for flirting with him at the café and then making him feel like I hadn't meant it. I mean, I didn't know anything about him, but he was still attractive—just as attractive as his brother, obviously. They were twins.

Did that make me shallow? Enough to flirt, sure. But I never wanted to make someone feel like...less.

"I may have asked you, thinking you were Jamie," I clarified, "but that doesn't mean I don't want to know you, um..." I reached toward him to let him fill the space.

"Brendan," he offered. Reluctantly.

Twins going to the same college could be an interesting story, part of my mind whispered, especially good-looking twins. And while Brendan was the same height as Jamie, I could now see that maybe he was a bit leaner. Or, I just couldn't stop picturing Jamie in those hockey pads. I imagined the photo that could accompany the story; it would be the two of them looking at each other, as if through a mirror. What if I interviewed them both? That would definitely be worth Professor Lewis's time. I know *I* was curious to learn more about them. The school would be, too.

"Please, sit." I gestured to the plastic seat beside me. "While we wait for your...brother, you can tell me about yourself."

The cool air of the arena slowly seeped into my skin. I rubbed my hand over my opposite arm to stay warm as he sat beside me. I needed to move around a bit soon or I'd become an icicle.

Brendan reached into his backpack to pull out a black sweatshirt.

"Cold?" he asked, offering it to me.

I waved it away, though I found the offer very sweet. "Nah, I'll be fine as soon as I'm out of here in a few minutes. Thank you, though." Clearing my throat, I angled myself toward him, determined to show him I wasn't passing him over for Jamie, and that his promise to me earlier to be interviewed mattered. "So, Brendan, what's your major? What are you into?"

"Is this for the article you're writing?" he responded. "Or do you just want to know?"

"Can't it be both?" I smiled, doing my best to be charming, but he looked at me with a certain wariness that bothered me. It made me wonder how often he'd been overlooked. If his brother was a prominent hockey player, did that mean he was the twin in the shadows? Or did he have his own way to shine?

Brendan leaned back, his gaze sweeping over the empty rink once more as a side door opened and a Zamboni began cleaning the ice. "I'm majoring in Economics."

"Okay, and what do you plan on using SRU's fine education in Economics to do?"

"Make money," he answered, voice gruff.

"Sincere, I like it. But I'm sure you could make money with a whole bunch of different degrees—why that one?"

He turned to face me, his eyebrows pinched with annoyance. "Look, I know you wanted to interview Jamie. You don't have to ask me these things."

"Hey, I'm a reporter of my word." I leaned forward, putting my palm on his knee. A tingling in my fingers and a flutter in my chest clued me in to that ever-fleeting *spark* I was chasing. Brendan was someone I could connect with—someone I'd enjoy being around—if only he'd let me. "I asked you to spill your guts and you agreed. I promised to make it quick and buy you a coffee. I still plan on keeping my end of the deal. How about you?"

He cleared his throat, something warming in his features. A tick of his lips, maybe. The roar of the Zamboni vibrated through the ground while I waited anxiously for his answer.

"Jamie and I, we don't come from money," he said, eventually.

I noticed he didn't move, barely even breathed, and I thought it might have something to do with my hand. Either he didn't want me to remove it...or it made him uncomfortable. I was a pretty tactile person, and I got that not everyone liked that, but for now I'd keep my fingers where they were, lightly resting on his leg. I wanted to see where this went, to satiate my own curiosity, though it was an ever-hungry beast.

"When I was little I had these dreams of pulling together what money I had in my piggybank and throwing it into some stocks—not that I really had any idea what stocks even were," he continued, "and it would double and double until I'd have so much money I could buy my mom the house she deserved, and make it so she never worked again. I'd finance all the dreams I had, and the dreams my brother had...and live life free of worries."

He breathed deep then, eyes darting back to mine. I got the feeling he was surprised at himself. That he'd said so much.

"So, you're studying Economics to make that a reality?" I asked.

Brendan huffed a quiet laugh, the sound swallowed by the immensity of the arena. "No. Well, sort of. I know now that it doesn't necessarily work that way. I just saw too many movies about men in suits with briefcases full of papers, and somehow they made more money than they could ever need. I picked Economics because I want to make my own path to that kind of success. I want to learn about all those paths." His voice was soft, sincere, and utterly endearing. I had no inkling of greed from him, despite his childhood dreams, only a beautiful and genuine desire to...provide.

The image of him as a young boy, those hazel eyes too large for his face, that floppy hair in his eyes while watching television and dreaming about taking care of his family, tugged at something inside me immediately. It would make a great story. *He* would make a great story.

"And if you had more money than you could ever need, what would you do?" I prompted, drawn into the fantasy. "What are those dreams you would finance?"

"I play music," he said, and now his eyes brightened; he became less wistful and more excited. This was Brendan with passion. "I'm in a band, and if I had the funds, I would buy better instruments, a good producer, recording time. I would play where and when I wanted, and not worry about making ends meet. I wouldn't worry as much about failing."

"Hey, Sadie, ready to go?" a voice asked behind me.

Turning in my seat, I saw Jamie, hair combed back and damp from a shower, with a bag of gear hanging from one hand. He was wearing another graphic T-shirt, this one reading "Make Hockey Violent Again." That tracked. It stretched nicely across his biceps, tight at his shoulders, and I reminded myself not to stare. I reminded myself that his brother—who I was actually having a great conversation with—was right beside me.

"Yeah," I said, tone wry. "I was just getting to know your *twin*."

"Caught that, did you?" He smirked.

"It would have been nice to know."

Not that it wasn't sort of a fun surprise, but I did feel like a jerk for flirting with Brendan, thinking he was Jamie. Did that happen a lot to these two, I wondered? Maybe they had a habit of swapping girls like switching classes. I blushed at the thought, but while I could picture Jamie being into it, that didn't seem to fit Brendan's serious vibe. I'd add that to my list of questions, filing it into the cabinets of my mind. No amount of information would ever be enough to fill them. I always wanted more.

"Where would the fun be if you knew all about me right away?" Jamie cocked a hip against one of the plastic seats.

"You make a good point," I said. "Investigating *is* my favorite."

"And hoarding knowledge."

I nodded. "That too."

Brendan shifted beside me and stood up. "Well, this has been lovely, but I really need to get to work."

Jamie gestured for us to follow, and we trailed him through a side door and down a long, empty hall, the shuffle of our feet against the linoleum the only sound. I wasn't a big fan of silence, and with Jamie ahead of me and Brendan behind, it felt like I was somehow caught between them.

I cleared my throat, turning a bit to see over my shoulder. "So, Brendan, where do you work?"

"Daphne's," he answered, "it's a grocery and convenience store. I work nights."

I twisted further, almost walking backwards to look at him. "That must make classes difficult."

He shrugged. "I only do six-hour shifts, so it's not so bad. We can't all be banking on a career as a big shot." He said this last bit with more humor in his tone than anything, but I could tell there was an undercurrent of tension there. "You were running late," he added, and I realized he was talking to Jamie.

"Coach wanted to talk to me."

"What about?" Brendan asked.

We reached the end of the hall and Jamie pushed open another metal door, revealing a parking garage behind him.

"After you," Jamie said with a roguish tone and a sweeping arm.

The garage was one of those creepy multi-level underground monstrosities. The only lights were a series of pale-white disks hanging every ten feet or so, shadows gathering between them. I would hate to have been there alone.

"Jamie," Brendan pressed, with a hint of warning.

"Don't worry about it," said his brother.

I turned and caught them staring at each other, some kind of unspoken message passing between them.

"Was it the lack of backchecking?" I asked, trying to lighten up whatever tense moment was happening.

Jamie used the distraction to break away from his brother and lead us down a row of cars, stopping at an older model gray Civic. It had a couple scratches on it but looked well-cared for. Jamie popped the trunk and threw his bag of equipment inside.

"It wasn't anything to worry about," Jamie continued, climbing into the driver's seat. Brendan opened the back door, which I guess meant I was being treated to the passenger's side, but I couldn't relax into the seat. There was something going on I was missing, and all that made me want to do was ask more questions. Still, I decided to stay quiet—for now.

I had to remind myself I barely knew these two. It wasn't my business or my job to get to the bottom of their problems, no matter how much I wanted to.

The ride was awkward, and too stilted for my taste. Jamie put on a radio station that played some hip-hop and pop and it made me want to ask Brendan what kind of music he played—what his band was like and where they typically performed. But I still had my actual interview to finish, so I simply added the questions to my ever-growing mental list.

"I'm taking Sadie around town," Jamie said suddenly, glancing into the rearview mirror to meet his twin's gaze. "But I'll have the car back for Mom."

"Thanks."

And that was it.

We dropped Brendan off just a couple miles from campus. Daphne's was a squat building with a green-shingled overhang and bright twinkle lights lining the front windows. I could see something like a deli inside, and a sign on the door advertised fresh produce, fudge, and gourmet sandwiches. The parking lot was crowded, and I figured this was the main source of non-campus food for students who lived nearby. The chain grocery store closer to me wasn't nearly as charming.

"Have a good time, Sadie," Brendan said, climbing out of the car. "I guess I'll...see you tomorrow for that interview."

"I'll be there," I called.

He smiled then, more than the weak twist of lips he'd offered me earlier, and those dimples I adored on Jamie's face made their appearance on Brendan's. With his dark clothes, headphones, and silver chain around his neck, his smile suggested a sinful series of thoughts—like he was a criminal slinking into the dark, or a mobster with a secret. He was guarded, but that mischief in his eyes was eerily familiar, if only shadowed with a bit more severity.

"Ready to be wowed by what Spindle River has to offer?" Jamie asked, and I turned back toward him.

"Sure. Let's do it."

The first thing he did was drive me into the downtown area, which I hadn't yet been able to explore. It was getting dark, but the main street was lit with garlands of Edison bulbs hanging over restaurant patios, and neon signs for everything from late-night salons to package stores. The people walking by were mostly around our age, which didn't surprise me in this college town. But every now and then I'd see parents with strollers meandering down the sidewalk, their expressions relaxed and easy, like the oncoming twilight was a satisfying end to an accomplished day. I found myself studying them all as we drove slowly past, feeling suddenly enamored by my new town.

"So, you're interviewing Brendan for something?" Jamie asked, tone innocent.

"Yeah." I turned away from the window. "I'm working to be a staff member for the *Weekly Prowl*, and I have to do a story on an upperclassman. I asked him...thinking he was you."

He nodded. "Ahh, now I understand what you meant back at the rink. Here I thought it was a sexy strip-type game when you said you couldn't wait to interview me."

"Afraid not," I said, shaking my head sadly.

"So, you're looking for potential story ideas?"

I grinned. "Always."

Jamie hummed, as if trying to think up some topics for me, but he needn't have worried. Spindle River's downtown was full of interesting spots, just as he'd claimed, and the tidbits he threw out about each street or business were plenty to keep my mind occupied.

We passed more than one bar claiming to be historic, and when he slowed by a hole-in-the-wall bar called Dio's Wine Club, I saw a hanging wooden placard claiming they had been in business since 1921.

"You could definitely do a story on this place," he said, continuing his commentary. "It used to be this old-school wine-tasting place that only rich, white people could go to, and then it got bought by this schoolteacher in the seventies. He turned it into a bar that minorities could enjoy, and since he's Black, the town gave him a hard time at first, but he made a crap ton of money and paid a high bracket of taxes, so they let him stay. Eventually, it became iconic to downtown. He stocks whatever weird foreign alcohols he can get his hands on, but also beer and wine and regular cocktails. Still, if you know what to ask for, you can try stuff like South American grape brandy or weird-flavored soju."

"He's still there?" I asked, trying to do the mental math as we turned the corner, the pink neon sign for "Dio's" lighting up the back windshield.

"He shows up once in a while to introduce the staff to whatever new concoction he's found, but he doesn't consistently work there anymore."

The streets in this part of downtown were cobbled with rough stone, and the car trembled and shook as we pulled into a small lot on the side of the road.

"It sounds amazing," I said.

"I'll take you there sometime, if you like. You twenty-one?"

I shook my head. "Not quite."

"Ah, that's a shame. But there's a space in the back where SRU kids go dancing. So even if you can't drink, there's still some nightlife to enjoy."

"Is that what we're doing now?" I asked. "Enjoying some nightlife in a—" I peered around past the lot we'd parked in, "vacant industrial complex?"

He barked a soft laugh. "Nah, this is just one of the only free spots to park. Come on."

The night air had grown colder, so I kept close to Jamie's side as we walked across the street and headed toward what looked like an esplanade. There was a dip up ahead where I imagined a river would run through, but as we got closer, I watched the spotty tree line devolve into shrubs and dry grasses, then mud. What lay at the bottom of the riverbed was only a shallow stream of slow-moving water, maybe thirty feet across.

"Not much of a river, is it?" Jamie asked, echoing my thoughts.

"This is Spindle River? The one the town is named for?"

We ambled down a well-trodden path along the waterfront, my eyes constantly drawn to the river rocks that shone with each lamppost we passed.

"It was much bigger before the nineties, and then dwindled down to this. We have wet summers that tend to fill it back half-way, but then in autumn it retreats again. It's not like anyone really swam in it or fished from it before," he shrugged, "but the city's been working to fill it back up to help tourism or something. Either way, it's a solid line through town, so if you walk along it you can see all the older businesses."

He pointed out a few as we walked: a closed florist shop that specialized in Halloween and Christmas arrangements, a jewelry store that was apparently the first to be founded in the state, and a carpentry business that had supplied all the booths and seats at Dio's Wine Bar. There was an entire, intricate story somehow being woven between all of them, and

Jamie seemed to know just enough pieces to keep me absolutely hooked.

As the night got chillier and I shivered, he put his arm around my shoulder, tucking me into the heat of his body. That scent of coffee and cologne wafted into my nose, comforting and exciting at the same time. The hard strength of his torso was intoxicating; my whole body felt alive with it, aware of every inch we had contact. And when we stopped at a cart that sold hot pretzels, he held his out to me so I could try the cinnamon-sugar coating he got on his, which was almost as good as the asiago cheese sprinkled onto mine.

In short, it may have been one of the best dates of my life, and I wasn't even sure it was a date.

"So," he said, finishing off his pretzel, "ever thought about doing a piece for the *Prowl* about the university's sexiest hockey player?"

"Why, who is he?"

I smiled around my cheesy pretzel as he stumbled, holding a hand to his chest and pretending to be wounded while laughing this deep, surprised chuckle I immediately wanted to record for posterity.

"Okay, what about the team, then?" he asked after a minute. "We could always use some good press. More chances for sponsorships and counsel money and all that."

"Are you having funding problems?" I asked.

He shrugged, then put his arm back around my shoulders, but I could feel there was more he wasn't saying. I remembered his beat-up laptop, the car he apparently shared with his mother and Brendan, as well as the way Brendan had talked about their home life and not wanting their mother to work anymore. But before I could tactfully attempt to wriggle some truth out of him, he gently turned us around, so we were headed back to the car, weaving through the other couples enjoying a nighttime stroll. It felt so natural, walking beside him, like we were in step, nestled perfectly together as a comfortable unit. The gentle shushing of the weak river was a pleasant background noise.

Jamie cleared his throat. "If you wrote about the team, I bet I could help you come up with some sick one-liners. Like all those alliterative headlines reporters love."

"Oh, yeah? What you got?" I threw out my napkin in a trash can as he did the same and then snuggled back into his side, our stride picking up as if it had never stopped.

"*Rink Rats of Spindle River...Rise to the Occasion*," he quoted.

"That *is* pretty good. Or what about *Hockey Hounds get Hat-trick*?"

"*Kings of Puck Kick Posers to the Penalty Box.*"

I shook my head, chuckling. "Damn, that one's good."

"Okay, I might have been working on that one for a bit." His tone was sheepish, and I looked up to see his profile illuminated by a passing streetlight, that dimple like a dark divot I wanted to poke at. He'd been trying to impress me? My chest fluttered at the thought.

I smiled up at him. "It shows. Quite impressive. Got any more?"

We kept up the banter, coming up with silly headlines, and quicker than I'd have liked, we were back at the Civic.

"I have to grab dinner at home and make sure my mom has the car in time for work, so I gotta go," he said as an apology. "But this...this has been good."

I nodded. It really had.

I let him drive me back to the university lot where my Buick was parked, and he spent the entire ride answering my dozens of hockey-related questions. I learned quite a bit, and had already started to mentally pitch a story about the leading line of the team, just in case one hadn't already been done recently. I'd have to check the archives.

When Jamie turned off the car and pivoted to me, I thought for sure the night would end in a kiss. The lot was dark and empty except for my car and a smattering of others, and the world seemed hushed—like it was waiting for this romantic moment as much as I was. I hadn't intended this to be a date, but he was so fun to talk to, and so handsome and playful and warm and outgoing. It was engrossing just to be near him.

Jamie opened his mouth and then closed it, changing his mind about something. I watched his features shift from hesitation back to that charming, easy grin.

"Have fun interviewing Brendan tomorrow. Don't let him get too serious."

"I'll do my best. But I must let the story take me where it goes." I held out my hands, as if helpless.

"Damn, there go all my family secrets," he said.

He leaned over then and pressed a soft kiss to my forehead, which I hadn't expected. I almost let my eyes drift closed like a lovesick middle schooler, but instead, I tilted my head up in invitation.

His eyes dropped to my mouth. He leaned closer, barely, by the tiniest fraction of space. I could feel the wet heat of his breath.

My heart tumbled and swelled, excitement making my palms sweat, but then he pulled back.

"So, I'll see you in class next week?" he asked.

I nodded, fighting disappointment. Normally, I would take that as a flat-out rejection, but his eyes were dark with intent. He was interested. He just wasn't going forward with it. Because of my interview with Brendan? Or because this was all just a little fast? He didn't seem the type to keep these things formal, but maybe he was more old-fashioned than

I realized.

I smirked, refusing to feel down. "Yeah, if I don't catch you before then."

We said good night and I left his car, and I was pleased to note he didn't drive away until I settled inside the Buick and turned on the engine. Chivalry for the modern age.

Still buoyed by a great night despite the romantic slowdown, I started my arduous trip home.

CHAPTER FIVE

The winding road that led to my pond-laden cottage seemed a bit more beautiful that night. Trees had begun to lean over the lane, their branches heavy with drooping leaves that drifted occasionally onto the asphalt. When autumn was well and truly underway, I imagined it would feel like driving through a rainbow tunnel—something to look forward to. Or maybe the beauty was simply a reflection of my good mood. Even though Jamie hadn't kissed me, it had still been an excellent night. Worst case, if nothing romantic developed between the two of us, at least I had gotten my feet wet at school. I was learning about the town and the people in it. I was making connections that would hopefully last me the next few years at SRU.

There was a letter sticking out of my mailbox at the bottom of the driveway for the first time ever, and even something as simple as my first piece of mail at my new home felt more special than before.

I slowed the Buick and rolled down my driver's side window, reaching into the mailbox. The house was dark and there were no light posts nearby, but in the glow of the dashboard I could see it was a letter from the school. Probably some form I needed to sign or—

Someone yanked open my door.

I had been partially leaning on the open window, looking at the envelope, and my elbow slipped down, my body tilting.

In a state of shock, I almost fell out of the car.

"Hey! What the—" and then something sharp grazed my arm. A hand had darted out from the dark and clutched at my elbow, pulling me from my seat.

The smell of wet earth and rot assaulted my nose, a cloying tinge to the air that stuck in my throat as I took in a breath to scream. But then a hard, cold hand smacked against my mouth.

My ass hit the ground, my feet still hanging from the lip of the open car door, and the hands started dragging me backward.

I tried tilting my head to see who had grabbed me, so I would know what I was up against, but it was dark, and my body wouldn't cooperate. My limbs were too busy twisting and churning in their hold, trying to get free. Now it was the inside of their elbow around my mouth as they yanked me against them. Mud streaked across my face, blurring my glasses.

I couldn't tell if it was a man or a woman. All I could discern was they were wet and cold, like they'd been waiting for me outside in the woods, and that they were so, so strong. I bit down on the flesh at my mouth, the skin damp and bitter on my tongue, and they jerked my head to the side so hard I heard something pop. My glasses flew off my face and clattered somewhere to the side.

Breath hitching with terror, I watched the car get farther and farther away from my kicking boots. The concrete scraped their soles, and then it was dirt.

Fighting and thrashing against my captor, I was able to turn my body like a crocodile in a death roll, finally surprising them enough to drop me.

My knees hit the ground and my palms scraped along rocks and brambles as I attempted to crawl away.

A hand pulled at my shirt, but the cloth simply ripped under their strength. There was another sharp sting against my ribs, and my already frantic heartbeat stuttered with terror. Had that been their nails? Or a knife?

"Help!" I screamed, managing to clamber to my feet.

Not that anyone would hear me.

There was another house a bit up the road, but it would be a miracle if my voice made its way there.

The car. I had to get back to the car. I could lock myself inside and call for help. That is, unless they broke the window. What if they had a gun?

Too many questions tumbled around in my head, but nothing could break through the fear cycling over and over, louder than anything else: *Get away, get away, get away!* I didn't know how to fight, only some basic self-defense like "Don't be afraid to hit them in the throat, or kick them in the crotch, anything to get free." But I had no desire to turn around and deal a blow, I only wanted to escape.

I could hear whoever it was shuffling behind me, the sounds of crunching leaves and displaced gravel loud in my ears. That hand grabbed me again, this time with a fist full of my hair, and my head was yanked backward. I swung my arm behind me as hard as I could, catching them at their shoulder. My nails grazed skin. I heard a hiss, and then they released me.

Clamoring up into the cab of the car and wiping a hand over my grimy eyes, I reached for the door handle, but my leg was stuck. At first, I thought my pants were caught on something, but then I saw grimy, long-nailed fingers clutching my pant leg.

They pulled.

I screamed again, my body already half out of the car once more. I grabbed the edge of the driver's seat and pulled myself forward with every ounce of strength I could muster, my arms shaking, my heart pounding. Hot tears leaked from my eyes, helping to clear my sight, and I spotted the glove box ahead of me. I didn't have a weapon, but I did have a road flare. I was supposed to keep it in the trunk, but with all the boxes from moving, I'd stored it there and forgot to move it back.

Kicking my legs and trying to dislodge the hand there, I inched myself forward, lifting one hand to strain toward the box. My fingertips groped against the latch and it released, the door dropping down and junk tumbling onto the floor. Tampons, napkins, air fresheners—*there*!

I snatched the road flare just as I was pulled again from the car. Using both hands to pull the cap free, I flicked off the top to expose the striker. My elbows slammed into the concrete drive, my attacker seemingly unconcerned with what I held and more interested in pulling me back toward the dirt. I struck the top of the flare anyway, ignoring the pain in my arms, and heard the telltale sizzle of the flare coming to life.

The flame was bright red and hot enough to severely burn you if you put your face or hands too close. So, I bent at my waist as hard as I could, dragging my body along the rough, damp dirt, and curled myself toward my ankles, and the hands that held them.

Shoving the light forward with a shout, I caught my first warped glimpse of my attacker through my blurred, murky vision. It was a woman, bedraggled and covered in mud, her eyes dark and wild. I thought maybe her hair was red under all the muck, but that could have been the light from the flare. Her skin also seemed tinted some shade that made her appear lilac. Either way, my aim landed true, the flare striking her in the face.

She shrieked, the sound rough and broken, releasing me once more. Her hands were curled as she cradled her face, nails so long and curved they reminded me of a hawk's talons.

I was gearing up to hit her again, ready to shove the light directly into her eyes if I could, but she spun and fled, her body moving too fast to track. And then, she was in the pitch-black woods.

Gone.

Not waiting to see if she'd return, I scrambled into the car and slammed the door shut, locking it. I reached for my phone, my hands trembling so badly it took me multiple tries to dial 911.

***

The rest of the night was a blur of flashing lights, repetitive questions, and a very sweet EMT who apologized for every sting while cleaning out the scrapes on my hands, knees, and elbows. The cuts along my side were also impressive, which I could now fully appreciate since my glasses had been retrieved—somehow undamaged—from where they had fallen by the car. I reassured the EMT multiple times I didn't want to go to a hospital; I hadn't hit my head or gotten anything more than a few scratches and bruises, and I was worried they would contact my father if I was admitted. The whole ordeal had been terrifying, but I didn't want to risk the chance he would drop everything he was working on in Texas and come running to my side. I was a big girl; I could handle this. And I'd done everything right—I'd protected myself and called for help. Just because some insane woman accosted me off the street was no reason for my life, or anyone else's, to screech to a halt.

The cops arrived to take a statement, scraping the bits of the woman's flesh I'd trapped beneath my nails as evidence, though the policeman was skeptical anything would come of it.

"Looks like the sample is tainted with something she had on her skin," he said, when I asked if they'd be able to identify her. "The stuff under your nails is blue, and there's no blood. Might be some kind of paint."

They assured me it was most likely a one-time incident of a disturbed woman who was probably under the influence of some kind of narcotic, maybe even a topical one, given the weird substance I'd scraped off her. Still, I wasn't so sure. She hadn't seemed to want money, or my car. She didn't speak or threaten me. All she'd done was drag me towards the woods like some fairytale monster. Acting that troubled *could* be the result of drugs, but wouldn't she have been aiming for something particular or raving aloud? She had been so...silent.

I decided to push those thoughts away, urging my frazzled mind to accept that sometimes violent acts didn't make sense. It was best to let this go and move on to the best of my ability, back to my new life in Spindle River, which had seemed so vibrant and hopeful only hours before.

My house was locked up tight, with all the new curtains drawn, and after some ibuprofen and a guided meditation session via phone app, I slept for almost twelve hours. I woke up feeling sore and shaky, and not up for putting on a happy face and driving to school, so I emailed my professors to let them know what had happened. Thankfully, Statistics was still warming up in difficulty, so I didn't anticipate any issues. However, I hated the thought of missing my first History of American Media class, especially since it met only once a week. The TA—a guy named Jesse who replied with a lot of flowery language and a heap of sympathy—emailed me back and promised to provide me with notes for the missed class, bless him. Professor Lewis gave me an extension on my article and told me to come to next week's newspaper staff meeting prepared to pitch multiple story ideas.

I spent the day relaxing in front of my laptop, binge watching *The Bold Type*, and drafting a few paragraphs for my Psych paper on bondage. Occasionally, I could hear the brush of wind against the windows, or the passing of a car, and my body would tense, my pulse loud in my ears, but soon enough it would fade, and my focus would return to the here and now.

My phone buzzed, startling me, and I saw a text light up.

Jamie: *Hey Brendan says you weren't in class today. U ok?*

Oh shit. The interview. I shook my head, debating how much to tell him, and how to formulate a short apology he could relay to Brendan for missing our coffee date. What I ended up telling him was that I was attacked near my house, but I was fine, and I was taking the day off to recuperate. All true, and yet somehow missing the key elements of my experience—the panic, the violence, the weirdness, and the fight for what might have been my life.

Jamie: *Holy shit that's insane. Sure ur alright? He wants to know if he can bring you stats notes? Check on u*

Me: *I live pretty far, I can just get them on Tuesday. Thanks tho.*

Jamie: *He'll bring you...a vanilla latte?*

I could picture them now, standing side-by-side, looking down at the phone. I glanced at the clock—Statistics would have let out an hour ago, and it wasn't too late for caffeine. A warm latte sounded wonderful, like it would somehow cure the aches in my body and the tension headache I'd been on and off ignoring all day.

Me: *How can I say no to that?*

I gave him the address and told him Brendan could have my number, in case something went wrong, or he got lost. Looking around the rented cottage, I debated tidying just for something to do, but it was clean enough since I hadn't moved much from the couch. I snuggled deeper into the pleather seat and my plaid blanket, pulling up the doc on my laptop that listed all the questions I'd thought of asking him.

A knock woke me. Apparently twelve hours of sleep hadn't been enough.

I rubbed my fingers over my eyes, feeling for just a second the grime that woman had wiped over my face last night, and then—after my heartbeat calmed back down—hurried to check the peep hole in the front door.

It was Brendan. Or Jamie. He wasn't wearing headphones, and I couldn't tell if that silver chain was around his neck—which I hoped was a standard accessory for Brendan—so I wasn't entirely sure which brother was on my porch.

I was going to have to come up with some kind of code word for each of them, or get them both to wear tight enough shirts so I could tell who had the slightly leaner chest.

"Hey," I said, pulling open the door.

His eyes widened with concern. "Fuck, I thought you said you were okay." He looked me up and down, and though my pajama pants covered the bruises on my knees, and my T-shirt hid the long scratch at my waist, I guess it did display the scrapes along my arms and elbows. My palms also sported thin bandages. At least my face wasn't too banged up.

"It's really not that bad," I assured him, letting him in.

I couldn't help but check the space behind him, scanning the drive for anything out of the ordinary. The police assured me they'd be on the lookout for a dirty and potentially blue-painted woman wandering the area, and they would drive by the house a few times each night to keep an eye on things, but I couldn't be too careful. Thankfully, next to the gray Civic and my Buick was nothing but quiet, sun-dappled woods.

"Who was it that attacked you?" he asked, looking around the sparsely furnished living room and kitchen.

"Some crazy lady the police think was on drugs. Maybe homeless."

"Jesus Christ." He rubbed a hand over the side of his neck, and I caught a peek of silver under the black hoodie he wore—the same one he offered to me yesterday. It was truly Brendan after all. "Did they catch her?"

I shook my head, sitting gingerly back down on the couch. "Not yet."

Suddenly his gaze became sharper, like his perusal of the room was now from the perspective of someone in danger. His eyes tracked each window and door, looking for threats.

"She didn't break in here," I hurried to explain, "it was at the start of the driveway, right on the street. They think she was walking by and saw an opportunity to rob me or something. Please, don't freak me out more than I already am. I need to tell myself the house is safe."

Brendan sighed. "Sorry. Okay. Well, here—" he gingerly put a backpack he'd been wearing onto the ground and pulled out a red thermos. "I poured it in directly from the campus café—I didn't make it myself. Vanilla latte, hopefully still warm."

"My hero." I beamed, taking the thermos, and unscrewing the top to smell the sweet caffeine inside. I took a sip. It was heaven.

"And..." he pulled out a couple sheets of paper, "I copied my Stats notes for you. All we need to do is read pages 23 to 40 in the textbook and do the worksheet at the end."

I put the papers down on the floor by my computer and shifted sideways, offering him a seat. Unfortunately, the couch was barely more than a loveseat, and even after I moved my blanket aside, there wasn't a ton of room for him.

"This was really nice of you," I said, honestly, as he fit into the cushion beside me. "I know it's a bit of a drive. And I'm sorry for spacing about the interview—it's really not like me. I should've messaged Jamie to tell you."

He raised an eyebrow. "I think you're off the hook this time. Besides, I don't have work this afternoon, so I figured I'd bring the interview to you. And any excuse for a vanilla latte, right?"

"Exactly." I tried to ignore the heat of his body along my side, feeling strangely guilty as I looked around for a spot to put my drink. The side table was small and covered with magazines, an empty water glass, and a wrapped-up phone charger, and I would already have my laptop on my lap once I started. Man, I really did need some furniture.

"How about we go sit outside?" I asked, and then immediately regretted it. The outside wasn't *exactly* where I wanted to be right now, but it was too cramped in here.

"You sure?"

I think he could see the unease on my face, but I nodded, trying to appear braver than I felt. After all, this is where I lived. I needed to face the discomfort head-on, so I could put this horrible experience behind me as quickly as possible.

"Like I said, I need to feel like the house and yard are safe, right? And you'll like the view, believe me. Plus, you're here. I'll just push you toward any crazy person who shows up so I can get away. Sound good?"

Brendan gave a low chuckle, but his words were soft and sincere. "Works for me. I'll protect you."

My heart did a little flip at the way he said that, though I hated the idea I needed to be protected at all.

CHAPTER SIX

I carried my laptop and latte out the sliding kitchen doors and gestured for Brendan to take one of the two wicker patio chairs placed in the weak sunlight. My drink fit perfectly on the small, round table between them. It was chilly for just my pajamas, so I ended up going back into the living room to grab my plaid blanket, wrapping it around me with only my head and hands poking out. I would have felt foolish, but Brendan was smiling at me. Where Jamie always seemed to be smirking or grinning, I got the feeling Brendan's smiles were rarer. It made him all the more handsome as he settled into the chair.

"Yes, I'm so fashionable, aren't I?" I asked.

"Fashionable and adorable. A double threat."

"That's what they teach us at reporter school," I replied, ignoring the slight thrill of being called adorable. "Okay, you ready?"

He nodded and I looked at my list of questions, the laptop warming my thighs.

"What's it like being a twin?"

He barked out a laugh, deeper and louder than I expected. For a moment it drowned out all the other sounds in the yard—the tapping of a woodpecker, the spare croak of frogs, the buzzing of dragonflies along the water. It was truly a gorgeous laugh, and I caught myself watching his throat as he did it.

"What?" I asked. "Dumb question?"

"It's just always the first one people ask us, and we never know how to answer. What's it like not being a twin?" He looked at me. "It's just...the way it is. And no, we don't have some secret language with each other, and no we don't feel each other's pain. I imagine it's like having any other kind of sibling, except people can never tell us apart. The one cliché thing we do is swap classes—or at least, we did in high school."

I raised one eyebrow, expectant, and his expression became sheepish.

"I was better in math and Jamie was always better at bullshitting in English, like he'd read whatever was assigned, so once in a while we would trade places. Pretty sure it's the only reason he passed geometry."

I typed down everything he was saying, mentally crossing off a few other topics I'd planned on. Maybe them being twins wasn't the right angle here.

"Okay, well let's focus on you," I told him. "How was your childhood? Jamie said you've lived in Spindle River your whole lives?"

Brendan settled back into the patio chair, looking out over the pond, and it reminded me of how he had acted at the rink, not willing to meet my eye while he talked. I didn't know if it was because he was shy, or if—like a typical guy—he was having trouble being vulnerable.

"Yeah, we grew up here. My mom...she worked a lot, so we didn't see her much. Our childhood was...fine? Nothing beyond the usual dumb kid stories where you try to jump out of a tree and sprain your ankle, or you fall asleep on the bus and end up in Bredham."

"What about high school?" I asked. "Besides swapping classes."

He paused again before answering, and I had this feeling like he was carefully weighing out his words. "High school was fine, honestly—that's when I met my bandmate, Andrea, and we started making music. Jamie was off playing hockey, and I was working at Daphne's and playing music when I could. Nothing much has changed since then, really. We went to the high school close to the SRU campus, so when we graduated it didn't really feel like we moved on, you know? Like, we could walk back in any day and sit down in that same geometry class."

I noticed he said most things were fine, but I could tell there was more to his story. Still, I let it go, trying a different tactic.

"What does your mother do for work?"

Brendan licked his lips, covering what might have been a sigh, and he took so long to answer I didn't think he was going to reply.

"She's a nurse," he said eventually. "Did a lot of hours at night so she could get us to and from school. But she hasn't worked as much lately. Shifts here and there."

I kept quiet, waiting for him to say more.

"My mom...she's always been sort of unwell. She was diagnosed with mild schizophrenia, and usually she's okay—just restless, and dizzy sometimes from the medications she's on—but it's gotten worse lately." His eyes darted back to me. "You won't publish anything about this, will you?"

I shook my head. "I won't print anything you don't want me to."

A breeze ruffled his hair then, and his scent, warm and sweet, like a sugared version of his brother's coffee and spice, brushed my nose like a caress. I wanted to lean into it. His features were calm as his hazel eyes watched mine, something akin to gratitude in their shadowed depths.

"It's not like she hears voices telling her to do violent things, she just sees things sometimes," he explained, his mouth twisting into a wry smile. "Even when we were born, she swore for a while she only gave birth to one son. She thought there were two of us because she was hallucinating the second one."

"Wow." I blinked. "That must have been tough."

He shrugged. "She's never said that directly to us, it's something our uncle told us. She swore she was only having one baby, and then when there were two, she didn't believe the doctor or the nurses. She was confused. For a few years after that she was pretty bad—seeing shadows, not able to distinguish what was real or not—but when we got older, she got better. I've always tried to take care of her, and get jobs when I could so she wouldn't have to work as much. Stress seems to trigger her symptoms more than anything else." He straightened, as if suddenly panicked that he was painting her in too negative a light. His expression was nervous as he finally turned his head to meet my gaze. "She loves us, though, more than anything," he said, "and it's always been her mission to give us whatever we needed, no matter the consequences to her own health: ice time, skates, pads and jerseys, money for school trips or training camps for..." he trailed off, biting at his lip.

"All things for Jamie," I summarized, though it was partially a question.

"He needed more than I did," Brendan said, simple and quiet. "Once I had my guitar it's not like there was anything else to get, and I bought it used."

"What about music lessons? Or rehearsal space?" I could imagine it had felt very unfair, growing up where one son needed to spend money, so the other son needed to make money.

He lifted one shoulder. "I taught myself using videos online and Andrea has a basement her parents let us use for practice."

"And you don't...resent him?" I asked.

Brendan seemed to think hard about this, and I appreciated that he wouldn't give me a flippant yes or no. A mourning dove fluttered over the pond, the hushed rustle of ferns and cattails like a series of tiny sighs, and I watched something ripple in the water—some fish hunting a skating bug, or maybe a turtle coming up for air. A cloud passed overhead, blocking out the afternoon sun.

"Sometimes I do," he admitted. "I resent how he has things now; he doesn't know what it's like to work a shit job every day to bring money home. He enjoys the games and the travelling, but I know he's putting in work for the future. Jamie thinks once he makes it into the AHL it's only a matter of time before he moves onto a national team, and then mom and I will be set for life. The support we give him...it's sort of like an investment." He paused. "Sometimes I just want a little of that investment for myself."

Scratching at his cheek, a hint of a blush bloomed around his neck. "Sorry. I really...I don't think you should write any of that. It's pretty whiny."

I held up my hands. "It's not whiny, it's your truth. And I haven't taken notes since you mentioned your mom."

"I don't think I'm being a very good interview subject," he said, his smile a bit sad.

"There will always be another story," I told him, and I meant it. If this 'twins' angle wasn't right, I'd find something else. I always did.

"Why do you want to work for the *Prowl* anyway?" he asked, clearly eager to turn the attention away from himself.

"I've always loved journalism," I said, adjusting in my seat so I could lean closer to him and that sugary smell. "I enjoy asking people questions and doing research. I like digging around until I find the truth. Plus, my dad and I moved around a lot when I was younger, so I never really got into any sports or clubs—nothing that meant you had to stick around, anyway. Can't really be an actress or athlete when you might need to pack your bags at a moment's notice."

"And you don't resent *him*?" Brendan asked, mimicking me. He turned his chest more toward me, and the wide backyard seemed to grow smaller, more intimate. We were close enough that I could reach out and touch his arm, like I had the other day.

I opened my mouth to answer, but halted, my body locking up. There was a shift in the air around us, a discordant change. The hair on my arms stood for no reason.

A mosquito flew by my face, startling me, but I waved it away. And then I realized why I felt that sense of danger.

The whole yard had gone silent.

There was no wind, no bird calls, no ripples of pond water. The frogs had stopped croaking and the buzzing of insects had vanished.

Something screamed inside me to stand up and leave. To hurry. To run.

I looked at Brendan and saw the same unease mirrored in his features; not fear, exactly, but something like it.

"That's weird," he said, voice quiet, as if afraid of being overheard. "Let's...go inside."

I nodded and gently took the hand he offered, which was warm and calloused, if just a little damp. He was careful of my bandages while pulling me backward, and I hurried to gather my blanket and laptop with my free hand while he snatched the thermos. We rushed inside, sliding the door to the kitchen shut and locking it. Standing at the glass, we both peered outside, but nothing had changed. The clouds moved, and sunlight once again blanketed the sloping lawn and sparkled over the pond. The breeze resumed once more, making the long willow vines dance.

"Weird," I agreed.

Brendan hummed, like he was thinking through a difficult problem.

"So…" I looked up to study his profile. "You definitely felt like something spooked the wildlife, right? That wasn't just me?"

He shook his head. "No. It wasn't you."

Well, at least the attack wasn't making me paranoid, I reasoned.

"Maybe a coyote was nearby," said Brendan. "That could have scared the birds, at least."

"Which could have scared the frogs and the bugs, right?" I didn't know much about coyotes.

Brendan raised one shoulder, the move reminding me of his brother. He wasn't convinced, and neither was I. That wasn't reassuring.

I tried to keep the rest of the interview a bit more casual, though we were crammed close together once more on the loveseat. Brendan talked to me about his band, Shady Tree Lane, and the running bi-weekly gig they had at a restaurant and bar downtown with an all-ages night. He asked me about my favorite articles that I'd written, and what topics I would cover if I had free reign. I told him local interest stories or environmental impact studies, and he let me know about a hiking path clean-up event happening next weekend, which I took note of along with the sparse record I had made of our chat.

It wasn't enough for an article, not yet, but we were getting there. Either way, I was happy to have the company for the rest of the afternoon, especially after that creepy moment outside. I really didn't want to feel afraid in my own house, but I had been attacked at the start of the driveway, and there wasn't any fence or gate in the back to stop someone from wandering through the woods right onto the property. I really needed to stop thinking about that—or get my hands on a baseball bat or something.

When Brendan left to go pick up Jamie from class, I spent the rest of the night researching the clean-up initiative, and then organizing my thoughts about the Barreto boys and what I knew about them so far. Sitting with Brendan had been...peaceful. At least until that weirdness outside. He was like deep, dark waters I hadn't yet explored—tranquil but mysterious. Jamie, on the other hand, was more like a set of rapids. It was easy to get swept up in him. He set my heart racing. Both had their own temptation, and their own dangers.

I felt like I'd gotten a sneak peek at a very intricate puzzle and had only just gathered the edge pieces. If anything, it just left me craving another chance to dig deeper.

CHAPTER SEVEN

I spent the weekend being somewhat of a hermit. I had no classes, and the long break gave me a chance to heal, letting the bruises from my attack slowly fade from purple to green to a sickly yellow. By Monday morning, I'd completely finished my paper on bondage—a week ahead of schedule—and joined an online mailing list for updates on clean-up activities in the area.

I was truly, utterly bored.

Thankfully, Monday meant Psychology, where I could chat with Lynne; and Linguistics, where I could see Jamie for the first time in days.

Lynne took a look at my hands as I sat beside her and asked me, in a half-asleep voice, if I'd been experimenting with my bondage topic.

I choked out a laugh, the sound so loud and abrupt that half the class turned to look at me. My face flushed bright red.

"God, I wish," I told her, then gave her a pared-down version of the traumatic events of the last week. Her eyes were saucers by the time I finished, and when Nina walked in to start her lecture, Lynne quietly offered to take me to the school counselor if I needed someone to talk to. It was very sweet, but the idea of rehashing it all to yet another person made my palms sweat, so I declined. She then offered to get me drunk, which held slightly more appeal, so I told her that was definitely an option.

"Any time," she offered, and I could tell she meant it. It made me feel normal again, like things were back on track—friends and classes and fresh starts.

When I walked into the Linguistics classroom, Jamie was already in the seats that had somehow become permanently ours, his bag on my chair to keep it saved and a paper coffee cup sitting on the retractable desk arm. It seemed unlike him to be so early, but all that did was enhance my good mood.

"What's this?" I asked with a grin, sitting down.

"Brendan's not the only one who can supply you with lattes." There was a slight edge to his words, but when I met his gaze, his face was full of cocky pride. But then he caught sight of my hands. The mischief in his eyes dimmed into worry.

"Shit, Sadie," he said. "Brendan made it sound like just a couple scratches."

"They are just a couple scratches," I assured him. "I'm fine, I swear." The red marks on my palms and knuckles were taking longer to fade than the bruises, probably because I kept typing and cleaning and cooking—generally *living my life*—and the movement was agitating them.

He rearranged his laptop, as if killing time, building up to something before his hazel eyes, darkened with concern, focused on me. "I was thinking...if they haven't caught the woman who attacked you yet, maybe I should drive you home. Just to make sure you get in okay."

I took a sip of the latte, letting the warmth carry through my limbs. I was already feeling spoiled by all the afternoon caffeine the boys kept bringing me.

"That's really sweet," I said, placing my free palm on his arm. The soft heat of his skin beneath my fingertips was its own sort of delight. "But also, completely unnecessary. The cops are doing drive-bys at my place throughout the night, and now I know to be more careful. Oh, and thanks for the latte—between this and root beer I can never get enough sugar."

His mouth twisted with apprehension; I'd failed to distract him. "Do you have a weapon on you at least?"

I raised one eyebrow. "Um, no? What kind of weapon should I be carrying to and from a college campus?" Just the image of a giant metal baseball bat sticking out of my messenger bag as I walked out of the stately New England brick building would probably merit its own article, I reasoned.

"Mace? A taser?" he offered.

I shook my head. "I know some self-defense. Really, once they catch her, I'll feel so much better, but who knows how long that will take? It's a waiting game. I just have to stay aware and cautious until then."

"Yeah, but who knows how long the police will actually keep driving by your place?" Jamie retorted. "The force here is pretty small. I wouldn't be surprised if they only kept that up for a week or two before deciding to move on."

"Well, maybe they'll have caught the woman by then."

He groaned a bit in frustration. "I can't believe you were physically assaulted and you're not even worried enough to take a free escort home."

"Because I'm independent," I shrugged.

"Stubborn is more like it." He paused, scratching at the side of his neck. "What if I used the trip to your place to give you an interview? The other side of the twin-coin?" A wry smile lifted one corner of his mouth.

"I bet I know even more stories about the town that you'd love."

That had me reconsidering. I'd gotten Brendan's side of the story, but what if Jamie had a completely different interpretation? That alone would make for an interesting article, and it wasn't like I could use much of what Brendan had told me. Plus, the tidbits Jamie seemed to know about all the businesses and history of Spindle River would be helpful.

Still, I hesitated. "Why are you so determined to drive me home?" I asked.

He shifted in his chair, as if self-conscious, and I noticed the shirt he wore today was another screen-printed tee with the Pornhub logo, only the word "Porn" was replaced with "Pun." I almost rolled my eyes, but it *did* make a grin break free across my features.

"Maybe I just want to spend more time with you," he said.

I looked up from the logo on his chest to find him watching me, his stare so eerily similar to Brendan's and yet...different. I didn't know how to explain it, but I wondered if, after some time, I would be able to tell them apart just from the way they looked at me. With Brendan there was something like a soulful tenderness in his gaze while we talked. With Jamie it was more...intense. Fiery.

It made it really difficult to say no to him.

"I drove in today," I started, "and I won't lie, I felt a little nervous getting in and out of the car, but it is *really* out of your way so I understand if you change your mind, or if there are some days you just can't do it...but if you want to drive behind me tonight, or bring me to school tomorrow, that would be nice. Really nice." I could feel a blush creeping up my face and took a breath, wondering why I was rambling so much. "And again, still totally unnecessary."

I forcefully closed my mouth and chewed at my lip, beyond flustered.

Jamie and Brendan's concerns were so...endearing. I'd had so many brief flings and passing friends it made my heart skip to think of them caring about me so deeply. It was as if we'd been close for much longer than a few days.

"Then it's settled." Jamie nodded—case closed. "As long as you don't mind waiting until my practice is over."

A chance to get to watch him in action again? I wasn't mad about it. "Can I take pictures?"

"Sure."

"Then I don't mind." I grinned, sipping my latte, feeling all kinds of pleasure.

After class was over, we walked side-by-side to the arena, and I got my first taste of Jamie's popularity around campus. Guys greeted him with raised hands or quick words of encouragement like "Destroy the Eagles this weekend!" and more than one girl scanned him from head to toe as they passed, a chorus of "Hey, Jamie," following wherever we walked.

I raised one eyebrow at him, but he didn't seem to notice; he was all smiles and friendly responses. It really did seem like he had his finger on the pulse of the school.

When we separated so he could go to the locker room, I settled into a chair in the stadium seating—grateful for the thick sweater I was wearing—and opened my laptop, ready to take notes and do more hockey research. Opening the doc from my interview with Brendan, I scanned over the record I'd made of our conversation, wondering what questions I should ask Jamie. I could try to drive the conversation in the same direction to see if they answered differently about their mother or their approaches to the future. Or I could try a drastically different approach and let their personality differences take the wheel. I wasn't sure.

Regardless, once practice started it was hard to take my eyes off the ice. The team had a host of warm-up activities like stretches and sprints, and then they paired off into smaller groups to do rotating mini games. All the while, the mustachioed coach shouted out critiques that ranged from vaguely offensive to downright mean. But it *was* very entertaining.

"Might as well skate on your hands, Peters!" the coach shouted to one of the players. "Then maybe you'd be able to see the damn puck!"

I'd always thought girls who sat in the bleachers at their boyfriends' football or soccer practices were a bit vapid—having nothing else to do with themselves but sit around and cheer on their beaus—but I could sort of see the appeal now. I think I'd judged them too harshly. In between reviewing pages for Stats or googling sports terms, it was like watching a very messy hockey game mixed with a family-oriented drama. Some of the players knocked their helmets together or playfully smacked each other on the ass with their sticks. The goalie closest to me was singing some Taylor Swift song that was annoying the others into making harder and faster shots. I was quickly becoming entranced.

I kept expecting Brendan to arrive for a ride to work, but he must not have had a shift at Daphne's, because sooner than expected practice was over, and Jamie was following me to my car. Thankfully he hadn't gotten pulled aside this time by the coach, but the question of what that conversation had been about still rattled annoyingly around in my brain.

I sat in the Buick watching the sky grow darker with each passing moment, a far-off brontide of thunder creeping closer. Another storm. Checking my phone, I saw the severe weather alert warning of on-and-off rain for the next two days. Wonderful.

A honk pulled my attention up to see Jamie in his gray car, ready to tail me home.

This escort still felt silly, but also, knowing the winding roads ahead of me and the way the rain would darken my driveway once more, I was grateful to have him nearby.

I drove slowly, checking on him occasionally in my rearview mirror. It was a nice distraction, at least until I had to turn my wipers on to deal with the oncoming drizzle. And soon enough my driveway came into view, my mailbox empty, all the windows like black mirrors reflecting my headlights. I should probably have bought a floodlight while I was out, something with a motion sensor.

Jamie pulled in behind me after I parked, and I hurried to the front door, ducking my head to avoid the rain. Protected under the short awning at the door, I was able to turn and wave, but he didn't leave. My phone vibrated and I pulled it from my pocket.

Jamie: *I'll wait until ur inside*

I nodded and went inside, closing the door behind me. The house felt cold, like I had left a window open, or the heating had failed to kick on all day. I could almost see my breath.

Rubbing my hands along my arms to warm them, I hurried into the kitchen, doing a quick glance around the space. Everything seemed locked tight, and nothing was out of place—not that I expected any trouble. It was just some crazy woman wandering by, I reminded myself. The house was safe. I was safe.

My phone buzzed again.

Jamie: *everything good?*

I was debating my reply, typing and deleting messages that sounded too flippant, then too sincere. This was such a nice thing he was doing, and I didn't want him to worry, but also the trip had reminded me how serious the attack could have been. Should I just thank him again? Add a wink? Tell him a joke about visiting a shooting range? I wanted to examine this vibe between us—more than the one quasi-date we'd had driving and walking around town. He was sitting outside, and I could just *go out there*. Get his story. If I learned more about him then maybe I wouldn't have this damned hesitation about how to respond. I'd know what was too glib, or too deep.

If I didn't hurry up and respond he would probably think I'd been attacked again.

Frustrated by my own indecision, I grabbed my keys in one fist and my phone in the other and rushed back out into the rain, locking the house behind me.

"What's wrong?" he asked, leaning his head out of the driver's side window.

Ignoring him, I rushed around the hood and climbed inside the car. "You don't have somewhere to be right now, do you?"

He shook his head. "No, why? What's going on?"

"I don't want to be alone," I replied, taking off my glasses to wipe at the splatter of rainwater. It was a partial truth. An excuse. "And I want that interview now, instead of tomorrow. I want to hear your side of that twin-coin. Is that...okay?"

There was a pause then, with just the sound of rain pattering against the roof, and the car's engine rumbling softly around us. Being surrounded by it created a sense of anticipation, like a breath about to be taken.

He grinned, those dimples drawing my attention like magnets. It really did make his smile seem magical. "Sure, let's go."

Jamie took us back onto the main road, heading downtown. He cranked the heat up high, and though the windows started to fog at the corners, it made the rain outside less intimidating; I felt bundled and safe. He drove slowly, bringing me down one twisting, curving road, and then another. I watched the trees pass like a messy watercolor, colors melting from yellow to green and back again.

"I'll have to bring the car home eventually," Jamie said, pulling back my attention, "but for the next couple of hours, I'm all yours."

The heat in those words hit me like a full-body wave, but I shook away improper thoughts and put on my metaphorical reporter's hat. I was going to approach this interview differently. No softball questions. No leading.

"What is your greatest fear?" I asked.

Jamie whistled. "Whoa, really?" He used one hand to rub the back of his neck, keeping his gaze on the road.

I let him think about it, let the silence do the talking for me. Sometimes it was the most effective tool at getting someone to open up.

"Letting my family down," he said, eventually. "Failing them."

"By not making it big in hockey?" I surmised.

He looked over at me. "How much did Brendan tell you, exactly?"

"Enough to know why being successful might be so important to you. But still...I want to hear it in your words."

We came upon a small park, and through the rain-drenched window I could make out a gazebo in the center of a circle of short hedges. It was painted a faded white, and on a sunny day it might look like a romantic place for a picnic, but as the clouds choked the sky and the trees swayed in the storm, it seemed more like a rock thrusting from the ocean, battered on all sides by the tide.

He pulled the car alongside the park and turned off the engine, the hush of the rain growing louder. I wondered if this place was a common make-out spot for teens—if Jamie or Brendan had brought any girls here while they were in high school. But kissing seemed to be the last thing on Jamie's mind. He was lost in thought, staring out into the rain.

"I know he thinks I'm living this high-profile life right now," he said. "The games are streamed on local channels, and I get a lot of attention for my time on the ice. But just because it's called a game doesn't mean it isn't...taken seriously. Any time I go out there, I could break a leg or get a concussion or worse, and all my opportunities would be gone. All my chances to help him and my mom would go down the drain like that—" he snapped his fingers. "I don't have much to fall back on."

"Do you feel like you need to be a good player for *them*? Or is hockey something you started doing for yourself?"

He placed his hands on the steering wheel, then removed them. I could see he'd rather be walking or running—something physical—but with the storm, he just sat beside me in the car, our breath clouding the windows.

"I loved playing when I was growing up. But I knew what it cost my mom to keep me in the sport. Brendan thinks I take it for granted, but I don't. Every time I needed a new stick, or for my skates to be replaced when my feet got too big, I knew she'd be working extra shifts just to get them for me."

"That must have put a lot of pressure on you."

"Yeah," he lifted one shoulder. "But it was worth it. Every time I stepped out onto the ice, I felt more alive. I had so much energy as a kid I didn't know what to do with it, and suddenly, I could skate and hit and practice shots in my spare time. It kept me focused. And I was good at it. If you were good at something you knew could drag your family out of a financial hole the size of Maine, you'd do it too, wouldn't you?"

He stopped suddenly, as if aware of what he'd said. Brendan had implied they didn't have much in the way of money, but from Jamie it sounded like they were buried in debt. I debated asking about it, but decided against it, figuring it had to be a sore spot. Plus, I wanted to bring the conversation closer to his life with Brendan.

"How did your brother feel about your hockey prowess? Was he athletic growing up too?"

Jamie shook his head, then seemed to decide something.

"Come with me."

He pulled open the car door and ran out into the downpour. Stunned, I watched him dash to the gazebo.

"What are we doing?" I shrieked, following him. Within seconds I was soaked. I hadn't worn a jacket today, and the sweater I wore stuck to me, heavy and cold, as I climbed the two steps up into the shelter. The gazebo had a hexagonal platform, with benches lining the inside. Jamie was already settled into one of them, holding out his arms.

His T-shirt was wet, clinging to what looked like a very solid stomach I was sure had at least a handful of defined muscles.

God, what was up with me? I'd never felt this kind of magnetic pull to a guy before. Friendly flirting was one thing, but as he spread his legs a bit on the seat, the hems of his jeans dark with rainwater, all I could imagine was crawling on top of him, straddling that lap. Taking his damp hair in my hands and kissing him senseless. Usually, I needed to date for at least a couple weeks before my mind drifted in that direction. Feeling this out of control was a bit...unnerving.

"This is one of my favorite spots," Jamie said, dragging my mind out of its spiral. "Brendan and I used to play card games on the floor here. The hospital our mom works at is only two streets away, and our house is just a few blocks beyond that. Sometimes we would wrestle or bring our friend, Pete, here to do some generally stupid shit, like smoke pot or sneak a beer."

I took the seat next to him, looking around the gazebo with new eyes and trying to picture two teen boys calling this dainty gazebo their own hideaway. And then I peeked down at the bench. By my thighs was a carving: "ONE DAY."

"Yeah, we did that," he said, following my eyeline. "Or, well, I did."

"Is Brendan not a fan of defacing public property?"

Jamie smirked. "Not as much as I am."

"What does it mean?"

"That one day we'd make it. We'd be rich and get out of here. Take our mom somewhere warm and sunny or just...different."

"I thought you liked Spindle River?" Jamie talked about the history of the town with so much affection. Also, he and Brendan had both chosen to stay close to home, instead of going to college in another state. Although it was obvious they both felt a responsibility to their mother and her health, which I was sure had a lot to do with that decision.

"I like it well enough," he said, tone nonchalant, "but I've always wanted to see more, you know? Once I make it into the national league, I'll get to fly all over."

I tilted my head, the feel of my wet hair heavy on my shoulders. I pushed it aside and Jamie watched the movement in a way that had my pulse racing.

"Is that your dream, then?" I asked after a moment. "Travel around and play hockey? Have enough money to keep your family comfortable?"

"Yeah," he said, wistfully. "That would be pretty damn perfect."

A streak of lightning arced through the sky, followed swiftly by a booming peal of thunder. I shivered a bit, scooching closer to Jamie. He put his arm around me without asking, the move already familiar and comforting.

"I wouldn't mind a girl to come home to either," he said, all sly.

I huffed a silent laugh. "Trust you to take this deep conversation and pepper some philandering in there."

"You and your big words," he teased. His thumb stroked my arm and we sat for a while, watching the rain drip off the gazebo roof. He got a text and pulled away to check his phone, his calm, easy expression going a bit troubled.

"Everything ok?" I asked.

He nodded. "Yeah. Fine." Putting the phone away, he turned to me. "Go on a date with me."

"What?" I was a bit confused. Wasn't that sort of what we were already doing?

"A real one," he added, reading my mind. "One where I pick you up and the time is decided in advance. Where I can actually take you somewhere fun." His eyes were hopeful, that tilt on his mouth turning his smile into an impish smirk.

I pressed my lips together to stop myself from grinning too widely. "Okay. Yeah, I'd like that."

Jamie's hand settled once more along my shoulder, as if he wanted me to stay put. The heat from his palm seeped through my sweater onto my skin, so hot it might have been a brand, marking me. "Great. It's a date."

CHAPTER EIGHT

Jamie drove me back home, and the energy between us seemed to shift. There was that anticipation, but also something else—a buoyancy that bounced between us, like the giddy dynamism of first love. I'd been in relationships before, gone on dozens of dates, but I'd never felt this level of excitement for some future date I knew nothing about. I think he felt it too.

The radio played some love ballad from the eighties, and more than once I caught his hand moving from the steering wheel to hover over the gear shift, getting close to my own palm that rested on my lap, like he wanted to take it in his own. There was no reason the idea of him holding my hand should have been so exhilarating, and yet it was. It was almost embarrassing.

The rain continued as we drove, forcing the wipers to their maximum speed. While the air between us was hot and damp, the windows always seconds from fogging, the brumous night was unable to reach us.

We pulled into my driveway too soon, not having said much, but when he killed the engine and looked over to me, his eyes darted to my lips then back up. I tried not to grin too stupidly.

"Thanks for this..." I started, feeling oddly shy and gesturing to the house. "The ride and everything. And spending time with me."

"You know me, I'm a giver," he replied with a wink, and then he rubbed a thumb over his mouth, like he regretted saying something so cheesy. "So..." his gaze landed on my lips once more, quick, but not quick enough to miss, "I'll see you tomorrow morning? I usually drop Brendan off on campus for Stats anyway, so I can just grab you and drop you both off."

"Yeah, that sounds good. If it's too much trouble though, just text me. Mornings aren't as scary, you know?"

He nodded. "Makes sense."

I waited a beat, wondering if he would make a move. If we'd kiss before our first official date. I wanted to, and I could tell he wanted to. But I understood it would be too fast, like we were jumping in without looking. There was a connection between us, obviously, and a chemical attraction. His body, his smell, and his vibrant hazel eyes—always sparkling at me like he wanted to let me in on a private joke—they all drew me in. I wished I had asked him more questions at the gazebo and gotten to know him better. Normally conversations with guys I liked were more interview than not, even if there was no potential article involved, but I just liked hearing him talk. Too bad I'd also enjoyed sitting snuggled up to him in the quiet.

When he didn't lean forward or say anything else, I opened the door, ready to duck out into the rain.

"Have a good night," I said. "Thanks again."

"Yeah, you too." He sounded preoccupied, but I waved and hurried up to my door.

I just about had my key in the lock when I heard his car door open and close.

Turning, I watched him jog up to me.

"What—"

"Sorry, I meant to do this," Jamie said, reaching me. He wasn't breathing hard from the jog, but his cheeks were tinged with pink. He pulled in a harsh breath, as if getting ready for a dive. And then he held my face in both of his hands and leaned in close.

There was a pause as he breathed against my mouth, his eyes dark and serious as they met mine. I nodded, hearing him ask without any words.

And then he kissed me. I stood there on the front steps, the rain cold on my shoulders, but his lips were so warm as they moved over mine softly. Once, and then again. He started to pull away, keeping it sweet, but I had my hands in his shirt, and I couldn't help but pull him closer. The firm length of his body pressed into me from knees to shoulders, and his heat enveloped me, curling through my veins down to my toes. I trembled with it.

His tongue moved against my lips, and I opened my mouth for him, letting him tilt my jaw for better access. I almost groaned at the feel of his tongue sliding over mine. It was like a roaring in my ears, this kiss. All encompassing. His hands moved from where they cupped my face, one moving to my waist, dragging me somehow ever tighter, the other skimming down my arm, then up, curling around the back of my neck and fisting in my hair.

His fingers at my hip clenched, gripping me tight, and I flinched, hissing as he accidentally pressed into the long scratch that crazy woman had left behind.

"Shit, are you okay?" he asked, pulling back.

I nodded, slightly out of breath, feeling like I'd just been dragged from some unfathomable depth. My body was singing with adrenaline. "Yeah, just...still a little banged up, I guess."

He swallowed, and I was pleased by the rough cadence of his voice as he said, "God, I'm sorry."

"No, it's fine. Honestly." The rain was catching on my eyelashes and making my glasses a watery mess. I rubbed my hands over them so I could see.

Jamie chuckled. "I guess that's probably my cue to leave." He looked back at his car.

"Are you sure?" I asked. I didn't outright tell him he could come inside, but the idea was definitely present. I wouldn't have hated to have him on my couch, or on my bed. Just to dry off. I could only imagine what he would look like shirtless...

"Yeah." He rubbed a hand over his neck. "I need to get the car home. I'll, uh, see you tomorrow?"

"I'll be here."

Looking sheepish, he backed away from the front steps, then walked to his car.

He waited until I was safely inside to drive away.

In comparison to all the excitement of the kiss, the house felt as still and as cold as before. I turned up the thermostat and rushed to get out of my wet clothes and into some comfy sweats, pulling my drenched hair up into a ponytail. My curtains were all still drawn, but I felt braver tonight, steadier, so I opened the blinds on the patio doors and gazed outside.

The rain was rippling over the pond, the willows hanging heavy with water. Nothing seemed amiss, though beyond the first line of trees I couldn't really see anything in the dark. As I drew back, I caught sight of a puddle right by the door. It was muddy and wide, like a plant had sat there gathering rainwater until it was removed. The ground seemed level, but there must have been some dirt beneath the pavers, saturating and pushing water up from the ground, I reasoned.

Still, it brought back the nerves from the attack. The wet feel of that woman's skin. I remembered how dirty she was. How I could barely tell the color of her body or her hair. That had to be why my confused mind had decided she'd looked blue. Like an alien of some kind.

With a weak shudder, I pulled the blinds closed once more, blocking out the yard.

After putting together notes about what Jamie had told me, briefly Googling what could tint a person's skin blue, and then doing some Netflix binging, I lay in my bed replaying the quasi-date and the kiss over and over again. The way he'd held my jaw. The feel of his hard body against mine. It was like a movie I never wanted to stop watching.

My body heated just thinking about it.

I wiggled deeper into my blankets, my skin suddenly oversensitive and my heart fluttering in my chest.

A chime from my nightstand had me reaching for my phone, only to find an email notification from one of my old classmates, Andrew, from my senior year of high school.

We'd dated for almost three months, and he'd been one of my closer boyfriends. He'd worked on the newspaper staff with me, though he had mainly been a photographer, who only wrote columns when the teacher forced him too, and always about whatever metal band he was into at the time. What I'd always liked about him was his proclivity for sending me links to interesting news stories he thought I'd enjoy. And this was no different.

The email was a regular update on his life at NYU, where he was currently dating a man named Donnie he'd met through an app, and links to some of the photos he'd contributed to his university's paper. I laughed at a particularly grainy shot of a pigeon sitting on an old man's head, flapping its wings as if about to lift the guy off the ground. It was for an article about bird migration patterns, but the photo was definitely the draw.

I couldn't help but compare the dates we'd been on to the night I'd just had with Jamie. I was attracted to Andrew, sure. He had beautiful brown eyes and short hair that he lathered with mouse and gel until it was a decorated mess. It fit his dark, skater-type aesthetic. I recalled the way his hands had felt on my hipbones and the way he would crowd my space when we kissed, enveloping me. The sex had been pretty good, though he'd also been one of my firsts, so I hadn't really amassed a particularly good scale for that yet. But I'd never looked at him and felt my heart go heavy. Never had trembling hands and heat curling down to my toes. It had been nice but not...intense.

God, how was I feeling this way already? And why was my next thought about Brendan, wondering if he kissed the same? Wondering if he had the same kind of passion looming behind his soulful expression.

I put the phone down, shaking my head. Obviously, my brain was just a mess of hormones. There hadn't been anyone serious at South Carolina, and while I'd hooked up with one guy spring semester, my summer had been a hectic time—scrounging to get my transcripts and schedule in order at a new school, packing and moving into this house, leaving another life behind. I hadn't had time to feel this...ache.

In the dark of my bedroom I released a long breath, bringing my hand up to the soft cotton of the shirt I slept in. I was safe in this room, in this bed, and I'd been kissed just hours ago. The feeling of being *alive* coursed through me, hot and wet. That was why I couldn't think of anything else, I decided. If I could get it out of my system, maybe I could think straight.

My hand grazed over one of my breasts, the peak there hardening between my fingers. I closed my eyes and imagined Jamie there, watching me, that smirk fading from his mouth, his eyes going heavy-lidded as he stared. My fingertips stroked and tweaked my nipple beneath the shirt, my other hand drifting lower.

Hips shifting beneath the blankets, I teased myself through my underwear, wondering what it would feel like if he was here—if this was Jamie's hand instead of my own, his hard-won muscles bunching in his forearm. I was already wet, still keyed up from how he'd left me at my front door, and it was easy enough to push the fabric aside and dip one finger against my center.

I was soft and slick already, my body begging for attention. I curled one finger inside myself, then plunged in another, lifting my hips off the bed.

More. I wanted more.

Pressing the heel of my palm into that bundle of nerves at the apex, I pushed and rubbed, letting my fingers slide in and out, slow at first. And then faster. Deeper. My breathing and the rustling of the sheets were the only sounds in the room, but I could practically hear his voice. "Sorry, I meant to do this," he'd say again, climbing on top of me. He'd kiss me hard; all tongue and hands and teeth. And then he'd grind into me, just like this.

Gripping hard at my breast, I jerked my hips, pressing up into my hand, imagining the rough way he'd pound into me, the strength in his athletic body pinning me down.

I came with a soft moan, keeping quiet despite the empty house, as if he'd somehow know my thoughts if I were too loud. I huffed out a tired laugh at my own foolish musings, relaxed and sated, my breathing returned to normal as I removed my hand and the image of Jamie faded.

Curling onto my side, I felt sleep sneak up behind me and take me over, my mind finally blissfully silent.

***

I woke to a dark room, wondering what had pulled me out of a deep, dreamless sleep. The alarm clock on my nightstand read 2:44 a.m. and I groaned, rolling over, trying to get back to it.

But then I heard a thud.

My heart pounding, I sat up, trying to pinpoint where the sound had come from.

There was a screech, like the sound of something sharp on glass, and I wondered if there was a tree on the side of the house banging against the window. The first storm had done that, I remembered—made the branches sway and scrape against the siding. It had to be that. Right?

There was another thud, like something heavy falling, but I couldn't tell if it was inside or outside.

I felt around for my phone and pressed the numbers 9 and 1, cautiously making my way out of the bed. Maybe I should have been more serious about getting a weapon or taser like Jamie suggested, but the house was locked up tight and I'm sure I would have heard glass shattering if someone was breaking in. It had to be the storm.

My legs wobbled as I moved through the room toward my open door, debating if I should turn on the light. It would be safer in the dark if someone was in the house, but I didn't know my way around well enough. If I bumped into something or hurt myself, that could be worse. I turned my phone's flashlight on, wishing there was some kind of light source from outside. With the heavy storm smothering the sky there was no visible moonlight, and the house was too far from the street for any of the sporadic streetlamps to make a difference.

The hardwood creaked under my bare feet as I crept down the stairs. My phone light moved over the floor, casting an eerie, blue-tinted glare along my sparse furniture. Nothing seemed out of place. No one stood in my living room, waiting to attack me.

Another thud had my whole body jumping, spinning toward the kitchen and the patio's sliding doors. They were closed, the blinds reflecting my phone's light back at me. I was too afraid to move closer.

Instead, I kept my finger hovering over the "1" button, ready to bolt into the bathroom and lock the door if needed.

I waited, counting my breaths. First two, then five, then ten.

The wind howled, and something screeched once more. It was quieter this time, though. Like it was further away, or maybe the branch wasn't hitting the window as forcefully.

After a full minute of standing there petrified, when no other sounds but the howling winds echoed through the room, my shoulders lowered, and I rolled my neck.

This old house was going to give me a heart attack.

I made my way back to the bedroom and crawled under the covers, waiting for my pulse to slow, and after more than an hour of tossing and turning, I finally made it back to sleep.

CHAPTER NINE

Tuesday morning was gray but blissfully rain-free, and knowing Jamie and Brendan were on their way to pick me up, I spent an inordinately long time working on my hair and makeup. With a red lip and my blonde tresses curled into gentle waves, I tucked a plain, white T-shirt into the best-fitting jeans I owned and layered on a burnt-orange cardigan for a pop of autumn color. With some brown, heeled boots, I was the picture of casual, feminine confidence. At least, that was the attempt. I'd had to use a lot of concealer to make the under-eye bags from my poor night's sleep disappear.

When the gray Civic pulled up to the top of my drive, I locked up the house and got into the back seat. Both guys were in the front, but I wasn't sure who was driving. They were both wearing dark hoodies this morning, and there wasn't a pair of headphones in sight. I wondered if this was some kind of test.

"Morning, gentlemen," I said brightly.

"Morning, Sadie," said the guy in the passenger seat. He smiled, and the glimmer there made me think that was Jamie.

But then the guy in the driver's seat turned his head and gave me a wink. Brendan hadn't winked at me before. Had he?

"So..." I started, pulling my phone from my shoulder bag and pretending to scroll through my email, "how was work last night, Brendan?" I made sure not to look up at either of them.

"No robberies," muttered the driver. "So, could have been worse."

That was Brendan.

"Could have been more exciting, you mean," said Jamie from the passenger seat.

Brendan lifted one shoulder, and then his eyes met mine in the rearview mirror. "How are you doing? You okay?"

I bit my lip, debating how much of my late-night freak-out I should tell them. "I'm still a little frazzled, I think," I admitted. "I thought I heard some banging and scraping sounds last night, and I know it was the storm, but it still made sleeping difficult."

Brendan shared a glance with his brother as he expertly maneuvered through the winding roads toward campus. "See?" he said. "I told you one of us should have stayed."

"Hey, getting her to agree to the rides was difficult enough," Jamie replied with a huff.

I leaned forward. "And *again*, it was just the storm, and these rides are very kind and still totally unnecessary. I don't need someone staking out my house or constantly worrying about me."

"See?" mimicked Jamie, looking smug.

"Fair enough." The words were more of a sigh, but Brendan let it drop, keeping quiet the rest of the ride.

There was an awkward tension between us all then, which was odd because I wasn't sure exactly what had caused it. Their protectiveness was sweet, but also one notch above what I felt was deserved, considering how new our friendships were. It was almost...irksome. It made me feel smaller than I was, more helpless.

"I'm going to buy pepper spray," I blurted into the silence, as we neared one of the school lots. "And I've seen the police officers go by the house."

Technically, that wasn't true, since I left all the blinds and curtains drawn, but I believed that the officers were staying true to their word and doing drive-bys.

"There's really no need to worry about me," I added.

"Sorry," said Brendan, and his tone surprised me. He sounded genuinely remorseful. "We'll rein it in."

Jamie looked over at his brother, eyebrows low with concern, or maybe confusion. I watched them interact like a pair of interesting specimens under a glass. Brendan had told me they didn't have their own language, but I thought they might. Maybe they just didn't realize it.

Either way, Brendan pulled into a spot and turned off the car.

"All yours," he said to Jamie. "Come on, Sadie, Stats awaits." The excitement was forced, but I followed him out of the car, waving to Jamie. I did my best to match Brendan's long strides as we headed toward the Janus Building.

I waited until we were far enough from the car, and then I caught him with a hand on his arm, his dark expression too serious for me to ignore.

"Hey, are you okay?" I asked. "What's going on?"

He stopped, and his eyes closed for one moment, as if pained. "Yeah. Sorry. I just..." he cleared his throat. "Our mom was having a bad night last night. She hasn't been great the past couple days and it always puts me in a mood. I think it just makes me want to do something, you know? Be proactive."

"Wow. Yeah, I can only imagine. You must feel sort of...helpless."

He scratched at his neck, just like Jamie did when he was nervous. I found it strangely charming that they had the same tell.

"I guess," he said eventually.

"Well, as someone who has been to three whole Psychology classes, I would say you're projecting your need to protect your mother onto me."

A weak smile peaked through his features, like a single ray of sunshine between the clouds. "Wow, that sure is some Psych program we have here."

"What can I say, I'm very studious. And intuitive." I paused. "And hey, I appreciate your concern, I really do; you don't have to feel bad for wanting to keep the people around you safe. If this is your way of exerting control on an uncontrollable situation, maybe—maybe—I could allow the rides to continue, despite my forthcoming shopping trip to grab Mace and the fact that I am capable and self-reliant. Just...don't go overboard."

"I won't," he promised.

"Now, let's go suffer through some math." I held out my elbow and he put his arm through mine, his steps now noticeably lighter as we walked to class.

The week passed in what was quickly becoming a pleasant, albeit unconventional routine. Jamie—or both brothers, depending on their schedules—would pick me up in the morning and drive me to school. Then, after classes and/or hockey practice, one or both of them would drive me home. I used the opportunity to ask them more questions about life growing up in Spindle River—what changes the town had gone through, what their experience being a twin had done to affect their education and social experiences, and even how their dating histories differed.

I learned that Jamie tended to be a serial monogamist, jumping from one serious relationship to the next, which surprised me given his flirtatious nature. Brendan, on the other hand, was more of the casual dater. He'd been on dates with a handful of girls he met at his music gigs, and none of them had lasted more than four dates each. According to Jamie, each girl had been gorgeous and funny and smart, all great catches, but his twin grew bored easily.

Taking notes about all of this felt like keeping a very odd diary, but soon I saw a pattern emerge: while one brother focused wholeheartedly on the future, the other was very much entrenched in the present. It made for an interesting dichotomy, and I had a rough draft of my article ready for my first *Prowl* staff meeting. I made sure to pass it by Jaime and Brendan first, and despite both of them feeling a bit uneasy with the attention—although Jamie less so—they gave me the go ahead.

The staff meeting was housed in a room on the basement floor of Artemio Hall where Professor Lewis had his office. There were no windows, and the wide, white-washed room was bustling with activity when I arrived, reminding me of a frantic series of ant tunnels. The Editor-in-Chief, Kim Sann—a woman with her black hair in a high ponytail and wearing a sharp, emerald-green blazer—sat at a desk in the front. She was peering closely at the dual screens in front of her. I knew she was a senior, and even though she was only two years older than me, she gave off the energy of someone who had lived a long, stressful life. So I was surprised when I walked up to her desk to introduce myself and her entire demeanor changed.

"Oh, you're the one who wrote about the Barreto brothers? It was good work, breezy but with just the right amount of heart." She smiled, her teeth straight and blindingly white, her dark eyes crinkling at the edges with how wide she grinned.

"Thank you!" I said, a bit surprised. "I wasn't aware Professor Lewis had already shared it with you."

"Things move pretty fast around here." She gestured for me to look at the room behind me and the rush of the staff moving from desk to desk, all talking in hushed voices. "We're running a bit behind schedule today so things are too hectic to announce you to everyone, but if you want to claim a space in the back, I can email you something to proof in the next hour."

"Sounds good." I smiled, already empowered by the sheer energy of the room. It made me want to find some hard-hitting news story, blow the lid off a conspiracy, or scream into an old-fashioned rotary phone to "stop the presses!"

"Sadie," Kim called, and I turned. "Next week's assignments have already been designated—we started early today—but if you have any local interest pieces or blips you can get to me by Wednesday next week, we can see about squeezing it in. Just run the idea by me first."

"Will do." I saluted her like a soldier, and she chuckled before returning her attention to her screens.

I swerved through the masses, finding a small desk at the back with a built-in tabletop. It was similar to ones I'd had in high schools—easily movable and not a lot of space—but it was all I needed. Opening my laptop, I already saw the email from Kim with a story on a grassroots protest to proofread. Finally, I felt grounded. Like Spindle River had revealed an empty space and I was the missing piece that could slide into place there.

Brendan drove me home that night since Jamie had a late practice to prepare for a game on Saturday. He was excited to hear about the article being well-received, and even more enthusiastic when I told him I was thinking of using this weekend's clean-up of the Edgewood hiking path as my next piece.

"I was already planning on going, at least for a few hours," he said, "so I can bring you."

"How often do these things happen?" I asked.

"In the fall it happens once or twice to take care of the mess we get from summer tourists and prep the space for the October rush." He looked over to me in the passenger seat, maybe expecting my skepticism. "I know it doesn't seem like it, but we get an influx just like every other Massachusetts town with leaf-peeping roads and hiking trails. Southerners go crazy for that shit, and the campgrounds by the river are usually crowded from September to November."

"Even though there isn't really a river?"

"Like I said, it's mostly for the trees. But the trash won't clean itself."

"I'm surprised you're not going to Jamie's game," I said, and I watched Brendan's soft smile go flat.

"I go when it's a home game, but this one is across state. It would be a long drive. Plus, our mom usually works weekends and would need the car." He lifted one shoulder under his dark T-shirt, the move too casual. "This weekend it just worked out that I could go to this clean-up. And I'd rather do that."

I heard what he was saying underneath the words. His mom didn't need the car. "Your mom still not working right now?" I asked.

He shook his head but didn't say much else as he drove us into the night. It had been a week of quiet nights—clear skies and no obvious disturbances outside—so I wasn't as worried about the dark when he dropped me off. His silence, however, was disconcerting—not awkward, but solemn. Heavy. I wished I knew what to say to ease his anxieties. Still, I didn't know much about their mother, and I could tell from the grip he had on the steering wheel that tonight was not the night to ask.

Brendan's arms stiffened, like the quiet was making him uneasy as well, and he cleared his throat. "What does your mom do for work? You've never said."

"Well, she left when I was pretty young, so I have no idea."

His eyes darted over to me, but he kept most of his attention on the road. "Shit. That sucks. Sorry if bringing it up is—"

"No! It's fine, really. My dad is amazing, and other than a couple specific milestones I would have wanted her there for, I haven't felt…" I waved my hands, searching for the word, "bereft in any way. Plus, it's why I've gotten to move around so much, following my dad for his work. It's the reason I've met so many people and developed my drive for journalism. Like it was meant to be, you know?"

"So, you actually like switching schools all the time? Is that why you left USC? Got bored?"

"Oh. No," I said, and then I paused, unsure how to continue. I didn't *hate* moving around so much, but I had been looking forward to staying put. That is, until I'd been practically forced out.

This time, his glance was longer, his expression pinched. He didn't like that he'd hit on something sensitive. "You don't have to talk about it if you don't want to."

I shrugged, shifting in my seat. "It's not a huge deal, it's just…something that spiraled out of control, you know? It took on a life of its own."

He stayed quiet, waiting to see if I'd tell him more, and I decided, in that moment, that I wanted to. Brendan wouldn't hold it against me, and if I graced him with my own nugget of painful truth, like a peace offering, maybe he'd be more open to sharing his own inner turmoil. This was how you built trust, wasn't it? I wanted him to trust me. I wanted to know everything about him. His warm, sugared scent wafted around me, comforting and sweet, and I took a deep breath of it to steel myself.

"So..." I started, "the whole story is that I was investigating this teacher that one of my roommates said made her uncomfortable—the way he watched her in class and such. There was nothing on his record, but I followed him for a couple weeks. I ended up finding him one afternoon coming out of a closet, holding a girl's underwear and shoving it into his pocket."

Brendan made a sound somewhere between surprise and disgust.

"Yeah," I agreed. "I got a picture, but I didn't know for sure what was going on until a few days later when I caught him buying more underwear from a freshman girl in the parking lot. A girl, I found out, who was in his class. He constantly snuck away into closets and bathrooms afterward, and I didn't even want to think about what he was doing in there, but it was obviously sexual and *not* meant for campus. Still, the girl who'd sold the underwear refused to talk to me when I asked her about it. I was eager to expose him for the creep he was, so I wrote an exposé and my editor agreed to publish it so long as we brought it to the university board first. He was fired for soliciting, and for abusing his relationship with his student, so I thought everything was good." I licked my lips, hating this next part, wishing that by divulging it all again I could somehow fix it. "But then the girl accosted me on my way to class. She was *furious* I took part in dismantling what she considered honest sex work. She'd needed the money, and she hadn't been coerced or threatened into selling him the underwear like I'd alluded to in the article."

"Holy shit," Brendan murmured, then he turned to me with one eyebrow raised. "Still, he was in a position of power, buying an obvious sex-related item from her. That has to be some kind of violation, right?"

I sighed, a headache brewing at the memory of how she'd grabbed my backpack right off my shoulder, screaming at me in the hallway. "Yeah, but it didn't matter. She tore me to shreds online, and then some guys on campus started a protest group about me, saying that I was punishing men who had harmless sexual desires. It just spiraled into this horrible shit show. I got death threats pushed under my door, and the article had to be taken offline since the comments were all about *me*. I was essentially cancelled and I just...didn't know if I could claw my way back from that, you know?"

"I don't blame you for wanting to escape that," Brendan said, after a moment. His tone was soft and low in a way that felt like a physical caress, as if he'd touched my cheek. "Especially since you were trying to do the right thing."

We pulled into my driveway, and I took an uneven breath as he parked the car. "Sometimes it feels like I took the cowardly way out. I know being a reporter will always come with negative comments and critique—it's just something I need to get used to. And it was an important lesson to verify everything and never jump to conclusions. But...even though part of me understands I had the right to take that step, I still wonder if a fresh start was the best thing, or if I should have stuck it out."

Brendan shook his head, twisting his torso toward me as if to emphasize his full attention. "I think it was the best thing. You got out of a bad situation with the only real option that was left to you. And there is no way I would consider you a coward. Just smart. Besides, it brought you to us, right?"

I smiled, my cheeks warming. "Right."

He smiled back. "Goodnight, Sadie," he said, voice quiet. "Sleep tight."

"You too. See you Saturday."

Just when I was about to climb out of the car, he reached over, the movement slow and purposeful, and took my hand. His eyes were concentrated as his fingertips grazed my palms, ghosting over the mostly-healed scratches there. I had the feeling he was testing them to see how well I was recovered without asking, trying to keep his promise by being less overtly protective.

"Thank you for telling me about that," he said, looking up from my hand. "And for not asking about my mom. I know you wanted to." His smile was wry. "It's just...hard to talk about sometimes."

"It's okay. You can talk to me about it whenever you want to," I told him. "*If* you ever want to."

The calluses on his fingertips drew my attention, narrowing my focus to their slow glide back and forth along my skin. It felt better than it had any right to, like he was touching other parts of me. My breathing hitched. And then he released me.

My legs trembled under me as I left the car and headed into the house, guilt gnawing at me for the way my body had responded. Jamie and I hadn't kissed again since our make-out at my front door, but the intent was there to build something between us. And I had a real date with him scheduled for Sunday at some undisclosed location.

But now I was worried this hiking-trail clean-up on Saturday would feel less like an opportunity to write a story and have a friend tag along, and more like its own date.

CHAPTER TEN

I'd just finished some overdue cleaning when Brendan picked me up
Saturday morning, and I was pleased to note that, despite knowing
he *would* be the twin to come get me, I was pretty sure I would've been
able to tell him apart from his brother even if they'd both been there. His
hair was a bit wilder than Jamie's, now that it wasn't pressed down by the
wide band of his headphones; a soft wave of it brushed over his forehead.
I could also see the silver chain around his throat, winking at me from the
neck of his plain gray T-shirt. Definitely his signature accessory.

I felt a bit overdressed in a raincoat that draped low over my thighs and
a dark turtleneck underneath, but the weather had called for a cloudy,
windy day and I wasn't going to chance another rainstorm unprepared.

The Edgewood hiking path turned out to be only a ten-minute drive
from my house. The parking lot, which was already full, was only big
enough for a dozen cars, so minivans and trucks lined the road on either
side of the entrance. A small crowd of people were gathering by a rusted
metal gate on one end.

Brendan seemed quieter than usual this morning. His gaze was
somber as we walked up to the volunteer organizer, but I remembered
the way he'd reverently taken my hand yesterday and decided to continue

my new method for getting him to share: keeping my mouth shut, but in an obviously caring, I'm-here-when-you're-ready, sort of way.

A chill breeze tangled the loose strands of the braid I'd wrestled my hair into that morning, and in the shade of the mighty trees around us, I was glad to have my coat tied tightly shut.

"How are you not freezing?" I asked Brendan, scanning his T-shirt and jeans. We were handed a sheet of paper with a marked path and told we'd be working in small groups to cover various sections of the hiking trails, including the rest and view spots as well as the picnic areas. It looked like we were handling a northwest section.

"We'll be moving around a lot," he mused, studying the map, "and in an hour or two I think it'll warm up."

"If you say so." I crossed my arms, snuggling into my coat.

After collecting yellow arm bands that marked us as volunteer cleaners as well as a set of trash bags and mechanical grabber-arms, we set off with our group and headed into the dense woods.

"I feel kind of like an inmate," I said as we started the hike.

"They actually used to make prisoners do this until a few years ago," he replied. "Not sure why." His voice was far away, like he was only half paying attention, but his steps were sure as he led the way up a twig-strewn dirt path that was packed down from years of venturing outdoorsy types. Of which I was not.

I was already out of breath when we reached the first rise.

Our group consisted of a few middle-aged women I assumed were long-standing hikers, and one teen boy who looked very sullen to be here—probably forced to join the clean-up by his mother, or maybe as community service for some minor crime—and they were all doing much better than I was.

"Do you need to stop?" Brendan asked.

I shook my head, taking a deep breath of fresh air laced with pine and maple. It was invigorating. "Just need my forest legs."

He cracked a smile then. "Yeah, you strike me as a city girl."

I hurried to match his longer strides up a gently sloping trail, the brush and grasses buried under a thin layer of autumn leaves. At least the crunch underfoot was intensely satisfying.

"What makes you say that?" I asked, huffing. "The fact that I'm already dying? My glasses? My love for computers and the internet and specific latte drinks?"

"The way you watch people."

That took me aback. "What do you mean?"

"You would be bored stiff without tons of people to watch and catalogue. You've probably already made up a story about our volunteer group, and definitely everyone in our Stats class. Probably even the barista at the campus café."

"Oh, Alina? Oh yeah, I'm pretty sure she's a dancer, the way she moves behind that counter. All grace." I was trying not to pant, and failing. "I keep looking for her name to pop up on a campus poster for some performance arts piece."

Brendan chuckled at this, and I grinned, feeling strangely appreciated. It was rare for someone to see me so clearly, especially only having known me for a couple of weeks. Brendan was more observant than I gave him credit for, and I wondered if his quiet, moody attitude was only disguising a detective after my own heart.

Sweat started to gather at my armpits and under my breasts, and I took a minute to pull off my raincoat and tie it around my waist.

"Told you," he muttered, but his voice was full of humor.

"Okay, so I like to watch people and I was not made for strenuous exercise," I admitted. "What about you? Is this your idea of an easy stroll in the woods?"

"No, it's rough. But I do walk a lot. After classes, once my mom has gone to work, I like to walk around the neighborhood, just to stretch my legs. It helps me think. Plus, I've done this hike twice before, for the clean-up."

We reached a fork in the path and thankfully took the more level route, so my aching thighs could enjoy the stretch of easy walking. I rolled my shoulders. "So, on the record, why *do* you take part in this yearly excursion of trash pick-up?"

"I live here," he answered. "Why wouldn't I want to help?"

I waited, sensing more.

He sighed. "Fine. So, a few years back I got caught smoking weed on school grounds. My history teacher sentenced me to this clean-up as punishment, but it felt good to do something. I walked the whole path that fall, and I was proud it was clean, you know? So, I kept coming back."

The path opened ahead, revealing the picnic area that heralded the northwest trail. I took in the sight and released a long, low breath. It was charming. There was a series of wooden tables arranged in a loose square shape, the center taken up by a wide but clean fire pit. Bursts of color edged the clearing, mostly red maples to one side, and some vibrant yellow-leaved trees on the other. They glowed as the cloud cover above shifted momentarily, letting through some soft, warm sunlight. There were bushes ripe with dark berries at my knees as we wandered into the space, bright purple flowers growing lush beside them. A pair of squirrels skittered under one of the picnic tables then raced up a tree.

"It's like a different world," I marveled aloud, then turned to Brendan to find him watching my expression. "I know I love the city," I added, "but...this could be nice too."

He pressed his lips together, as if hiding a smile, then held out his hand. "Give me your phone."

I forked it over without a thought, barely paying attention to the rest of our group as they went on ahead. Maybe they were used to the scenery already, or had been here a handful of times before, but I couldn't help but stop and admire the way the trees towered at the edges of the clearing, creating this little sanctuary in the middle of the woods. I could imagine families having reunions here, cookouts around the fire, children plucking berries from the bushes, staining their fingers blue.

Brendan held up the phone toward me, which almost startled me out of my musings.

"I thought you were going to take a picture of the beautiful scenery," I said.

"I did," he replied. A shy smile finally appeared, transforming his face.

I grinned back, though it felt dangerous to do so, and when he handed me back the phone, I inspected the shot he'd taken. There I was, gazing ahead, dappled sunlight streaming on my cheeks. My dark turtleneck was stark against my blond, messy braid and the yellow-tinted trees behind me. I looked like an autumn witch communing with the sun. It was a good picture, beautiful even, just like he'd said.

"Too bad you didn't catch me actually picking up trash," I said, putting the phone away. "Then I could use it for the article."

"We've got time." He gestured for me to follow, and we continued our trek along the path, eventually making it to our designated cleaning assignment.

There was more trash than I thought there would be. At first you couldn't really tell what was decaying leaves and what was muddy refuse from campers, but sure enough after a few minutes I could spot candy wrappers and crumpled water bottles under the ground cover. We plucked detritus like a single sock with a hole torn into it, some beer cans, an empty cannister of sprayable sunscreen, and even a condom—make that two condoms.

"Wow," I muttered, using my grabber to put it into my trash bag. "People really like to get lucky around here, huh?"

Brendan laughed, picking up a beer can. "Late nights, far from the campground...teens sneak away to do all types of dirty deeds."

"Speaking from experience?" I asked. His silence had me looking at him over my shoulder, my grabber forgotten in my hand.

"You didn't!" I hissed, scandalized.

He laughed again, this time loud enough that it caught the attention of our group members. I'd never heard him laugh like that before. It was like Jamie's but...different. Deeper, maybe? It resonated inside me like heavy bass at a concert, sticking to my ribs.

"You should see your face," he said, still chuckling. His whole body was lit up, as if being in this space made him freer. Or maybe it was being active that gave him a new radiance. He wanted so much to be *helping*, I realized. Helping anyone, anything. It was attractive. As was the way his muscles ticked under his shirt as he tugged another half-buried scrap of trash out of the dirt. His body seemed fuller under the sunlight, as if shadows were the only thing that made him seem leaner than his brother.

I shook my head and went back to picking up litter as we moved our way up the trail in a slow line, taking photos with my phone here and there of our group—with their permission—to add to my article. Even halfway through the clean-up they looked cheery and pink-cheeked. As anticipated, I had sweat through my turtleneck before lunch time.

Exhausted and sore, I followed Brendan back down the sloped trail to the parking lot around one in the afternoon. Our section of the woods was successfully cleared of summer trash, ready and waiting for a new host of guests to pollute the area. But I did feel accomplished, even proud, like he'd said.

I handed my full trash bag over to the organizer, a man with a military-short haircut, the wiry frame of a runner, and a plastic name tag reading, "Ronald Highland." I then took out my phone and turned on the voice recorder. After explaining I was writing an article for the university newspaper, he was happy to answer all my questions: how this was planned each year, how many people usually took part, and any changes he'd noticed throughout the years. It was all very banal and ordinary, until that last question.

"The trash has actually gotten better in the last couple tourist seasons," he informed me, which was surprising. Usually, pollution and trash problems tended to get worse over time and not better, according to my research. "The clean-up used to take close to five hours with a group this size, but it's dropped down to four."

"And what do you think the reason is for that?" I asked. Brendan waited patiently behind me, scrolling through something on his phone, but I could tell he was listening.

"The park has seen fewer guests in the summer since the river levels have dropped," Ronald replied, taking another trash bag from a leaving volunteer, and thanking them with a firm handshake. "It wasn't as noticeable until the last decade or so…but with less water comes less boaters and water-skiers. We used to have a crew competition here, if you can believe it, until about 2016. But the water level has dropped an inch every couple years and now it's too low to even swim in."

"Do you know what's been causing this?" I remembered the ravine Jamie showed me, and how it used to be a wide river he could barely remember.

Ronald shook his head. "No idea. It's been happening so slowly and for so long it's sort of just become a way of life. I think for a while the mayor was looking into it—something about the rising temperature of the watershed—but nothing came of it. A few buddies of mine think it's the Santa Elena plant down the way, but there's nothing to back that up. Might just be the way of the world, you know? Global warming and all that."

He paused and crossed his arms, as if considering something else. "We've seen some nearby trails go too dry and rocky to safely traverse, like the whole area is shriveling. It's a shame though...soon enough there won't be much tourism at all except for the peepers."

Something tugged at me then, like a finger pulling at my sleeve—something I wanted to remember. After a moment I nodded, turning off the recorder.

"Thanks, Ronald. I appreciate the quotes."

"No problem." He turned, immediately making small talk with another volunteer.

"What's wrong?" Brendan asked as we walked back to the car.

I shook my head. "I'm not sure. I mean, it's upsetting about the river, obviously. It's strange no one has figured out what's going on. But the idea of the town dying around the riverbed...it reminds me of something I can't quite put my finger on."

"Maybe it's just how much the land here agrees with you."

"Don't let the glow fool you," I retorted, "it's all sweat."

We reached the car and Brendan pulled out his cell, an older model with a smaller camera than mine, and a crack along the screen. He unlocked it and pushed it into my hands. I stared, looking at...me. There were candid photos of me picking up trash, one of me interviewing the older of the middle-aged women who'd been in our group, and another one of me looking up into the treetops. In each one there was a sense of movement, of sweetness. He had captured each instant with a good, clear eye, and even managed to get the shadow of a bird in flight against the bark of a tree in the last one. It was like art.

"These are amazing," I said, stunned.

"You're an easy subject. Plus, it's the autumn effect. All the colors make the background more detailed, so the subject is contrasted against it. It's more beautiful that way..."

I looked up to see a harsh blush pinkening his ears, his hazel eyes straight ahead on the road as he started to pull away from the parking lot.

"You didn't tell me you were a photographer." Scrolling back through the images, I could imagine each one framed and on display. He'd made me look delighted and full of wonder, instead of sweaty and red-faced like I know I'd actually been.

He shook his head. "I'm not. I just take pictures once in a while for fun. When my band releases an album, I want to take the cover photo, but other than that it's not really serious."

"Can I send these to myself?"

"Sure," he said, lifting one shoulder. "I'm just glad I was able to capture you like that."

"With the land agreeing with me?" I laughed, wrinkling my nose.

What a strange way to phrase it.

"It just looked like you were having a moment," he explained. "You were connecting, or something."

"You're a bit of an odd duck, Brendan."

But he was right. Somehow, despite my love for lattes and libraries, the woods had rejuvenated me. An energy tingled at my fingertips, and I couldn't wait to get home and write about everything I'd seen and all the people I'd met. I was ready to tell the story of the Edgewood trails and its connection to Spindle River, the town and the waterway. Maybe I'd even use one of his photos instead of mine.

"Thank you for taking me," I added, hoping he didn't take any offense.

"Odd ducks gotta stick together," he replied, and when I looked over to him maneuvering the curved road back to my house, the desire struck me to reach out and tug the necklace he wore free from his shirt. My fingers even inched forward before I pulled them back. In that instant, I imagined using the chain to tug him over. To press my lips against his. To feel if his arms were as strong as they looked, his fingers as deft and sure. I imagined Brendan's kiss would be soft and slow, dragging in its leisurely glide.

Instead, I sat back harder against my seat, wondering why my heart was tripping in my chest. Was it because he made me feel beautiful, taking these pictures of me? Was it because he looked like Jamie? Was it because he was *different* from Jamie?

I just didn't know.

CHAPTER ELEVEN

My phone pinged.

Jamie: *Ready for our date tmrw?*

Me: *Not really, since you haven't told me what to expect.*

Me: *Did you win your game??*

Jamie: *4-2, Prowlers ;)*

Me: *Awesome, congrats! How many people did you beat up? lol*

Jamie: *Only 1, but he deserved it - called our goalie a bitch. Dress warm for our date tomorrow*

Me: *How rude of him. And warm like hiking? Because I'm full up on outdoor adventures.*

Jamie: *Guess you'll have to wait to find out*

Me: *:(Monster.*

Despite the emoticon, I was grinning as I put down the phone, re-reading my messages from the night before.

There were genuine butterflies fluttering around in my stomach while I checked my reflection in the mirror and adjusted the hunter green scarf around my neck. I'd gone for a thicker sweater today in a creamy white color, and skinny jeans that didn't have any holes. This was as warm as

I could get, since most of my wardrobe still consisted of clothing from last year in South Carolina. Besides, how cold would we be getting? It was luminously sunny out and already over sixty degrees when I heard Jamie pull up outside to pick me up.

The air had a crisp, fresh smell as I climbed into the Civic, and though my arms and legs were a bit sore from trash clean-up the day before, the scent energized me. Or maybe it was the grin Jamie aimed my way as he scanned me from head to toe.

"Wow. It's perfect."

"Really?" I asked, looking down at my outfit. "I was nervous since you still *refuse* to tell me anything about today." But it was hard to even put on a fake frown.

Jamie was in a navy hoodie, like the first morning I'd met him, but I could see a dark button-up beneath it. His jeans were gray and tight around his thighs, at least from where I could see. Not that I was looking too closely.

I dragged my gaze north and met his dazzling eyes, only vaguely noticing the soft shadow of scruff around his jaw.

"Don't you like surprises?" he asked, pulling out of my driveway.

A shadow seemed to move under the cover of the trees that lined the road, like the twist of smoke from a campfire, and my head twitched, following the movement. But there was no one there.

I released a breath, wondering how long I would feel so skittish around my own house.

"Sadie?" Jamie prompted.

"What?" I whipped my head back toward him. "Sorry, yeah. Surprises can be good." I offered what smile I could, and did my best to live in the moment, to enjoy the warm coffee smell of him and the crooked way he smiled while he detailed for me the game he'd won yesterday. Normally I wasn't too interested in sports, but he had a great way of narrating it like it was a hard-hitting news story. He laid out the brutality of each hit and the facts of each pass and goal, so I couldn't help but ask more and more follow-up questions: How did they decide what hits were illegal boarding? Where was the "crease"?" What was the difference between backchecking and forechecking? He answered each with obvious glee.

Sometimes my mind's constant craving for information could be a source of annoyance on dates; I'd learned early on that asking a couple questions was fine, but guys didn't like to feel grilled. Jamie was different—with each question he only grew more animated.

When he pulled the car into the SRU parking lot, which was surprisingly crowded, I turned to him with one eyebrow raised.

"For our date you're taking me to campus?"

"You'll see." He took my hand in his as we walked up the now-familiar path toward the Silenos Arena, the afternoon sunlight reflecting off the glass ahead like a snowy prism. Jamie's hand was calloused and hot in mine, and I prayed I wouldn't start sweating. I wasn't nervous, per-se, more like excited. Eager. When his fingers tightened around mine, my heart thumped harder in my chest, those butterflies returning to do flips and dives in my belly.

The arena was surprisingly loud as we walked into the lobby. Music played through the speakers in the lobby—something bright and pop-y I recognized from the radio—and a few kids wobbled by on plastic-capped ice skates, gripping tight to their parents' hands as they awkwardly maneuvered the short trip to the ice. Laughter and happy screams echoed beyond the metal double doors.

"Tell me, Sadie, do you know how to skate?" He turned to me with a wink.

"Not at all," I said with a smile.

"Perfect."

He directed me to the counter where skates were rented and paid for a pair, then asked the girl manning the booth—a freshman I recognized from my Psychology class, with her hair in intricate braids and a nametag that read "Stacy"—to pull his hockey skates from behind the counter.

Making our way down toward the ice, Jamie pulled me to a bench and crouched in front of me. He laced up the daintier figure skates for me with steady hands, which I couldn't help but stare at while he worked. They were large and a bit rough, his nails cut short, a vein on the back of his hand catching my eye and not letting me go. I didn't know a hand could be so attractive.

"The thing to remember is you're more likely to fall backward than forward, so always lean toward your feet and you'll do fine." He tugged at the laces, his bent head putting his dark, slightly wavy hair on display. I itched to run my fingers through it, then remembered the way he'd kissed me on my front steps. The way he'd held my hand on the way into the arena. Who said I couldn't touch him just as easily as he touched me?

His hair was just as soft as it looked. It sifted easily through my fingers like strands of silk, and I used the tips of my nails to graze over his scalp.

He looked up, a tuft of swept hair falling over his forehead, and I pushed it back, enjoying the feel of it under my palm. His eyes went heavy-lidded.

"Hey now," Jamie warned, his tone a bit gravelly. I could see the promise in his expression. His eyes darted to my mouth.

"Sorry," I said, not sorry at all. "I had to."

He cleared his throat and took a steadying breath before going back to pull the last laces over the tiny metal prongs on the boots. "If your ankles start to hurt, let me know and we can adjust the boots. Or I can just carry you around the rink." His mischievous smile was back as he held out that gorgeous hand, helping me stand.

The sensation of skates on my feet was strange. I'd been roller skating before and those were heavier, but these were more...precarious. I could feel my ankles wobble a bit from side to side as they tried to balance on the thin blade.

"Alright?" He asked.

I nodded, gripping his hand tight as he led me toward the ice.

There were maybe a hundred or so kids skating in slow, uneven loops around the rink. A few adults in black-and-white striped shirts meandered back and forth, helping those who needed it, picking kids up off the ground and dusting the ice off their jackets. There were maybe a handful of people our age, but it was mostly a younger group.

"Is this a kid's hour or something?"

Jamie tilted his head, as if unsure how to answer. "It's a learning hour for new skaters, which—in Spindle River—are usually pretty young. Skating is big here, and there's a discount on Sundays so the place gets packed." His cheeks seemed to flush with color then. About the discount? I wasn't sure.

Hand steady in mine, he gently tugged me to stand at the open door to the ice.

"Ready?"

I nodded, and then immediately regretted it as my skates met the ice and my entire equilibrium changed. I slid forward, then back, then wobbled side to side.

Jamie chuckled as he held me steady.

"Try grabbing onto the railing for now, then push off one skate at a time at an angle, like this—" he swept each of his black hockey skates out at a forty-five-degree angle, the motion reminding me of swimming.

"I mean, I watched your practice, and I've seen ice skating before," I told him, trying out the motion, though at a much shorter distance, "but it's so much harder than it looks." I giggled nervously as my skates wobbled again, which turned into a shriek of laughter when I almost toppled backward. Jamie's hands were on each of my arms then as he skated backward, leading me inch by inch.

"Now lean forward," he reminded me. "That's it." His smile was wide and white and completely gorgeous. That dimple appeared and I would have preferred to spend time memorizing it, but I had to look back down to my skates. At the angles of my blades as my feet drifted forward in unsteady jerks.

"You're actually doing pretty well," he said. And it sounded surprisingly honest.

Feeling brave, I took a longer stride, and then another, leaning forward and holding on to his forearms for dear life. Children were racing past us, emphasizing how slowly we moved, but it was still exhilarating.

Jamie pulled to the side so he was skating in the same direction as me, holding on to my left arm so my other hand could hover over the low wall.

His jean-clad legs moved with grace and power beside me, and though I was still getting my ice-legs, it made me want to dash into the center of the rink and watch him chase me. As if I would survive getting even a foot away from the boards.

"How fast can you skate?" I asked.

"Not sure," he said. "Maybe fifteen miles an hour? Maybe more. I haven't clocked it."

"Your coach should have a skating contest, to see what your speeds are," I suggested. It was easier to talk now that my legs had sort-of figured out how to move. A bit to the right, then a bit to the left. Lean forward. Hold Jamie's hand with a death grip so he can lead the way gradually around the outer edge of the ice.

"I'll mention it, though what matters more is maneuverability," he said. "That, and how accurately you can swipe for the puck. How close you can get to another player's skates."

"Well, you're doing pretty good now," I said with a nervous chuckle. His skates kept drifting so close to mine they almost touched.

"That's why I'm good—I don't mind getting right on top of somebody."

I barked a laugh at the innuendo. "Does that confidence come free with the skates?"

A boy with a bright yellow puffer jacket zoomed past and when my attention drifted to follow him, my feet went too far forward. One slipped out from under me, and then the other, but Jamie was fast. Pulling me up before I could hit the ice, he yanked me close. My chest and stomach crashed into his hard body, the hoodie doing nothing to temper the feel of those solid muscles beneath.

A breath whooshed out of me. "Thanks."

"No worries."

I looked up to see him grinning, that languid look back in his eyes. I imagined him leaning down and kissing me, right there surrounded by a bunch of squealing kids, but he carefully released me. My feet touched back to the ice, and he let me get my bearings before returning to my side.

"The confidence is all just part of being a player," he said, and I struggled to remember what we'd been talking about before he'd held me against that built, wide body. "It's kind of like playing a part."

"You mean you don't actually feel sure about your abilities?" I asked. "But you're one of the best players. I've looked at your stats, the points or whatever. Assists and shots and time on the ice—it's all pretty high."

I could see him shrug from the corner of my vision, but I couldn't risk looking away from the ice to see the expression on his face.

"I'm good, but it's not like I've made one of the feeder teams yet—the ones that lead to the NHL. And there's a lot of pressure to keep those numbers up, to keep training and getting better." He paused, and I could tell he was thinking hard about how to say something. "The scholarship I have isn't based on grades, or even the fact I grew up in town. It's about how well I play and how good I can make the school look. I don't have something to fall back on like Brendan—he's got the grades and a job and other talents besides his music—all I've got is this."

I hadn't thought about Brendan this entire date, I realized. Despite the identical person currently shuffling me around the rink. I'd forgotten for a second that Jamie was a twin, and that I'd spent all day yesterday with his brother.

"You say that like your scholarship isn't incredibly impressive," I replied. "You have a dream and you're working toward it. Even though there's pressure...it's not something you can't handle, because you already are."

I squeezed his hand so he would look down at me. His frame was tall enough that when I peeked up, his head was blocking an overhead light, so he seemed haloed. "You're going to class, and practice, and games—which you've been winning, might I add—and you even have time to drive me around, as well as Brendan. I think that's enough."

I thought I heard a hitch of breath, like a sharp inhale, but Jamie looked as solid as ever. His hand shifted in mine, so our fingers were laced, and he squeezed. It was like something loosened in his posture and smoothed out his features. Instead of mischief there was...peace. The gesture felt like a "thank you."

"If only I could keep it up," he said, eventually.

I would have stopped, but our momentum kept us moving forward, my feet still shuffling in uneven, shallow glides. "What do you mean?"

He waved a hand, as if it wasn't important. "I'm just going to have to be here a bit more often. I'm trying to get an agent so I can score a professional contract, but my grades were slipping last semester. My coach is reducing my ice time at games to try and motivate me." He sighed. "It's what he was yelling at me about last week. I have to train better and really show up at practice while getting my GPA in order." With a jerk, he turned his head to me. "Don't mention this to Brendan, by the way. I don't want him to think I'm in trouble, or that I'm not...pulling my weight. This is all temporary—if anything, in a couple weeks I should be back on track, once our classes start posting temp grades."

I did my best to keep the concerned expression off my features. "Sure, I won't say anything. I'm sorry things are hard for you right now, though. I could always help you study," I offered.

"I might take you up on that. And don't be sorry. It's just life, right? Besides, you make things better just by keeping me laughing."

"How am I doing tha—" I slipped, windmilling one arm while clutching onto him with the other and he laughed, loud and fierce, as he righted me. I guess that was how.

Jamie and Brendan were both fighting their own battles to meet their goals, I realized, and all while supporting their family. A fissure of guilt cracked through me. I'd always had whatever I wanted growing up, and no trouble making good grades since I didn't have to worry about working side jobs or playing a time-consuming sport. I would make sure I was more available to help Jamie study, but would that be enough? Should I ask Brendan to drive me to and from school more often, so Jamie had more time for schoolwork? But Brendan needed his spare time too. I shook my head, resolving to think about it until I came up with a solution that worked for everyone. They were already doing so much for me, and I wanted to repay the favor somehow.

My ankles started to throb after another turn on the ice, which we skated in companionable silence, and Jamie made good on his offer to carry me around the rink. Putting an arm under my knees and another around my back, he lifted me against his chest and proceeded to speed around the arena, closer to the center, breaking us both out of our thoughts and plunging us into the moment.

I yelped, keeping my arms tight around his neck, my face pressed into his shoulder, until one of the referees yelled at him by name to put me down. Apparently, the guy had known Jamie for years, otherwise we would have gotten banned from the rink. But we were ready to leave anyway, so Jamie gingerly steered me back to the safety of a dry floor.

"I need to grab my gear from the storage closet," Jamie said around a satisfied grin, holding my skates in his arms. His hair was mussed, and there was a pleasing glint to his eyes that made me think of how he might look in bed. Slightly out of breath. Intent. Euphoric. "Gotta bring the stuff home to wash it. Be right back."

"I'll come with you," I offered. "Can you show me the locker room or the coach's office? It couldn't hurt any future hockey-related articles to have a behind-the-scenes view."

"Sure, come on."

I pulled on my normal shoes and followed him back to the skate rental booth where he handed over my boots to Stacy. His own were laced and hung over his shoulder, emphasizing the broad strength there.

As he led me down a long, well-lit tunnel, with concrete sides and a gray-blue painted floor, it felt like we were traveling deep into a mountain, like an underpass for miners.

"First stop," he said, gesturing to a dark metal door labeled "storage." There was a keypad beside it, and he typed in a four-digit code I had a suspicion was just 1, 2, 3, 4. The inside was the size of a walk-in closet, lined on three sides with metal racks full of cardboard boxes and mesh bags loaded with pucks and loose padding. There wasn't much room, so I could have stayed in the hall, but I was curious what other odds and ends an arena storage room might hold—some weird mascot uniform, maybe, or a secret alcohol stash. Just the idea made me want to write a story about the seedy underbelly of ice rinks and the proverbial skeletons in this storage closet.

Jamie turned to see me behind him. "Oh, don't let the door cl—"

I heard the hushed click of the door sliding shut behind me.

"What, why?" Reaching for the handle, I gave it a jiggle, but the door refused to open.

"It's okay, it just sticks a lot. Most of the time we prop it open with something, but I thought you'd stay outside. Sorry." A black mesh bag full of gear dangled in one hand while he gently eased me aside.

His own attempts to open the door were more impressive, yet ultimately useless. No matter how he shook the handle or pulled it, the door stayed shut. He sighed.

"People go down this hall all the time, so it's just a matter of time if we keep knocking." He looked over his shoulder at me while methodically hitting his fist on the door, the pounding like a drumbeat. "I swear I didn't mean to lock you in here with me." His laugh was nervous. "That's a fourth date move if anything."

"If you say so," I teased, only half-joking. I wasn't claustrophobic or anything, and the closet was big enough to pace a small circle, but there were other places I would prefer to be trapped with a handsome hockey player. Like a comfortable movie theatre, shrouded in shadows, or a hotel room with a very large bed.

I pushed those thoughts out of my head as I took the opportunity to peer more closely at the boxes on the shelves, reading the half-faded labels for rolls of duct tape and blank jerseys. If I got too cold at least I could layer up, but the room wasn't frigid like the rest of the arena.

If anything, it seemed to be getting warmer.

I loosened the scarf around my neck, pushing up the sleeves of my sweater.

"You okay?" Jamie asked me, his fist a metronome against the door. He looked genuinely concerned.

"Yeah, I think I'm just still warm from skating. I've been more active the past couple days than I have been in weeks." I sat on a cardboard box that seemed sturdy enough to hold me and attempted to smooth down the errant strands of hair that had fallen out of my braid.

"Well, if it helps, you looked good out there. Once you stopped flailing." His nose crinkled a bit, making a face at me.

"It does, thanks." I stuck out my tongue.

He turned back to the door and started pounding harder on it, almost unconsciously. I noticed his shoulders moving more with each breath, his lungs pulling more and more air.

"Hey," I said, standing. "Are *you* okay?"

He nodded but didn't look at me. "Yeah, just showing off my awe-inspiring strength. I'll probably break it down any second now." His voice shook a bit at the end.

The bravado wasn't fooling anyone.

"Like you said, people walk down this hall all the time, right?" I asked. I suddenly worried he'd said that more for his own benefit than mine, and that we were about to be trapped in this closet all afternoon. All night, even. I thought about asking when the next hockey game or practice would be held, but I was worried how far out that answer might be.

"Oh, I can call someone," I suggested, pulling my phone out of my pocket.

Jamie rolled his shoulders, then continued banging on the door. "I don't have Stacy's number. But anyway, yeah, there are always people going in and out of the locker rooms if they're regulars, so it should only be a minute or two. I don't know why I'm..." *freaking out*. He didn't say it, but I heard it loud and clear.

"Jamie," I said quietly, now really worried, but he didn't answer. He just kept pounding his fist on the door. "Jameson."

I didn't want him hurting himself trying to get out of here; I imagined he needed both hands in working order to play hockey. Leaving my perch, I walked up behind him and put my hand on his shoulder as lightly and unobtrusively as I could. His fist stopped. I could feel his muscles ticking under my palm, a slight tremor working its way through him as I pulled him around. The sudden silence of the room felt thick with tension.

Jamie was breathing in through his nose, doing what he could to remain calm.

"I swear I didn't do this on purpose," he said, almost a whisper. His eyes were wide, his cheeks more flushed now than when he'd carried me around the ice. He slumped a bit against the door.

I nodded. "I believe you."

If anything, now I knew this was the antithesis of his idea of a good time. He was obviously not a fan of being in small spaces.

"Everything is going to be fine," I promised. "We're in an arena full of people, including referees who will probably be stashing their uniforms or whistles or something in here, right? Let me text Lynne. She lives on campus; it wouldn't take her long to get here and let us out."

I typed out a quick message to Lynne, asking if she could make a run to the arena, and while I waited for her respond I put my hand on Jamie's jaw, scratching at the rough stubble there.

"I haven't seen you with a five o'clock shadow before," I added, trying to keep him distracted. He leaned the tiniest bit into my hand, like he was enjoying the sensation, so I rubbed my thumb over the skin there.

"We thought it might be a good idea." His voice was a bit choked. I kept up the motion of my thumb, trying to emit what I hoped were soothing vibes.

"We?"

"Brendan and I...so you could more easily tell us apart." He gave me a wobbly, uneven smile. "Don't think we missed the whole 'how was work last night, Brendan' thing."

I giggled, caught off guard. "How kind."

"I try. When this is coming in all patchy and the guys start making fun of me, I expect...ample appreciation."

My hand stilled. While I knew he was talking to keep steady and didn't really mean it, the image in my head that developed, like the slow clarity of a polaroid picture, was something I very much wanted to see. Me kissing him. Me climbing on top of him, wrapping my forearms around his neck and twining my legs around his. Me showing him just how much I appreciated the gesture.

His chest rose with a deep breath. Was he thinking the same things?

Those hazel eyes darkened under his lowering eyelids, almost as if in answer to my unspoken question.

The space between us seemed to dissolve, inch by inch, and the climbing heat in the room was making my skin overly sensitive to my sweater and the tight stretch of my jeans. I tilted my head up, thinking a kiss surely couldn't hurt in this situation, as it would distract him. Plus, I wanted to. I wanted it so much I just...let myself have it. It would be worth it, so long as I could make him feel better, even for a moment.

Taking the dive, I gave in, my mouth crashing up onto his.

At first, he seemed surprised. Frozen. And then his hand was at the back of my neck, fingers tangling in my hair, the other pulling me tight so his body was flush against me. My feet almost left the ground.

Jamie opened his mouth, his tongue instantly stroking against my own, and the wet heat traveled straight to my core. I moaned. The sound seemed to invigorate him and he tilted my head the way he wanted me, his lower body grinding into me as we spun, so I was pushed against the door. With the cold metal at my back and the hot feel of his chest at my front, I became a hurricane of sensation.

The kiss was like something out of my dirtiest fantasies, his lips moving over mine like a man starving for my taste, dragging and pulling at my mouth. His breathing was ragged, but then, so was mine. I clutched at his shoulders and then wrapped my arms around his neck just like I'd imagined. He took my new leverage for all it was worth, using his hips to pin me against the door. My legs lifted to lock onto his waist. He was hard against me, grinding up into my center so the pressure and friction of our jeans rubbed into the bundle of nerves at my core, sending sparks through me like wildfire.

"Jamie," I hissed at the sensation, wanting more, but his kiss swallowed the sound.

His strong arms had no trouble holding me still while he pushed up and into me, the rhythm growing faster, more frantic. This was insane. This was a *closet*. And yet I never wanted him to stop. I felt so...*alive*. My breasts were crushed into his chest, and I held his face with both hands, licking into his mouth, letting him control everything else. A noise pulled out of him, deep and low, and I knew if we kept going, if he kept moving against me, we were both going to—

I squealed when the door behind me disappeared.

If Jamie hadn't been gripping my hips so tightly, I would have fallen straight onto the concrete floor, but thankfully his hold on me was secure, and we somehow managed to stay upright.

We both blinked and looked at the person who had opened the door—a baby-faced guy with a goatee and a look of shock he quickly schooled into a wry smirk.

"Barreto," he said, nodding.

"Silvera," Jamie replied, his voice rough.

"Can I just scooch behind you?" He gestured to the closet and Jamie inched to the side, gingerly lowering me to the ground while the guy reached for one of the smaller cardboard boxes at the top of a rack.

Normally this would be when I turned bright red and buried my face in Jamie's shoulder, but as I caught my breath, I felt oddly brazen. I didn't care how it seemed, or how I looked. If my lips were puffy and swollen, or my hair was askew or my sweater was rucked up an inch too high, so be it.

My phone buzzed and I looked down.

Lynne: *I can be there in ten!*

"As you were," Silvera said in a voice laced with humor, leaving us. "See you at practice."

I sent a "never mind!" text to Lynne, while Jamie made sure to stop the door from closing again.

CHAPTER TWELVE

As Jamie drove me home, I expected what we'd started in the storage closet would continue, either in the car or at my place, but he surprised me with a chaste kiss goodbye, and something uneasy drifting across his expression.

I almost asked him what was wrong, but decided it was probably leftover emotional confusion. After all, the afternoon had gone from fun to nerve-wracking and then to spicy, until it had been doused with a bucket of cold water *à la* Silvera. Even I was a little discombobulated.

I tried to corral my frayed nerves and calm my unsettled libido by drinking a cup of chamomile tea and sitting by the patio doors, enjoying the view of the sun drifting down below the pond from the safety of the kitchen. A turtle meandered slow and easy around the southern edge of the water, as if looking for a smooth way out. I watched it, enjoying this private slice of nature I could call my own. The turtle was small and blended into the murky, brown mud, but now and again it would raise its head, as if sniffing the air.

Just as I considered going outside with my camera to get a picture of it, something reached out from the water and snatched the creature. It was so fast I wasn't sure what I had seen. A hand? The mouth of a catfish, or maybe a bigger turtle? There was a widening ripple on the water that hadn't been there before, so I hadn't imagined it.

The tea felt grainy on my tongue as I put the mug down, my fingers trembling. It was just a turtle, I reasoned. It could have fallen in the water, or dived, and only looked like it was grabbed. My mind could have been playing tricks on me, or the setting sun might have been in my eyes, distorting the glare off the pond.

I waited, the minutes passing as I sat, hoping the turtle would resurface or some other explanation would appear, but the clouds continued to gently drift by the setting sun, and the turtle didn't return. The colors of the sky shifted from tangerine to pink to plum, the shadows of the cattails reaching across the lawn like long, spindly fingers. It was stark and beautiful, and I thought again of going outside to take a photo, or just to enjoy the cool air, but something held me back—a latent sense of fear.

Then I got angry. Why was I still scared to leave my house? I was just being weird about the turtle. It had been almost two weeks since that woman had attacked me. There'd been no sign of her, and no news from the police. She had probably moved on to the next town or been caught by someone and arrested. Maybe she'd died. My backyard wasn't visible from the driveway, where my attack had happened, so it would be as safe as anywhere, I reasoned. Feeling determined, I stood, leaving my tea on the table. I wouldn't let myself be held captive by the hypothetical threat of another attack. I wouldn't let that woman control my life.

Grabbing the small container of Mace, which I'd bought the day before at an Army & Navy Supply store one town over, I tucked my phone into my back pocket and placed a hand over my racing heart, begging it to calm. After a deep breath, I unlocked the patio doors.

I hadn't been out back here since that day with Brendan, which had been much less frightening, even as we fled. Probably because I wasn't alone.

But I was very much alone now.

The sound of geese honking overhead and the swish of field grasses in the breeze were the only noises as the doors silently opened and I stepped outside. I walked down the sloping lawn, my eyes scanning from left to right and back again. There was no one around. It was just me and the landscape laid out before me.

The willows gently leaned over the water, creating a tunnel that the dying sunlight could barely penetrate. The few rays of the sunset that did make it through twinkled on the water and painted the tall reads a glowing amber. I tugged out my phone and took a picture, moving closer.

Another ripple on the pond caught my attention and I stopped, freezing in place. It became shallow, like the smallest of waves as it stretched toward the water's edges. I waited, my gaze focused and searching for any sign of...something. The turtle. A fish. But the ripple died down and vanished, the surface going as smooth as glass once more.

White and yellow wildflowers swayed tall and proud under my hand as I got close to the water. I could hear a gentle croaking sound by the miniature dock. Zooming in with my phone camera, I caught the shape of something brown on a lily pad.

My foot crunched on something, and I looked down, expecting a mound of leaves or an errant pinecone, but instead found a rough, tan piece of cloth bunched under my boot. I lifted my heel, and on closer inspection the fabric was more of a...mesh, or a skin. It was porous and crisp at the ends, folded on top of itself like a snake had wiggled its way free of it and then curled up on top for a nap. I didn't even think there were snakes that shed this far north. I'd have to do some research to see what it could be, but at least that explained what may have grabbed that turtle. *If anything actually did grab it*, I reminded myself.

Being sure to check the ground as I walked, I made my way toward the dock on the right side of the pond, admiring the way the grass was peppered with bits of clover. If I could get a picture low to the ground, using the dock, I could probably get the sunset and its own reflection in the water. Brendan would appreciate the artistry, and it would be a great keepsake for whenever I moved away, whether to the dorms or another apartment. This was one of the most beautiful places I'd ever lived, and I wanted to remember it.

My phone buzzed in my hand.

"Speak of the devil," I muttered to myself.

Brendan: *Hey, if you're free Friday I have a gig in town. If you want to see the band.*

I'd forgotten he even had my number—it seemed he typically did his communication in person or through Jamie—and there was a strange thrill at him messaging me. I wasn't sure why.

Me: *Sure! What time?*

Brendan: *We go on at 9.*

Brendan: *No pressure tho.*

Me: *I'd love to hear you play. Who knows, maybe I'll use it for my next exposé – Local Band on the Rise :)*

The sound of a twig snapping had me looking up sharp, scanning the trees to make sure I was still alone, and then searching the ground for a snake. My fingers inched toward the pepper spray in my front pocket. There was nothing there, I assured myself. All around me was an open field and then dense wood. The house was bright behind me, a beacon against the rugged landscape.

I turned away from the dock, ready to head inside, when my foot slipped on something. I almost tumbled backward, but at the last second, I used my now-aching core muscles to lean forward, as if I was on ice skates. My arms swinging, I righted myself before I could tumble into the wood of the dock or the wet earth around it. My momentary panic disappeared, and I almost laughed with relief. This place was really throwing me for a loop.

Peeking down at my boot, I saw the dark smudge I'd slid on. It was grimy and brown, like mud, but there were streaks of a purple-tinted red in it. I wondered if this was the spot where some unfortunate animal had met its end. Maybe another turtle.

My arms pebbled with goosebumps.

The darkening sky suddenly felt unwelcoming, so, with careful steps, I made my way back into the house, closing and locking the patio doors behind me and feeling as if I had barely escaped something treacherous.

The snakeskin I'd seen outside wouldn't leave my thoughts, and I spent a lot of that night pouring over Wikipedia and various articles about snakes in New England, the fragility of pond ecosystems, and then Spindle River pollution in general, wondering if the drying river was forcing wildlife into my backyard where they normally wouldn't reside. Unsurprisingly, there was plenty of information about the flora and fauna found in Massachusetts wetlands, but there was almost nothing about this town and its falling water levels—just a couple of blog posts from the early 2010's citing rising water temperatures, and a cancellation notice published in the town newspaper, the *Spindle River Chronicle*, for the summer regatta in 2016. That guide at the trash pick-up, Ronald, was right. It was like the decay of the river was so slow, the landscape changing so gradually, that not many people had tried to find the cause. It just...was.

And that felt suspicious to me.

The earliest record I could find of the water levels receding was in 1988, and I used my college credentials to pull copies of the *Weekly Prowl* for that year. They were copied and scanned, and therefore not easy to read, but my brain was hooked on this lead now, as sure as any gullible fish. My gut said to follow the line.

There were hundreds of pages to sort through, however, and the night was deepening outside my porch doors. I reluctantly left the hunt for another day, my eyes crusty with fatigue.

***

Monday morning was rough; I'd barely slept the night before and the last thing I wanted to do was get ready for my morning Psych class. The paper was almost due, and though I'd finished it days ago and we'd be starting some new topic, which I'd normally find exciting, I was too preoccupied. I wasn't sure which Barreto twin would come to pick me up for class, or if things between Jamie and I had now changed—if I should kiss him when I got into the car, if we were dating now, if we were exclusive—and I also wasn't sure if I was wasting my time with this river-based obsession. My thoughts refused to settle down, just buzzed in swirls that grated on my attention.

A honk sounded outside, and I rushed to the car.

It was Brendan who was waiting for me. His jaw was smooth, and I could see his tell-tale silver chain hanging over his dark gray Henley.

"Morning," I said, climbing in.

He nodded in response, then paused to look me up and down, his eyebrows creased with concern. "You okay?"

"What? Yeah. I'm fine, just tired. Why?"

Lifting one shoulder, he pulled the car onto the street and started the drive toward campus, the muscles of his arms prominent beneath the long sleeves. "Nothing."

I looked down at my blouse, making sure the buttons weren't crooked or that my fly wasn't open. I'd put on makeup, and I knew my glasses were on straight, but now I was self-conscious.

"So," I started, trying to dispel the odd tension suddenly clogging the air, "what should I know about this gig on Friday? Is it an all-ages thing? Or will I need a fake ID?"

"Do you have one?" He sounded astonished and I took a small measure of pride pulling out the license to show him.

"Back in Tennessee I had a friend who loved going to clubs," I said, tucking it away. "Zara. She only wanted to go to dance and not drink, but we needed them to get in—this was my senior year of high school. She had a brother who made them for us, but we still had to pay a crap ton. Thankfully, he did a good job."

"Wow, you're more of a rebel than I thought," he said, obviously amused. "But the place is all ages. You probably shouldn't tell Jamie you have a fake, though."

"Why not?"

"He'll immediately drag you to some bar party full of sketchy people, and when he's drunk he always starts talking about getting tattoos. Don't let him rope you into one."

I hummed as if deep in thought. "Well, I do think I'd look good with a 'live, laugh, love' tramp stamp, don't you?"

He tilted his head on a laugh, as if considering it. "There are worse ones to pick, I guess. Butterflies are way overdone."

"Oh, and Chinese symbols," I added.

"You don't want your restaurant order inked on your skin?" he asked. "I think that would be handy."

"That's a good point. But I definitely wouldn't do it alone. One of you would have to get one first. A butterfly."

"What if I already have one?"

"A butterfly?" I asked, incredulous.

"A tattoo."

I tried to discern his expression, somewhere between gravity and embarrassment, and my first instinct was to ask where, and what, and why, or if he was just teasing me. But I held off. It felt too personal, especially given that he refused to meet my gaze, so I let that silence stretch between us once more. Until I couldn't take it.

"The idea of a bar party doesn't sound horrible, you know," I said, fighting the urge to chew my lip. "I'm up for a good time, is what I mean." My eyes closed of their own volition, mortification making my pulse tick at my neck. "Not a good time like...like *that*, I'm just saying I like parties. I can party."

"I never thought you couldn't." He chanced a look at me. "Jamie's just got some friends I don't particularly like, that's all. Sorry, I'm being protective again. Reeling it in," he said on a nod, as if commanding himself.

"As long as you acknowledge your shortcomings," I teased. "But seriously, tell me more about the show—will you introduce me to your band members?"

"Of course. I want them all to know you." His voice was lower then, serious, and I turned to watch his profile, oddly touched. He was clenching his jaw, the muscle there pulsing, and then he cleared his throat. I turned back to the road.

"Andrea's the one on keyboard," he said, "and she has an incredible voice. Really husky and low. When I'm not singing it's usually her on vocals. Then we have Frank on drums and Sam on bass. They're brother and sister but you'd never know it. They don't look anything alike."

"You sound jealous."

He barked out a laugh. "Well, it must be nice to be seen as your own person is all, but no, I'm not jealous. I met Frank in middle school, and we started hanging out together. Then when we started fooling around with music, he brought Sam in. Andrea joined last."

We pulled into the parking lot then, and I finally drummed up the courage to ask where Jamie was.

"He's getting a ride later," was all he said, voice flat.

"Oh. Okay." I moved to get out of the car and felt his hand, soft as a falling leaf, touch my arm. When I turned to look at him there was something...wounded in his eyes, his expression damaged and sorrowful.

"Sadie, I..." He took a breath. "He's not the only one that likes you."

For a heartbeat I sat there frozen, watching his eyes track mine. Inside, my emotions were turbulent. I liked Brendan and I wanted to know more about him. There was this mysterious energy to him, this quiet tenderness I craved to explore. Being out on the forest trail with him had been easy, and there was no denying the attraction. But Jamie—the passion I felt with him, the way I lit up from the inside when he touched me...I couldn't ignore that. And I didn't want to betray the relationship we'd started, even if we hadn't put a specific name on it. We'd kissed. We'd almost...more than kissed.

"You don't have to say anything," Brendan added, pulling back his hand. "I realize it's a shitty thing, what I just did. I know you and Jamie have something going on, but I...I actually *like* talking to you, which is rare for me. I liked sitting with you in your backyard and going on that hike with you. I want to spend more time with you." His eyes darted down and then back to mine, his dark lashes lifting to reveal those dark hazel pools, drawing me in. "I just feel like I need to be honest about the circumstances." He rubbed a hand over the back of his neck and then up into his hair, making the wavy strands fall crookedly over his forehead. I itched to move it out of the way, to feel if it was just as soft as Jamie's.

And then guilt started churning in my stomach for daring to wonder.

"Thank you," I said. I clenched my hands in my lap and focused on the chipped nail polish there, unsure how I could feel such a strange attraction to both of them, even though it was in different ways. "Thanks for telling me."

"And Jamie knows."

My head whipped up. "He does?"

Brendan nodded. "We don't let things like this get between us. He, uh...he let me drive you today so I could tell you."

I gaped at him, my mind racing too fast to form any singular, coherent thought. It was only my phone buzzing in my pocket that pulled my stunned gaze away from his.

It was just an email from Professor Lewis about the next staff meeting, but then I saw the time.

"I have to go..." I said, somewhat apologetic. "My class is going to start in a minute."

Brendan raised one hand. "Sure. I'll see you later, Sadie. Have a good day."

"Thanks."

I climbed out of the car, feeling ten types of awkwardness, and hurried toward Psych class. My heart pounded all the way, the confused muscle pulsing in time to the questions repeating in my head. *Did I like Brendan? Did I like Jamie? Did I like both?*

CHAPTER THIRTEEN

Lynne was half asleep in her chair, but she lazily turned to look my way as I dropped into the seat beside her. I was trying—and failing—to get my breathing under control. Dashing into class and having your almost-boyfriend's twin brother confess his feelings for you will do that.

"Yo. You okay?" Lynne whispered.

"I think so. It's just..." I paused to take out my laptop and then lowered my head toward hers, "do you know Brendan and Jamie Barreto? The twins?"

She shook her head, then half-heartedly copied down one of the notes from the whiteboard. "No, but twins could have been a good pleasure fantasy topic to write about," she mused. "Insanely hot."

"Not a great fantasy topic when it's your life," I replied.

Her eyes widened and she suddenly seemed more awake. "Tell me more words, please."

Nina's lecture was on various personality disorders linked to sexuality—only a slight deviation from our previous subject—and though I wanted to pay attention, telling Lynne about my experiences with the Barreto brothers was too much of a draw to ignore. It was abbreviated, but I went through everything: thinking Brendan was Jamie, then interviewing them for the article, getting kissed, going on that hike and the ice-skating date and subsequent closet dry humping that followed, then the car ride this morning.

Lynne's jaw was slack, but it wasn't from her usual lethargy.

"Gal, whatever perfume you're wearing, you need to let me borrow it."

"It's not all it's cracked up to be," I hissed. "I've only known them a couple of weeks and already I feel weirdly torn between them. Like some...*hussy* intruding on their family bond or something."

"Well, it doesn't sound like they're fighting," she replied, keeping her voice low. "If anything, it sounds like they're being really mature about it. Maybe you should just...see where it goes?"

"Honestly?" I slinked down further in my chair so Nina wouldn't see my surprised expression when she turned to the class.

"Why not?" Lynne propped her chin on her hand, looking wistfully out the windows on the right side of the room. "You've got two hot guys interested in you and they're not assholes. Sounds like a win-win."

"Yeah, but they decided this between them, like they're handing me back and forth or something."

Lynne shook her head. "I don't think so. It feels more like the hockey one told the broody one to give it a shot."

"Yeah, but isn't that *weird*? I thought we—"

Nina cleared her throat at the front of the room, and we turned to see her staring up at us. The rest of the class was silent. I straightened in my seat, but embarrassment and shame kept me from looking anywhere but at Nina's shoes.

"Sorry," Lynne and I both mumbled, ending the discussion for now.

As class ended, I felt no closer to sorting out the complex emotions I was feeling about Brendan's admission this morning. And my next class was Linguistics. With Jamie.

"Do you want to come over to my room after your class?" Lynne offered, as we scurried out of Nina's sight. "We could have that drink I promised last week. Talk about your boy troubles."

"You sure?"

She smiled. "Of course. It's either that or do the reading on…" she looked down at her messy notes, "dependent personality disorder."

I nearly hugged her; I was so relieved to have someone to hash this out with. "That would be amazing, thanks. I'll text you when I get out."

We parted ways and I walked toward Linguistics and Jamie with a sense that—even if I didn't know quite yet how to feel about all of this—I'd at least have the chance to figure it out later.

Jamie wasn't in class yet when I settled into my normal seat.

I waited, pulling up my notes document and debating how I should play this. I wanted to ask him what his conversation with Brendan had been like, but I simultaneously didn't want to know anything about it. Was Jamie upset at all that his brother liked me? Did I want him to be?

But class started and Jamie still wasn't there.

He ended up being about ten minutes late, walking in with a swagger and an easy smile directed at the professor, who pointed to a seat at the front—punishment for being tardy.

I could see the dark swoop of his messy hair from my seat, and I thought about texting him to make sure he was okay, but it felt needy. I'd leave the first move to him, I decided.

My mind was half-gone all of class, but I did my best to take notes and not let Jamie's slouching posture and periodic movements distract me. I purposefully didn't watch when he rubbed at his neck, or scratched at his stubbled jaw, or yawned and used the movement to surreptitiously check back at me. I also didn't retain any Linguistics-related information.

When we were released, I felt so keyed up and anxious my hands shook as I gathered up my things.

"Hey."

I looked up to find him by my chair, his bag casually slung over one shoulder, that rakish smile aimed my way with expert precision. There was something off about it, though. It was too flat. Insincere.

"Hey, yourself," I replied.

"How was your ride this morning?" he asked, following me down the stadium-style steps and out of the room.

"I don't know, how did you want it to go?" There was a tiny bit of bite to my words, and I wasn't even sure why, so I made sure my expression was friendly when I looked over my shoulder at him.

He didn't answer.

The hallways were mostly empty, with only a few rooms on this floor in use, but the lights were blindingly bright above us, making the space feel full. It was almost giving me a headache. I used a palm to shield my eyes and turned, peering up at him, expectant.

He put both of his hands in his pockets, his shoulders dipping, and stood still in front of me while the rest of our classmates wove their way around us and down the hall. His breath released like a sigh.

"My brother and I...we have this agreement," he started. "We've seen all those movies and TV shows about brothers or best friends being torn apart by someone they like. We made a deal when we were in high school that we would talk about that shit; we wouldn't let it ruin the relationship we have. Not that we don't have our rough spots, obviously.

But he told me how he felt and I...I couldn't fight him over it. It has to be about you. Who you like. And whoever that is, we'll accept it."

This is all so fast, is what I wanted to say, but I couldn't deny the flurry of feelings I'd developed for both brothers over the past couple weeks. For any normal pair of guys, this would definitely have been the time for posturing or ultimatums, which would have been hard to take; and it was downright refreshing for them to be so communicative about it. But still...

"This is kind of...intense," I said.

"It doesn't have to be. It can be casual, if that's what you want." Jamie lifted one shoulder.

"So, you don't feel..." I wasn't sure how to finish my sentence. He didn't feel the same deep connection? He didn't feel this all-consuming craving to touch me, like I felt about him?

But he didn't need me to finish.

Hands still in his pockets, he moved closer, crowding me against one of the walls. His chest brushed mine as he leaned in close, his mouth by my neck.

"I feel plenty, I promise. And if you want to spend some time with Brendan, I understand. But—" Jamie pressed a kiss to my pulse, uncaring if anyone walked by, licking the spot just enough to have heat pooling in my core, "I'm hoping you'll come back to me."

There was a promise in his eyes as he backed away, and I knew if I wanted it, we would finish what we had started in that supply closet. The fire was there. The passion.

It wasn't like they were handing me off to each other, I realized. They were giving me space to choose. And Jamie wanted me to choose *him*.

"Do you have practice now?" I asked. I sounded slightly out of breath, and I swallowed, trying to regain some composure.

He nodded. "I do. Brendan will drive you home."

I shook my head. "I'm actually going to spend some time on campus with my friend Lynne. I'll text him that he can go."

Jamie paused, as if trying to decide if I was telling the truth, or just avoiding his brother.

"Well then," he said, after a moment. "I guess I'll see you Thursday—if I don't hear from you before then." A smirk wormed its way over his features, and then he turned with easy grace, walking down the hall to the south exit. I'm not ashamed of the way I watched him walk away.

Releasing a breath, I texted Brendan the change of plans and asked Lynne for directions to her room.

I was going to need more than one drink.

CHAPTER FOURTEEN

Lynne had plenty of ideas about how to handle the Brendan-Jamie situation, and most of them involved nudity. She made it easy to laugh about though, which I appreciated. We had a glass of some white wine her older roommate had stashed in their mini fridge while we talked. And then another glass. And another.

My mind was pleasantly hazy and my vision a bit crooked when I finally called an Uber to bring me home. Lynne offered to let me stay, but in a suite of six girls with only a short, lumpy couch as an option, I passed. My own bed was calling me, and I was willing to pay the surcharge to get to it.

I didn't remember the road home being so bumpy, but the trees flew past as my driver—an old man named Brian with thick glasses and a bristly, uneven beard—maneuvered the winding roads with impressive speed, his headlights cutting into the night like a heavenly knife. My stomach sloshed uncomfortably, so I closed my eyes for half the drive—and then he was calling my name in a loud but concerned way, waking me.

"What?" I looked around, spotting the familiar mailbox in the dark. "Oh, sorry."

I climbed out of the car, said something about giving him five stars, and then watched as he nodded, still looking a bit uneasy, and drove away.

"Well, at least I didn't puke," I muttered to myself. Taking out my keys, I ambled up the driveway, being careful to scan the area for anything amiss. Not that I could see much. The woods were swallowed by the night sky, the trees barely breaking through the wide, starlit expanse. My body swayed as I looked up, trying to find the Big Dipper, but the stars seemed to shift as soon as I focused on them.

I was at my door, keys in hand, when I heard it. A hiss like the air leaking from a radiator.

It sliced through the quiet and I looked down, expecting to find a snake at my heels, or slithering up the steps, but there was nothing. All I could see was the vague outline of my stoop, murky and uneven.

And then something struck me. I think they were aiming for my head, but the blow landed high on my shoulder, the force of it pushing me into the siding of the house. My skull cracked against the wall, and I fell. My vision blinked out, returning so slowly I wasn't even sure my eyes were open, except that I could see something moving.

No, *I* was moving.

The ground was cold and sharp beneath me, scraping my lower back as my blouse rode up toward my neck.

I opened my mouth to take a breath, to scream, but dizziness overwhelmed me, and I wheezed instead. Turning my head, I blinked again and again, trying to clear my vision. I had no idea who had hold of me. I could feel something hard banded low around my legs. Rope?

Horror and dread flooded me, the dire situation I was in finally coming into focus. I was being *taken*. Twisting onto my stomach, I reached for the hard earth beneath me, scraping at it with my nails and kicking back with my legs, hoping to fall out of my attacker's grip, but there truly was rope of some kind around my ankles. My motion was severely limited.

Despite my aching chest, I took in one labored, full breath.

"Help!" I screamed. "Somebody, help me!"

The person carrying me dropped my legs and flipped me onto my back, their hands scratching up my torso and onto my face, scrambling to cover my mouth. Did that mean I was still close to the house or the road? I bit at their fingers as they smothered my cries, trying to scream around them, but they were strong. Too strong. I thought my jaw would crack under the pressure, or that they might twist my head and break my neck.

"Please!" I tried to yell, but the plea was muffled. I heard a cough, another hiss, and then something like "Hush," the voice gravelly and cracking, but feminine.

With an eerie swiftness, the woman stuffed something into my mouth. It tasted horrible, like bitter weeds and mud, but it was too big to spit out. Tears leaked from my eyes, tracking down my face, as she then pulled at my hands, using my arms to drag me instead of my tied legs.

My glasses started to slide down my nose and I lifted my head to keep them on. They were grimy and my vision was still tilting this way and that, but the last thing I needed was to be well and truly blind. I wriggled as much as I could, shouting through the gag, rubbing my ankles together in the hopes of loosening whatever binding kept me immobile, but it was no use, and I couldn't think of anything else to do. I couldn't twist out of her hold.

For all my reading and researching, I'd never investigated much self-defense beyond the easy "kick your opponent where it hurts" class. Nothing had ever covered waking up as an abductee. Now, as I struggled to breathe through aching sobs, I really wished I'd expanded my repertoire.

The dark woods were becoming sparse, the ground wetter, so I thought we were nearing some kind of swamp. Mud squelched under me, coating my body in freezing muck, and now I was crying harder. I didn't know what to do. Would someone come looking for me? Would Jamie or Brendan come to my rescue? My phone and keys were somewhere back at the house, so maybe tomorrow morning when Brendan came to get me for Stats he would see them. But would it be too late?

Minutes passed as I struggled. Now and then the woman would mutter under her breath; I caught snippets of her words through my whimpering.

"Don't want this…"

"Too late."

"Drink…or else…"

My heart was bursting from my chest as panic overtook me, and then finally, the woman slowed and released my arms. I tried to flip over, to crawl away, but she dragged me backward, my hands clutching uselessly at the wet ground. She then pulled me up into a sitting position and shoved me, my back hitting a hard surface.

Something emitted light far to my left and I looked there, blinking against the glow of a low and dying fire through my smudged glasses. And then I could finally see her.

Her skin was tinted a pale blue and coated in streaks of muddy water, her figure gaunt and long-limbed. She had longer arms than any person I'd ever seen; they'd helped her drag me with such ease. As she backed away a step, I could see her hands were curled, the ends tipped in black with curved nails that resembled claws, reminding me of a bird of prey. At first her hair appeared brown, but then beneath the grime I could see the firelight reflecting on strands of a bright, unearthly red. If I hadn't felt her immense strength, and couldn't see her stretched, inhuman arms, I would think she was in some kind of cheap, faded Mystique costume.

But when she opened her cracked, blue-tinted mouth and I saw the sharp, pointed teeth within, I knew she was a predator. It was in the way she seemed to scent the air like a snake. This was no costume.

I scrambled back up against the wall, which I could now discern was one side of a narrow cave, trying to get as much space between me and this inhuman...*thing* as possible. I kept blinking furiously, praying I was hallucinating.

"Please," I said, the word indecipherable around the gag, and then—realizing my hands were now free—pulled it out of my mouth, spitting mud onto the ground. "Please let me go."

The woman's eyes were so dilated it seemed the entire space was black, but she looked at me with a resigned stillness, a fatigue. She plopped onto the muddy ground by my feet, startling me with her sudden drop, and let out a long, moaning breath.

"I will..." she started, in a grating voice I imagined was rarely used. "I will take...drink."

Her long, bedraggled hair stuck to her face and when she pushed it aside, I caught the glimmer of something opaque between her clawed fingers. Webbing? Was she some kind of fairytale monster? A ghoul?

"What...are you?" I dared to ask. Nausea crawled up my throat, but I swallowed it down. The lingering taste of my gag—which was a bundle of moss wrapped in some sort of leaf, I could now see—still sat bitter on my tongue.

She didn't answer, just continued to stare.

"Please let me go," I whispered in a watery voice. "Please, I won't tell anyone." I looked around the cave, hoping to see a weapon, but other than maybe grabbing one of the burning pieces of wood in the fire, there was nothing but dirt and stone.

"Will heal me," she groaned.

"Heal you? Are you—are you hurt?" I asked, feeling foolish as I shook with fear under her black gaze. This creature, though she *almost* resembled a woman, had knocked me unconscious and dragged me into the woods. Surely if she was strong enough for that she couldn't be too injured. Her clothing was torn and dark and I couldn't make out if it was a dress or just some ripped amalgamation of cloth strips, but I saw no obvious blood.

"Dying," she responded, then cleared her throat. "Like the water. Under the dock. Your blood...will drink it—" she coughed, the sound wet and labored, then wiped her hand over her muddy hair. "Then find him. I can smell...it. Your blood. Special."

"What are you talking about? Find who?" My voice shook, and I could barely keep from crying hysterically, but I had to keep her talking. The longer she raved her crazy nonsense the more chance I had of making an escape, and if she truly was dying maybe she would eventually just...keel over.

"My child. Dark boy...I left him."

She breathed in a slow, rattling gasp and I licked my lips, searching for another question, anything, to keep her sitting and not disemboweling me with those clawed hands. To keep her from drinking my blood, like some sort of horrific swamp vampire. A manic giggle pushed at my mouth, but I shook my head.

"Why did you leave him?" I asked, sniffling. "Your...child?"

"So, I would wither...alone. Sick like the land. Maybe he would escape." Her mouth lowered at the corners, shoulders slumping, as if she was genuinely heartbroken. "Years and years holding on, and then to smell you. So close. I'll drink some, then bring you...to him."

"You're dying and need to—" I stopped before using the word *drink*, hesitant to confirm it, and watched the sad way she peered up at me through her lank, dirty hair. "But, why me?" I added, bending my legs so my still-bound ankles were closer to my hands. If I could untie them, I could run. I could fight. Sad or not, crazy or not, I would hurt this woman to get away.

"You share my blood. Naiad," she grumbled, her voice sounding stronger with each word. "Or sylph. Some ember lingers...in your human scent. You cannot hide it." She reached forward and I held up my hands.

"Wait, please! Your son...he's nearby? We could go to him! Where is he?"

The woman looked toward the mouth of the cave, and I hurried to dig my nails into the rope, only to find the material more closely resembling vines. They chipped and leaked water under my fingertips, sturdier and thicker than they had any right to be, but not impossible to break. The creature turned back to me, and I stilled, her big black eyes now wider. She suddenly looked almost wistful.

"He is close. I smell him in the river. The land. I will find him...once I have your blood. Tall and strong now...I left him," her wistful expression became dazed, almost confused, "sleeping next to a boy. All human." Her mouth twisted in a disgusted sneer, those dagger-like teeth making another appearance. "To change and blend, like frogs in the reed. My dark boy...growing up like you. Weak. Once I am free of this drying, we will be together." Her eyes closed, as if relishing the dream and the strength it gave her.

I dug at the vines once more, careful to shift when her eyes reopened, pretending to find a more comfortable spot on the ground.

This woman was a *monster*—a real-life verifiable demon of some kind. I had no other choice but to believe she meant what she said. That she was something unnatural—a creature that defied logic. I was seeing it with my own eyes: her webbed claws, her blue-tinted skin, her spindly arms, and the wet, rasping way she spoke through teeth sharpened to wicked points.

I was trapped in a nightmare; my world spun upside down into an unrecognizable place. Meanwhile, my mind was still jumping from option to option. I just needed to *get away*. I needed to say or do whatever I could to run and regroup. I could figure this all out later.

"I will share you with him," the woman growled, opening her eyes once more. And then her hands were on my arms, pulling me forward, her claws piercing my flesh.

"No!" I screamed, trying to pull back. "No, stop! Wait! My blood—you can have it!" The woman halted and I tried to rein in my pounding heart. "You need something to put it in, right? I'll give it to you. As much as you want." I was rambling, but I didn't care. "Do you have a...a bottle? Or a bag? How will you get it to him if you hurt me here?"

She paused, her head tilted in an inhuman way, that stringy, filthy hair dragging over her features. I could imagine her face rising from the water, a mythical beast coming to drag you down into the depths. I shivered, all the while trying to look innocent.

"I'll give you the blood," I repeated. "I can help you." My feet shuffled and I felt the vines start to loosen.

The woman released me, slowly, and then her head dipped as if she was so exhausted she could barely keep upright.

"Days to recover...trying to get you before," the creature whispered. "Just a taste." She leaned forward, but I snatched her hand, shoving those pointed claws at the vines all the while using every ounce of muscle I had to strain against them, pulling my legs apart. I heard a snap just as the creature attacked.

She must have actually been as tired as she claimed because her movements were delayed and uncoordinated.

I kicked at her face, feeling my heel land solidly on flesh, and she screeched. Her trembling hands rushed to her eyes.

Scrambling to the side, I crawled on my hands and knees until I could climb to my feet. Then I ran.

Sprinting, I could only tell I was in a wide copse of trees, the ground wet and sinking beneath my boots. It made each step that much harder, but adrenaline raced through me, pushing me on, keeping my headache and roiling stomach at bay. Every few breaths I checked behind me, looking for her, but as far as I could tell, she wasn't following. Still, I couldn't slow down.

My lungs were burning, and I had no idea if I was headed in the right direction, but eventually I saw an open space ahead. A field or clearing of some kind.

When I broke through the tree line, I instantly recognized my surroundings—directly ahead was the pond. My pond. And beyond it, my house.

Dashing across the lawn, I passed the dock and then the patio, coming up around the side of the house and hurrying for the front door. A sharp, relieved exhale punched from my lungs when I saw my keys and phone on the ground.

My breath heaving, I halted, debating where to go. Into the house? Into my car? Where could I drive? I could head to campus, since I at least knew where Lynne was, but should I call the cops first? The idea was almost funny—telling the Spindle River police that the crazy homeless woman who'd attacked me weeks ago was actually some blue, claw-fingered monster. A naiad, she'd said. And she wanted my blood.

No wonder the sample they'd pulled from under my nails had seemed tainted.

The police would probably blame my blood-alcohol levels—not that I could fault them—and send me home. *Home.*

I looked up at the house, remembering the bangs and scrapes I'd heard during storms. Was that her trying to get in? The doors and windows were always locked...maybe she hadn't been strong enough to break them? It had been two weeks and she'd only attacked me outside, but it seemed too easy for me to go into the cottage. Like I'd end up in a horror movie of my own making, trapped in my house with a killer.

Keys in hand, I raced to my car and prayed when I turned on the headlights I wouldn't see her gruesome features in the woods, watching me. And I didn't. As the engine turned over, there was only an empty driveway, dark shadows between the trees, and the house as it sat innocently atop the stoop, its windows vacant.

I started driving aimlessly, wondering where I should go, but my thoughts were muddled. The alcohol had mostly vanished from my system, but that woman—that *naiad*—had clobbered me pretty good. My head throbbed on one side where it had smacked the house, and my hands were once more scraped open from scrabbling against the ground while she'd pulled me. There were puncture marks on my forearms from her claws and I probably had cuts and bruises on my back from being dragged, but that was future me's problem. Present me needed to find somewhere to go.

The clock on the dashboard read 12:08 a.m. and I blinked. Hadn't I only left Lynne's around ten? How long had I been in the woods?

A car honked at me, bringing my attention back to the road, and I realized I'd been drifting across the lane. With a jerk, I righted the wheel, feeling suddenly faint.

There was a vehicle repair shop up ahead, closed at this late hour, but I pulled into the mostly empty lot and turned off the car. My whole body was trembling as I took in measured breaths, counting my way through the panic attack. I was too afraid to close my eyes. Too afraid to open my window for some fresh air. Had I driven far enough? Could she still find me?

But no, she was weak, I reminded myself. Right? She'd been obviously tired from attacking me and dragging me into her lair.

Her *lair*.

A weak giggle broke out of me, which then grew into a chuckle. Suddenly I was baying, my laughter somewhere between frantic and gasping, my chest blowing up like a balloon. I smacked the steering wheel, feeling close to losing my mind, as my laughter became wracking sobs.

How was any of this real? How did that *creature* exist?

Minutes passed and my body finally settled. It was as if I'd just purged the entire night's worth of lunacy. My crying slowed to a hiccupping stop, and I took my first deep breath in hours. The passing headlights of a car every few minutes brought me back to a state of near normalcy.

Through sheer force of will I was now able to focus on my next steps. Taking out my phone, I opened my voice recorder app.

"These are the facts as I know them." I took a breath, gathering my thoughts. "When: September 24th...now 12:36 a.m. Where: behind the cottage I'm renting in Spindle River, somewhere beyond my backyard, there is a swampy area in the woods, and a cave. Who: a creature-like a woman, but not. Light blue skin, muddy hair that may have been red, webbed hands ending in claws, and...jagged teeth. She claims to be a naiad. What: my blood. In her own words she said she needs it for herself and her son, who she apparently left here years ago with another baby...to blend in."

I turned off the recorder, shaking my head. Even listing it all out like a report I was drafting into an article, I couldn't believe it. No one would believe it. But still, that last part felt eerily like a story I'd heard before.

I opened the Google app and searched "naiad." Wikipedia defined the term as, "A type of female spirit, or nymph, presiding over fountains, wells, springs, and other bodies of freshwater, who were tied to the land or water source they hailed from. Described as peaceful and usually benign in various mythologies, unless threatened, they heralded fruitful crops and game and were often seen as beautiful, ethereal creatures." Not really the impression I had gotten from the monster who'd just threatened to drink my blood, and there was nothing about leaving babies. When I searched, "creature that leaves babies," the first few results were just about different animals that were apparently horrible mothers: lizards and pandas and...quokkas. Further down, though, there was an entry for "changelings."

I turned the recorder back on, reading the entry.

"Historically, changelings were human-like beings found in folklore and some religions, believed to be a fairy or supernatural creature that had been left in place of a stolen human, in their bed. Sometimes as early as in the birthing chamber."

I paused; the idea of a mythological creature disguised as a human baby finally clicked in my mind. The idea of a baby that didn't seem to belong...

The story of the Barreto twins.

Their mother swore she'd only had one son, and then was presented with two. No, that was insane. Right? Just because Brendan said their mother was sure she'd only given birth to one baby...that was her schizophrenia. It was mental illness, not gruesome mythology.

And how would a mud-caked creature walk into a hospital and drop off a baby without being noticed? And why was I actually considering that this could have happened, even as a passing thought? If I hadn't seen the woman for myself, I'd think I was mad.

"A common way a changeling would reveal itself is through displaying unusual behavior when it thinks it is alone," I continued reading. The list of strange behavior was long and varied, from having uncanny sight or intelligence, to dancing without music, to growing a beard as an infant. Some of these changelings disappeared once they were weaned, supposedly to go back to their fae parents, but some would forget they were not human...proceeding to live a human life.

I sat back in the car seat, feeling oddly boneless as I digested the impractical idea that Jamie or Brendan could be something less than human. No, this was all ridiculous. Maybe I had hit my head harder than I had thought. Maybe this was my brain trying to draw connections where there were none, looking to make sense of a nonsensical event.

It would be too convenient for one of the three friends I'd made so far to be a *fairy*. Or naiad. Whatever. But she'd said his scent had been nearby. She knew her son was close. Both the twins had been at or in my house. Add that to the story of their mother...

A car zoomed by, reminding me that I was parked in an empty lot. The night swallowed the parking lot around me, and the woods further behind the car shop seemed to creep closer. What was it with this town and all these fucking woods?

I groaned in frustration, hitting the steering wheel while I debated what to do.

"Okay, I can't just sit here all night," I muttered. "I either go home, or I..." *I find Jamie and Brendan.* There was no way I could tell them what had happened—it would be equivalent to accusing one of them of being a face-snatching fae baby—but I needed to see them. I needed to look them in the eyes and put these crazy thoughts and this crazy, violent night behind me.

"It's just a story, Sadie," I grumbled to myself, turning off the recorder. "Just a raving lunatic woman with paint on her skin and bad nails who's lived outside for too long. Right?" I felt eerily close to another laughing fit, but I pushed it down.

Maybe if I could observe the twins enough, I could prove to myself it wasn't true...or I could determine which brother wasn't human. No matter how absurd, I didn't have many other options. And even if it was true, which it couldn't be, I still liked them, didn't I? I trusted them. They'd protected me by driving me to and from school...*almost like they knew.*

No. I refused to think that.

Before I could change my mind, I started a group chat with both of them, hoping someone would be awake.

Me: *Hey, I know it's late, but I kinda need someplace to stay tonight. Any chance you have a couch free?*

I sat and waited, my pulse still thready and uneven, but at least my breathing was under control.

Brendan: *Of course. U ok? Do you need me to come get you?*

Me: *No, I'm already on the road. Just give me your address?*

He replied and I plugged the address into my nav system, still half-convinced this was all a horrible misunderstanding. A fever dream brought on by alcohol and an overactive imagination.

But that wasn't me. I was about facts. What I could see, and research, and confirm. And if I was going to be able to put this all behind me, that's what I had to do.

This was the first step.

CHAPTER FIFTEEN

I pulled up to a single-story house with a one-car garage and a cute old-fashioned lamppost glowing at the start of the walkway. It was too dark to see much else. The road was dead quiet, but one of the windows on the far-right side of the house was lit.

Feeling oddly scandalous to be visiting so late, I made my way to the front door, which opened before I could knock.

Brendan stood backlit by some lamp inside; he was wearing a black T-shirt that hugged his chest and a pair of gray sweatpants low on his hips. There was a tiny sliver of skin visible between the two as he rested his hand at the top of the doorframe.

"Jamie and my mom are asleep," he whispered, looking down at me with a mix of confusion and concern. "But I can wake Jamie up if you want. Do you need—" he stopped abruptly. I wondered if he'd noticed how messy my hair was, or how my clothes were rumpled, or how there was dirt and specs of blood all over my jeans and under my fingernails, though I doubted he could see any of that. *Unless he had a changeling's uncanny vision*, an annoying mental voice prompted.

"Jesus, Sadie. What happened?"

"Oh." I looked down at my palms, which were really the only obvious injury I had. "That woman...she came back."

"What?" he hissed, gently taking my elbow and pulling me inside. "The one who attacked you in your driveway?"

I nodded dumbly, trying to wrangle some form of the truth together that would be plausible without leading to any additional questions or problems.

His house was warm inside, and I smelled garlic and some kind of roasted meat as he closed the door behind me. He stayed close, his steps quiet as he led me through a cozy living room and down a hallway to a small bathroom.

The overhead light in the bathroom was blinding, the robin's egg blue walls vibrant behind a series of frames with pressed flowers between the glass. I looked around, as if there might be some clue hidden next to the tub about which Barreto brother may or may not be a fairy changeling—if that was even a thing—but then Brendan took my hands in his, his touch soft.

"We need to clean these out. Did you talk to the police already?"

"Yeah. I, uh—I called them right away. I was getting out of an Uber and lingering at my door. Stupid, I know, but I didn't think..." I cleared my throat as he brought out a plastic box from beneath the sink and started rummaging through gauze and various packets of pills and creams. "Anyway, she pushed me down—that's how I got the scratches—but then she ran off. I told the cops and they said they'd do increased patrols, but I just didn't want to stay in that house tonight." I only felt the tiniest twinge at the lie. After all, it's not like I could tell him the truth.

"Of course." He dabbed at my palms with a small, damp wipe. It stung but he paused every few strokes to blow a stream of cool air across my skin, easing the pain. "You can stay as long as you'd like."

The sight of him leaning forward, his mouth close to my hands, tightened something inside me, making me aware of how small the room was and how warm his fingers were as they held my wrist in place. I smelled sugar and something like cinnamon as I leaned the tiniest bit forward, inhaling the scent drifting off his hair. His tall frame seemed to cradle mine, and I wondered if his torso was as firm as Jamie's. And if I touched him...

Brendan looked up at me, those hazel eyes almost glowing in the bright bathroom light, and I shot my gaze down, pretending to look more closely at my hands.

"Thanks, I appreciate it," I said, swallowing against a suddenly dry mouth. "You're a lifesaver."

"I should really wake up Jamie," he said, like he was doing something wrong by helping me. He placed a sterile bandage over one of my palms and then unraveled some long gauze.

"No, it's fine," I insisted. "I feel stupid for not using my Mace, anyway. I didn't have it on me, but I'll be carrying it in my purse from now on."

"And what? You think he'll be mad about that?"

I shook my head, watching him gently wrap first my right hand, and then my left. He was so cautious with how he touched me, so light, and though the room was crowded he made sure to give me space. It made me want to stumble into his chest, just to see that careful façade break away.

"Not mad," I said. "I just...would rather not give him any more evidence that I'm an idiot." I gave him a wry smile. "Let him sleep. I can tell him about it in the morning. Besides, there's nothing he could really do about it that you haven't already taken care of."

"I think we both know you're not an idiot," he replied, but I could swear his chest expanded, as if he was proud to be taking care of me. In being the one to help me in my time of need.

He put the metal bracket in place around the last wrap and sat back. I examined his work; my hands were as cleaned and bandaged as they could be.

"Are you tired?" he asked. "Hungry? I have some weed if you want to relax."

I shook my head. "I'm okay. But laying down does sound nice. Will your mom freak out if she sees a strange girl on the couch in the morning?"

"She might, actually," he replied, straightening. "That's not something we—I mean, if we stay out for the night, she assumes we're getting into trouble, but she knows we can handle ourselves. But we don't...bring girls home."

I raised my eyebrow, unsure then why he was so confident I could stay here as long as I wanted.

"You can stay in my room," he offered, his tone calm but lower than it had been just a minute before. "Or Jamie's."

The decision had never been laid so clearly out before me. Two bedrooms. Two brothers. A late-night request to hide. Jamie most likely had an early-morning practice tomorrow, though the idea of waking him by crawling into his bed was tempting. Still, Brendan was already awake and helping me. Taking care of me.

"I'll stay with you, if that's alright."

He nodded and led me from the bathroom to continue down the hall. There were two doors, one on either side, and he opened the door on the left, closer to the front of the house. The light I'd seen from the road was his.

His room was somehow exactly what I expected, and yet also a surprise. There were two guitars propped up against the far wall—one acoustic and one electric—a desk covered in notebooks and his signature oversized headphones, a full bed beneath the window that was rumpled and unmade, and a bureau by the door that looked well-worn, with scratches and chips in the wood. A framed photo of him and three friends that I assumed were his band members sat on top of the bureau, but where I expected there to be band posters on the walls, there were actually hundreds of photographs—sunsets and bridges, buildings in shadow, and crowds at a bar. As I continued to gaze at the wall, I was able to pick out portraits and nature shots, a strike of lightning over water, and a dozen or so self-portraits of Brendan himself—or possibly of Jamie—laughing or driving or scowling into a book. His work was displayed in batches that begged to be dissected and studied.

"Yeah, I—like I said, I like photography, but it's just a hobby," said Brendan, watching me scan them. "Something I do for myself."

"They're amazing," I whispered, taking a closer look at one by his bed. The photo showed a series of out-of-focus branches that divided the leaf-strewn ground and the dark, motionless water of a lake. Sunlight streaked through the frame, like the brush of a fingertip.

"You can have the bed," he said, heading for his closet. I looked over to see his profile, a pink splotch spreading across his nose and cheeks. He and Jamie didn't bring girls home...did that mean no one had seen this collection before?

Pulling a sleeping bag from the back of the narrow closet, he started shaking it loose.

"Honestly, I can sleep anywhere," I told him. "It's one of my gifts. I can fall asleep on buses and planes and literally anywhere with a flat surface, so please, take your bed. I did show up here in the middle of the night after all."

"My mom would smack me upside the head if she knew I'd made a girl sleep on the floor," he replied.

"Wouldn't she smack you upside the head to know a girl was sleeping in your bed?"

He paused, a short, muted laugh curling the edges of his smile, revealing a dimple. "You have a point."

I paused, picturing the night ahead of us. If I slept on the floor and woke up not knowing where I was, would I panic? Would I feel like I was right back in those woods, with that woman's claws in my arms and her teeth by my neck?

A shiver wracked through me, and Brendan's eyes narrowed.

"Sadie. Are you sure you're okay?"

I shook my head, but then nodded. "Yeah. I am. Just...maybe you're right and I'm still kind of frazzled. If you don't mind, we could share the bed." *One of you might be a monster, but I don't want to be alone*, I wanted to add. But Brendan was no monster. He couldn't be. His eyes were trained on me with a softness that had my insides heating.

"Even though you know how I feel about you?" he asked after a pause.

The sincerity was refreshing, but he was right to ask—wouldn't it be cruel to have him sleep beside me, knowing he liked me? Or was it worse to make him sleep on the floor, knowing I was so close by?

I swayed a bit on my feet, the night catching up with me. I wanted to sleep, and having a warm, solid body beside me would be comforting. He was willing, so I couldn't feel too shamefaced for taking him up on the offer, could I? Though, if I was being honest, some selfish, base side of me found the idea of sharing a bed with him thrilling.

I licked my suddenly dry lips as my heart started pounding harder in my chest. My body's response was so contradictory. Was this my mind's way of trying to forget the trauma of the night I'd just had? Wanting to lose myself in someone else? I cleared my throat, ignoring all the warring signals my body was sending. "Yes," I told him. "I don't mind. Honestly. If you don't."

Brendan nodded, deciding something for himself, and then went to his bureau, pulling out a large T-shirt and some basketball shorts. "You can change into these."

He turned to face his closet while I took off my wet, dirty jeans and my blouse, which he thankfully hadn't noticed was ripped in the back.

"I'm decent," I said, and he turned in this slow, purposeful way, as if he suspected I might be lying—or like he hoped I was. His hazel eyes scanned me from head to toe in the baggy shirt and low shorts, causing my cheeks to flush. It felt good to have him look at me like that. Except...I was with Jamie. Wasn't I?

I'm hoping you'll come back to me, Jamie had said. It was like he knew this would happen.

Brendan gestured to the bed, which—though mussed—at least seemed clean. The sheets were a heather gray, and I could tell from the indent on the pillow he usually took the left side, so I aimed for the right.

It was pleasantly comfortable as I wriggled between the sheets, exhaustion making my limbs heavy and slow almost as soon as I was horizontal.

"Goodnight, Sadie," he whispered as he joined me, his body causing a slight dip in the mattress beside me. I heard a click as he turned off the bedside lamp.

"G'night," I replied.

The dark of the room was only broken by the lamppost outside, creating the shadow of windowpanes over his collection of photographs.

"Thank you," I said into the night. "For letting me stay."

"Anything you need," he murmured, sounding already half-asleep. "Whenever."

I could smell his sugary scent on the bedspread and hear his slow exhale. He was still wearing the T-shirt and pants, and I wondered if that was his usual outfit for sleeping, or if he'd kept layers on for me. Was it normally all warm skin against these sheets?

Turning away from him, I attempted to wipe those thoughts away like fog from glass. Jamie was just across the hall, sleeping, and here I was picturing his brother shirtless—pants-less—wondering what his secret tattoo depicted, if he did truly have one, and trying my best to ignore that he might not actually be human. Brendan shifted at my back, and I wondered if he had turned toward me or away, but I was too nervous to look over my shoulder to find out.

Sleep eventually pulled me under, with a catalogue of images running rampant through my mind: snakeskin and music notes and tribal shapes and smears of blood. And then I was dreaming.

***

What woke me was the sound of a door slamming.

My eyes were crusted and dry as I pulled on my discarded glasses and attempted to blink the room around me into focus. Right. Brendan's room. It was early morning, the sun barely risen, but Brendan was missing from his side of the bed.

I sat up, my body now an aching patchwork of sore muscles and tight skin, and looked around for my clothes. The pile I'd left them in last night was gone. He must have taken them to be washed. Damn—I hoped he hadn't seen the scratch marks and holes the rough ground had made in the fabric. That would be hard to explain. Maybe he wouldn't look too closely.

I had to pee, but I was really hoping to avoid an awkward encounter with Jamie and Brendan's mother. There was a chance she might be at work; the boys said she sometimes had early shifts, sometimes late, so there was no telling. And that was if she was even well enough to be working today. But leaving her son's bedroom in his borrowed clothes would definitely send a message I did *not* want to explain.

Opening the door, I peeked into the hall, finding it empty. Jamie's door across the hall was still shut tight, and part of me desperately wanted to investigate his space, to experience the smell on his sheets, and see what photos decorated his walls. He was probably still asleep, though, and I didn't want to wake him. Instead, I snuck toward the bathroom.

Before I could reach it, the bathroom door opened, and there was Brendan.

No. It was Jamie. Scruff darkened his jaw, and there was no necklace in sight. He wore almost identical sleepwear to his brother—low-slung sweats—but no shirt.

"Sadie?"

I lifted my hand in a weak wave, my cheeks going pink. "Hey."

His gaze snagged on the bandages over both palms.

"What the fuck?" he whispered, then met my eyes with his own. I was trying hard not to stare at his chest. It was built from long hours at the gym, his pecs defined and smooth, a thin trail of hair leading from his navel to drift below the waistline of his pants. I wondered if his skin would be hot and soft over those hard muscles. At least my eyeline didn't drift south of the equator—more than once.

"I, uh...I came over late last night," I told him. "I needed a place to stay, and Brendan answered. Did you see my text?"

He shook his head, looking down at my clothes. "My phone's charging. You...you slept here? With him?"

"Not *with* him," I said, waving both hands like a flailing bird. "Just in his room. I swear." The last part came out as a squeak, though I wasn't even sure why I was anxious. He was the one who had practically opened the door to me trying things out with Brendan if I'd wanted to. Not that I was sure I didn't...

He chuckled then, the sound low and deep, rumbling up from his stomach. I wanted to bottle the sound. "I believe that. I just—it's a surprise to see you." He winked. "You could have always crawled into *my* bed, you know."

I didn't tell him I had considered it, but from the blush on my cheeks I think he could tell.

"Mind if I..." I gestured toward the bathroom behind him.

"Oh. Sure." He shifted to the side, but the hallway was narrow enough that our chests almost brushed as I moved past him. "Are you okay, though? What happened?"

"Jameson?" A voice called before I could answer, freezing me in place. That wasn't Brendan.

I peeked to the right and saw a woman who had to be their mother. She was beautiful, with long, curling dark hair pulled into a messy ponytail, her skin an olive tone that almost hid the lines at the corners of her eyes. A pair of faded jeans hugged her legs, and a bulky pink sweater hung on her short and narrow frame. She was thin in a way that made me think she sometimes forgot to eat, but her eyes seemed alert.

"Shit," muttered Jamie.

"Who's this?" she asked, coming forward.

Somehow, I had expected her to be charismatic and confident like Jamie, or quiet and reserved like Brendan, but she was somewhere in between, her smile warm and earnest.

"This is Sadie, Ma," said Jamie. "She needed a place to sleep for the night. Stayed in Brendan's room." His voice was more serious than I was used to, more authoritative.

At this, the woman cocked an eyebrow. "Not yours?"

Jamie shrugged, that easy, poised persona taking over. "I'm just as surprised as you are."

"Are you in some type of trouble?" she asked me.

"No, ma'am." I shook my head, and then reconsidered. "Well, I mean, I was attacked, but I didn't do anything."

Jamie's head snapped back toward my own. "What? Is that why your hands are wrapped up?"

"Yeah." I smiled sheepishly, showing the bandages to his mother. "There's this...woman who's been hanging by my house. She tried to hurt me last night, but I got away. The cops said they're going to be checking on my place, but I just wanted to stay somewhere that felt a little safer. I didn't know where else to go." I felt like I should apologize for sleeping in her house while she was unaware, but before I could wrestle the feeling into words, the woman gasped.

Her face transformed from suspicious to concerned, her hand coming up to her breastbone. "You poor thing. Do your parents know where you are? Do you need to call them?"

"I'll ring my dad later today; I didn't want to wake him up. He lives pretty far away."

"Still, I'm sure he would want to know." Her voice was soft now, and so maternal I felt a pang in my chest. "You're welcome to stay here as long as you need. I can make up the couch for you. Are you hungry? I'm making breakfast before I head to work."

"You should have woken me up," Jamie said before I could answer. When I turned to look at him, I saw something tortured in his expression—almost like betrayal. It was fierce, and it reminded me of the way he could crowd me into walls and the way he could lift me so easily. It reminded me again that either he or Brendan might not be human.

He took a step toward me, and I backed away instinctively, my shoulders hitting a photo frame hanging in the hallway, so it almost toppled to the floor.

"Oh, sorry." I wrapped my arms around my middle and shifted back toward the bathroom. "I just...I need to pee. But—yes, I would like some breakfast, Mrs. Barreto, thank you."

"No problem. French toast coming up, and please, call me Mia," she said, and then left us alone in the hall.

"I..." I looked at Jamie, unsure if I should explain my decision last night, or the odd panic I felt when he reached for me, but a cowardly sense of self-preservation took over and I closed the bathroom door in his face.

Breathing in deep, steady counts, I looked at myself in the mirror over the sink. My hair was still tangled in a loose braid over my shoulder, my skin a bit too pale, but other than my bandaged hands I looked mostly unharmed. The punctures and scratches were hidden beneath my shirt. Thankfully.

I washed my face and peed, then took care to re-braid my hair so I looked less bedraggled, wondering if I had time to look around the house more. Maybe if I peered into every corner and studied their belongings some clue would make itself known that would prove I was losing my mind, and they were both human. *Sure, as if I'd find a DNA test just lying on a table.* I shook my head, releasing a trembling breath.

Brendan was waiting for me in the hall when I walked out. His shaven face was a giveaway, as was the fact his chest was decidedly covered.

He had my clothes cleaned and folded in his hands, ready for me.

"I hear you met the matriarch," he teased. "Did she give you a hard time?"

I took the clothes with a weak smile. "Your mom is so sweet. I don't know why you'd worry. She's going to make French toast."

"She has her good days and her bad days; looks like today will be good." Brendan's smile was half-hearted, and then he shifted on his feet, seeming uneasy. "I better go give her a hand."

When he left me in the hall, I couldn't help but feel like I'd missed something. I rushed into his room and changed back into my clothes from last night, grateful to find the wear and tear at the back wasn't as drastic as it had seemed covered in dirt. Still, I spotted a hooded sweatshirt hanging on Brendan's closet door and decided to pilfer it to avoid any additional questions.

It was soft and warm and smelled like his bed, and I enjoyed the baggy feel of it around me, like a comfortable blanket.

When I walked into the kitchen, which was small but bright, with lots of yellow accents like lemon-patterned hand towels and potholders, the table was already set. It was circular and built for four, with Jamie on one side and Brendan on the other. Jamie was already eating a plate of eggs and there was a bag of hockey gear by his feet.

"Early practice?" I asked, sitting down. Their mom—Mia—had her back turned to us, and I could smell the browning butter and cinnamon of breakfast cooking.

He nodded, rushing a bit through his meal.

"You're going to be late if you don't leave now," said Brendan.

The look they shared was heavy with some unspoken message. Jamie's eyes went flat with annoyance.

"I'm waiting for Luke," he said. "Since you need the car."

I had a feeling he said this more for my benefit than anything else, but before Brendan could reply, a car honked outside.

Jamie sighed. Taking one final bite, he picked up his half-full plate and put it on the kitchen counter beside Mia as she puttered away at the stovetop. I watched as he kissed her hair—the twins towered at least five inches over her—and told her not to work too hard.

When he walked back to the table, I almost expected the same treatment, but as he picked up his bag of gear, he leaned his face close to mine, creating the sense that we were having a private moment. Despite his brother sitting only one foot away, watching us.

"Promise you'll tell me about what happened last night when you get the chance?"

I nodded, and my eyes drifted to his mouth just as it ticked up into that rakish smirk.

"Good."

He kissed me.

It was chaste, nothing like the intense meeting of lips we'd shared before in the storage room or in the rain, but the heat was there in the softness of his mouth. The seconds he lingered turned the peck into something just a little bit...more.

As he pulled away, I was aware that his mother was in the room, and so was Brendan, but for that singular moment when he'd kissed me all I'd thought about was him. Thankfully, with a quick glance, I saw that Mia was still facing away from us.

With a wink, Jamie turned and left the room, and I heard the front door shut behind him.

Breakfast became a little awkward after that. Mia served me a heaping plate of French toast with a kind smile and multiple offers to make me bacon or a side of eggs. She was as happy and sweet as could be, but I could tell Brendan was a little...perturbed by Jamie's goodbye. He kept his eyes down at his food, not making much in the way of conversation unless I asked him a direct question.

"Do you have other classes today besides Stats?" I asked.

"Econ."

"And do you like it?"

"Sure." He took a bite of his breakfast so slowly I thought he was studying the flavor to write a paper about it.

"But you have work after our class, right? At Daphne's?" I prompted.

"Yeah. Econ is later."

I bit my lip. "Wow, four whole words that time."

He finally looked up just as Mia sat in the seat across from me.

"Oh, don't mind him, Sadie," his mother said with a gentle smile. "He's just my sullen, little gremlin. Such a dark, broody boy." She reached out and patted his hand with her own, then tilted her head. "Hmm?" Looking to the left, near the fridge, she seemed to see something, or someone, and withdrew her hand, but I couldn't see what had made her move.

I met Brendan's gaze, and he gave the slightest shake of his head.

So…this was her schizophrenia in action, seeing things that weren't there. I could imagine that was what made Jamie and Brendan so protective of her—keeping her safe from the judgements of the world, but also safe from the world her mind made seem real. And then her words registered.

My body chilled, the delicious breakfast drying in my mouth.

Dark, broody boy. Brendan really could be like that monster who attacked me. There could be something lying in wait inside him, biding time until his nails would curve, his eyes would blacken. I didn't want to believe it. But last night had really happened, and what that woman had said wouldn't stop repeating over and over in my head. *I left him…to change and blend. Powerless. My dark boy.* While the naiad was dying under the docks of my property…was Mia raising her son?

"Anyway," Mia continued, startling me out of my thoughts. "You just let me know if you need to stay another few nights. We'd be happy to have you."

"Oh. Thank you," I said, a bit embarrassed, but my mind was back in the cave, with that creature and her blue skin and her inhuman strength. Her shark-like teeth.

"You okay?" Brendan asked.

"Yeah. Fine. I just—I realized I need to go home to get my stuff for Stats."

"I can come with you," he offered.

Shaking my head, I finished what few bites left of my meal I could stomach, and then rose from the table. "I need to talk to my dad and take a shower and…I'll just meet in you in class, okay?"

"…okay."

"It was nice to meet you, Mia," I said to his mom. "Thank you so much for breakfast."

She smiled, her face open and flushed with compassion, and gestured for me to leave the plate.

I'm ashamed to say I rushed out of their house like a rude guest, forgetting to return Brendan's hoodie. The pounding in my chest was a drumbeat that urged me to run. *My dark boy.*

Brendan's story about his mother had been so heart-breaking—a woman who was so unwell she didn't remember giving birth to more than one son. But now I could see the malicious layer of darkness between his words. It was possible there was another, more disturbing side to the tale; one of her sons might not be human. If that creature had somehow placed her infant beside Mia's own, Mia had been right. Maybe she'd never actually had a mental illness. Or at least, not before her world was upturned and no one had believed her claims. Her sad story was now one of potential horror.

And despite the incredulity of it all, my scratched hands burned, and that bitter mossy taste returned to my mouth. My instincts were screaming at me that it was all somehow true.

CHAPTER SIXTEEN

I drove back home with my thoughts tumbling over one another, struggling to line up everything I'd learned back into facts and timelines. When I added up everything I knew about Jamie, and then everything I knew about Brendan, I hoped some picture would emerge—some clue that exposed the truth. But all I could see were two different, beautiful boys, each with their own struggles, their own goals and dreams. Their own faults.

Before reaching any clarity, I was already sitting in the driveway to my rented abode, my fingers clenched tight on the steering wheel. That...*naiad* had only attacked me at night, but I couldn't be too careful. Dashing to the door while scanning left to right, I almost tripped up the steps, but I made it inside and slammed the door shut, sliding the lock home.

My small bottle of Mace was sitting on the living room table, and I sighed. It was time to start carrying it more regularly, instead of just when I thought I'd need it.

It was the size of a travel bottle of shampoo and disguised to look like hairspray—which I thought was genius—and came attached to a metal ring. I added it to my keys, feeling some measure of relief with its weight in my hands.

I looked around the apartment, viewing the rooms with new eyes. I spotted places the naiad could break in, and places she could hide. Was I safe here at all? Should I go stay at a motel far from the woods? But she had waited days between attacks, and she had only struck when I was outside. The cottage *seemed* secure...

I dialed my dad's number, expecting his busy schedule to mean I'd be talking once more to his answering machine, but he actually picked up his phone.

"Hey Sadie-lady, how's my favorite intrepid reporter?"

"Oh, you know," I laughed, though it came off more like a cough, "living the dream: classes, parties, uncovering conspiracies."

"That's my girl. Any word about that crazy woman?"

I'd told him a very watered-down version of my attack, worried he would demand I leave school until I could get safer on-campus housing, or that he would quit his current position in Texas and show up on my front door with a suitcase in hand. Now, I almost wished I had come clean. Maybe then I wouldn't have been dragged through the woods last night and nearly chomped on.

"Um, no," I said. "Nothing. I think the cops may have found her downtown, but that hasn't been confirmed." I closed my eyes, as if I could hide from my own lies, but there was no point in telling him a mythological water spirit was squatting in the pond here, hoping to feed my blood to her changeling child. He wouldn't believe me, and if he did, then I'd never get answers; I'd be carted off somewhere. "Actually, Dad, I have a...research question for you."

"Shoot."

"When you found this house for me, was it through a regular online listing? How did you pick it?"

His voice was tinged with guilt when he answered. "Oh, well actually, I had an old co-worker look for me, and he picked the place. Sorry, Sadie, I just didn't have much time with the move and the new job here, and he said he knew the area. Is there something wrong with it?"

"No, it's fine!" I assured him. "It's got some quirks, but the land is so beautiful, and I just wondered about the history of it. You know me."

"I think I have the link he sent me somewhere..." I heard the line crackling as he put me on speaker and started navigating through his email. "I'll send it to you once I find it."

"Thanks, that would be great."

There was a pause then, an extended stretch between us, and I swear he could tell I was drumming up the nerve to ask my next question. Instead of cracking a joke or starting a weird anecdote about the people he was meeting at his new company, he let the silence linger.

I swallowed; my tongue suddenly swollen in my mouth. "And...one other quick question. Was Mom—I mean, did Mom have any family in the area? Do you know?"

While most of my mind was focused on the naiad and her potential connection to the Barreto brothers, one other crazy thing she'd said followed me like a shadow: *You share my blood. Some ember lingers.* It's why she wanted to drink from me, and why I was in danger in the first place. She thought there was something inside me that was like *her*. I knew my father's parents, and they were as normal as you could get. So, if there was some mystical creature hiding in my family tree, there was only one other direction it could come from.

"I don't think so," Dad answered. "She was from Virginia originally, and that's where her parents met." His tone was overly casual.

I tended not to ask about Mom. She'd left when I was little, and the story was that she'd just...decided being a mother wasn't for her. In solidarity, I stuck to dad like a barnacle on a boat, keeping those "before times" in the rearview, but in moments like this, when the answer could turn my world upside down, questions needed to be asked, no matter who they hurt. I still hated doing it.

"Oh," I replied, keeping my tone light and carefree. "What about her grandparents?"

"Her grandfather was adopted; I only know because when he passed, they thought he might have had a congenital heart disease, which would have been hereditary, but they had no way of checking. That was right before you were born. Honey...why are you asking?"

"It's this weird family genealogy thing I'm working on for an article. About someone else," I rushed to add, "but it made me curious. He...he found out he had family in the area he didn't know about. Anyway, I actually have to get ready for class now, but I just figured I'd ask."

"Alright, well make sure you're careful up there," he said. His tone was uneasy, as if he didn't quite believe me, but the familiarity of his deep voice, and the concern lacing it, had my own nerves easing.

"Yes, Dad," I said through a smile. "Will do."

"I'll send you the apartment listing now—just found it. Love you, kiddo."

"Love you too."

After a quick shower, where I pondered the idea that my mother's grandfather could have been some changeling himself, or the son of a water sprite, I checked my phone to see he'd sent the listing through.

It was on a local site, and the picture of the house was taken in the winter, the lawn covered in pristine snow, a wreath over the door and lit garlands in the windows making the scene warm and inviting. I read the description, and then scrolled through room sizes and years the heating and roof had been updated, until I got down to the last line: "Previously owned by a retired general, windows have been upgraded to insulated ballistic glass, and additional layers of mineral wool insulation were added to the walls—great for saving on your heating bills in winter!"

So, this place was a veritable fortress, then, despite its charming small-town exterior. I walked over to the patio doors in the kitchen, lifting the blinds and moving aside the curtains, looking again at the beautiful scenery of the yard.

I knocked on the glass. It sounded dull and low when I hit it, almost like plastic, and I knocked again. Harder. So...as long as I kept everything locked up tight, I should be okay, I reasoned. At least for now. And since the naiad had been so tired from dragging me to her lair, I expected a couple days' reprieve before she made another appearance. It could be her scratching against the walls I'd heard at night, or her trying to get in through the windows, but I would have my Mace on me from now on. And I would keep a weapon by my bedside every night, I decided.

I could do this. I could hold her off while I investigated her claims.

I hoped.

Brendan was quiet that morning in Stats, and so was I. There was no good opportunity to discuss last night or ask him anything about his mother as we sat down and were immediately handed a quiz on scatter plot correlations. When the teacher dismissed us—him to Daphne's and me to head home—I returned the sweatshirt I'd borrowed, which he thanked me for with a nod, and then we went our separate ways.

Grateful for the chance to really dig into my theories, I spent the afternoon studying more on changelings and naiads, reading strange stories about children who could levitate, or who were so sickly their skin was tinged blue—which now seemed a legitimate claim given the naiad creature's azure tint. There were even stories of women who dragged unsuspecting boaters into the depths of rivers and lakes, picking at their flesh until nothing but slimy bones remained.

Could Jamie or Brendan really be born from something like that? Could I share even a small percentage of my heritage with a creature that dangerous? I had poor eyesight, I couldn't swim, and I'd never been physically fit. Surely, those genes had to be far-*far* removed. Right?

I kept reading.

"Changelings and other fae in mythology who appeared human could usually only be controlled by using their true name, which was concealed and kept secret for that very reason. Fairies of all genera, therefore, use nicknames or false names in most historical ballads or poems. It was said that possession of a fae's true name constrained them to marry the keeper of the name."

While that was interesting and made me think about how Jamie was a nickname for Jameson, it didn't really help me. And while I couldn't find anything about naiads drinking blood, or blood-sharing fae in general, I did find more stories about various fae-folk torturing humans, forcing them to create art or music while working them to the bone—literally—until they met their untimely end.

When I couldn't look at those gruesome images any longer, I switched to my never-ending list of articles about the Spindle River ecosystem and its record of dropping water levels. It all jumbled together to the point where I thought I should stop, but I couldn't sleep, so I read through the night. And then another. And another.

My days became a blur of watching Jamie and Brendan a little too closely, blotting the dark circles under my eyes with concealer, and drinking the sweetest coffee drinks I could find to keep up with my deteriorating sleep schedule.

I needed to understand this incredible situation I found myself in, and though I learned everything I could, it didn't seem like it would ever be enough.

CHAPTER SEVENTEEN

Throughout the next week, I simultaneously tried to avoid the Barreto brothers—partly because I was moderately concerned about one of them being inhuman, but also because I dreaded the idea of having to choose between them—while still being drawn to them. I watched them like a hawk through every interaction, hoping for some kind of "eureka moment" to occur.

Jamie was just as bright and charismatic as ever in Linguistics, nudging my shoulder with his while making dirty jokes out of the various vowel sounds we had to practice. Brendan showed up on days we had Stats to drive me to class and it would have been both foolish and rude to send him off alone only to trail after him minutes later, so we spent the ride with an uncomfortable tension between us. I asked him questions and he answered, but the easy way we'd talked before was now halting and troubled. Still, the urge to reach out and touch him absorbed my attention more than once. I wanted to erase the worried look in his hazel eyes and bring him out of his shell once more.

While Brendan was worried about me, his expression ever serious, Jamie kept things light and easy. I wanted them both.

I was also afraid of them both.

Every time Jamie leaned close for a kiss, or Brendan slowly extended a hand, I thought of that naiad and how one of these boys might have something similar lurking beneath their skin. Each day that passed I found myself wound tighter.

Come Thursday evening, I was proud and relieved to find that Kim and Professor Lewis liked my article about the Edgewood trails clean-up, and that only minor copyedits were needed. The piece would be published in Monday's issue. It would be my first, since the comparative interviews with Brendan and Jamie had only been a warm-up, as opposed to an assignment. However, Kim said the 'twin piece' might be included come the end of the year, when they liked to do profiles on students looking forward to being seniors. Regardless, I couldn't be happier that my Edgewood article would be printed. It would be another for my portfolio, although hopefully not so I could cart it to another school next year.

It was late when the staff meeting ended, and I tried to stop my feet from dragging as I made my way to the lot where Brendan would be waiting. I was surprised he was willing to come get me, given his shift at Daphne's, but he'd sent me a text asking when I needed a ride, and there he was—dependable to a fault.

I climbed into the Civic, my eyes aching from staring at the same redlines for hours, and gave Brendan what I hoped was a friendly, appreciative smile. "Hey. Thanks again for the ride."

"Of course," he said. "Newspaper always go so late?"

"The *Prowl* never sleeps," I joked, and then yawned. "I just wanted to go over my story a few extra times. It's going to be in the next issue."

"That's awesome, I can't wait to read it." We pulled out of the lot, and I noticed he was wearing a white T-shirt, which by itself didn't seem so alarming, except that I realized I'd never seen him in anything but black or gray. It made his arms seem tanner, and his dark hair shinier. It was a good look on him. His bicep ticked once as I stared, so I quickly averted my eyes.

"Thanks," I said, blinking myself more awake. "I...I ended up using one of the photos you gave me, too."

"Oh, yeah? Which one?"

"You'll just have to wait and find out," I teased. I was happy to see him grin, his white, even teeth highlighted by the reflection of the headlights on the road.

"So, what's your next piece going to be on?" he asked.

"Not sure yet. I was thinking I might write about your gig tomorrow night, if you don't mind."

"You really think people will want to read about me and my garage band buddies?"

"Only if you put on a good show."

"Oh, well that I can promise," he said, turning to me with raised eyebrows. "Andrea wrote a new song we're debuting, and we're pretty sure it will be our next hit. Very Billie Eilish meets Bad Omens. Plus, we have a few dedicated fans who show up to these things—they tend to lift people up and all that. It gets pretty entertaining."

"And you'll be singing too, right?" I asked.

He nodded, but his eyes met mine then darted back to the road, like he was nervous.

I was glad he was back to talking to me like this, with more than one-word answers, though it had taken a while post-kiss from Jamie, and I was looking forward to seeing him perform more than I let on. I'd seen Jamie in his element at practice, slamming hockey players into the boards, slashing across the ice, making raucous jokes to his teammates and slapping their shoulders. Now I'd finally have the chance to see Brendan in action. I hated how badly I wanted to compare them. To find a fault I could utilize to take a step back.

After we said goodnight, I clutched my Mace bottle tightly in one hand and tried to act casual as I hurried to the front door. It was dark, but I had left the living room light on all day so there was enough light to see the space around the driveway.

Brendan waited until I was safely inside before leaving.

Thankfully, Fridays were very low-key for me. I didn't have any classes, and currently I had no need for a job—though I was thinking of looking for one to build up my post-graduation savings—so I spent my day relaxing on my couch and doing research on watershed pollution between bouts of homework. I was ahead in my class reading so I practiced Stats problems until it was time to reward myself with some TV binging and a long, hot shower to get ready for tonight.

Since this was my first experience with Spindle River nightlife, I spent a good deal of time debating what to wear. I decided on a cut-off leather jacket over a gray tank top, some ripped jeans, and heeled boots. With a red lip, some dangling earrings, and mascara that made my eyes pop behind my glasses, I was ready to go.

I'd gotten a text from Jamie that he would be driving me to and from the concert, which was fine, except it felt oddly like he was chauffeuring me on a date with someone else. After all, I was heading out to see his brother's band. To be there for *Brendan*. It was all very unconventional.

Jamie: *I'm outside. U ready?*

Taking one last check in my hall mirror, I grabbed my keys—Mace included—and a small purse, and then went out to the car.

"Damn. You look good," he said as soon as I climbed inside.

"You too." He was in a tight, emerald green long-sleeve shirt which stretched impressively over his chest and arms. I remembered seeing that chest sans-shirt, with that trail of hair down his abs, and thought about how easy it would be to reach out and touch him. And from the delicious way his eyes raked over me as I settled into the seat, I had a feeling he would welcome it. He'd feed that heat right back to me, and I realized if I kissed him, we would be all over each other in this car. I wouldn't stand a chance.

I shot my gaze forward.

The show was at a venue called Caisse's Bar & Grill, which hosted an all-ages night for musical performances twice a month. As Jamie drove there, we kept the conversation light, talking about our classes and his upcoming game against Eastborough College. More than once, I caught his hand drifting between us, like he was about to rest it on my thigh, but he held back. Whether his restraint was for Brendan's sake or not, I wasn't sure. And then we were pulling up to the bar.

It was a square, brick building, with a set of tall windows cracked open vertically to let in the cool, evening air. A green-striped awning stretched over the front door. Music spilled into the night, mixed with laughter and the scuffle of dozens of people meandering about inside.

Jamie took my hand as we walked in.

The entire right wall of the restaurant was one giant chalkboard, and though it most likely typically sported a menu, there was a lineup of tonight's entertainment there instead. A band called Fathom Biddies would be performing shortly, but the obvious headliner, name written in a much larger font, was Shady Tree Lane.

While the floor was a bit sticky under my boots, the place seemed relatively clean. It had wooden panels on the other walls and dozens of dark tables pushed along the edges of the room to make a wide, open floor before the slightly raised stage. A group of guys was setting up there, plugging in instruments and checking microphones, their dark clothes almost blending into the black backdrop behind them.

"Hey, glad you made it," Brendan said as he walked up to us. And if he wasn't nearly identical to the guy currently holding my hand, I might not have recognized him. His hair was wild with mousse, curling over one side of his forehead. There was a piercing glimmering in his ear, and he wore a baggy T-shirt ripped in a few places that hung loosely over his frame and what I thought were...leather pants? I licked my suddenly dry lips. I could so easily picture him drenched in sweat and curled over a microphone, his mouth grazing the grille, captivating the audience with his penetrating gaze.

"Of course!" I said, voice a bit squeaky. "Wouldn't miss it."

His eyes darted down to my hand, which Jamie had loosely laced with his own. Jamie didn't grip it tighter or show it off, but he didn't remove it, either. I spent a moment deciding if I should pull away, but while they made it clear the decision between them was mine, I didn't want to fight against the tide of the moment. I'd go with the flow as much as I could, and if the flow meant letting Jamie's warm, rough palm rest against mine, then so be it.

Clearing his throat, Brendan turned to a small group crowded near the stage, huddled in some discussion, and waved them over. "Frank! Bring the girls over here."

Frank turned out to have a startling number of tattoos traveling the lengths of both arms, which he showed off with a white tank top. He had Japanese features and a smirk that made me think he lived for the kind of attention this band offered him. Sam, who I remembered was Frank's sister, had the same delicate nose and sharp cheekbones, but Brendan was right in that they didn't come off as siblings; her long hair was dyed light blonde, she wore sky-blue contacts, and her frame was hidden by a tan sweater she had on over jeans.

"You must be Sadie," said the third band member as she ventured up to us, who had to be Andrea. She was beautiful, with a smattering of freckles over her cheeks and strawberry blonde hair in a thick braid hanging over one shoulder. She was fair-skinned and thin, and the dark eyes she trained on me were just a tiny bit too large for her face. She reminded me of a doll. A doll who, at the moment, was scanning me from head to toe with something like suspicion.

"That's me," I replied, as Brendan introduced everyone.

"You here to be Brendan's new groupie?" Frank asked. He pulled a pair of drum sticks from his back pocket and started twirling them between his fingers.

"Shut it, *Franklin*," said Brendan.

He shrugged. "Just asking. We could always use some more rabid Laners."

"Laners?" I asked.

"We are not calling our fans that," scoffed Andrea. I noticed she edged closer to Brendan, as if to pull him away.

Jamie tugged at my hand. "We're here to support, groupie-dealings aside," he said. "We'll see you up there?" The dismissal was clear, and though I was eager to learn more about the band members, I let him pull me through the growing crowd to a few high tables near the back.

The first band started playing, their sound heavy with screams and fast guitar riffs. For a group with the word Biddies in it, they were vicious.

The main singer was shouting into the mic something about blood and darkness before the words were drowned out with a sharp solo from the guitar.

I winced.

"Yeah, they're a mess," Jamie agreed. I hadn't been aware he was watching me. He had to shout to be heard over the music and we both leaned over our elbows on the circular high-top. We spent the entire first song pointing out everything ridiculous about this band, starting from their all-black ensemble and off-beat drummer, and ending at the way the singer had to lick his lips between every line.

I was laughing and having a surprisingly good time, inching ever closer to Jamie while the set played on. It was almost enough to make me forget the way I was supposed to be investigating him, looking for clues he wasn't human—not that I had any idea what those clues might look like.

And it was ridiculous I was even looking. They were both obviously normal guys; neither had fangs, or claws, or a cool tint to their skin. Maybe I had it wrong. It could be a coincidence that their mother didn't remember having a second baby, I mused as I watched Jamie's mouth in profile twist into a smirk at a particularly discordant chord. Their mother may have been genuinely confused, or blacked out from pain, or having a schizophrenic episode. If I told Jamie and Brendan about what I had really been through, maybe they would have some logical answers. However, I had already learned my lesson about opening my mouth before I had all the facts. If my time at USC taught me anything, it was that I had to have the whole picture before making my thoughts public. I didn't want to ask them for clarity while subtly hinting one of them may be a naiad.

"I'm going to get a drink," Jamie yelled, just as the band was nearing the end of their last song. "You want one?"

I shook my head, and Jamie nodded, leaving the table to fight his way through the throng. Despite the mediocre performance of Fathom Biddies, the place was now packed. Brendan's band was clearly the real draw.

Watching Jamie shoulder his way across the floor, I focused on the way people reacted to him. Some of the myths I'd read said people could instinctively tell when a fae creature was among them—that they'd move around them and give them space without even realizing it—but Jamie was engulfed on all sides, brushing up against people and gently moving them aside with an open hand. I saw him smile and nod at someone he moved past, and then heard more than one guy call his name. He was popular, which was the opposite of what a changeling was supposed to be. At least, according to obscure medieval literature.

The Fathom Biddies finished their set to a smattering of civil applause, and Brendan and his group started taking over the stage with practiced ease, changing out their equipment.

I watched as Brendan plugged in the electric guitar I recognized from his room, and when the rest of his group was ready, he sauntered up to the mic, all confidence, and smiled at the crowd.

"Thanks for coming, everyone. We're Shady Tree Lane, and this first one is called 'Smoke Signal.'" He wrapped his palm around the microphone and rolled his shoulders, twisting to put his lips close to the mic, eyes closed, as Frank counted them in at the drums.

The sound was so different from the first band, I wondered why they'd been grouped together—Brendan's voice started soft, blending with the opening beats of the bass that Sam expertly strummed at his side. She kept close as he sang, the lyrics hauntingly sad. The song was about begging for someone to recognize a call for help, even from far away. Andrea was on keyboards, the tune a lilting undercurrent for Brendan's voice, and Frank played the drums like a weak heartbeat against it all. Together, they created a sound that painted a picture in my mind. I could see the pain and loneliness in the lyrics and could imagine the gray skies and lengthening shadows in the story.

And then Brendan's eyes opened, and he pulled his guitar forward.

His long fingers were steady over the strings, his arm muscles ticking as he played the beat. The music grew more layered and less harmonic, like a person falling to pieces. Brendan's voice became hoarse, moving from crooning to almost tortured as the song crescendoed, his eyes finding mine through the crowd.

I inhaled, stunned by his emotion and the power and range of his voice as the dark melody swept through me. Andrea switched the key, then Sam, and finally Frank's attack on the drums grew violent. I couldn't look away. It was like Brendan held my jaw in his hands, pulling me forward. His chin tilted up and I almost mirrored him. It was like sex—a push and pull—connecting us as he sang directly to me.

His voice got softer then, drifting away with a promise to hold on, until someone could see the smoke signal and take him home. When he sang the word "home" it felt like he'd called my name. My body was flushed with the attention. *This* was the Brendan I knew was hiding under that quiet, chivalrous protector. This was him *unleashed*. I watched him close his eyes again, as if pained.

"Hey." Jamie came up behind me, wrapping one arm around my collarbone and putting his mouth close to my ear. It startled me out of the moment like a splash of cold water, and then the pressure of his hand by my neck had something like panic flashing through me.

Images of the naiad, her webbed hands grabbing my arms, her claws dragging me along the ground, had me stepping out of Jamie's embrace. My heart pounded in my chest, the ghost of adrenaline flooding my limbs.

"I got you a root beer," he said, moving his way back to his side of the table. "Since they don't serve lattes here." He gestured to the drink he'd apparently placed by my elbow without me noticing, his smile tilted and sardonic, though he had one eyebrow raised. He'd probably caught the way I'd jerked away from him.

"Oh. Thanks." I struggled to take a deep breath and lower my heart rate, pleasantly surprised he'd remembered I like root beer.

The song ended and I cheered and screamed with the rest of the crowd, doing my best to bring myself back into the moment as I applauded Brendan. He gave a sheepish smile and then nodded to Andrea.

"This next one is a new song, so be gentle," Brendan said into the mic, and then backed away. He wouldn't be singing for this one, and I found myself extremely disappointed. All I wanted was to hear his voice again, to dissect its differences from the way he talked to me in the car or in my backyard—like he was only beginning to find his voice—to this gritty, confident tenor.

Andrea was the star of this song, and Brendan was right that her breathy, low voice was reminiscent of Billie Eilish, but the keys reminded me of something a bit more emo than pop. Still, she had presence and talent, her fingers moving over the keyboard like the patter of raindrops, her expression full of longing as she looked to the crowd, and then to Brendan as he played the chords of the chorus on his guitar.

"They're amazing," I called to Jamie.

"Yeah, I'm really proud of him." He took a sip of his own drink, which looked like mine but was most likely alcoholic, and though he sounded honest, his eyebrows were a bit low, his mouth tense. As Jamie put down his drink, a change came over his face, like he was determined not to be bothered by whatever was on his mind. "Good thing they warmed up the audience with that Biddies garbage before the main course. Really sells the whole 'indie scene' feel. You know, I hear they have the record for the second-loudest audio feedback in the state of Utah."

I muffled a giggle by sipping my root beer, then looked around to make sure none of the aforementioned Biddies members were lingering nearby. Seeing the coast was clear, I widened my eyes at Jamie, trying to smother my laughter.

"The actual loudest was another indie band featuring the same singer but..." he put on a pompous, nasally tone, "you probably haven't heard of them."

At this, I snorted an actual laugh, then covered my mouth.

He winked. "You think this is good, you should have seen B play the recorder when we were six. He was hot crossing *all* the buns."

"Stop," I hissed, chuckling as I swatted his arm. "I'm trying to listen." But my smile didn't dim for the rest of the Shady Tree Lane set, and I was back to feeling like I was somehow on a date with both brothers at the same time, pulled between them in a game I didn't know if I could win.

And part of me didn't mind.

CHAPTER EIGHTEEN

When Shady Tree Lane finished their set, my palms were sweating, and my chest felt like it was glowing with heat. It had been an impressive show. Brendan and Andrea had taken turns as the main vocalist and finished with a duet about cheating on each other that was simultaneously sensual and sad. Between Jamie's humor and Brendan's intensity, I found myself eager to spend time with both of them, and ashamed of how equal that craving was.

The bar switched to a DJ who set up on the stage, the songs decidedly more dance-oriented, and the crowd went from a concert rush to the grind and sway of a nightclub.

"Wanna dance?" Jamie asked me, putting down his empty glass.

"Sure!" I grabbed his outstretched hand, and he pulled me away from the table, leading me toward the center of the floor. After the set, Brendan had drifted off to the side with his band members to accept praise and maybe do some post-show discussion. I didn't see him now as we moved through the crowd.

Jamie's hands were hot as they found my hips. The music thumped through my ribs as we twisted and swayed, my arms thrown into the air to caress my body on the way down. Sweat started to gather under my breasts and on my stomach as we were pushed closer together, his head dipping toward mine. My body unraveled, moving on its own as he stroked his fingers up my sides then back to my hip bones. It was as if a circle of space had opened around us, a pocket of warm, wet air secluding us so that when his mouth dipped to my own, his lips softly dragging up mine just once, I had no sense of our surroundings.

I felt the caress of his lips down to my toes, and if we were alone, I knew all it would take was one look, one word, and we'd be in some hallway or back room, clawing at each other.

If Brendan was a force on the stage, Jamie was a force in my arms. I ran my palms up his muscled arms, cupping his neck as I threw my head back, feeling the hard length of his body against mine while we moved, grinding to the rhythm. The song's tempo increased. I turned so my back was facing him, my ass cradled against his hips, and he held me there with one hand, the other scraping up the over sensitized skin of my arms and then brushing the edges of my breasts.

I tensed as he accidentally grazed the still-healing cuts on my side, and suddenly all my focus was on my injuries. My near-death experience. My escape. My mission.

I spun in his arms. "I'm getting kind of warm," I shouted over the music. "Can we sit this one out?"

He nodded and I followed him back to the edges of the dance floor, looking for somewhere I could catch my breath.

A girl in a minidress tapped Jamie on the shoulder, her pink lips all smiles. Her long, brunette hair hung down her back in loose waves and she flicked the tresses away as she leaned close. "Jamie! I need you to talk to Miles," she yelled, her mouth becoming a pout. "He keeps trying to get Charlie to go in on this off-campus apartment for next year and I *cannot* live with both of them. I need you to remind him how gross guys can be—tell him more stories about the locker room or something!"

Jamie laughed, his head thrown back. "I feel so honored. Want me to tell the snake one again?"

"Yes! Exactly!"

He turned toward me. "Wanna meet some of the guys?" he asked.

I shook my head. "No, I could really use a breather. I'll get some water and meet you in a few?"

His head was cocked as he studied me, eyebrows pinched with concern. "You sure?"

"I'm sure." I gave him an easy smile, patting him on the arm. "Go play."

The bar was crowded, but within a few minutes I was able to get a bottle of water and move toward the windows, hoping for an errant breeze to make its way in. Drinking deep, I then put the closed bottle against my neck, trying to cool down. If I had danced through one more song without being reminded of the naiad, I might have ridden Jamie's thigh right there on the dance floor, in full view of everyone nearby. The attraction was that powerful.

"There you are," said a voice behind me. I thought it was Jamie, already back from his chat with the popular crowd, but when I turned it was Brendan behind me, his hair a sweaty, tousled mess, his shirt sticking to his skin.

"Hey. Aren't those pants uncomfortable in this heat?" I asked, looking down at the leather pants.

He tugged at the silver chain beneath the shirt, his expression distressed. "You have no idea." Moving to stand beside me at the window, he took a deep breath of the fresh air. "Wanna go outside for a minute?"

"Jamie might come looking for me," I replied, and then I wanted to kick myself. I wasn't anyone's property; I was allowed to go where I wanted, with whoever I wanted. "Actually, yeah. Just for a bit."

I followed Brendan easily through the edges of the packed bar, though he didn't take my hand or pull me along, and then we were out underneath the green awning of the restaurant. There were a couple guys to our right smoking cigarettes, and Brendan edged to the left, so we were by the windows. The club music was all bass and synth as it spilled onto the sidewalk, pulsing through the soles of my boots.

Brendan released a long breath. "God, these things are exhausting."

"Don't you mean exhilarating? You seemed to be having a good time up there."

"For the show, sure," he lifted one shoulder, "but afterwards it's always this kind of...schmoozing while we try to get people to buy CDs or any merch Frank and Sam have brought."

"Ooh, I want to buy something!"

He huffed a laugh. "I don't think you'll feel the same once you see the weird-ass font Frank used for the band name."

I took another swig of my water, then offered Brendan the bottle, but he shook his head. He seemed to take in the cool night air like its own form of sustenance.

"Why don't you offer one of your photographs as part of the design?" I asked. "Make something into an icon for the band."

He considered that. "Well, the name is based on this street Andrea used to live on, and a photo of the sign might be cool. But that's across the state, not easy to get to."

"Could be a fun adventure," I said, smiling up at him.

Brendan's gaze drifted from the buildings across the street down to my face, and the slowest, sweetest smile bloomed over his features.

"It could," he said, nodding his head. "That's a nice way to look at it."

There was a moment of silence between us as we enjoyed the cool night air, and then his voice found me like a physical caress. "You always seem to have a positive spin on things." With his hazel eyes intense on mine—so much so I almost wanted to look away—I could only take his words as complete honesty. "I really like that about you."

I swallowed, embarrassment crawling up my cheeks. "Thanks. I—I really liked seeing you perform tonight."

He shifted so his shoulder was resting against the brick facade, his hands now tucked into the pockets of those tight, leather pants. "I'm glad you could come. It means a lot to me."

"Trying to get me to be a groupie?" I asked, with a grin. "Frank seems to think you need one."

I expected him to laugh and make a joke, to feed on the lighthearted energy of our banter, but this was Brendan, I remembered, as his easy smile drifted away. His tone was serious as he twisted more toward me. "I'd take you in whatever way you'd let me," he said, and I wondered how much it cost him to be so open and vulnerable. "I just want to keep you in my life."

"You say that like you're worried I'll disappear." My voice became breathy, and I found myself drifting closer to him. I could feel the heat pouring off his body.

"I'm always worried people are going to disappear," he admitted, his voice low. "My dad...he left before we were born. And I've always worried Mom is just one bad episode away from being declared unfit, or worse." He cleared his throat. "We're not minors anymore, so it's not like anyone could take us away now, but I spent a lot of my life being anxious about it."

"Wow," I said, blinking. "I'm sorry. That must have been really hard on you, growing up scared like that." That's why he was always so dependable, I figured. Working hard for his family, keeping his dreams on the sidelines. Sacrificing. I imagined it was why he was so quiet—so good at keeping himself contained until he could let it all go, like he did on stage, intensity and passion flickering just under the surface.

I put my hand on his arm, my heart aching for him, and those dark, hazel eyes met my own. I wanted to be open with him, too.

"I have a bad habit of bouncing from place to place, and I've never had a real relationship because of it," I admitted. "One that could stick. But I hope...I hope I can stay here. I don't want to disappear from your life—"

Like a lightning strike without warning, he bent his head and pressed his lips to mine.

I pulled in a breath through my nose, my whole body rising to meet him like a magnet was yanking me into the air. The kiss wasn't a peck like I'd expected, but harsh and violent, a clash of tongue and teeth that put my mind into a state of shock so all I could do was let instinct take over.

He pulled me against his body, his back against the bricks as we kissed and breathed into each other's mouths like we were drowning and searching for air. His head tilted and I opened further for him, reveling in every sensation.

It felt exciting, like a pure rush, but also...like I was stepping off the edge of a knife. I didn't like the idea of how far I could fall into the darkness below.

Brendan had one hand cradling the back of my head, and another at my lower back, clutching me fiercely against him, fingers gripping my shirt like a lifeline. I could feel his hard body against mine, frantic to line us up like two puzzle pieces waiting to click into place. My hand drifted up his firm chest and the cool metal of his necklace tickled my palm. Stroking my fingers farther up, they found the soft, full waves of his hair, messy and damp with sweat. And then my mind caught up to the hot blood roaring through me and I broke away, panting for breath.

"I..." I started, unsure what to say. Jamie and I weren't exclusive, and hell, he had practically told me to give Brendan a chance, get him out of my system, but this felt too...consuming. Too much like losing control. My lips were wet and swollen and I fought back the desire to lick them and savor the sensation. "I should probably go back inside," I said.

My foot bumped up against my water bottle, which I hadn't even noticed I'd dropped. I bent to pick it up, my face flushing with shame.

Brendan didn't say anything, just watched me with a steady gaze, his chest rising and falling as he struggled to get his breathing back to normal. His lips were dark.

I left him there, feeling cowardly and confused, hoping wherever Jamie was, he hadn't seen us kissing and groping against the wall.

Opening the door to the bar was like entering a cacophonous nightmare. All the bodies sliding against one another in the dim light had seemed so erotic and wild moments before, but were now a chaos I desperately wanted to escape. My brain was stuck somewhere outside, against the brick wall. We'd kissed. I'd liked it. And I didn't know what that meant or what I should do or if—

My shoulder bumped into someone, and I mumbled a rushed apology, but they stopped me with a hard grip. It was Andrea, her eyes like flint. An overhead light made her freckled cheeks stand out like a porous skull. I tried to back away, the vision startling me, but she held tight.

"What were you doing out there?" she demanded. "Are you playing him?"

Shit, she must have seen us.

"I'm not playing anyone," I said, trying to remove her hand. With one jerk, which nearly caused me to trip and fall, Andrea had her mouth at my ear.

"Don't even think about hurting him," she hissed. "I've seen how he looks at you, and if you—"

She was pulled away, and I found Brendan back at my side.

"That's enough, 'Dre."

He threw down her hand, and I could tell his hold on her wrist had hurt her. Her eyes were wide with betrayal. I thought she might argue or cry, but instead she spun, heading back into the fray of the room—to lick her wounds in peace.

"You didn't have to do that," I told him. My voice sounded weak to my own ears. "She was just looking out for you."

"Still, she shouldn't have come after you that way," he said. His expression was dangerous as he looked around us, like he was searching for other threats.

I almost rolled my eyes, but I was too frustrated with him. "I had that handled. And you need to *stop* being overprotective like this, no matter how you grew up."

He reached out to touch me—my arm maybe, at the place where Andrea had grabbed me—but I pulled away. The last thing I needed was to be manhandled, even if I had craved his touch so intensely just seconds ago.

My emotions were swinging too fast for me to get a grip on—wanting him, wanting Jamie, being afraid of their touch, suspicious of their motives, fighting all my instincts to give myself to one and then the other. I needed to get out of here.

"I'm going to go find Jamie," I yelled over the music. "Thanks again...for inviting me."

Brendan nodded, his mouth tight-lipped with disappointment, but he let me go.

I found Jamie at the left end of the room, still in a circle of people, that minidress-wearing brunette at his right, her arm wrapped around another guy. They were laughing at something, but when Jamie saw me, his grin went from wide to downright beaming.

"Sadie, there you are!" He waved me closer. "Feeling better? I want you to meet some of these idiots."

"Actually, I think I might need to head out."

"Are you okay?" he asked, his smile dropping. He made his way through the small circle, so he could lower his voice. "What's up?"

I shook my head. "Nothing, I just...I'm not feeling great." *I kissed your brother, and his bandmate maybe wanted to attack me, and I feel really confused and overwhelmed*, was too difficult to say out loud.

"Okay, let me take you home."

"No, that's fine, I can take—"

"Sadie." Jamie shook his head. "I can see these guys literally any day of the week. And I drove you here. It's safer if you don't go home alone."

"I have my pepper spray," I argued.

He pursed his lips. "I'd really feel better if I could make sure you get there safe. If I'm worried, I might not sleep, and if I don't sleep, I'll be horrible at practice tomorrow and my coach will make me run suicide drills until my legs fall off. You haven't seen my bare legs yet, but let me tell you, it would be a travesty to future swimsuit covers if something happened—"

"Okay, okay," I said, bemused despite myself.

Jamie turned back to the crowd. "See you guys later!"

A chorus of "'Night, Jamie!" followed us as he muscled his way through the dancers, keeping one hand clenched in mine so I could trail behind him. I thought I would feel nervous about his grip, given how I kept reacting to being touched, but maybe it was because I could see his tan, short-nailed fingers in front of me. Or maybe it was because I suddenly felt...safe, like he would take care of me.

We didn't see Brendan on our way out into the night.

The ride back to my house was quiet at first. Jamie kept the heat cranked up high and the music turned low; I finally had some space to think. I replayed every moment of the evening, from joking and having fun with Jamie to the intense attraction I felt to Brendan on that stage. The dancing, the kiss, and now the ride home had me yo-yoing between them, and it was making me dizzy.

"Hey, I hope you didn't feel abandoned when I got pulled away," Jamie said into the dark, after we were about half-way to my house.

"No, it was fine," I assured him. "I get it. I'll have you know I was very popular at my last couple of schools."

"I believe it. You seem like the type who can make friends with any-one."

"Because of how much I talk?" I joked.

"That helps," he said, teasing. "Or maybe it's the way your reporter brain works—seeing someone and instantly wanting their story. Asking them questions and being genuinely interested probably has a lot to do with it."

I paused, impressed he'd discerned something so intrinsic to the way

I worked. He was right, I did love to ask questions, and I was always looking for a person's story. It's how I'd felt about him when we'd first met.

"Do you think that's why I'm with you?" I asked, worried he viewed this all as a long experiment in investigative journalism.

"Nah, I know part of it is because I'm hot." He smirked. His hand found my knee and squeezed, and normally it would have sent all kinds of ideas racing through my head—climbing into his seat, or putting my own palm on his thigh, wondering what tension I could build—but instead I flinched, that feeling of safety replaced by images of claws and mud.

Jamie removed his hand. "Sorry, I...are you okay? You seem a little off tonight."

"Yeah. Like I said, just not feeling very good."

He nodded, and though I expected him to be a bit bothered by the shutdown, he simply changed the subject, asking me what my favorite song of the night was, and if I thought leather pants caused chafing. He managed to turn the ride back into something easy and light, and when I arrived home, I didn't feel as jumbled. I almost felt like myself again.

CHAPTER NINETEEN

October started and I found myself stuck in a see-saw type of routine. On Monday and Wednesday Jamie gave me a ride to school, and after rehashing any ongoing drama to Lynne in Psychology, I would sit beside him in Linguistics. Jamie and I joked together and sizzled with chemistry, but other than a forehead kiss Wednesday afternoon, we were decidedly hands-off. His hockey game against Eastborough College was on Saturday and he asked me to be there. Of course, I said yes, but then my first concern was if—like the Shady Tree Lane show—his twin would be there to support him.

On Tuesday and Thursday Brendan was the one to pick me up and drop me off, and he now sat directly behind me in Statistics. His notes were impeccable, and he let me borrow them after each class. Math was never my strong suit, but he had a way of sorting out each problem into an idea I could understand. Thursday night ran late, considering my American Media course and *Weekly Prowl* staff meeting, but he didn't complain. He just turned the music down low so I could rest my eyes, the curving road like the rocking of a gentle hammock beneath me.

I craved both of them—the brash playfulness as well as the sweet calm, the intensity and the sensitivity. My moments of panic slowly receded as

I spent more time with them, my concept of the naiad and her violent behavior becoming ever more separate from the Barreto brothers, like a widening trench. But as I grew to accept that one of them might have had a potentially supernatural heritage—even though I couldn't determine who—I still then had to face the struggle of choosing between them.

While Jamie seemed to think nothing was amiss, Brendan was observant enough to see my apprehension. He asked nothing of me, only made himself available to talk or sit quietly together. But while Brendan was easy to be with, it was Jamie who made me feel like my skin was burning to touch him. He made it clear with heavy-lidded glances and the quick stroke of his thumb over his lips that he would pull me over to the driver's side and taste me if I let him.

By Friday, the filing cabinets of my mind were wrecked, papers spilling over onto my mental floor. My lists had revealed no obvious lean for which brother might not be human, and they had both noticed that their touch—if sudden or unexpected—tended to make me flinch. I was trying to show them I was fine, but I couldn't deny that I wanted to pull them both closer, and also push them both away.

To take my mind off this bizarre struggle, I did a deep dive on Santa Elena, the shipping company Ronald had mentioned at the trash clean-up. They were expanding every year, more shipping and receiving centers opening along the coast, their plants and warehouses boasting eco-friendly machinery, fair wages, and room for growth within the company. I searched for environmental studies on the cities where they built plants, but the internet had surprisingly little information to offer. The campus repository of academic articles had a few more hits, but only mentioned Santa Elena as a footnote; an example of a corporation with a good image but bad waste practices, but there was little in the way of evidence. The only article that seemed promising was littered with black-out over the text, redacted like some government conspiracy. I noted everything down, my hunch growing into a full-fledged compulsive need to know more. There was something here.

Jamie: *What r u up to today? Wanna be study buddies?*

I re-read the text, my pulse jumping at the idea of having him come over. Neither brother had been inside my house since Brendan's interview weeks ago; I was too worried the naiad would make an appearance. If she did, I'd either have to explain, then keep him and myself safe, or worse—he'd know immediately who she was, and I'd be caught between a couple of murderous fae thirsting for my blood.

But they didn't know they were fae, I reminded myself. Or that one of them was. Nothing about my investigation indicated Jamie or Brendan thought of themselves as anything but human.

By telling some stories of my own childhood and asking some subtle questions, I'd learned both had broken bones before and ended up in the hospital—Jamie had even had his appendix out. Would a naiad even *have* an appendix? They'd both been in Spindle River their whole life, they had separate but reliable social circles, their own obvious responsibilities, and their own very human-like issues. Jamie's knee clicked from a bad fall on the ice when he was fourteen, and Brendan had once broken three fingers on his left hand in a bicycle crash as a kid which made playing his guitar for more than a few hours, even now, nearly impossible. Neither sounded like a mystical fairy who consumed power from their connection to the land or water. And there were witnesses and corroborators for every tale.

My last option was to talk to their mother, in the hopes she would have some kind of maternal instinct that could shine some light on one of her sons being a bit...different, but that would definitely be crossing a line. Still, I was running out of ideas.

Me: *I'm free*, I eventually typed out. *How about I come over there? I could use some time away from the house.*

Jamie: *If ur sure. I could always come get u tho*

Me: *I'm getting too spoiled. Gotta make sure the Buick still works after all this time rusting in the driveway, lol.*

Jamie: *Yea but I like spoiling you*

I licked my lips, knowing his voice would drop to a husky whisper if he was saying that to me in person.

Still, if I was caught talking to their mom and my investigation was exposed, or if one of them revealed a darker, naiad-type nature, I wanted an easy getaway.

Me: *Too bad. Be there in a bit! :)*

I was jittery with nerves as I pulled a pale jean jacket over the long sleeve shirt I'd been lounging in. With my boots tugged on over the cuffs of my jeans, and my pepper spray in hand, I scanned the driveway to make sure the coast was clear before dashing outside.

Panting, I locked myself in and started the car, then checked the back seat to make sure the creature hadn't somehow broken in to lie in wait. I was being paranoid. Or maybe I was being smart. Either way, I felt like an escaped convict as I backed slowly out of the driveway, my eyes darting to either side of the wooded land bracketing the property. I saw something move, a shadow maybe, or just tree branches swaying in the wind, and I slammed my brakes. Studying the tree line, I waited to see some glimpse of her. I expected her skin to be like lapis lazuli in the light, her hair like blood.

But no. Nothing. The forest only bristled in the breeze, autumn leaves tumbling to the ground.

I had only imagined it.

Once I was sufficiently far from the house, I was able to breathe deeply. And though my hands had stopped sweating, I was still nervous. Was I about to be alone with Jamie in his house, or would Brendan also be there? Would their mother? And which of those scenarios did I actually want?

I pulled into the same spot on the street as the week before, grateful it was daytime so I could see their house better. The siding was a light blue, with dark shutters bracketing the windows, and a few planter boxes below that were full of purple pansies. The Civic was gone, so either Brendan had it and was out, or their mom was at work. Maybe both.

Squaring my shoulders, I knocked on the front door, unsurprised that Jamie answered it.

"There you are," he said. He wore a T-shirt that read "Ask me about my goat," dark jeans, and a smile just for me as he shifted to the side and gestured for me to enter. The shadow of a beard on his jaw was growing darker with each passing day, and I was ashamed to admit it made him insanely attractive—manly and rugged while somehow also soft. His spiced coffee scent enveloped me, and his warm hand landed on my lower back. "I just made myself a coffee. You want one?"

Ah, so the smell wasn't just him after all.

"Nah, I'm good. Thanks, though." I watched him pour a mug from the pot on his kitchen counter, his hands dwarfing the handle. "So, uh...your goat?" I gestured to his shirt.

He looked down. "Oh, that," he said with a laugh. He then used his free hand to lift the edge of the shirt, until it was almost over his head. On the inside of the shirt, now imposed over his covered face, was an image of a screaming goat. I would have chuckled if my attention wasn't immediately captured by the bare chest and defined abdominal muscles he was flashing my way, and the trail of hair trickling down his navel into the waistband of black underwear peeking above his jeans. The way his pecs ticked, as if winking at me, had me blushing.

When he dropped the shirt, I almost reached out to stop him, but his self-satisfied grin made me pause.

Instead, I crossed my arms. "And how many times have you used that to show girls your abs?"

He tilted his head and gazed toward the ceiling, as if engrossed in some mental math. "You're only number...sixteen. You'd be surprised at how many more guys ask than girls." His smile was charming, and somehow also chagrined. "So, you ready to memorize some phonetic symbols?"

"Lead the way."

I followed him down the hallway, remembering the morning I'd bumped into him after spending the night with his brother. I looked at Brendan's door, but it was closed, and I couldn't hear beyond it as we passed. And then we were in Jamie's room.

It was more like what I'd pictured than Brendan's room had been: Prowlers pennants on the walls, and a few posters of NHL players on his closet door. There was a small desk against one window that was littered with more clothes than books, and an unmade bed pushed into the corner, the dark blue sheets rumpled and half-covered with textbooks and his scuffed-up laptop.

"Sorry about the mess," he offered, shuffling most of the books into piles on the floor so there was somewhere to sit, and then shrugged. "I'm just...messy."

I sat on the corner of the bed, and as he bent to brush away something from the sheets, the back of his hand grazed the outside of my thigh. I looked up, finding his face only inches from mine. He went still.

"Fair enough," I breathed.

His eyes met mine and I watched them drift to my lips and back. That tingling sensation started in my fingers again, only this time it traveled into my chest. My stomach. Lower.

He licked his lips. And then, backing away in one slow, smooth movement, he pulled the wooden chair from his desk to sit facing the bed and started thumbing through our Linguistics book.

"Should we start with pulmonic consonants?"

I blinked. "Oh. You were serious." And then I blushed. I had basically just admitted I'd expected this study session to be an excuse to get me alone. And that I'd gone along with it.

Jamie looked up from the book, his eyes glittering.

"Well...I was."

The book fell onto his wooden floor with a smack. He put one knee on the bed, kneeling over me and crowding me backward onto the bed in a slow, languorous move, with the grace of a predator. If it had been quick, like the strike of a snake, it might have frightened me. Might have put me back in that reflexive place where the fear of claws and teeth locked me up tight. But he was slow—intent. He put one large, rough hand on my jaw, pulling my mouth to his inch by inch. I gasped against his lips.

My mind went blissfully quiet as I focused on the way he hovered above me, the way his thigh slotted between my own. Kissing him became a sport, a game we might win if we could only taste the other more thoroughly. His tongue brushed and grazed against my own, the heat of it coursing through me until I was moaning beneath him, our movements becoming erratic.

"God, Sadie," he muttered, breaking away to press a kiss to my chin, my neck, my collar bones. One of his hands dragged up my shirt as he kissed the skin above my bra. Looking up to match my gaze, his hazel eyes were heavy with a question. I nodded, my breathing heavy. He pulled down the cup of my bra and licked my nipple once, twice, and then engulfed it. The hot, wet pleasure of his attention had my back arching off the bed just enough that he could use his other arm to wrap around my waist and tug me further up the bed.

With greedy hands I pulled him back up so I could taste his mouth again. The shift in his weight had his jean-clad leg rubbing against my center and I hissed, moving against him for more friction, wishing there were fewer layers between us.

It was like he read my mind, because with one swift yank, he pulled his shirt off sideways, the cotton ruffling his hair, and continued kissing me senseless.

My hands finally got their fill of his smooth, warm skin. The wide expanse of his shoulders shifting against my fingertips made me want to dig my nails into his flesh and pull him ever closer. I was being driven crazy by desire.

He palmed my sides, angling his hips so that if we were naked, he would have been inside me, and I groaned his name.

Dragging my fingers through his hair, I tugged at the strands. His hips jerked in response, pressing into me just right.

"Don't stop doing that," I whispered against his lips.

He grinned, then licked once more into my mouth. "Then keep pulling my hair."

I fisted the strands in my hand as he dragged himself against me. He was hard and hot, the length of him impressive, and I used my free hand to rub him through his jeans.

He rewarded me by yanking down my bra once more and suckling me deep into his mouth. His fingers found my other breast, plucking at my nipple through the fabric.

"Let's get this off you," he grumbled, and I let him peel my shirt off, watching as he flung it across the room.

He looked down at me, my pale bra slightly crooked, the waistband of my jeans rucked higher from our grinding. There was hunger in his expression. Wild, untethered want. And I wanted him back.

Was I really about to give my body to him? This guy who could potentially...not be human?

If he kept looking at me like that, maybe.

His eyes caught on the birthmark I had over my left hip bone, a wonky circle the size of a quarter, the color a few shades darker than my skin. He brushed a thumb over it, slowly, and a shiver worked its way up my arms.

"I have one of those too, you know," he murmured. "A birthmark."

"Do you have to take off your pants to show me?" I asked. I sounded breathy and desperate, even to my own ears, but the responding smile he gave me was worth the admission.

"Wouldn't you like to know?"

I pouted and he let out a low laugh, his hands now skating up and down my thighs as he kneeled between my legs.

"Can I?"

I nodded.

He unbuttoned my jeans and started gently tugging them down each leg, the anticipation of what would come next causing my heart to race against my ribs.

"It's actually on my back," he said, just as my feet kicked free from my pants. He threw them on the floor beside my shirt. I was glad I'd actually worn a nice pair of red, lace-edged panties today instead of something comfier and plain.

"Can I see?" I asked, breathless.

He twisted and showed me his back, his olive-toned skin perfect beyond a couple moles near the top of his shoulders, and the birthmark in question. It was a dark splotch, low and to the left of his spine. The shape was something like a narrow and crooked "C," the color a red-brown that stood out in sharp relief.

I reached out to touch it, knowing all his teammates and probably every teenager in Spindle River had seen this mark at least once—in the summer when he went swimming, or in the locker room—but I still felt special for seeing it now.

"Too bad your name doesn't start with C," I said as he twisted back around.

"My middle name does. Give you three guesses what it is."

"What do I win if I get it right?" I asked, all sultry as I shifted my bare legs against each other. I watched his eyes follow the motion, then drift and linger on the red underwear.

"Whatever you want," he said, voice gravelly.

He climbed back over me, and though I wanted him to take off his own pants, I couldn't muster up the determination to stop him. I loved the feel of his hot skin against my own, his hard muscles keeping him hovering just far enough to tease me. He was kissing me, but I wanted more. I wanted all of him.

And then a thought froze me in place.

"Does...does Brendan have the same birthmark?"

I tried to ask it casually, like this wouldn't possibly be the biggest break in the case. If Brendan didn't have it, then maybe as an infant he hadn't had the sight or the power to copy it. I wasn't sure if it made sense, but my gut said the one with the mark was the human.

"Yeah, he does," Jamie said, between kisses along the underside of my chin. "Why?" He didn't seem concerned about me bringing up his brother, even as he sucked at my neck once more.

Damn, so much for that theory.

"No reason," I replied.

"It's on the same side and everything," he added, as casual as reporting the weather, even as he bit the cord at my neck, startling a gasp from me. "Mom was mad it wouldn't help her tell us apart." He soothed the bite with a lick that had heat pouring through my veins.

"You mean your mirror side, right?" I asked, somewhat distracted. "You're mirror twins?" They were rare, but according to my research some twins had identical moles or birthmarks, just on opposite sides of each other, so if they faced each other it would seem like they were looking into a mirror.

He shook his head "no" against my neck, his breath tickling the skin there, so I squirmed. I wanted to ask more questions, wanted to confirm, but I also wanted him to keep moving. Keep kissing me. Keep driving my body higher and higher with sensation until we both crashed.

But my mind was stuck now. And I needed to know.

"Okay," I breathed, trying to ignore the climbing heat between us. His knee pushed up higher against me and I fought back a moan. "So, you both have the exact same mark, both on the same side?"

He must have finally noticed the tone of my voice was more than easygoing, because his lips stopped grazing over my pulse and his eyes met mine.

"Yes?"

"That's not..." I licked my lips, trying to find the words to describe how that was impossible without essentially mansplaining twindom to an actual twin. "I thought that wasn't possible."

He shrugged, then used one hand to tuck a few errant strands of my hair behind my ear. The touch was tender and affectionate and all together much more than I deserved. Because now there was no way my reporter brain was going to let this go.

"Do you remember when you noticed the marks? Did you two always have them?" I pressed.

There was a pause, and I watched the desire in his expression fade into something wary.

"What's this all about?" He pulled away and my body instantly missed his warmth. A chill raced over my bare arms.

"Sorry, I—" I sat up, feeling suddenly vulnerable, and like I'd somehow become a villain in this story. I couldn't keep investigating them like this; it wasn't getting me anywhere. I needed to do more than ask vague questions and read Wikipedia pages about changelings and naiads. I had to get this out in the open.

I'd been impulsive before, and persistent to a fault, but this was going to take the cake.

"Is Brendan here?"

Jamie cocked his head. "If I answer that, are you going to tell me what's going on with you?" He didn't sound upset, which I would have understood. Instead, he sounded disappointed. Hurt, even.

I nodded.

"Yeah. He's here," he said. "And look, I know I made it seem cool if you wanted to take a ride on the B-train, but I didn't mean the two of us—"

I waved him off. "What? No!" My laugh was awkward as I remembered Brendan's show—the fact I *had* kissed him—but if anything, this was the opposite of a ménage à trois; I was probably about to ruin my relationship with both of them. Wriggling out from under Jamie, I slipped off of the bed and started tugging my jeans back on, all while Jamie watched.

"Come on," I said, as I pulled my shirt back over my still-crooked bra.

I grabbed his hand and, though he easily could have resisted, he chose to be pulled along as I went into the hallway, knocked on Brendan's door, and then barged in.

He was sitting at his desk wearing his oversized headphones. A laptop was open under his hands, but he looked up as I walked in.

"Uh, hi," said Brendan, pulling his headphones down to rest around his neck. His clean-shaven face stood in sharp relief from his desk lamp, all angles and dark lines, like a tortured artist in a painting. God, it was unfair how gorgeous they both were. "What's up?

I looked around his room, wondering if I should sit on his bed, but it felt inappropriate after just being scantily clad with his brother in the next room, so I huffed a breath and abruptly sat cross-legged on the floor. Jamie stood by the door, his confused expression a mirror of Brendan's. And that was just the problem.

"So...this is going to sound insane," I started. "And obviously I try not to jump to conclusions without getting all the necessary background. I do my research, I follow-up, I ask question after question until I've covered all the angles, but this? This is something else. And I just don't know what to do anymore. Maybe I misread the situation, and I don't want this to be like what happened at my last school, where I open my mouth on a hunch and then everything goes sideways—" I was rambling, my mind getting away from me, until Brendan held up one hand, his eyebrows low and scrunched together in an adorable, puppy-like confusion.

"Is this about...choosing one of us?" He asked. He looked at Jamie behind me. "Is that why she's been weird?"

"No!" I offered, frustrated with myself. "I mean, well, it *was*. You essentially told me I needed to pick, though not in those exact words, but no. I've been weird because...what this is about is..." I took a deep breath. "Have you ever heard of changelings?"

Brendan turned his desk chair more toward me, like I now had his full attention. I turned to see Jamie with a blank look on his face. He was still shirtless, but he walked forward to stand by his brother, leaning against the desk and crossing his arms over his naked chest. At least now I could see both of their reactions at once.

"The woman who attacked me outside my house wasn't actually a woman," I explained. "And last week, when she came after me a second time, she was...successful. She kidnapped me—knocked me against a wall and suddenly I was being dragged into the woods..."

I told them everything, from start to finish—the haunting way her black eyes bore into mine, her webbed hands and blue skin and wet, straggly hair, and the story she'd told me about her child—her son that she left next to an infant to copy its face and join its family. I explained that there were myths of creatures like her, and I'd done the investigation to prove it. To prove one of them might not be human. I glazed over the position we'd been in when Jamie had told me about his birthmark, but pulled up a website on my phone to explain how matching marks were unnatural if they weren't mirror images or slightly different. If the moles on Jamie's shoulders were identical to Brendan's, that was a natural impossibility. Those kinds of marks were based on exposure to sunlight, dietary and hormone factors, and a whole other bunch of influences that could never be exactly replicated—not unless some other force was at work.

I showed them the webpage, but other than a precursory glance, both seemed uninterested.

Brendan listened to the entire story with a stoic expression, and I wondered if he'd had inklings of something like this before, or if maybe his artist's mind was more inclined to believe something supernatural was at work. Because in comparison, Jamie looked downright flabbergasted.

"This woman was obviously *crazy*, Sadie," he said, with something that could have passed for a laugh. He raised an eyebrow, shaking his head. "She's been drinking lake water or huffing bog fumes—maybe she was wearing gloves that just made her hands *look* webbed. People file their teeth just like they get piercings, and she could have been covered in paint. It was dark, right? I get that she freaked you out, but that just...that can't be real." He seemed to run out of steam by the end, as if by refuting each point he could hear the weakness in his own argument. It would have been an immensely organized and purposeful costume for such an ill-seeming woman to pull off. But I didn't say so.

Instead, I looked at Brendan. "What do you think?"

He scratched at his neck. "I, uh...I remember looking some of this stuff up when we were younger," he said.

"You what?" Jamie twisted to peer down at him and I watched them exchange some look heavy with meaning that I couldn't quite discern.

"It was some folktale I read, and it made me curious. But it didn't make sense," he added. "And I didn't believe it. Still don't. Mom's story about the hospital just always bothered me, about her not knowing I was hers, but it—"

"We don't know it was you that she didn't recognize," Jamie interrupted.

"Yeah, but you always got what you wanted when we were kids," Brendan argued. "She put you first over and over again. I think we all know who she thought was her real son."

"She's *ill*, B. And you know that's not true." Jamie dropped his arms. "She had to take me to practice and buy me gear, but it's not like she didn't drop everything when you got sick or broke your fingers." Jamie rubbed a hand over his hair, ruffling what was already a messy pile of curls, and it was hard to believe that only minutes ago I'd been dragging my own hands through those curls. Writhing underneath him.

"Look," I said, interrupting them as well as my own unruly thoughts, "I've been trying to figure out if one of you is...is fae. I'm sorry for how that sounds, and I know it still seems insane, but I have. If it was true I had to know. But...I haven't had much luck. Then when I saw Jamie's birthmark and he told me you had the same one—"

"Speaking of," interrupted Brendan, sounding annoyed, "could you put an actual shirt on?"

Jamie ticked his pecs in response, and I saw the glimmer of a familiar tease in his expression. Finally, at least one sense of normalcy in this otherwise ludicrous encounter.

"*In conclusion*," I said, raising my voice. "I actually need both of you shirtless."

"What about pants?" asked Jamie, a full-blown smirk now hooking his mouth to the left.

"Do you have any pertinent birthmarks or distinguishing freckles on your legs?"

"No."

I shook my head. "Then no."

Brendan stood up from his desk and sighed. "Okay. Let's do this then."

CHAPTER TWENTY

When Brendan took off his shirt, I'm not sure what I expected—a paler, slightly leaner version of his brother, maybe, or that secret tattoo he may or may not have—but it must have been the looser clothing he wore that made me think he would be thinner than Jamie.

He was identical. I know, a shocker.

Given Jamie's hockey workouts, I wondered how Brendan managed to develop and maintain the same muscles. Maybe he did push-ups in his room, or there was a more physical aspect to his job at Daphne's—lifting and carrying pallets of goods or something. There was a thin trail of dark hair down his stomach, the same as Jamie, and though he wasn't the type to tick his pectoral muscles for fun I had the feeling he could do so without much effort. Their darker skin tone, which I originally thought was from summers in the sun, had no hint of a tan line, and must have been from their Portuguese heritage—I'd also googled their last name and its origins.

"Having a good time there, Sadie?" Jamie asked.

I realized I was staring and tore my gaze away from their chests.

"Just, you know...studying the similarities."

"Uh huh."

I cleared my throat. "Turn around?"

The boys did so, and the power of telling them to do something and watching both comply without complaint gave me a bit of a thrill. I flushed with heat.

I took a step closer, so I could touch my fingers to their skin if I wanted, and my blood ran cold. It was all identical. And I mean, *identical*.

Both had the C-shaped birthmark, in the same place low on their back, and both had two dark moles on their shoulders. Even their freckles were the same. There was a smattering of six dots on the right, and a paler bunch on the left. A darker one close to the spine. Using my hands, I measured out the distance between each mark and, while Brendan twitched a bit under the touch, there wasn't a singular difference I could see.

"It's...unreal," I whispered.

"Unreal how attractive you find us?" Jamie teased, but I could hear the strain in his voice, the unease.

He turned when I didn't respond, and Brendan followed.

I blinked. "It really is true."

They looked at each other, and then Brendan bent to put his shirt back on.

"So...what does that mean?" Jamie asked. "That the woman you saw was a mythical creature? That one of us—" he pointed between himself and his brother, "is an evil fairy kid?"

I shook my head. "I don't think there's anything inherently evil about it, but...yes?"

There was a pause, and I watched them both absorb the information in different ways. Brendan sat on his bed, arms folded across his chest as he stared at some spot off to the side, lost in thought. Jamie looked angry, hands twitching at his side and his body swaying slightly, as if he wanted to flee from the room. I couldn't blame him.

"This is a lot to take in," I said, my eyes going from Jamie to Brendan and back again. "I know I'm kind of springing this on you, but if this is true, then the woman I met really is a naiad, and she might be dying from some mystical disease. One she thinks my blood will cure."

Brendan shivered a bit at that, clearly more freaked out than he was letting on. "And she wanted to drink your blood and also give some to…"

"Her son." I nodded. "I assume that's one of you, so yeah."

"There has to be another explanation," said Jamie. "A prank or just some mentally deranged woman who *thinks* she's—"

Brendan scoffed. "Who went through all the trouble of transforming herself physically into a monster?"

"So, you buy this then?" Jamie asked, incredulous. "You really need to believe that you're some special creature. That you're different from me."

"This isn't about being different from you. This is about what Sadie saw, and—"

"This is *always* about being different from me! How you hate being compared to me and my 'idiot jock routine,' right? You'd rather be a goddamn fairytale creature than my brother."

Brendan shook his head, half sympathetic, half aggravated. "That's not true."

I took a step forward, hoping I could stop this argument from escalating. "She was real, Jamie. I swear it. The way she moved…the way she spoke and acted—I truly believe it wasn't an act. And I've never believed in the supernatural. I've never seen a ghost or even been superstitious."

Please, believe me, I wanted to add. *Believe me like Brendan is trying to believe me.* But I knew how much that would hurt him.

Jamie took a deep breath, his fingers shaking as he ran them through his hair. "I know that you saw something that you can't explain. And maybe she really was this...*thing*, a naiad or whatever, but the idea that one of us is involved is too much. Brendan just wants to be his own person." His jaw clenched. "He would believe anything you told him if it meant he could step out of my shadow."

"This isn't about Brendan." I was pleading now, but I didn't care. "I'm sorry, I know this is insane, and you're both freaked but—"

At this, Brendan stood up. "Sadie, I think Jamie and I need to talk about this...alone. You shouldn't have to listen to this."

"What?" I blinked, feeling like cold water had splashed across my face. "Are you sure?"

He nodded, turning his back on his brother. "You drove here, right? Just...be safe. We have some things to hash out, but I'll call you, ok?" He paused. "One of us will call you."

I waited for Jamie to argue against it and ask me to stay, counting the heartbeats, but he was silent. That was answer enough.

The betrayal stung as I left Brendan's room. How could Jamie be so adamant that I was wrong? How could Brendan ask me to leave? I could see that Jamie was more conflicted than he seemed, and Brendan was more distraught, but that was only because I had spent so much time studying their faces. Not because they trusted me enough to clue me in.

Logically, I understood that I had just upended their lives, and that they needed to fight this out in private—finding out you might be a mythological creature who could apparently grow webbed appendages and potentially breathe underwater had to be a shock—but I still wanted to be a part of the discussion. And besides, did they miss the part where

I'd been attacked—*twice*—by the woman who might be their mother? She'd tried to bite me with her pointed teeth and drink my blood! I could go home but…did I want to? I would be safe locked inside but just the idea of walking down my driveway alone had my pulse racing.

Their house was eerily quiet as I made my way down the hall and out the front door. It was as if they were waiting to make sure I was gone before things got nasty.

I pulled out my phone and texted Lynne.

Me: *Any chance I could bunk with you tonight on campus?*

She responded immediately.

Lynne: *Only if you promise to try out my game! <3*

Me: *Done.*

Thankfully, Lynne didn't ask any questions about why I wanted to spend the night in her dorm. She shared a suite with five other girls, but her snoring roommate was gone for the weekend, so her bed was available.

We ordered pizza from a nearby shop, and she walked me through her fantasy-adventure video game where you played as a cat lost in a magical wood, defeating wizard dogs, sampling bowls of cream, and collecting bird parts littered on the ground to complete puzzles. It was a little graphic for my tastes, but the cat character was trying to find its missing child, and the idea of a kitten lost somewhere in the dark forest was enough to keep me playing. The sound of a tiny meow would period-ically make its way through the rustling and hooting sounds Lynne had built into the background, and each time it made me smile. It was an impressive game. I asked her if I could do an article on her for the *Weekly Prowl* about hidden student talents, and she agreed. I just hoped I could get Kim and Professor Lewis to sign off.

The distraction was refreshing; it took my mind off the potentially inhuman Barreto twins and the odd pang of hurt that echoed in my sternum when I remembered how we'd left things.

As I lay in Lynne's roommate's bed, I wondered what my time at Spindle River would look like if they both cut me out of their lives. If I'd pushed too hard and ruined this thing for good. Suddenly Linguistics wouldn't be my favorite class, and I'd have no one to complain to about Statistics. I'd drive myself to and from my creepy little house with its creepy little pond and diseased naiad infestation and hope the creature didn't find a way to break in and suck me dry.

I shivered, pulling my borrowed blanket more securely around my chin.

"Hey, Lynne?" I asked into the dark.

She hummed, the sound close to a groan, and I could tell she was much closer to sleep than I was.

"Do you know anything about the river here?"

"Not really," she mumbled. "Just that we shouldn't swim in it. Tour guide mentioned it during freshman orientation." She yawned, and I heard her rustling deeper into her bed. "That we shouldn't go near any of the water sources, 'cause the ground is all...boggy now."

"It wasn't always like that?" I thought about the wetlands in the woods by my house, how the dry, leafy forest had gotten muddy and damp, my feet sticking in the mire.

Lynne didn't answer, except for the sound of a soft snore.

I sighed. It was going to be a long night.

***

The next morning, I had breakfast with Lynne and her suitemates in the cafeteria. They were a boisterous group of girls, adding vodka to their orange juice and spilling secrets about who had hooked up with who at various parties, and whether or not they'd overlapped in their conquests. I envied them their college experience, wishing I'd been with them to pick strangers out of a crowd like selecting fruit at a grocery store, drinking Fireball shots and dancing to club music someone was blasting out of a portable speaker. Instead, I was worried about this town I lived in, and the two boys whose lives I'd crashed through. How desperately I'd miss them both if this was the end of our relationship. *Relationships*, I corrected. It wasn't the longest romantic entanglement I'd been a part of—even adding them together—but I was still heartbroken at the prospect. Despite how odd the situation was, what I shared with Jamie and Brendan felt more...real than other bonds I'd made. They had both brought out and helped me explore the various sides of myself—by giving me the choice, they had made me pay closer attention to what I wanted. They were both wonderful. Determined, caring, passionate, and beautiful. I didn't want to lose either of them.

"So," said Lynne, taking a piece of bacon off my plate and interrupting my glum reverie, "I take it our impromptu girls' night had something to do with your twin debacle?" She spoke low enough so the rest of her suitemates continued their own conversations unaware, which I appreciated.

I nodded. "Something like that."

"Didn't try my nudity plan?" she asked, and I laughed, nearly choking on my sugary coffee. Believe it or not, I sort of *had* tried her nudity plan. It just hadn't gone well. I shook my head.

"Well," she continued, "we're all going to be at the game later. You still gonna show?"

Shit. Jamie's hockey game. I had forgotten it was today.

"Um, I think so?" I focused on my food, pushing around my slowly deteriorating cereal in its bowl. I didn't know if Jamie would still want me there; he'd been so shut down as I'd left their house yesterday. But it was just due to shock, wasn't it? I hoped.

"Great, you'll be the perfect addition to our cheering section," Lynne said with a smile. She seemed to read the tension on my face, because she put a warm hand on my back and rubbed an absentminded circle there, as if I was suffering from a hangover or a headache. "Don't worry. The hockey games here have a habit of bringing out the wild side of people." She gestured to one of the girls on the opposite side of our table—a redhead with a septum piercing and a plastic choker around her neck. "Last home game, Casey broke up with her boyfriend, Matt, during the first intermission and was dating this girl Evelyn from her speech writing class by the second. They started making out in front of a concession stand and would *not* get out of the way."

The girls all laughed.

"Such a good night," Casey said with a contemplative sigh.

"Wild, huh?" I mused. I wasn't sure that was what I needed, but it looked like I wouldn't have much of a choice.

I drove home after breakfast so I could shower and change, feeling slightly braver in the daylight. Keeping an eye out for the naiad was easy, I just opened the blinds on the patio doors every hour or so, checking the pond for movement and scanning the woods for shadows that seemed out of place. No sign of her.

I couldn't stop turning over what she'd said about my blood—that it was special. She'd said I was part naiad, or something like it. My hands were pale and human as I looked down at them, and the more I tried to imagine webbing between my fingers, or my nails curving into claws, the more uneasy I felt about that part of the story. The boys hadn't focused much on how this was all tied to me and my blood, and while I understood their attention had been on themselves and each other, it irked me that they hadn't considered much of my experience with this woman and what it meant for me. How it felt being *hunted*.

I thought about texting Jamie to let him know I'd be at the game, but worried he'd tell me not to. That kind of rejection was the last thing I needed on top of everything else. Besides, I was meeting Lynne and her suitemates there. I had friends who had nothing to do with mythical creatures or sexual tension. I was going.

Pulling on my cute leather jacket and changing out my glasses for rarely-worn contacts, I spent extra time on my make-up, even putting on some blue eyeshadow to show school spirit. Thankfully, Spindle River U's colors were black and royal blue, so with jeans and my jacket it was easy—and fashionable—to be supportive.

Before it could get dark, I rushed out to my Buick, pepper spray in hand, and drove to the school. Neither Brendan nor Jamie had texted me all day, and I tried not to feel bothered by that as I pulled into the multi-level parking garage near the entrance to the arena.

I was early, but the merchandise stalls and concession stands were already open. I paid for my cheap, student-priced ticket to the game and made my way around the arena. The air was crisp and cold, the smell of salty popcorn tickling my nose, covering up the scent of fresh ice. A few students meandered around, covered from head to toe in royal blue. Some had black foam-hands that ended in curved claws, the Prowler emblem diagonal across their palms. If it didn't remind me so much of the murderous creature living in my backyard, I would have bought one. Instead, I just took my time walking the lanes, buying a root beer to sip while I browsed the various merchandise, finally landing on a black-and-blue-striped scarf stamped with "SRU" at the ends. The tassels were soft under my cold fingers and gave me something to nervously fidget with while I looked for Lynne.

But who I found instead was Brendan.

He was standing up ahead, leaning on a stone wall by one of the open doors to the arena seating, arms crossed and eyes unfocused ahead of him, like he was deep in thought. Loud music blared from inside, echoing off the near-empty stadium. I debated turning around and walking the other way, but before I could make a firm decision, he saw me and raised a hand.

Everything about his ensemble screamed "rock star," from his black T-shirt with a hole at the hem to his dark gray jeans. His headphones were sitting around his neck and his tall, lean body was tense as I approached. Those hazel eyes, which were always gentle, seemed cautious.

"I'm...happy you came," he said, pulling away from the wall. "Jamie will appreciate it."

"Will he?" I asked. "Because I haven't heard from him at all."

"We had a pretty rough night, and well...he's pretty freaked out," said Brendan, as if that was enough.

"And I'm not?" I replied. "You're not?"

He sighed and I could see from the slump of his shoulders and the tightness around his mouth that he hadn't slept much. Looking to either side, as if to make sure we weren't being overheard, he gestured for me to walk with him around the promenade.

"I'm not saying this is *easy* for me," he started, voice low, "but it's something that I had already thought about, and…it didn't really bother me."

I looked up to him in shock and he just shrugged one shoulder, looking so much like his brother in profile as he walked beside me that I almost reached for his hand. Almost double checked to make sure this wasn't some prank Jamie was playing on me, masquerading as Brendan.

"When I was a kid and I read that folktale, I thought…well, that would explain it—my mom, I mean," he said. "And it would be cool, wouldn't it? If one of us was secretly magical? Like getting a letter from Hogwarts, or finding out you're a demigod. I liked to imagine it was me who wasn't human and one day I'd start to fly or control plants or something. It wasn't scary, even though now, yeah, I'm a *bit* freaked out." His chuckle was stilted, and I had the feeling he understood exactly how bizarre this conversation was. "Jamie was right in that I…I liked the idea of being special."

"Doesn't being a twin already make you feel special?" I asked, genuinely interested.

"Not really. It just makes it easier for people to compare you and confuse one for the other. If anything, it makes you feel less special, because there's another version of you. And this other version just happens to be popular and good at sports."

So, Jamie *had* hit on something true last night, I realized. I could see the pain in Brendan's expression for admitting it. It took a certain amount of strength to be this vulnerable, and again that desire to hold his hand nearly overwhelmed me. I let it, taking his hand loosely in mine. Maybe I shouldn't have, but it felt right, and I wasn't going to limit myself to what was…proper, in this moment. Nothing currently happening between the three of us was normal, so normal rules didn't seem to apply.

"Still," I said after a pause, "being jealous of Jamie while you were growing up, is that really a reason to hope you're a changeling?" My voice rose at the end, and I watched a couple of students turn their heads our way.

"No, I don't hope that—I never did," he hissed, and then he used our linked hands to pull me toward an arena entrance where the loud music was just fading to announce the warm-up skate. "I'm just saying it had crossed my mind and when I was a *kid* it wasn't a terrifying possibility. But to Jamie...this is all nuts."

We started down the arena steps and I spotted Jamie on the ice with ease. I'd grown familiar with the shape of his torso under those hockey pads, the length of his legs with the added skates. His helmet was on, but I could make out the grim line of his mouth as he raced by, pumping his arms as his strides ate up the ice. The number 26 blazed in bright blue below his name.

Brendan and I found a mostly empty section of seats and sat while I sipped my root beer, watching Jamie go through his pre-game routine, which apparently involved short sprints, then a stretch low on the ground, some puck handling, then back to sprints.

"He looks okay to me," I muttered.

"He's not," said Brendan. "He's been off since last night." His tone had me worried and I turned to see him watching his brother with even more focus than I was. "We fought...and it wasn't like any other fight we've had." He turned his gaze to me, his eyebrows scrunched with unease. "When I told Jamie how I felt about you, he accepted it right away. We'd made this deal as kids not to let a girl come between us—"

"Yeah, he told me about that," I said, nodding. "Impressive decision for two teenage boys to make."

"Thanks. But when it came to how we should handle this monster business, we couldn't agree. There's no way for us to tell which son might be hers, and so we can't worry about that part, but about how to address her as a—well, not a *person*, but you know what I mean—he started shouting, then I started shouting. I said some things I'm not proud of."

"Jamie said some cruel things, too," I added. "Even before I left."

Leaning his elbows on his knees, Brendan bent down, his voice aimed at the ice as if Jamie might then be able to hear him. "I'm sorry you had to see any of that. And I hate that we're fighting, but I'm not sorry for the stance I took."

I paused, biting at my lip. "And which stance was that?"

"I think we should help her. Try to heal her."

My mouth dropped open.

A buzzer sounded, and the skaters retreated off the ice so the Zamboni could smooth over any skate marks on the surface.

Placing my paper cup of root beer on the floor by my feet and folding my hands together, I took in a long, uneven breath. "You think that we should give the woman who attacked and kidnapped me some mystical first aid? You realize that means...my blood?"

Brendan rubbed a hand over his face. "I know. I realize it sounds insane. But if Jamie and I were with you, we could protect you. We wouldn't let you be in any danger. The other option besides helping her is, what? Kill her? Trap her in a giant net and drop her in the ocean?" His voice was brittle.

"Is that what Jamie suggested?"

He shrugged, refusing to look at me now, even though the only thing to watch on the ice was the old man driving the Zamboni. "The killing her part, anyway. He was torn, but the more we talked about it, the more that's what he thought was right. It's just, we should at least meet with her and hear her out, don't you think? Talk with her. Maybe there's something we can do. Maybe we can learn something from her. Figure out another way."

I shook my head. "She wasn't exactly a good conversationalist," I argued. "Not to mention...violent. I may have hidden some of my bruises and scratches from you both. She was about to *kill me*, Brendan."

His face paled a bit, but that gleam of determination was still reflected in those hazel eyes. "That's awful. And I'm so sorry you went through that. I wouldn't forgive it. I won't. But you said that she's desperate, right? That she's dying. She might be our—" he paused, and I know he'd been about to say *mother*. "I just think, if you were on the brink of death and knew there was a cure in someone's blood...wouldn't you do whatever you could to get it?"

I huffed a sharp laugh, lacking in any humor. "I wouldn't kidnap them and try to hurt them."

"So, you're on his side," Brendan murmured, sounding disappointed.

"No." I put a hand on his knee, forcing him to look at me. "I don't want to kill anyone, or anything. And I don't think we're going to find a whale-grade net anywhere in Spindle River, so capturing her might be out of the question. But I also don't want to be her lunch. It's the right thing, to help someone if you can, but..."

"Sadie!" A voice called, and I looked up to see Lynne, Casey, and her other suitemates in a collage of black and blue gear, waving me over to a seat two sections away, closer to center ice.

Brendan leaned his head close to mine, his voice a near whisper. "Just think about it, okay? What we should do. Obviously, I don't want you to get hurt, and I would *never* let you be anyone's...lunch. There just has to be a middle ground here. Another option." He paused, and those dark circles under his eyes suddenly seemed more pronounced. "And maybe you can get through to Jamie. He might listen to you, but he sure isn't listening to me right now. I'm worried about him." *About what he might do*, was what he seemed to mean.

"Okay," I told him. "I'll think about it."

I grabbed my cup and left Brendan to his contemplative brooding, my mind churning over the argument the Barreto brothers were apparently in the middle of. I'd been so focused on figuring out who was the human, I'd neglected to think too much about what should be done with the dying naiad in my pond. Really, I'd just imagined going about my life the way I was now—avoiding her—but that wouldn't last. Even if we knew who her son was, that wouldn't change her mission, or the strange illness that seemed to have befallen her—one that could potentially befall her child. One of these boys might soon want my blood as much as she did.

I thought about the spark I'd felt for each of them, and wondered if that was my own fae heritage at work. Was that moment of connection I'd always relied on some inhuman design settled into my genes? The thought had me shivering as the cold air of the arena brushed over my face.

Lynne and her group welcomed me with open arms, and as we waited for the game to start, I glanced back to where Brendan had been sitting.

He was gone.

CHAPTER TWENTY-ONE

The plastic seat was cold under my thighs as the noise of the crowded arena grew louder, the students roaring as the mascot—Spindle River's own feline Prowler—skated onto the ice and raised its arms. I joined Lynne and the others in chanting "Let's go Prowlers, let's go!" while pumping our fists in the air.

Lynne pulled a tiny bottle of vodka out of her purse and gestured towards my open root beer. I nodded. Why not? We were here to have fun. I wanted to spend the next few hours thoroughly forgetting any weird supernatural or romantic problems I had and enjoying a brutal, entertaining game of hockey. Plus, now that I'd spent time with Jamie at practice and researched the rules, I'd know what was going on.

I took a sip of my drink, the alcohol burning on the way down, and popped my lips. "Let's go Prowlers, let's go!"

The game started, a hush falling over the stands as the puck was dropped at the face-off. And then I understood what Brendan meant when he said that Jamie was off.

His skates cut up the ice in vicious slashes, and he attacked with a speed and ferocity that was almost illegal. With a brutal shove, he cross-checked the skater on his right, nailing him into the boards. The wobbly, plastic wall on that side of the arena shook hard, and the reverberations carried all the way to our end of the stands. The stadium screamed, cheering him on, but my heart thundered in my chest. That should have been a penalty, but the ref had apparently missed Jamie using his stick to push the player.

There was a desperation in Jamie's actions that was hard to describe, but it was visible in the tense line of his arms, and the quick jerks of his stick as he batted away at the puck. Smacking the rubber disk from between his opponent's legs, he gave one final shove and backed away, returning to the fray. It was a great break-out play as he and his teammates went on the attack, entering the Eastborough zone, but my mouth was dry with nerves.

"Damn," said Lynne, "your boy is a beast!"

"Yeah," I replied, feeling uneasy. Tonight, he sure was. He moved the puck to the weak side of the ice, creating an odd man rush despite his defensive position, setting up three Prowlers to their two Falcons.

When the Prowlers scored their first goal at the top shelf of the net, halfway through the period, Jamie got an assist credit for it. He celebrated by briefly lowering to one knee, sliding along on his pad and yelling to his teammates as, one by one, they clapped him on the shoulder. Anything he shouted was swallowed by the cheers of the students around me, but one of the opponents must have chirped something unsavory in response to the goal, because I watched Jamie's helmet whip to the side, his chin notching higher.

His sights were trained on the offensive player in Eastborough red, like a bull aiming for a matador's cape.

When the whistle blew and play started once more, Jamie wasted no time sprinting after that player, waiting until he had his stick on the puck before turning to bodycheck him. He slammed them both into the boards at an angle that had me gasping. I watched the number "26" on his back twist as he jammed his shoulder into the guy, pinning him.

The whistle blew again, and Jamie's teammates rushed over in case the scuffle dissolved into a fight, just as the referee started pulling the two apart. Jamie used his elbow once more to shove at the guy's back. A warning of more aggression to come.

The Eastborough player dropped to his knees, obviously dazed, and his red-clad teammates converged, shouting and demanding a penalty. Noise erupted into a riot around me as the Prowler fans stood and screamed over the ice and the referees debated the call.

I couldn't help but feel weirdly responsible for the violence happening in front of me. Jamie was clearly trying to work through some frustration and internal dilemmas, but he was going too far. He was an enforcer, sure, but this kind of rough conduct was definitely not allowed on school ice. It made me think about the naiad, and her impressive strength. If Jamie was the changeling, was this fury and power only the tip of the proverbial iceberg? Or were these nature-dwelling fae as peaceful and serene as the stories made them out to be, only turning vicious when threatened? More like who Brendan seemed to be.

I groaned, forcing those thoughts away with another sip of my alcoholic root beer. Debating the possibilities in circles like this would only drive me crazy. I couldn't be paranoid about every little thing they did.

Jamie got two minutes for boarding, and I watched him roll a shoulder as he drifted down the rink toward the penalty box. The Eastborough player shook off the hit and rejoined his team on the ice, which was the only reason his penalty wasn't more severe. Still, I could see the mustached coach scowling at Jamie with disappointment.

I released a breath I hadn't realized I'd been holding, and chugged my remaining drink, really hoping for some semblance of calm as I watched Jamie take a seat. He stretched his left arm backwards and forwards like he'd hurt himself on that last check.

Jamie didn't get back into the game for the rest of the first period, and I could tell he was irked by his time on the bench. His line had switched him out for a different defenseman, and there was no telling if it was due to his potential injury, or as a punishment. I couldn't make out his expression from this far away as the Prowlers meandered down the hall back into the locker room for their first intermission. Either way, I knew those mirthful, mischievous eyes would be flat with anger—anger he wasn't dealing with well, even though hockey was usually his outlet.

From the way an assistant coach—or maybe that was a medic—crowded him as they strode away, I had a feeling he'd be lucky to be back out on the ice at all tonight.

Lynne and I took the break in play to go back to one of the concessions stands. We got a bucket of habanero pretzel bites and some more soda, into which she immediately poured another tiny bottle of vodka.

"Where are you keeping these things?" I asked. I hadn't even seen her pull the bottle from her clutch-sized purse.

She gestured to her boots, which ended at mid-calf and had a wide brim. I leaned over to look inside. There were two more bottles resting there against her striped socks.

Laughing, I put my arm around her shoulder, letting her pick at my pretzel bites. "You're a genius, you know that?"

"I know," she said with a smirk, popping another pretzel into her mouth. I gulped down some more of our makeshift cocktail and this time I was able to do so without making a face. My stomach felt warm, and my chest felt a bit lighter as we made our way around the outside of the arena. There was no sign of Brendan, and though I had to admit I was looking for him, I was also grateful he couldn't be found.

The second period of the game was much tamer than the first, mainly because Jamie was as absent as his brother. He wasn't on the bench, and I didn't see him in the hallway to the locker rooms. I had no idea if he'd been pulled from the game for his attitude or was indeed injured. I hoped it was the former.

With him gone I thought I'd be able to focus more on the game, but if anything, my mind started to wander worse than before. If he was hurt, would they take him to the hospital? Would they call his mother? Or Brendan? Was there a way for me to go check on him?

The Eastborough Falcons scored, then the Prowlers; it was a tight game offensively, but it became clear that without Jameson "Jamie" Barreto the Prowler's defense wasn't nearly as cohesive. Eastborough scored a second time. Then a third.

I tried my best to enjoy myself, giving Lynne a play-by-play of what was happening in my best sports-announcer voice, explaining what "icing" was and why it kept being called, and drinking my fair share of alcoholic root beer. It felt like I was playing a part, making up the lines as I went. And then I remembered Jamie saying this was how he felt sometimes—like a pretender.

My head was floaty as the game ended, my vision swaying a bit, but after hours of trying to forget Jamie, or at least not think of him for two consecutive minutes, I'd given up on doing anything except finding him.

"I'll text you later," I told Lynne, and she gave me a tipsy salute as we headed our separate ways. The arena was quieter now, the crowd much less raucous; we had lost by two goals.

It was easier than I thought to make my way through the lobby and down the hall toward the storage closet where Jamie and I had been trapped together. I remembered that room almost fondly, and as I passed it, I brushed my fingers over the door. Maybe all Jamie needed was a night locked in a room with me, I thought wickedly. But I shook my head. No, that was tipsy Sadie talking.

There was a man standing at the end of the hall, his arms crossed against his bulky chest, and I thought maybe he was security, except he was wearing the royal blue polo all the assistant coaches had been sporting.

"Hi," I said, offering him my most charming smile, "I'm here to see Jamie. Is he still getting changed?"

The man looked me up and down, the sensation immediately making the hairs on my arms stand on edge. His chest puffed higher as if to show off his muscles, and his eyes landed somewhere below my neck. I stopped myself from rolling my eyes in disgust. Did he think I was some groupie who'd flash him to get inside or something? The man was at least as old as my father—something like bile crawled up my throat.

"Fans stay outside," he said eventually, in a low, guttural voice.

"Oh, I'm not a fan. Well, I mean I am, but...I'm his girlfriend." I tried to imbue my voice with a sense of entitlement and boredom, like this was a casual, everyday occurrence for me and he should know better. "Can you just tell him I'm here?"

The man paused, then looked away as he darted a tongue over his lips. Gross.

"One sec." He turned and opened the door, saying something in a quiet tone to another man in a blue polo. I blinked, the booze in my system making the exchange feel inexorably slow, but then the door was closed again, and the coach-slash-bodyguard shrugged. "He'll be out in a minute."

"Great, thanks. I'll just…wait back there." No way was I going to stand next to this guy any longer than I had to.

I backed up to stand near the storage closet door, wondering if I'd hear the sounds of a couple inside, maybe making out against a metal rack, or being pushed up against the wall. I shook my head again, pulling out my phone to distract myself while I waited.

I typed "common hockey injuries" into a search engine and started reading about concussions and broken collar bones, wondering if Jamie's shoulder had ever been injured on the ice before and if that's why he was taking so long.

"Hey." I looked up to find Jamie hovering over me and I was so startled I almost dropped my phone.

His hair was wet from a shower, and he wore a T-shirt that said, "Shut your five hole," which made absolutely no sense to me, tipsy Sadie or not, and over that was…a sling. His right arm was supported by a black drape of nylon fabric, and he looked extremely annoyed as he adjusted it.

"Oh, God," I muttered. "You did get hurt."

"Just a minor shoulder separation," he said. "Should be good to go by next game. I could have played afterward but the coach was being an ass. Says I'm on the bench next practice, too." His voice was strange, a combination of dull and edgy. It reminded me I should be angry with him—he'd given me the silent treatment as I left his house last night, and then he hadn't messaged me at all today—but as he glanced anxiously from one end of the hall to the other, I realized there was enough going on with him without my issues piled on top of it.

"Yeah, you, uh...hit that guy pretty hard, huh?"

"He was running his mouth," Jamie bit out from clenched teeth.

An awkward moment of silence stretched between us, and my face started to heat. Suddenly checking on him felt like such a stupid move. He obviously didn't want to talk to me; he was still dealing with the fight he'd had with Brendan, the debate over how to handle the naiad, and now this injury and reprimand.

"Well, I'm glad it's not more serious," I mumbled. "I'll, uh, see you later?"

I turned, ready to flee down the hall, but his hand reached out to stop me, his fingers gentle on my forearm. "Wait. I'm sorry," he said.

Looking over my shoulder, I could see the lines of tension around his mouth, the crease of those unruly eyebrows as he gazed down at me.

"I'm still trying to absorb all this mystic junk, but I shouldn't have let you leave last night like I did."

I let him pull me closer, and I could smell that coffee scent drifting off his skin, under the powdery smell of soap.

"I wanted to call you all day, I just...I didn't know what I should say. I was worried it would turn into a fight."

"You mean, like the one you're having with Brendan?"

"So, he already talked to you." He nodded, as if his fears were confirmed, and released my arm, moving to take a step back. I grabbed his hand.

"Yes, he talked to me," I said. "But it wasn't to gang up on you or make any kind of decision about all this. It's something we can all discuss together...once you've both cooled down a bit."

At that, he released a quick laugh. "As if Brendan was anything but *cool* when he told you."

"I mean, he didn't body slam some hockey player into a wall, but he was still obviously upset." I grinned without meaning to.

That cocky glint appeared in Jamie's eye. "It was a pretty impressive hit though, wasn't it?"

Playfully shoving him backward, I was about to scold him when I caught that creepy coach-bodyguard at the end of the hall watching us.

"Do you need a ride home?" I asked. "I'd like to get out of here."

He nodded. "Yeah, let me grab my bag."

The walk to the parking garage was sobering. Somehow it was colder outside than in the arena and I shivered in my sweater, the odd silence on this level making each step echo against the concrete pillars. Jamie walked at my side, his good arm holding a duffel bag full of gear. His pace was slow and measured, like he was tired. He didn't have dark circles under his eyes, but I had to imagine he'd been up most of the night like Brendan, debating what to do next, thinking in circles until he was dizzy.

As I climbed into the Buick and Jamie's frame piled in beside me, I realized I'd never had him in my car before. He seemed to take up more space than made sense, or maybe that was just the warmth pouring off him. I couldn't believe he was only wearing a T-shirt.

"So..." I started as I pulled out of the garage, turning my heat up as high as it would go, "want to tell me your side of the story? About last night?"

He looked over to me and ran his left hand through his hair.

"Why? It's pretty easy to tell what my stance is. That thing tried to hurt you. We should keep away from it. Stop it for good, if we need to."

"Simple as that?" I asked. "You're not worried that thing might...be your mother? Or Brendan's? That she's just trying to survive?"

"Are you going to write an article about this?" he quipped back.

"Strictly off the record."

He paused, and I got the sense he was genuinely trying to sort out his complicated feelings on the matter.

"Brendan doesn't want anything bad to happen to anyone," he said, taking a turn I hadn't expected. "He's protective of you, but also of this creature you talked about. He sees the...*innocence* in people. He sees her as a dying woman, sure, but to me she's a dying woman who kidnapped you and would have hurt you. Water spirit or mythical thing, whatever she is, she's dangerous. And when you do bad things, you lose the right to be protected like that. Brendan disagrees."

"He thinks she made a mistake," I presumed.

Jamie nodded, and suddenly the air in the car was so warm it was stifling. I turned off the heat and cracked a window, the refreshing stream of cool autumn air brushing over my face.

"Debating life and death like this..." I said into the quiet that clouded the air between us, "it's good that we can at least talk about it."

"Brendan and I aren't talking about it. Not anymore."

I turned my head to see his jaw clenched tight, a muscle ticking there. His left hand was a fist on his thigh, and I reached over, placing my palm over it, trying to imbue him with some semblance of serenity.

"He probably just needs a breather. Just like you did. Brothers fight, don't they?"

"Not like this," he muttered. "B and I hardly ever fought growing up. We may be different from each other, but it's always been us against the world. Now...now it feels like it's me against him."

"Wow. That must have been some argument."

He pulled his fist out from under my hand and my stomach dropped in disappointment before he turned my palm over, lacing his fingers with mine.

"It was. But you coming to my game, that helped."

My smile was sweet, and I may have blushed a bit as I tried to focus on the road. "Glad I could be of service."

"And...you look really beautiful tonight," he said.

"Is it the contacts?"

"No, you look beautiful with glasses too. Maybe it's the leather jacket, or how mad you were earlier. You look extra...fiery tonight."

I squeezed his hand in thanks before releasing him to navigate the turn onto his street. No need to tell him that fieriness had been the result of annoyance mixed with alcohol.

There were lights on in his house, but no car in the driveway as I pulled over and turned off the engine.

"You need a place to stay tonight?" Jamie asked. "I feel bad that you spent last night alone." I could see the tinge of pink at the tips of his ears, and it brought to mind the flush over his skin as he'd pulled off his shirt just the day before. The heat that had streaked through me as his knee pressed between my legs, rubbing me through my jeans.

I cleared my throat, which suddenly felt tight. "No, I'm okay. I actually stayed at Lynne's yesterday, but it's like...now that I know what I'm up against and I have my pepper spray, I feel a bit better about being home, you know? Plus, the place is apparently built like a fortress. I should be good. I don't want to run away from it anymore."

"You sure? You could come inside."

It was tempting, but I was pretty sure spending the night would be like adding a spark to the Barreto household powder keg. Things were bound to explode.

"I'm okay," I said again. "I'll be careful."

He nodded. "Alright, then text me when you're inside. Actually, text both of us. Brendan will want to know you're safe too."

That was oddly...considerate of him. It was so strange that they could handle this odd three-sided relationship, or at least the potential of one, when they couldn't stand each other's position on how to deal with a bloodthirsty naiad. But what did I know about siblings? Being an only child, and one who never had friends close enough to feel like family, I had no reference.

"Will do," I said with a small salute.

Jamie paused before leaving the car, and I saw him glance from my hands back at the wheel to my lips. There was something like restlessness in his posture, and then he leaned forward. Slowly. Giving me a chance to stop him.

But I didn't.

His mouth met mine, his lips warm and firm, and somehow so incredibly soft. It was chaste and sweet, but I pulled in a sharp breath anyway, my heart racing in my chest. The scruff along his jaw scraped at my chin, making my skin sensitive.

I leaned into the kiss, hating that he was pulling away, but I knew I couldn't keep him. Couldn't push this forward. I needed to sort through my own emotional mess before I took this any further. Still, that energy between us was invigorating. I craved more.

"Goodnight, Sadie," he whispered, his breath brushing my cheek.

"Goodnight, Jamie."

I sent them both a message in the group chat when I got home, having successfully dashed into the house, keys and Mace clutched in my fingers, and locked the door behind me.

Me: *Home safe.*

Brendan: *Good, text if you need anything.*

Jamie: *If you change your mind, u kno there's a bed for you here*

I wasn't sure how to answer either of those, so I just replied with a thumbs-up emoji and went about my night, drinking tea and researching more information on Santa Elena waste practices. It was late—past midnight—when I got ready for bed. I peeked outside my windows once I'd turned the lights off to make sure there was no creepy fae creature lingering in the shadows. I heard an owl hoot as I double-checked the front door, and though it was dark outside, with clouds blocking any moonlight that might have trickled down, I could see the outline of something on the street that made me pause.

A car that wasn't my own, its lights off.

At first, I thought maybe the police were still keeping their end of the bargain, checking in on me to make sure the "homeless woman" who'd accosted me weeks ago didn't return, but I could tell from the outline that it wasn't a police cruiser. It was too low to the ground—too rounded. Too similar to the gray Civic that typically drove me to and from campus.

I wanted to send another group message, asking who it could be, but I worried about starting another fight between Jamie and Brendan if one of the brothers was here without telling the other. Maybe they were protecting me, but maybe they were looking for the naiad to talk to her. Or potentially kill her.

Pulling on my slippers and a heavy coat, I grabbed my pepper spray and the largest kitchen knife I had and went outside.

The same owl hooted, and I heard the responding clicks of bats overhead as the night wind tugged at my hair. It was like the surrounding wilderness watched me walk down the driveway. The car didn't move, and I couldn't see the driver, so I crept further, surreptitiously scanning the area around me. A truck drove by, the sound of tires on wet asphalt comforting. Its lights briefly illuminated the man in the driver's seat.

A dark sweatshirt and closed eyes, a silver chain resting at his neck. Clean shaven.

Brendan.

He was sleeping, head tilted toward the driver's side window. I leaned forward, debating whether or not to wake him. Was it safe for him to be out here if the naiad came this way? She couldn't break into my house, but smashing a car window would be a much easier feat.

I tapped on the window with my fist, watching Brendan startle awake.

"Fuck," I heard him mutter as he rubbed a hand over his eyes. He rolled down his window.

"What are you doing here?" I asked.

"Just...checking in on you," he said. He looked behind me, as if suddenly worried there'd be someone else with me. "I didn't mean to fall asleep."

"Yeah, it would suck if *you* got kidnapped this time." My tone was wry, but I was serious. "Look, I'm okay in the house, really. You don't need to protect me."

"Somebody does."

"Well, not tonight. I was safely inside, and I've got my weapons," I said, brandishing the knife and Mace like an air traffic controller. "I don't want to feel responsible for something happening to you."

His gaze dropped and I could tell from the tenseness in his shoulders that he felt guilty. He nodded. "Okay, well...I guess I'll go. I was just worried."

"I get that," I said on a sigh, "and I appreciate it. You're thoughtful, and sweet. But I'm more worried about you and Jamie right now."

Brendan shrugged. "We'll be okay. We always are." He didn't sound very sure, but at that he started up the car and gestured toward the house. "Go back inside. Once you're in, I'll leave."

"You promise?" I asked.

"I promise."

I did as he asked, and watched his car leave from the safety of the window, but all the while I had a feeling he wasn't being entirely honest. The Brendan I knew was a good listener, and respectful, so he'd left, but he was so protective I worried he'd be back before the night was over. Whether it truly was just to protect *me*, or to also protect the naiad, I wasn't sure.

CHAPTER TWENTY-TWO

On Sunday I did my best to stay out of the boys' hair. I had this feeling like I'd somehow crashed into their lives, an investigative wrecking ball, and broken something between them. I mean, it wasn't my *fault* that supernatural creatures like the naiad existed and thirsted for my blood, but still…I hoped that if I stayed away and gave them some space, their fight would fizzle out into something manageable.

I ended up at the SRU library that afternoon, looking for any print articles that may have been left out of the electronic archives that mentioned water levels, Santa Elena, or Spindle River ecosystems. And while the chairs and old-fashioned writing desks were comfortable, and the fractal patterns on the windows were making the dark floors glow, the magic of this research haven still couldn't keep my concentration.

I kept imagining Jamie visiting me between the stacks of books, crowding me into the shelves with his imposing body and that damn smirk of his. And then I'd picture Brendan leaning over me as I sat at the computer, the silver chain at his neck dangling at my shoulder, his smooth jaw brushing along my cheek.

The old Sadie whirled into a town like a gust of wind, staying as long as fate allowed before her father got some new job and picked her up to flit away once more. That Sadie didn't worry too much about the mess she left behind; that girl saw broken hearts and half-formed friendships as a way of life. Not that I was careless or cruel—after all, I still kept in touch with most of the people I'd left behind—but nothing was serious. This...*thing* happening between Jamie, Brendan, and I was the definition of serious—life or death, love and lust and hate. I couldn't let them go.

The idea that I was here for good scared me. It still felt impossible, and yet, more than anything, I wanted to clean up this mess I'd somehow contributed to. I wanted to keep this thing between us alive, and figure out what it meant. That longing rode me hard while I scanned over newspapers and town notices.

I didn't find much.

On Monday I wasn't sure if Jamie would come pick me up, so I was almost at the front door, ready to drive myself to campus, when the Civic pulled into my driveway.

The shadow of beard on his face was fuller now, rough and dark along his jaw, and as I climbed into the car, I gave in to my desire to scratch at the hair with my fingernails.

"It looks good on you," I told him, my hand retreating.

His expression was torn, those hazel eyes warm and wanting, while the rest of him was tense, as if unsure what to do. I noticed shadowed circles beneath his eyes and a wan pallor to his cheeks.

"At least something good has come out of this, huh?" The false cheer in his voice tugged at my heart.

"Are things that bad?" I asked.

He took the car onto the main road and started toward school. I recognized the hoodie he wore as the one I'd seen him in that first day of classes. I remembered the soft feel of it under my hands, the firm chest muscles beneath. The way he'd winked. What a carefree, jovial guy he had seemed then. Not this edgy version whose muscles ticked as he drove. His whole body was wound tight as a guitar string.

"Brendan spent the night with the band to get away from me," he said, sounding unhappy. "Not that I blame him. Every time we talk there's all this..." he struggled to find the word, his hand lifting from the steering wheel so he could flip it through the air, "this strain. I talk about hockey, and he brings it to how violent I am. He mentions class, and it becomes about learning from mistakes, being on the right side, peace versus war, all this stuff. And then when I try to actually talk to him about mom's episodes or one of us being connected to that...*thing* it gets even worse." He shrugged and I noticed his arm was out of the sling. I felt like a jerk for not realizing earlier.

"Your arm is better already?"

He turned to look at me, a bit confused. "Yeah, it was just a minor separation, I told you. As long as I don't use it to shove somebody I'm fine." But the tight clench of his jaw and his paler-than-usual face made me think he was lying.

"I'm sorry you're still fighting," I said, after a long pause. "I feel like this is all my fault, and if you want me to—"

"This is *not* your fault," he bit out. "This is about Brendan and me and how he wants to be this good-guy hero and make me out to be some brainless brute. It's always been there, under the surface. This whole thing just...brought it out."

I didn't think Brendan was arguing for some perceived image, but I understood what he meant. Their differences made them beautiful and interesting and unique, but they could also make them clash like lightning on water.

"Still. If there's anything I can do…" I offered.

"I'll let you know," he said with a nod.

I hoped he meant it.

The next couple of days felt like an awkward game of keep-away, or maybe hot potato. I was handed off between Jamie and Brendan for rides to and from school. They had both suddenly decided it was imperative I was watched over, and the tension was palpable. Jamie didn't make his typical jokes or innuendos, and he didn't try to kiss me. Brendan was quieter than usual, answering questions with simple, one-word responses until I dragged full sentences from him. Conversations stayed bland, avoiding the topic of the naiad and my blood and their potential inhuman genes, and instead focused on things like Linguistics papers about speech disorders and Statistics projects on conditional probability.

The project topic Brendan and I had chosen was about the likelihood of a rainstorm on any given day—which involved lots of research on my part, and formula creation on Brendan's—and while I should have found the whole thing both relevant and engrossing, instead I was burnt out. The unease between us all was draining.

Come Thursday I was fed up with the lack of progress and began debating the merits of an intervention. Though, if I put both of them in the same room, I had a feeling the conversation would devolve into some kind of intense confrontation.

Brendan was taking me home after my staff meeting for the *Weekly Prowl,* and the long day plus the strained quiet in the car had me biting my cheek so hard I tasted blood.

Clenching my hands together in my lap I looked over to him in the driver's seat, his clean-shaven face a constant reminder of my indecision between him and Jamie.

"Have you had sex?" I asked.

Brendan jerked, the wheel going a bit to the left before he corrected course. He turned to look at me, one eyebrow raised. "Where did that come from?"

"It's a simple question," I said with a shrug.

He took a deep breath. "Yes, I've had sex."

"And did you sprout claws or grow webs between your fingers? Did your eyes go black?"

"Obviously not."

"So, would you say that potentially being a fae has impacted your relationships thus far?"

Brendan stretched his neck, as if hoping to pop the joints there. "Are you going somewhere with this?"

"I'm trying to point out the obvious." I kept my eyes trained on the road, the trees sweeping past us like dark hands, blocking out the moon. "This connection you or Jamie have to that naiad—and that's also not one-hundred percent certain—is something neither of you have noticed before. And if someone just comes up to you and tells you who you are without any evidence, you wouldn't believe them, right? You'd be curious, maybe look into it, but it wouldn't immediately reform your image of yourself."

"That's not the issue here," he replied.

"No. The issue is that it's changed the image you have of your brother."

He had no response to that.

"You're both looking for some clue that the other isn't human. And I admit, I'm guilty of that too." There was warmth pooling in my cheeks, and not from the Civic's heat blasting from the vents. "I spent those first days studying you both like insects, getting paranoid that the way you moved or spoke meant one of you was dangerous, and I feel like an ass for it. It was foolish, and it was based on fear. Besides, if we believe what that naiad has to say, I have some distant fae relative in my lopsided family tree too."

I watched him from my seat and clocked his hands loosening on the steering wheel.

"But don't pretend this never-ending fight between you two is anything other than that," I continued. "Fear. You're both suspicious and on edge, and this one disagreement has gotten completely out of control. No decision needs to be made right away about how we handle—"

"That's where you're wrong."

We turned into my driveway, the wind roaring over the hood of the car. It was a damp night, heavy with the promise of rain, and while I'd enjoyed a few days of pleasant weather, it was only a matter of time before the New England climate reared her ugly head. I was in for a night of thunder and lightning and the wail of wind over the windows. The idea made me shiver.

"What do you mean?" I asked.

His voice was low; I could barely make it out above the idling engine. "The way I feel protective over you...I just want to make sure you're safe. But Jamie is protective of you too. And his version of keeping you safe may involve killing someone—or *something*—if the chance comes along."

I tried to picture it in my head—Jamie hunting through the woods at the edge of my foggy pond, a bat in one hand, his face stiff with determination, eyes steely. But I couldn't compute the image with the laughing jokester I'd kissed in the storage closet—the one who hated small spaces and wore silly T-shirts.

"I think you're wrong," I murmured.

"You hope I'm wrong," he replied, equally as quiet.

Holding in something that might have been tears, I said goodnight and rushed toward the house. The smell of atmosphere was thick in the humid air, and I could hear a psithurism of wind above me, at turns soft then deafeningly loud. My heart pounded, but I made it inside and locked the door, watching Brendan leave before drawing the blinds closed. Defeat lay heavy on my shoulders, almost overwhelming me. There seemed to be little I could do to get them to see reason.

After a lazy dinner of ramen and some peanut butter cookies, I cuddled into my warmest blanket on the couch and watched mindless television on my laptop, trying to ignore the storm outside as it began in earnest. Every crack of thunder made me jump and every scrape of branches along the house's siding made my skin crawl. The naiad was probably out there right now, in the cold, wet reeds, cattails moving around her clawed hands. Her rasping, growling breaths probably panted out of her as she watched the house. Maybe she was even now crawling forward through the muck.

The power went out around me, the lamp in the corner of the living room dying with an audible *click*, and I flinched, looking around to see my entire apartment had gone dark.

I paused the show playing on my laptop, and the sudden silence was so intense I could hear my own pulse. It thrummed a beat like a warning drum. It had to be the storm—that was the logical explanation. It wasn't her. She couldn't get me when I was safely locked inside. She might even be dead already, caving to whatever illness she suffered from.

My cell phone chimed at my knee, the unexpected sound causing my entire body to seize with fright, but I looked down to see a text message, and then another.

Jamie: *I know its late but u awake?*

Jamie: *I need to get out of here*

Jamie: *please tell me I can come over*

I paused, taking in my dark living room. The glow of my computer cast an eerie blue glare over my furniture, and the storm was still raging outside. Having Jamie here would at least make the space less terrifying.

Me: *So long as you don't mind me not having any power. Everything ok?*

Jamie: *tell you when I get there*

I got up and went to the kitchen, using my cell phone's flashlight to rummage through the cabinets. There were a couple of tea lights and a box of matches that must have been left by the previous tenant—Mr. General himself—since I hadn't really made the apartment homey yet. I had no decorative candles or throw blankets or framed art. Scowling to myself, I realized that even though I'd now been here for almost two months, I still hadn't really settled in. The place didn't seem like it was *mine* yet.

Still, I lit the tea lights and placed them at either end of the kitchen. At least that way I wouldn't need my cell phone to avoid bumping into things.

My gaze drifted to the blinds across the patio doors. It was dark in here, so if I peeked through and looked outside, the naiad wouldn't be able to tell, would she? Through the rain and the wind, she wouldn't be able to see me. Unless she had some special night vision—which, I guess, she might.

"It's fine," I muttered to myself. "Just sit. Don't scare yourself more."

I made my way back to the couch and cozied myself into a corner, keeping my phone close. The Mace was on the table, and I left the show on my laptop on pause; without Wi-Fi, the episode was doomed to start an inevitable, unending buffering cycle if I dared to press play.

The sounds of the house pressed in on my ears, at first a heavy silence and then something like breathing. There was a slow, cumbersome creak and groan as the wind battered the roof and the wooden floors adjusted to the saturated air, the moisture causing the boards to swell and shift. More than once a scraping noise had me tightening into a ball, though I knew it must only be the trees outside. I eventually played saved music on my phone to drown out the storm, knowing I was draining my battery, but too keyed up to sit in this unquiet.

When Jamie knocked on the door, I practically flew off the couch, checking the peephole to make sure it was him before I opened the door and yanked him inside.

"Wow, Sadie, happy to see me?" he said with a weak laugh. And then he presented me with a bulging plastic bag. "Need some candles?"

"Oh my god, yes." I took the bag from him, letting him follow me into the kitchen where the remaining matches sat in their open box. The bag was full of a random assortment of candles —some obviously meant for Christmas, with holly berries strung around them and pine scents strong enough to make my eyes water—and some were in jars with labels like "Eucalyptus Spa" and "Lavender Dreams."

"I take it these are your mom's?" I asked, lighting one after another.

"She won't miss them," he replied, and I looked up to see him scanning the room, as if cataloging my meager possessions. It hit me then that Jamie had never been inside my place before, and I viewed it with new eyes: the sparse living room with its single loveseat and table, the desk in the kitchen and the built-in display that held my collection of rocks.

"Besides," he said, clearing his throat, "we still have power, and Brendan is there if we lose it. I figured you needed me more."

"I seem to remember a desperate text from *you* needing to come over, not the other way around," I teased.

He strode to the patio doors, and I wondered if his mind went to the naiad like mine did every time I thought of opening the blinds. Or maybe he was just avoiding the question in my tone. I wanted to know if there had been another fight between him and his brother, but I could tell he didn't want to talk about it.

"I just—I can't be in the same house with him right now," he said eventually. "I needed a break. So, can we...I don't know, just forget everything for a night?" He turned and I could see something bleak in his usually mischievous expression. The tiny glowing flames from a dozen candles made his features appear warm and smooth, the shadow of his beard stark. He looked like a lumberjack, or some other rustic log-cabin advertisement. The long-sleeve shirt he wore didn't have a funny saying on it—just an emblem for some hockey team I didn't recognize. It stretched lovingly over his shoulders and was darkened with speckles of rain.

"Sure," I said, when I found my voice. I held out a couple candles. "Help me spread these around?"

We arranged the lights so I could shut my laptop and still see all the corners of the living room and kitchen, then put another couple in the bathroom. It was oddly domestic, the two of us adjusting the little flames and moving them around the counters. And then we were sitting on the couch together, my mind full of questions I wasn't allowed to ask.

I watched Jamie lean back into the cushions and release a breath, forcing himself into a picture of ease before he looked over to me with one eyebrow raised.

"So, you finally have me all to yourself," he said. "What do you plan on doing about that?"

I smirked. "I plan on beating you at a game of UNO. Or maybe playing another, more *dangerous* game." I paused for dramatic effect. "My favorite game."

"Oh yeah, what's that?" His gaze went to my mouth.

"You sure you want to know?"

His eyes went hungry. "Yes."

I licked my lips, then curved them into a grin. "Twenty questions."

He barked a laugh, his head thrown back. "Of course that's your favorite game."

His whole face transformed when he laughed like that. It was lit from within, the dimples on either side of his mouth making me want to dig my fingers in. I wanted to kiss that laughing mouth. Damn him for being so attractive—I was trying to keep things platonic here. Not that I had many reasons to. I mean, I wanted him. He wanted me. But I had a feeling if anything happened it would be so he could forget his problems with Brendan, or avoid his confusion over the naiad and what that meant for him. It wouldn't be all about me.

And I wanted it to be.

"Maybe we *should* stick to UNO," I offered, sitting on my hands so I wouldn't reach out to touch him.

"Why? You afraid?" His taunt was a front, but it did manage to hit that spot in my brain labelled "challenge accepted."

"Fine," I said with a shrug. "I'll even let you go first."

He looked around the room, as if searching for inspiration for his first question, but I had the feeling it was all a ruse. He had something up his sleeve already.

"What's your favorite thing about me?" he asked.

What about me does Brendan not have? That's the question I read between his words. I could have been annoyed at having to compare them, but Jamie always came off as so confident, so himself. It was no surprise that underneath he would be insecure, especially if Brendan had told him about the...*encounter* we'd shared at his show. They were so open with each other, at least about their feelings for me, so it wouldn't surprise me if he had.

I took the question seriously and took a beat to deliberate.

"I love that you put people at ease," I told him. "You're good-natured, always joking and staying playful, even when I know it's sometimes an act. I think you'd like to be more serious and introverted, but it's in your nature to charm people. Keep them happy. It's your way of caring. I think that's my favorite thing about you."

I watched him bite his bottom lip and then look away, as if he needed a minute to absorb that.

Giving him an out, I pretended to flip my hair, adjusting my position on the couch to wiggle my shoulders and blink over at him, fluttering my eyelashes. "What's your favorite thing about *me*?"

His eyes were intense as he looked at me. "Besides the obvious?" He took a deep breath. "How stubborn you are."

That took me by surprise. "What do you mean? I'm not stubborn."

"Sadie, you're practically a bull mastiff with how doggedly determined you are."

"I'm sorry, did you just compare me to a dog?"

"A gorgeous, iron-willed, *stubborn* dog, yes," he said, nodding.

I huffed. "And how do you know so much about this particular breed?"

"My mom likes watching the dog show every Thanksgiving, and I usually sit there with her, but let's get back to you." He shifted closer, lowering his voice so it was a dark, rough whisper between us. "You are the definition of persistent. It's in the way you treat class, and the way you do research for articles, and probably the way you were looking into which one of us might not be human. You're always curious, and you've never let a single subject drop, at least not for good. Plus, you haven't given up on me. Or Brendan. Even with all this weird stuff it's thrown you into, and all the danger that comes with it. Bravery is a kind of stubbornness, I think. And...that's what I love about you." Somehow, he was inching closer to me, the heat and coffee scent drifting off his skin like a potion. It caused my heart to race while also lulling me into the comforting embrace of just being close to him. He'd said *love*, my dazed mind realized.

"Well, it's one of the things," he added, now so quiet I almost didn't hear him.

I breathed, overly aware of how my chest rose, almost brushing his. When had he moved to be right in front of me? Our knees were touching, his torso crowding me with the delicious strength of his arms, one of which was thrown onto the cushion behind me. I was being enveloped by him, and I didn't want him to stop. Places inside me clenched and heated.

"What's one of the other thi—" but I was cut off when his mouth captured mine.

His lips dragged and caressed my own, drawing the breath out of me so my body reached for his, trying not to drown. But it was too late. I grabbed onto his face with both hands, pulling him closer, sighing into him. My body moved without my control. I needed him closer. With what he'd just said about me...this wasn't just to forget. This wasn't about Brendan. It was about us.

This was a culmination of every look and touch we'd denied ourselves, bursting in one moment.

When his hands grabbed onto my waist I didn't resist him. He pulled me onto his lap, and I straddled his hips, feeling the hard press of him along the seam of my thin, cotton pajamas. It was so much better than the stiff fabric of jeans. I could feel every inch of him as he ground up into me, his firm length like heated steel.

I whimpered into his mouth, helpless to do anything but twitch against him, searching for more friction as I licked past his lips, tasting him.

"God, Sadie," he groaned, gasping for breath as his fingers pressed into the skin at my hipbones, pulling and pushing me so I was riding him through our clothes. His teeth found the skin beneath my jaw, and then he was leaving wet, hot kisses in a trail down my neck and to the collar of my shirt.

"Move it," he growled, and I complied, pulling the loose shirt down so he could access more of me.

He licked a stripe along the top of my bra before finally using one of his hands to tug the cup out of his way. When his mouth found my breast I gasped, liquid heat rushing through me in a line directly from my nipple to where he still pushed into me below. I groaned, head thrown back, while he kissed and sucked, his teeth tugging just enough to have my hips spasming against his own.

"Jamie," I said on my next inhale. Whether it was to ask for more, or for him never to stop, I wasn't sure.

He decided the meaning on his own, releasing my breast with a wet *pop* and then twisting us both. My back was on the loveseat, my head bent a bit unnaturally against the arm, but I didn't care. His torso blocked my vision as he settled between my thighs and took possession of my mouth once more.

Our tongues stroked and teased each other, delving into a type of exploration while we determined what the other person wanted—a language, a request, a demand. Jamie wanted long, forceful strokes. I wanted frantic passion.

And I think we could have both.

"Bedroom's upstairs," I huffed, panting between kisses.

"We'll get there," he said. His smile was wry against my lips. One of his large, capable hands swept up from my hip and along the side of my half-displaced bra, then back down again to grip at my ass. He pulled back a bit to watch my face as he thrust against me. I struggled not to let my eyes roll back in my head as Jamie pushed in one long, slow, grind. My body was already throbbing. Already wet. I wanted him *now*.

Instead, he hovered above me, moving in those agonizing thrusts, driving me crazy while he watched. With the candlelight off to the side, bathing half his face in an orange glow and throwing the rest into shadows, he looked like a figure torn out of an erotic dream, half-concocted by my own dark desires.

"Sadie," he whispered, and then pulled back to replace the hard length of him with his hand. His fingers dipped into the band of my pants and underwear, going straight for the slick center of me. I gripped onto his forearms while he tortured me with teasing pressure and gentle glides.

Opening my legs wide, I practically begged him to go further, to push into me and let me ride his hand like I wanted to ride *him*. But with a dark chuckle he only pressed one finger in an inch or so, then retreated.

I groaned with frustration.

His smile was wicked as he dipped his finger in again. "I want you so crazy that you let go of every inhibition when I'm inside of you."

"Getting there," I breathed, still annoyed as he toyed with me.

"Nah," he shook his head, confident and dreadfully sexy. "I'll know when you are." Pushing his finger deep inside of me, I clenched my inner muscles, trying to pull him in, trying to feel full. It wasn't enough.

"You're such a tease," I whined, panting.

"The idea of such a stubborn, studious reporter letting loose, being wild beneath me...it's worth a little teasing, don't you think?" He sounded a bit breathless as he curled his finger inside of me, pressing closer so the heel of his hand met the bundle of nerves beneath it.

I cried out.

"Yeah," he said above me. "Getting there."

"Worth a little teasing?" My voice was almost a whimper, but I let go of his arms, where I had been holding on for dear life while riding through the way he keyed up my body, and stroked him through his jeans.

He was so hard under my palm, and I fumbled at the button and zipper, trying to get to him the way he was getting to me. I'd have my revenge.

Sure enough, as soon as my hand reached inside his pants, gripping him through the boxers he wore, he hissed, hips twitching. There was already a damp spot at the tip, and I rubbed my thumb there, feeling the moan he released travel through his body. His finger pumped harder inside of me, then he added a second.

There wasn't enough room on this couch for me to spread my legs wider for him. I already had one foot on the floor.

"Now," I pleaded, and he understood. Nodding, he withdrew his fingers and helped pull me up. Almost dizzy with want, and my hair and body in complete disarray, I followed him up the stairs and into my bedroom.

In pitch blackness he pulled me against his chest, and I realized we'd put no candles in here. The power was still out. I didn't care, except that I wanted to look at him.

"One sec." I danced out of his hold and rushed down to the kitchen, grabbing two of the jar candles he'd brought. I carried them to the bedroom, placing one on my bureau and one on my nightstand. When I turned back to him, he was standing still, arms at his sides, breathing in steady counts but looking every inch like some animal ready to pounce, ready for me to wave the flag and release him. His jeans were still open and slightly low, his shirt wrinkled and begging to be removed.

"Take off your shirt," I said, feeling bold.

He did as I said, yanking it off with one hand. It mussed his already-wild hair, the waves falling briefly in front of his forehead before he pushed them back. The sight of his bare, muscled arm caught and held my sight as he dropped his shirt on the floor.

"Now the shoes. And pants."

"You want the socks to stay on? Dirty."

I laughed. "Those too."

He toed off his shoes, tugged off the socks, and then pushed down the jeans, stepping out of them so he stood in just his boxers.

"Now what?" he asked, taking a step forward. "Are we done teasing?" His tone was gritty and deep. It caused chills to pepper my arms.

I debated dictating to him every single thing I wanted—where he could put his fingers, where he could put his mouth, how deep I wanted him inside me—but instead, I nodded, giving him back the reins.

Jamie closed the space between us, and then he was kissing me with a ferocity that matched his energy on the ice. Just when I thought I'd recovered from the hand he stroked up my bra, plucking my nipple through the fabric, suddenly his other palm was on my ass, kneading there while he edged me backward onto the bed, laying me down. I couldn't catch my breath. My body was being played like a sport, and he was winning.

He bit at my bottom lip, and I groaned beneath him. Suddenly, I was right back to the edge I'd been riding on that couch. The way he kissed me, like a give and take of control, full of yearning and rolling pleasure, had me nearly senseless with the need for more.

With a gentle push I got him to lift his head.

"Do you have..." I started.

"Yeah." He rushed back to his jeans, pulling a foil packet from somewhere inside. I took the opportunity to pull my shirt off and kick my pajama pants down, so I was just in my crooked bra and underwear. And then he was back on top of me, his bare chest filling my hands. I stroked up the smooth, warm skin of his shoulders, then his back, feeling the strength of the muscles beneath. I'd had sex before, but the power and width of his body made me think I'd be in for more than I was used to.

One of his hands reached behind my back, unhooking my bra, and I let him pull it from my arms, baring myself to him.

He paused, and in the low light from the candles I could see his mouth was wet and plump from kissing me, his eyes dark as they trailed down my mostly naked body. Condom forgotten in one hand, he used the other to take one of my breasts in his palm, latching on with his mouth once more. This time he sucked *hard*, and the sound pulled free from my mouth was almost a scream. He licked and bit while I threaded one hand into his hair, pulling at the strands. The harder I tugged the harsher he laved and sucked at my breast, and something that had always been a simple, quick part of foreplay for me took on more. My body temperature skyrocketed. My heart pounded. My body shook with need as I splayed my legs wide open beneath him, wet and so, so empty I couldn't stand it.

"There we go," he said, all gravel.

He pulled down my underwear and I watched him put on the condom with a few quick rolls of his wrist. I wanted to sit up, to study how long and wide he was, to prepare. But before I could, he was kneeling between my open legs, the head of him already nudging into me.

With his elbows on either side of my arms and his firm stomach pressing into mine, he began to grind in subtle thrusts, slowly pushing his way into me. Every inch gained felt like a revelation, a burst of sensation I almost couldn't bear. His chest brushed my oversensitive nipples, his knees pushing my thighs further apart in a lurid display.

I kissed him, his short beard rough and almost painful against my chin, but I didn't care. He breathed into me as he edged further inside. All I wanted was for him to slam home, but he was determined to keep this part slow.

"More," I moaned. "Jamie, more. Please."

His laugh was just one short burst of air, but he must have felt the same desperation, because his control snapped. He jerked forward, his hips hitting mine, and then I was full of him, surrounded by him. Without delay he pulled back, long and slow, and then hammered home. I cried out. He did it again and I raised my hips to meet him, trying to drag him back faster. His thrusts became punishing. Pounding. Exhilarating.

There was a sound, like a low thump, and I thought it might have been the bed hitting the wall, or something downstairs, but before I could lift my head to check, Jamie used one arm to pull my leg higher, changing the angle so he was slamming into me quick and hard, my body bent beneath his.

I held onto him as I cried out, my nails digging into his skin. There was a sense of possession as he moved me, and I had no complaints. He could own every part of me if he just kept thrusting—kept bringing me higher. Pleasure shot through me as his teeth found a space low on my neck, his body plunging into mine with a power I knew he'd been containing. I was lost to anything but the sensations that wracked me as he pushed me closer to the edge.

When the sweet agony of each thrust became unbearable, I came, my thoughts shattering into nothing but the sound of my moans and the groan he made against my throat. I could feel him pulsing inside me as I shook through the aftershocks, my limbs instantly limp, my breathing labored.

Returning to awareness was a gradual process. At first it was just the sweat sticking between us, and then how heavy his chest was. I must have taken a deeper breath because he pushed up to his arms, adjusting to give me space while we were still connected. His expression held something like astonishment.

"Damn," he said, letting out a breath.

I giggled, and the sensation of him inside me while I did so was almost startling. "Yeah."

"Should I...?" he gestured with a dip of his head, and I nodded as he pulled out of me. It felt unnatural then, to be empty when he had just been thrusting madly inside of me. I already missed it, though I was deliciously sore.

Collapsing on my left, Jamie was still breathing like he'd gone through a heavy workout, but as the minutes passed, it calmed to an easier rhythm.

"Fighting with my brother has never been so rewarding," he said, absentmindedly, just as my heart rate returned to normal.

My lazy grin dropped a bit, almost into a frown. I hadn't thought of Brendan—or the naiad—since Jamie first kissed me. He had been all-consuming.

His gaze jerked to mine, his expression nervous. "Not that I...I mean, that wasn't what this was—"

"I know," I said, nodding. It wasn't about Brendan, but it *was* in spite of him. And the naiad. A whirlwind of unknowns battered us from all sides, but regardless we wanted each other. Wanted to be with each other.

I felt a bit guilty for enjoying myself while so much was going on, but as I looked over at Jamie's defined chest and ab muscles, and at the long length of him that I wanted inside me once more, all the guilt drained away. For one night we could both escape our troubles, until we were satisfied. And I knew, as I reached for him, I wasn't quite there. Not yet.

CHAPTER TWENTY-THREE

My morning with Jamie was blissfully easy. We woke up to watery light streaming through my bedroom window and the soft, low-pitched whistles of birds in the trees. Thankfully, we'd remembered to blow out the candles we'd had littered throughout the house before succumbing to sleep. I could see the living room lamp was on, so the power coming back on hadn't woken us.

We moved around each other like seasoned roommates. He brewed some coffee while I straightened the living room, and he casually poured in extra milk and sugar when I asked. Then I showed him where the bread was in the cabinet so we could make French toast. It wasn't as good as his mom's, but I still had a fun time cooking with him. He wrapped his arms around me from behind while I sprinkled cinnamon and sugar on top, kissing the place where my neck met my shoulder. It felt like we fit together perfectly, and even though I was in no shape for another round, a rush of warmth to my core had me nearly changing my mind.

Sitting on the loveseat together, eating in companionable silence, we both went through our phones to check news alerts and messages we'd missed from the night before. Only the sounds of our forks on our plates broke through the gentle sounds of the morning wildlife outside.

While I still had the blinds drawn, I couldn't tell if there were heavy clouds in the sky or if a cold morning chill was frosting the glass, but based on the warbling of the birds, I imagined we were in for a calm autumn day. Or maybe that was just wishful thinking.

"Shit," Jamie muttered, scrolling through his phone.

"What's wrong?"

"Brendan needs the car. He has a shift." His frown was serious, the look more intense than made sense.

"Is that all?" I asked, confused.

He put the phone down on the coffee table and slid it toward me. I looked at the screen.

Brendan: *Could you stop being a selfish prick already and bring the car home? I have a shift, and someone in this house needs to take home money. You know, if you want things like electricity and internet and food.*

"Wow," I said, reading it again. I knew Brendan was a bit resentful of having to work, since he thought Jamie's time on the ice was more a game than a career, but when I'd talked to him about it, he hadn't been nearly this negative. He'd been understanding.

"Ever since our fight he just keeps picking away at me like this," Jamie grumbled. "And..." he sighed, rubbing a hand over his growing beard, "to be honest, I pick back at him."

"What do you mean?" I took another bite of my breakfast, a sense of unease making my stomach roil.

"I mean, this thing between us—" he gestured at me and back at himself, "he was okay with it. It's our rule, right? But I...I may have rubbed it in a bit."

I was afraid to ask, but I did. "What did you tell him?"

"I told him about the storage closet. And I may have embellished."

"You mean you were a jerk about it."

Shame darkened his features, but he looked back at his phone. "To be fair, he started it—told me about how you kissed him, and I just forgot all about the rule. Our *one* rule—not to let a girl get between us. It's just the only weapon we have against each other right now, if that makes any sense. The only thing we can do to hurt each other."

And he was, I realized. Hurt. It was in the way his hazel eyes were now gazing down at his phone, then his plate, then back. He wouldn't look at me.

"Last night..." I started, and then took a breath. "You're not going to tell him as some kind of revenge, right?"

"No." He whipped his head toward me, his expression honestly surprised. "No, I swear." He took my hand. "It's not his business unless you want it to be. Last night wasn't about getting back at him or anything. Last night was amazing. And it was just about us. I hope that's how you felt too."

I nodded. "It was. It *is*. And that's good to know. I'm just...sorry about the kiss with Brendan. That you found out from him. But also, you *did* tell me to try and sus out my feelings."

"I did, and I'm not mad. I get it. Plus..." he offered me a shadow of his normal wry smile, "it's not like last night wasn't a pretty clear indicator of where we stand. That you have some *passionate* feelings for me."

"Pleased with yourself about that, are you?" I mused.

Lifting one shoulder, he took a big bite of the French toast, as if to stop himself from gloating.

"I don't like feeling like I'm in some sort of tug-of-war," I said into the silence. "You know that, right?"

He swallowed, his expression still sheepish. "I know. It's just...like I said. A weapon."

The rest of our breakfast was a bit strained after that, while my mind poured over our discussion. They were using me to hurt each other, and though the connection Jamie and I felt was real, I also cared about Brendan. I couldn't help but feel affection toward him, and even desire. When I pictured hands around my waist or the mouth I wanted to kiss, I pictured Jamie. The problem was Jamie looked identical to Brendan in most lights.

I cleared my throat, pulling myself out of those confusing thoughts. "I don't want it to be his business," I said decidedly. "I want last night to be something good. Not something used to start a fight."

I saw the muscle in Jamie's jaw clench while he deliberated something, but instead of saying whatever he was thinking, he just nodded once more and continued eating.

He left shortly after, so he could make sure Brendan got to work on time, and after I watched him back out of the driveway and head home, the house around me grew eerily quiet. It felt like there was cotton stuffed in my ears.

Rubbing the chill out of my arms, I went to turn the heat up, and then walked around the apartment, trying to determine why I suddenly felt so uneasy.

It was when I went to the kitchen that I saw it. There was a smudge of something dark at the bottom edge of the blinds. It caught my eye like a spider in the corner of a room—just enough out of place that my entire focus narrowed there.

Walking forward with cautious steps, I studied the smudge. It was wide and opaque, the color of mud.

I realized now that the heavy silence was the lack of bird calls outside, as if they'd sensed a threat and disappeared.

I thought about calling Jamie back. He was only minutes away—he could be here fast—but I was safe inside the house. I was just overreacting. Right?

Moving the blinds by just an inch, I saw the smudge was actually a series of streaks along the glass, dripping down into a thick pool at the door. It was a ruddy brown, like dried blood mixed with dirt and berry juice, and now that I knew what to look for, I could make out the trail of it that speckled the grass. Small puddles led down the hill toward the pond, but then they became too difficult to discern. And I did *not* want to go outside to investigate.

The lines at the bottom of the patio door looked like something had scrabbled at the bottom edge. Hoping to unlock it? Trying to somehow lift it? There was no question in my mind that this residue was from the naiad, and this muck was either dredged up from her watery home, or it was her inhuman blood.

I crouched low, looking at the mottled space, and felt the slightest hiss of cold air. There was a crack at the bottom of the glass, right along the frame.

Hands shaking, I placed my fingers by the thin fissure, feeling the cold air leak inside. She must have used all her strength to try and break through. And it had hurt her, if all the blood was any indication.

I stooped there on the floor, looking at the streaks where her fingers had groped to reach me, and instead of experiencing fear like I had in the dark the night before, I felt...sympathy. This woman was dying, and while Jamie, Brendan, and I sat in our indecision, she was growing sicker, and more desperate. I still didn't want to see her, or even be near her—she had *attacked and kidnapped me*—but Brendan's words came back to me. That we should at least meet with her, talk with her, before Jamie decided she was better off dead. Maybe there was something we could do to help her.

There was something *I* could do. And it involved giving her my blood.

This animosity between Jamie and Brendan had been going on for too long now. A pair of inseparable brothers who didn't let their different personalities, their dreams that fought for resources, or their interest in me get in the way of their relationship, were now being torn apart. All because we couldn't figure out what to do about this creature, who needed something only I could give. A creature that might be one boy's *mother*. My own mom might have been MIA, but this creature...if I believed she was a naiad, and her son was a changeling, then I had no recourse but to believe she'd left him for the reasons she claimed. She had been trying to save his life, and that tugged at me more than I cared to admit.

I released a breath, a sudden determination making me stand and head back toward the kitchen counter. This was stupid. I was being stupid. But sitting around waiting for some miracle solution to appear was only an option for so long. And really, I had Lynne to blame, because the idea was pulled directly from her video game, and the bowls of cream left out for the cat searching for their lost kitten.

"I can't believe I'm doing this," I muttered, pulling a mason jar from one of the cabinets, and then a knife from the drawer.

Looking down at my arms, I debated where to cut. I felt simultaneously like I was watching myself from afar, a disembodied head shaking in concern, and also like I was so entrenched in my body—in the racing pulse and shuddering breath of it—that I couldn't possibly be anywhere else.

The elbow, I decided, was the best choice. It was close to a vein, but not somewhere I would constantly use or touch like a hand or my wrist. Besides, that was where nurses drew blood, so that had to be for a reason, right?

I put down a series of paper towels and placed the jar beneath my arm, taking a deep breath. One quick slash and this would be over. I'd leave the jar for the naiad outside so she could drink it like the remedy she seemed so sure it was. If she got well maybe she'd leave. This could all be over with a minute or two of pain.

Before I could second guess myself, I pushed the tip of the knife into my arm, dragging down. My arm jerked reflexively, before I could even register the pain, but still, the knife did its job and I started to bleed. And damn, did it sting.

I held my quivering arm over the jar, watching the blood drip and slide down my skin to plop at the bottom of the glass. I never realized before how slowly blood could trickle, and though I maybe should have dug deeper or cut myself longer, I was afraid to do anything too damaging. So, for what seemed like an eternity, I bit my bottom lip and watched the slow *drip, drip, drip* of my blood until it slowed and nearly stopped. There was over an inch of blood in the jar, a much brighter red than I thought it would be. It wasn't a lot, but it would have to be enough, because I really, *really* did not want to do that again.

Grabbing the paper towels and putting pressure on the mostly-clotted cut, I cleaned myself off in the bathroom and put a couple of bandages over the wound.

With jerky movements, I placed the mason jar of blood on my back patio, right near the blue-brown puddles, and rushed to close and lock the door. Tonight, if she returned, maybe this offering would appease her, like some sacrifice made to an invisible god.

To block out the surreal turn my life had taken, I adamantly continued about my day as normally as possible. Research, homework, venturing to campus to hang with Lynne and her roommates, playing "Cups" and "Never Have I Ever" like we were at a children's sleepover. I spent the night tossing on her suite's lumpy couch and returned home in the morning, quick to check the patio.

The blood was still there, darker now and half-congealed. The puddles around the door had dried to a flaky, dirt-like consistency I wouldn't have looked twice at if I didn't already know what they were. It was as if her blood decayed back into nature if left untouched. I closed the blinds once more.

Another day passed, and another night.

On Sunday morning the jar was still there, dark with coagulated blood. I hadn't mentioned this little experiment to Jamie or Brendan, but I briefly considered texting them to ask what to try next. If the naiad was too weak, or maybe too far gone to find this blood, how could I get it to her? And should I even try? *Maybe*, like that vengeful voice inside me whispered, *I should leave her to perish.*

The trouble was, I wanted to see all sides of this story. A good reporter didn't let their personal experience taint the investigation, so even though she'd hurt me, I felt like it was my responsibility to see this through to the end. To try, if not for Jamie and Brendan's sake, then to satiate my own curiosity. It was crazy, and probably irrational, but the words were a recurring refrain inside my mind. *I have to try again.*

My fingers were cold with something like dread as I sat down and opened my phone, working on the next stage of my spur-of-the-moment plan. It was a dumb plan, but I would be smart about it—if that made any sense.

I opened my phone's settings and elected to change my voicemail message, having learned this trick from a friend of mine in high school who tended to go on dangerous hikes: "Hi, this is Sadie. I'm in my backyard...in the woods, hanging with my neighbor for a quick visit, where I may not have service. If my phone gets wet, or I don't return by..." I checked the time on my phone, seeing it was only a little after ten a.m., "noon, please contact Brendan or Jamie Barreto to come get me." I listed their numbers and hit confirm on the message.

It was time to make my gruesome delivery.

I grabbed a small tote bag from near the front door and put the sealed mason jar inside, followed by my Mace, a knife, and a stainless-steel water bottle. In my research on fae, I had found there were only a few items that could injure them. The main one was iron, but since I didn't have any old-fashioned padlocks or nails around, stainless steel would have to do—it was apparently 98% iron, according to Wikipedia. I just had to hope, if I needed to brain the naiad with it, that would suffice.

Changing into a warm, thick sweater and a pair of jeans, I was—hopefully—ready. I felt somewhat like a brave adventurer as I opened the patio doors, but also like the first actor on screen in a horror movie, about to get murdered. I was leaving the safety of my fortress and wandering headlong into danger.

If I hadn't thought Jamie and Brendan would have tried to talk me out of this, or that they could potentially become sick from the naiad's fae illness, I would have called and asked for back-up. But as it was, this was something I had to do on my own. This could put an end to all the arguing and fighting, all the strife. Maybe then our lives could go back to something resembling peaceful.

Thankfully, the trail of muck was easy enough to follow once I was outside. The morning was cloudy and gray, a brisk wind carrying the smell of damp earth and something like rot into my nose. Gusts hissed along the tall grasses by the pond, rippling the water as I drew closer, but the trail didn't lead toward the dock like I'd hoped. It went into the woods. If the naiad had been in the pond, it would have been much easier for me to leave the jar somewhere she would find it, but if she'd stumbled, dying, back into the cavernous rock formation she'd dragged me to, there was no way to tell if she was strong enough to make it back here one last time. I'd have to go to her.

I still almost left the blood at the water's edge, trying to convince myself it was enough, but I'd gone too far now to see the job half-done. What was the point of bleeding for her if she never got it?

Shivering a bit in the cold, I continued to walk beside the speckled blue-brown muck on the grass, watching it grow thinner and thicker by turn. If I'd thought this plan through a bit more, I would have carried some kind of vial to collect samples that could be tested later.

"That's what you get for being impulsive," I muttered to myself.

Fallen leaves crunched under my boots as I made it to the tree line, trying to remember the way I'd fled. This was close to the right angle, at least, so I breached the border of the woods, the shadows falling over me like a veil.

The woods were less terrifying in the daytime. Really, there was nothing special about them; they reminded me of the trail Brendan and I had hiked for clean-up work. Trees drooped orange and yellow branches toward the ground, the skittering of squirrels caught my eye more than once, and rocks jutted out into the path every few feet to stumble the unsuspecting. Weaving my way along the shoddy path, I stopped seeing signs of the naiad's blood, which was simultaneously relieving and worrying. I didn't want to run into her, but I wanted to get somewhat close to her hideout.

After maybe an hour of searching, with my legs grown tired and my heart exhausted from bouts of pounding anxiously in my chest at each unexpected sound, I spotted a rock cliff ahead with a distinguished opening at the corner. I was sure this was it—the ground had gotten damp and swampy around me, my boots sticking in the wet mud just like that night. It was as if a bog was rising up from below the earth, swallowing the trees and scrubs into its mire.

I struggled to keep my panicked breathing under control as I searched for a place to leave the jar.

A hiss like steam from a kettle had me turning, and my mouth went dry, my fingers almost dropping the straps of the bag in my hand.

I swallowed a scream.

CHAPTER TWENTY-FOUR

The naiad leaned weakly against a tree only a few meters away, her clawed hands gripping into the bark. There was dried, blue-tinted blood around her mouth and all over her front, covering the scraps of filthy linen she wore, emphasizing the pale hue of her azure skin. Her straggly, dark hair shielded half her face.

I backed up one step, and then another.

"You return," she said, her voice quiet and garbled.

"I—I said I would give you my blood," I bit out, backing away another step. My hands were sweating on the bag, and I reached inside slowly, fumbling for the jar. "I've brought it to you."

Her head ticked up an inch. "Part human girl, I am...no fool." She looked around, as if waiting for an ambush. "A trick."

"I'm alone. It's not a trick." I pulled out the jar and raised it so she could see the blood inside. "See?"

Crouching low, I did my best to roll the container over the uneven forest ground. It bumped against a rock, and I worried the thick glass would break, but it ambled toward her until it was only a foot away.

Her expression was skeptical, her wide mouth downturned at the corners, but after a moment she knelt, slow and with some difficulty, onto the floor. It was like watching an elderly woman move, her bony limbs shaking with effort. She unscrewed the lid and tipped the gluey blood into her open mouth, which seemed to grow bigger than any human's should. It reminded me of a snake opening its maw wide to ingest an egg.

I stared, entranced, as the blood slowly fell onto her tongue, like a gelatinous mass, and she worked to swallow it.

The woods around us went silent, to the point where I realized there *had* been noise before now—scuffles of critters in the brush, and the rustle of leaves thrown by the wind. But now it was so quiet I could hear the air moving in and out of my lungs.

She gulped, licking her lips, tipping the jar and her head back as if trying for more. A growl permeated the air, reminding me of an aggressive dog, and then with shocking force she flung the jar away. It shattered against a tree.

"Not enough!" She roared, her voice hoarse.

My gaze sliced from the broken glass back to her just in time to see her clawed hands reach forward, her thin legs pushing off the ground with a strength she'd hidden. My first thought was how foolish I'd been to assume she could be placated. To assume I was safe from her in any capacity. How could I have forgotten the power she'd used to smack me against the house like a plaything? She'd carted my body through the woods with little struggle, dragging me over twigs and rocks and uneven ground. I was an idiot. But my second thought was how, at least this time, I was armed.

Digging in my bag, I pulled out the bottle of Mace, and just as she reached me, I pressed the button on top, hoping it was pointed in the right direction. The spray hit her on the side of the face. I waved my arm, trying to get it into her eyes.

She shrieked, ducking low, her clawed hands coming around my middle to tackle me to the ground.

My lungs stuttered with the force of my fall, leaving me stunned. I couldn't breathe.

Not again, *not again*.

Scrabbling at my side for my bag, hoping for the knife or the water bottle—anything—I prayed the pepper spray had hurt the naiad enough to give me the precious few seconds I needed to start breathing once more. But she was back on me in an instant.

Her eyes were red-rimmed and nearly closed as thick, brown-tinted tears leaked down her bony cheeks. The sound that sawed in and out of her mouth as she breathed was a hiss. Sharp talons grabbed onto my arms, piercing the skin through my sweater as she struggled to rip it off me.

Her teeth clacked as she bit close to my skin, going for my throat, but I struggled against her hold, wiggling enough to avoid her.

And then I was twisted and pulled. She had ahold of both my arms. I kicked against the wet ground, trying to find a root or rock I could hook onto with my boots, anything to slow my progress along the floor. She was faster this time, as if the small amount of blood she'd consumed had revived her. I hoped that meant it would work; she would take a bit more and then realize she felt better. She would leave me alive.

It was a naïve dream.

My heels were dragging on the ground. I jerked my arms to the side, trying to break her hold, but she had too firm of a grip. My forearms were wet, and I knew the puncture wounds left by her nails were bleeding.

A darker shadow crested over my head, and I twisted my neck to get a better look, immediately recognizing the mouth of the cave. My pulse, which had already been frantic with the need to break free, now thumped so hard against my ribs I thought it might bruise them.

"Please, no," I whispered through my panting breath, trying not to cry. "Wait. Please. I said I'd give you some..." I changed tactics, raising my voice. "Wait, I—I know your son."

With no warning, the naiad dropped me onto the ground, my head smacking the hard rock floor.

I groaned, my eyesight going blurry while the pain crested and throbbed at the back of my skull.

The naiad crouched beside me, her mouth so close to my ear I thought she was about to bite my face, but she took a deep inhale, sniffing at my hairline.

I shivered, trying to reorient myself so I could sit up, but the cave ceiling was moving, and I felt like my head had been crushed in a vice.

"Smell...naiad," she hissed, and I thought I could hear astonishment in her tone. "But also, like life. Once I am free of this...we will be together. My boy."

"I know him. I can tell you—"

And then she pulled aside the collar of my sweater and bit down on my exposed shoulder.

I'd intended my knowledge of the boys to be used as leverage, thinking I was clever enough to stall her if I needed to, but I'd underestimated her bloodlust.

The teeth that struck my skin were jagged, tearing into the flesh with ease, sawing as she jerked and twitched, drinking me deep.

I tried to scream but the pain was blinding. The sound died in my throat.

I pawed at her, uselessly trying to push her face away, but her claws scratched at my skin, her body hunched over mine. Her presence was imposing and immovable; she was a fate I could not escape. Already I felt weak and tired. The pain was draining me as surely as the blood loss.

"Sadie!"

I heard the voice through my muddled thoughts and the lightning arc of pain in my shoulder, and managed to take in a breath, mustering my strength. I couldn't tell if it was Brendan or Jamie, but whoever it was—they were close. They were looking for me.

"Help!" I cried out, as loud as I could. It was more of a croak. "Here!"

The woman growled against my skin, her jaw moving like a beast ripping into a meal. My skin tore into shreds under her teeth, and this time I did manage a loud sob I hoped had sounded like a scream.

"Sadie!" someone called again, and then I could hear the displaced leaves and pounding feet of someone rushing toward me.

With a rip that pulled my chest up into the air, the naiad finally dislodged herself from me. Blood sat disturbingly warm against my sternum as I shivered on the ground, trying to edge backward.

We both looked to the cave entrance where a blurry figure—no, two figures—stood.

My vision blinked in and out, but as they moved forward, I could make out Jamie and Brendan, backlit so they were dense shadows, moving with purpose.

"Back!" The naiad hissed. She held up one clawed, blue-tinged hand, coated in blood. I could make out one of the twins staring down at me in shock, while the other took another threatening step into the cave.

I vaguely wondered if she had told them to stop so she could continue enjoying her meal, or if she was still worried about being too close to her son and potentially spreading the "drying sickness" she was hoping to cure.

Then she began to convulse.

It was a pulsing movement in the corner of my eye, and I tilted my head the tiniest bit, feeling my skin throb where life still drained out of me. My glasses slipped down my nose, and I wondered vaguely how they'd stayed on this whole time. The thought was like the whisp of a cloud passing over my vision, forgotten as soon as a sharp lance of agony pierced me.

Since the wound was at my shoulder and not the main artery of my neck, I had to hope that the blood loss wouldn't be fatal, but given the chill at my fingertips and legs, I feared the worst. Pain came in waves that made my vision spin, and nausea crawled up my throat.

The naiad's body jerked forward, then back, and she turned to the side, blood pouring out of her mouth. She was vomiting me up. At first what splashed onto the ground by my elbow was red, but then it grew darker—brown, then blue, and then black.

One of the twins groaned in disgust, covering his mouth, but rushed as if to reach for me and pull me out while she was distracted.

"No!" The naiad shrieked. Dark muck the color of coal still dripped from her teeth, and she started to mumble and moan. "Don't. It didn't work...still sick. Still..." She coughed up more liquid onto the cave floor, some of it trickling down her chin.

I stared, dazed, as he ignored her, pushing past his brother to kneel by us.

The naiad scrambled away, her expression furious. Garbled words fell from her mouth that I could not understand—a language more guttural than any I'd ever heard. With her eyes trained on the twin at my side, she snarled out something like a command, gesturing backward.

My sight cleared enough to look at the petrified, pale face beside me, tight beard and all. Jamie.

He fell backward, as if pushed by an invisible force, and then he was crawling back, leaving me behind.

"Stay away!" the creature wheezed. "I know your name. My boy...you will obey." She said that strange amalgamation of sounds once more, and I watched as Jamie stumbled to his feet but fell backward, further away. He retreated one step, then another, limbs moving in a staccato rhythm, like he wasn't in control of his own body.

I peered at him through my wobbling vision as he stood feet from the mouth of the cavern. His muscles clenched, like he was battling himself, and his hazel eyes were wide with terror. He couldn't move.

The naiad had controlled him, because she was his mother.

Jamie was the changeling.

CHAPTER TWENTY-FIVE

Now that Jamie was safely out of the way, the naiad glared down at me with betrayal in her dark eyes.

"Not enough. Not enough!" she screamed, shrill and piercing. My head was pounding as I tried to keep my eyes open. I was too weak to move, too scared to fight. Was I lying here dying? Should I try to turn over? My thoughts were becoming scattered and sluggish.

It was a shame, really, that my blood was not the cure she'd hoped for. Maybe I wasn't fae enough. Maybe I needed to be injected into her, instead of drunk. I imagined the two of us connected by needles and piping, moving my blood through her like a rudimentary dialysis machine, and the picture almost made me smile. How absurd.

"...have to let us take her," one of the boys said through gritted teeth. Brendan, I think. Had I fallen asleep?

"Not enough!" And then her teeth were back at my shoulder.

"No!" someone shouted, and then I saw Brendan leap forward. He shoved the naiad from my side, and I felt more than saw her tumble to the floor. Hissing, she crawled backward on her feet and hands like a crab.

Then her arms gave out. She moaned, turning her head, and I heard the wet gurgle of her throwing up once more.

"Come on, Sadie." Brendan was putting one arm under my legs, lifting me up, though it was a struggle. I was sprawled a bit ungainly, and I tried to pull my limbs together, tried to make it easier, but I was so, so tired.

My head lolled a bit to the side as he pulled me up, so I was able to see the creature trembling violently, her blue-tinted body an ashen gray. She collapsed onto her back, the dark blood around her drying into that dirt-like substance I'd seen on my porch. But it was happening so fast. Then her mouth was shriveling, her frame sinking in on itself.

She seized, and a mist-like pollen began to rise from her skin. There was agony in the way her claws stiffened and her back arched, and despite the sharp, raw pain of my own injuries, the sight made me cringe.

"Hurry!" Jamie yelled, still outside the cave. "Get her out of there!"

Brendan held me more firmly against his chest, taking quick steps that jostled me more than I would have liked. He carried me away from the naiad and all my blood on the floor. Soft, burbling cries echoed in the space we left behind and I knew the creature lay there, decaying. Wasting away into an inelegant death.

The light of day was sharp against my eyes as Brendan carted me into the thick of the trees, but then he halted.

"Jamie!" he called.

I guessed Jamie was still watching the naiad, helpless to step forward. Or was he stuck in place by whatever magic she'd cast? We couldn't leave him.

"Jamie?" I rasped, voice weak, hoping he could hear me. Hoping he wasn't forced to stay in the trauma of watching the naiad—his mother—die.

But then he was in my field of vision. "Yeah, I'm here. Let's go." He led the way out of the woods, holding aside branches and following some barely perceptible tracks leading back toward my yard.

"You found me," I whispered up to Brendan.

"Well, Jamie called you and that voicemail message just about gave him a heart attack. He grabbed me, and then once we were here...we saw the trail you must have followed. The blood. When we were in the woods..." his voice got quieter. "Jamie seemed to know which way to go."

My vision dimmed and I blinked, trying to focus.

"You have to stay awake, Sadie. We'll get you to the hospital, but you have to stay awake." Brendan's hands tightened on my arm and thigh, and I was grateful I could feel it. All I could do was nod and force my eyes open every time I blinked, the motion growing more difficult each time.

The next few hours blurred. The where and when of my own life was suspect as I found myself in the backseat of a car, then in a hospital bed, and all I'd done between those two moments was struggle to keep eyes on Brendan. Jamie must have driven. He must have explained something to the emergency room nurses who pulled me into a bay. He must have filled out my intake forms. Because Brendan never left my side.

I wondered if they'd lied about being related to me. I was woozy and my mind drifted in and out of thought, but I knew he wouldn't normally be allowed at my bedside.

When I woke next, there was a bag of blood hanging over my left shoulder, a stinging in my skin around an array of stitches, and a headache gnawing at the back of my eyeballs. But I was alive.

Brendan was sitting in a chair pulled up to the side of my bed, his gaze vaguely aimed at the singular window. He didn't notice I was awake, and I took a minute to look him over. He'd changed into a dark sweatshirt, and I wondered if his other clothes were ruined from my blood. I'm glad none of the doctors seemed to think he had hurt me.

There was stubble on his chin from a few days without shaving, emphasizing the pallor of his skin, but I had no trouble discerning him from his brother now. Those expressive hazel eyes were more haunted than ever.

"Brendan?"

His head whipped toward me. "Jesus Christ, Sadie." Though his tone was a combination of startled and relieved, his smile was all affection. "Don't do that to me."

"What? Get mauled by a naiad? Or interrupt your daydreams?" I tried to wriggle into a sitting position, but my shoulder throbbed at the movement. Brendan rushed to help me, pressing a button that raised the top of the bed, then adjusting my pillows. He handed me a cup of water, which I took eagerly using my uninjured arm; my mouth was stale and dry, like I hadn't used it in days.

"Thanks," I said with a wince. I chugged it down and then put on my slightly scratched glasses, which had been waiting for me on a table next to my bed.

A doctor came in then to check on me. She was an older woman with a messy bob and dangling earrings, who smiled warmly when she saw I was awake. I immediately liked her.

"Good afternoon, Sadie. We're glad to see you up and alert. Do you know where you are?"

"Spindle River Hospital?" I guessed. I didn't actually know the name of the local hospital, but how unique could it be?

The doctor chuckled. "Close enough." She came over to the machine beside me that held the blood bag, along with saline and some other liquids, and checked the readings. "Your vitals are greatly improved, and you have no oncoming signs of an infection, but we did administer a rabies vaccine and tetanus booster while you were out. How do you feel?"

"Sore," I answered honestly. "And I have a headache, but other than that, okay."

She nodded. "Good. I hope they catch that coyote. Damn things are always going after dogs. You were very brave to step in."

I wisely kept my mouth shut; I didn't need to look at Brendan to know it was the story he and his brother had cooked up to keep us all out of the loony bin.

Brendan patted my hand. "Our mom is really grateful you protected Coco."

"Yeah. Coco," I mumbled, trying not to laugh.

"We'll be keeping you one more night, but your father should be here by tomorrow morning to help with your release paperwork," she continued, unaware of Brendan clutching my hand in warning so I wouldn't giggle.

"Okay," I squeaked out. "Thank you."

When she left, I released a breath that turned into a snort.

"Coco?" I asked.

Brendan shrugged, and I saw the dimples at the edges of his mouth make their first appearance in days. "I panicked. It was the first name I thought of."

"So, I protected your dog from a vicious coyote attack?"

"That's the story."

I shook my head in disbelief. We were lucky the naiad didn't have more human-shaped teeth, and that the doctors weren't inclined to ask detailed questions.

The quiet stretched between us then, and while normally Brendan and I could sit in silence with no issue, this time there were too many questions lingering in the air to ignore.

"Where is he?" I asked.

Brendan hesitated. "He went home."

I tried to read from his tone how Jamie had left—if he was doing it to get their car to their mom, if he was going back to the woods to find his birth mother, or if he was too angry with me for going to her alone that he didn't want to see me—but I was too afraid to ask.

Brendan could see it in my expression though, because his hand gentled against mine.

"He's just...trying to deal," he explained.

"And he couldn't deal here?"

I sounded bitter, which I hated. Jamie was his own person, and he didn't owe me anything. It had been my decision to go after the naiad. But still, I was hurt he wasn't sitting in this hospital room like his brother, making sure I was okay.

"For once, he's being pretty quiet about how he feels," Brendan said, "but given all the guilt he's trying to bury, I'd say he's too ashamed to be around you right now."

"Ashamed of what?" I asked, stunned.

"Ashamed that you got hurt. That he didn't know who he is...*what* he is, I mean. You've only been here a day and a half, but in that time he's barely said a word. Just filled out your papers, sat in the waiting room until the doctors assured him you were going to be fine, then...fled."

Fled was a good word for it, I reasoned, since it sounded like a cowardly move, but I didn't say that. Maybe there was something I was missing here. Though I didn't think there was a good reason to abandon the girl you were dating—or sleeping with, or whatever we were doing—when she nearly got murdered trying to save your supernatural mother from a wasting disease.

I wished he was here. I wanted to know he was alright, and that he wasn't beating himself up for what had happened. It had been my choice. And, if I was being honest, I knew I'd do it all over again if I thought it would help them. Him. I cared about him. Maybe I even loved him.

I sighed, trying to ignore that last thought, since he wasn't even here.

"You're tired," Brendan noted. "I'll let you get some sleep—" he stopped as his phone pinged, and he checked the screen.

"Jamie?" I asked.

He shook his head. "The band. I've missed a practice and they're trying to meet up to prep for our gig next week at Dio's."

The name tugged at my memory. "Wait, the wine tasting place?"

Brendan raised one eyebrow. "You know about it?"

"Jamie told me about it when he was giving me a tour of the town. It's a big deal around here, right?"

"Yeah. They almost never do live music, but the new manager heard us play at Caisse's and asked us to do a show." He put the phone back in his pocket, looking embarrassed.

"That's great, I'm so happy for you." I grinned as I took his hand and squeezed it. "Go ahead and go, I'm fine. Just soaking up some O negative and lounging. You don't need to stay."

He tilted his head. "You sure? I don't mind."

"I need to think about some things and...I feel like some time alone could help."

"Things like Jamie?"

Releasing his hand, I took a breath. This might not be the right time, given that Jamie was AWOL, but Brendan needed to know where I stood. "Yeah. Jamie. He and I—I think we're pretty serious. You deserve to know that. I don't know what all this naiad stuff means for us, but I want to figure it out. With him. If he lets me."

"But you need to think about it." It was a question and a statement. An accusation and a plea.

"The supernatural aspect, yeah. About him, and about me. But not about how I feel." I met his eyes, the slightest bit darker than his twin's, and hoped this wouldn't cause the rift between them to grow. "I like you, and I'm not saying there isn't something here, but...I'm falling for him, Brendan. Have been since I bumped into him the first day of classes." I paused, licking my dry lips and debating if I should explain more—how right we felt together, and how he gave me what I needed, whether it was space or a laugh or a touch, without me having to ask—but I didn't. "I'm sorry," I said instead.

He shook his head. "Don't be sorry for what you feel." Still, there was a tinge of discomfort in his expression, his eyebrows low.

I may have kissed him at his show—more than kissed him, really—but this thing between Jamie and I was deeper. I wasn't going to string him along, and even if Jamie and I didn't work out, I wouldn't want Brendan to feel like he was a consolation prize. I needed to let him go.

He was quiet as he left, a mix of contemplation and discontent on his features. I realized I'd neglected to ask him how *he* was coping with the knowledge of his brother's supernatural heritage, but maybe I'd have the chance to talk to him about that later. I hoped he'd still want to be friends after this, but I wouldn't ask him for that yet. We all needed some time.

And I needed to get out of this hospital bed.

***

My dad showed up the next morning, full of outrage that I'd hurt myself protecting a *dog* of all things, and one that wasn't even my own. I'd talked to him the night before on the phone, but my chipper tone wasn't fooling him. The first thing he did was take in the bandages on my shoulder and the gauze at the back of my head and turn a nasty shade of purple.

"Sadie Emilia Shaw, are you trying to give me a heart attack?"

Thankfully, I was able to reassure him it looked worse than it was; I was being discharged with only minor instructions on how to care for the stitches. He packed me up and took me home, griping the whole time about how the city should be doing something about the coyote population and that maybe he should pay for some kind of fencing around the property where I was staying.

I let him rant for a while until he got it out of his system, which was always the easiest way to get him to let something go, and then he spent the morning tidying and inspecting my apartment while I lay on the couch. He wasn't very domestically oriented, so it was humorous to watch him try to figure out where my dishes went and where my hamper was.

After buying me some groceries, he then spent the day with me watching trash TV until it was time to help me to bed. Lynne came over the next day to keep me company while Dad worked from the kitchen, taking various meetings and typing way too hard on his keyboard. He stayed one more night—even though I promised him repeatedly I was *fine* and would be heading back to class soon—and then finally booked his flight home.

While it had been nice to see him, I was glad to be back on my own. I'd never needed much supervision, and the idea of everyone worried about me and monitoring me made my skin itch more than my healing stitches. However, there was one Barreto twin who was decidedly *not* monitoring me. He was giving me space, and while I enjoyed my freedom and the opportunity to sort out my thoughts, it was starting to feel like too much distance.

My head still throbbed a bit from time to time, and the skin at my shoulder was uncomfortably tight, but other than that I was recovering nicely. Still, instead of focusing on catching up on my schoolwork, or taking more glorious naps, all I could do now that I was alone was think of him. Jamie. Jamie, who was a changeling, or naiad—or both.

I still wasn't entirely sure how all of this worked, and I suspected he would have even less of an idea. I'd been doing research for weeks, whereas he was just getting the story from me—and his biological mother. I wondered if he'd understood the words she'd said to him to make him back off. If he'd heard his true name in all of it, or if her language had been just as foreign to him as it was to me.

I had too many questions to rest, so eventually that afternoon I gave in and pulled out my phone.

Me: *Can you come over?*

It took him almost five minutes to respond.

Jamie: *I don't think thats a good idea*

He wasn't going to keep running from me. We needed to talk. Already I had a mental list of what we should discuss and in what order, starting first thing with why the hell had he been avoiding me?

Me: *If you don't come here, I'll go to you.*

There was a delay, and I started to wonder if he'd called my bluff. No way was I getting off this couch.

Jamie: *Fine be there in 20*

I pulled a comfy blanket over my night shirt and pajama pants and waited for him, leaving most of the lights on. Already it seemed like weeks ago when the power had gone out and I'd kissed him in this very spot. I'd given myself to him and reveled in that spark between us. The part of me that wasn't upset with him admitted that if he leaned in close, I might very well kiss him again, which might be foolish.

But I liked him.

It didn't matter that he wasn't entirely human. After all, Jamie hadn't shown the slightest signs of naiad-ness, if that was a word—no claws or black eyes to speak of. He was physical and charismatic, wild and fun. But he hadn't hurt me, and I knew he never would. He'd risked his life—facing his claustrophobia and the potential to catch his mother's illness—trying to get to me in that cave, and those actions spoke louder than words.

Still, an annoying voice whispered in my ear that Brendan would be the safer choice. I enjoyed his sweet, quiet nature, and the way he always wanted to take care of the people around him. Maybe in the long run he might be the more stable, but it was too late. If only he made me *feel* the things Jamie made me feel—alive and completely consumed by the moment. Jamie was a flame, blazing and brilliant, drawing me in, and I wanted to burn with him. I wanted to see where this could lead.

His knock on the door pulled me out of my thoughts and I gingerly made my way to the door, checking the peephole before letting him in.

Jamie looked like he hadn't slept in days. His beard was unkempt, his eyes ringed with circles dark enough to be bruises. Even his wide shoulders were a bit hunched, his height reduced as if by some weight I couldn't see.

Rubbing a hand over the side of his neck, he took an awkward step inside, barely looking at me.

"Hey," he said.

"Hey, yourself." I took my spot back on the couch, knowing I wasn't supposed to stay on my feet for very long, but he remained standing. He chewed at his lip and looked off to the side, searching for something to say in the arrangement of my furniture.

"I'm sorry, I...I should have called you. Or texted," he said, eventually.

"Yeah, you should have."

Jamie winced. "It was shitty. I was shutting you out, but I was just..." He looked at me then, and there was something tortured in his expression. Something so dreadfully sorrowful that I worried something else had happened—that someone had died, or he had lost his hockey scholarship.

"What is it?"

"I was trying to figure out how much of a monster I'm going to become." His voice was a sob, masquerading as a laugh. "How utterly fucked I am. And how you already almost died. How it's my—" His voice broke off, so suddenly I thought he would turn and leave, but he just paced from one end of my living room to the other. "I shouldn't even be here."

"I asked you to come here." With a gentle pat, I gestured for him to sit beside me, and though he hesitated, he perched on the seat, his movements wooden. I'd never seen him so uncomfortable.

"Jamie, I don't blame you for anything that happened in the woods," I said. "I was the one who went after her with a jar of blood, thinking I was so clever and that all I needed to do was taunt her with the knowledge that I might know who her son was to stay safe. It was naïve. And stupid. And absolutely nothing you did."

"Yeah, but—"

I held up my hand, stopping him. "She smelled something about me, something not entirely human, and that's why she attacked me in the first place, remember? I'm not sure what that means, or even how common it might be that some ancestor of mine mingled where they shouldn't have, but that's not your doing either. What that means is we aren't so different." My hand landed on his thigh, and I could feel the tense pulse of his muscles beneath and the heat pouring off him. He was like a livewire ready to combust.

"It makes more sense now, I think," I continued. His gaze was caught on my hand, on the scratches along my skin from fighting and scrabbling at the sticks and mud. I gripped his thigh more forcefully, and he finally looked up. "I have this energy when you're around me, like I'm being truer to myself. I want to take risks and wrap myself around you. I want to try new things and dance and be in your orbit...and I don't think that's a bad thing. Maybe it's my supposed naiad heritage, maybe it's not, but it's not just some trick of biology, because this draw between us isn't just physical. It's how you try so hard to be the person who can support your family. How you joke and laugh and smile to make the people around you happy. It's your good-natured personality and your intensity and..." I stopped short of complimenting his self-satisfied smirk, and instead tilted my head forward so he could see how serious I was. "Jamie...if you being different makes you a monster, then I'm part monster too. And neither of those things is part of why I care so much about you."

I'd been so ready to read him the riot act about abandoning me these past few days, but the fury in my gut had tamped down the second I saw his tormented features. He was hurting and confused and, more than anything now, I just wanted to comfort him. To reassure him I was here, and I wasn't going anywhere. *For now*, that pesky voice reminded me. I almost never stuck around long enough to risk the pain of where this could end. But this time I wanted to be. I wanted to be with him.

Jamie released a breath and shook his head. "This isn't how it should be, though. My...my *mother* almost drained you dry. And she was dying from who knows what. That might happen to me, you know? One day I could start losing it, start getting sick like her, and then what would you do? You'd have to kill me."

"That's a lot of ifs," I said. "And I've been doing my research about naiads and changelings and the ecosystem here. I really feel like I'm close to figuring this out, and maybe then I can stop all of this."

He stood, leaving my side again, looking lost. "I don't think we should take the chance. It's a horror story waiting to happen."

"It's not!" I walked over to him on unsteady legs and grabbed his forearms, forcing him to be still. He was practically vibrating under my palms. "You're forgetting that it's not just your choice; it's mine, too. I did what you asked—I gave Brendan a chance, I spent time with him, I kissed him—but I want *you*. We'll figure out what this all means, but don't you dare shut me out again like suddenly that will protect me."

"It will," he insisted, though he looked torn.

"It won't. I live in this town, and I'm going to stay here, and if you try to push me away, I'll just dig my heels in deeper. Stubborn, remember? You being different isn't anything wrong. Not yet, and maybe not ever. It just...makes for a more interesting story." I shrugged, and then adjusted my glasses, feeling suddenly vulnerable, even though I'd been spilling my heart out for minutes now. "Please. Don't push me away. I talk a big game, but this is new for me too. I've never had a relationship last very long...but I want that for us."

Jamie took in a deep breath, as if collecting himself, and then with a delicate slowness he reached for me, taking my face in his large, calloused hands.

"You're sure you want to deal with this?" he whispered, his gaze searching my own.

I could see everything he wanted to hide behind those eyes—fear he was somehow not worth redeeming; affection for me, or maybe even love; and hope that something good could come out of this moment, where maybe he had expected rejection.

"I'm sure," I said. And I was. Utterly.

"Then I want you to know something. My name. In case you need it."

"Your..."

He nodded. "The name she used to control me. When she said it, it echoed around inside my head, and now I can't get it out. It's always there, in her voice, and I don't want to be controlled by it, but...I trust you. In case I get sick, or violent, or something happens, I want you to be able to use it. If you need it. I don't *feel* more like a...naiad, whatever that may mean, but just to be safe."

I held my breath, waiting for him to continue.

"Dorchaséifann Macàbeag," he whispered.

I scrunched up my nose, trying to mentally repeat it, but the vowels were jumbled in my head.

He laughed and spaced it out for me, saying it a few times, until I was sure I had it memorized.

"Thank you," I said, feeling touched by the admission—by the loyalty and control he was handing over to me. He was done hiding from me. He had bared himself to me in every way.

Jamie kissed me then, tentative and skittish, like it was the first time, but all I had to do was open my mouth beneath his and that familiar hunger took over us both.

"Sadie," he groaned.

I breathed him in, wrapping my arms around his neck, and he very nearly lifted me off the ground with the way he held me so tight against his chest. His heart pounded beneath my own, a beat I was coming to recognize. My body reacted to his like we'd been at this for years. The second he was pressed into me every other thought fled my mind. I wanted him and I needed him. Needed to reassure him I was here, safe, alive, and so was he. Things were finally set between us, and there was no tearing us apart.

"I don't want to hurt you," he whispered against my mouth.

"It's just my shoulder, I'm fine. Just imagine it's a minor separation." I tilted my head, kissing him through his smile, feeling the evidence of his desire press into me. He might have meant something different, something bigger, but it didn't matter. Instinct took over and I wriggled against him, though my feet barely touched the floor. Dizzy with want, or maybe just still recovering from blood loss, I broke free, gulping in a breath.

"Do you remember where the bedroom is?"

He nodded, giving me one more quick, fierce kiss, and then he reached down to grab my legs, pulling me into a princess carry to lead me up the stairs. Normally I would have protested the treatment, but it felt good to be held, and I could keep kissing him from this angle while he carefully padded toward my room.

When he put me down on the bed, I assumed he would tease me to death like he had the first time, but he surprised me by yanking off my pajama pants, and then my underwear, leaving me in nothing but my long-sleeved top.

And then he knelt on the bedspread, pulling my knees apart to crouch between them. Maybe this was some kind of penance, or possibly he was just so grateful I was okay, but there was a reverence in his heavy-lidded eyes I hadn't expected as he lowered his head and licked one gentle stroke at my center.

I arched off the bed, stunned by the immediate clench of my inner muscles. It made me want him more, made me *crazy* with it.

"Yes," I panted, as he licked again and again. He adjusted, getting comfortable in his place between my legs, and sucked at my flesh, pulling moans out of me one minute, and gasps of surprise the next. His fingers joined his tongue, teasing and torturing me until I was calling out his name, begging for more. His wide shoulders urged my legs wider, and he sucked hard, startling me into a screaming release under his attention. Every ache and worry was forgotten, drowned in pleasure.

And then, breathless and boneless, I lay there as he crawled atop me, this powerful, troubled man. I had no intention of leaving. And if finding out his mother was a murderous paranormal creature didn't have me looking for the door, I had faith in our staying power. I opened myself to him with my arms and my mouth and my body, feeling more at home than I ever had before.

CHAPTER TWENTY-SIX

The next few days involved some juggling. In addition to continuously reassuring my father I was fine every few hours when he called, there were also missed assignments from school to coordinate, and my Statistics project with Brendan to finish. I didn't want to go to class with a giant bandage on my shoulder, which would make for some awkward questions I didn't want to answer, so I emailed my professors a copy of my hospital release papers and was able to secure extensions for most of my homework, as well as the pieces I was supposed to have done for the *Weekly Prowl*.

Every spare moment I wasn't working on homework I was focusing on the atrophy of Spindle River's water-based ecosystems and comparing it to the growth of the Santa Elena company. I was sure there was a link there, if only I could find one piece of proof that wasn't redacted or behind some impossible paywall. There were no other companies big enough or close enough to the water to be the culprit.

Brendan buried himself in Shady Tree Lane business, answering my texts but not offering much in terms of conversation, always giving the excuse he was busy with practice for his show at Dio's. I had the feeling he was giving me time to figure out this new dynamic with Jamie, and the finality of our decision to be together, which I appreciated, but it also made me a bit uneasy. I didn't want to lose my relationship with him as a friend. There was no use pushing him on it, I decided. All I could do was accept his boundaries and see where we landed.

Once I'd gone back to the hospital to have my stitches checked and bloodwork done to make sure I hadn't incurred any infection from the "coyote" bite, a sense of relief had me practically floating back home. My cottage was safe from murderous naiads now, and with that realization came a certain amount of bliss. I didn't have to dash from the Buick to my door. I didn't need to clutch pepper spray in my fist when stepping out into my own yard. Hell, I could even leave my patio door open to the fresh, autumn air.

On that Sunday, I sat outside with my afternoon root beer, watching a heron drift lazily through the air only to dart down and catch an unsuspecting minnow in the pond within its beak. I'd ordered two more chairs for the patio, so I could invite Lynne and her roommates over soon, and they'd be here within the week. The idea made me fizz with excitement. This view was definitely worth sharing.

My phone dinged and I looked down. It was the group chat I had started with the Barreto brothers weeks ago.

Jamie: *B and I wanna talk to u about something. OK if we come over?*

Me: *Sure. I'm in the backyard, just come around when you get here.*

Brendan: *You sure that's safe?*

Me: *I mean, she was dying when we left...* I replied, and then cringed at how callous that sounded.

Me: *I just think she's definitely gone now.*

Jamie: *Thats kinda what we wanna talk to u about*

I put my root beer down and scanned the yard around me, that excitement now tinged with apprehension. There was no sign of the naiad's blood any longer. Morning dew and cool breezes seemed to have swept away any trace of her. Birds chirped and sang to each other in the trees to my right, the cattails swayed lazily at the pond, and there were no mysterious creaks at the dock or hisses in the woods. The sun was bright and warm on my shoulders, and the leaves—now a glorious burnt orange and wine-red—were no more frightening now than the autumns I'd experienced in New York or Virginia or anywhere else I'd lived. I truly believed she was now dead, so what could Jamie and Brendan be worried about? Another naiad? Something else?

When the boys arrived, it was their footfalls that announced their approach—the crunch of leaves beneath their shoes. I turned my head and there they were, side by side. I'd never seen them walk shoulder to shoulder before, and their similarities as they moved were eerie. And now I knew why. Their identical height, the way their shoulders moved in tandem, even the slight cock to their head as they saw me was the same—all of it was Jamie's nature as a changeling. He copied his brother without any purposeful attention, and I wondered if any future change Brendan made would be reflected on his false twin, or if they were old enough now to have some differences. Considering the neatly trimmed beard Jamie sported, while Brendan remained clean-faced, I had hope Jamie was now matured enough to be his own person—if that's even how this all worked. It would be a learning curve for all of us.

They both wore dark jeans, and while Brendan was back to his tortured musician roots with a black Henley, which was ripped and frayed at the edges, Jamie wore a white T-shirt under a partially-zipped hoodie.

I could just make out the words "ask" and "about" and I figured it was another goat-esque shirt that gave him an excuse to show off his abs. Not that I was complaining.

"Hey, beautiful," Jamie said with a smile. When he reached me, he leaned down and pressed a soft peck to my lips, but then lingered, a promise of what was to come on the date he was due to take me on in a couple days. I caught the word "ninja" on his shirt as he stepped back up and almost rolled my eyes, holding in a laugh.

"How are you feeling?" Brendan asked, and, though his tone was just as warm and gentle as usual, there was still an obvious distance between us.

"Better," I said. "Ready to go back to class tomorrow."

Jamie puffed up his chest a bit, looking adorable. "And I'll be here to bring you to campus."

"That's not really necessary anymore, is it?" I asked, but then at his down-turned expression I hurried to clarify. "I mean, if you just want the excuse to spend time with me, that's fine, but we're not worried about my trip to and from class anymore."

Jamie rubbed a hand over his hair, and I knew he was about to say something I didn't like. "Are we sure about that, Sadie?"

My eyes widened as I glanced between him and Brendan. "You think she might still be alive? But her body was literally...shriveling. She was turning into dirt. You can't think she's still there." It was a question, but I said it more as a statement, reading the confirmation in the stiff line of their identical mouths.

Brendan took a step back, looking over the backyard and moving his gaze from the pond to the edge of the woods and back again.

"We kind of wanted to check. If you're okay with that."

"What, like, go into the woods?" I stood, my root beer forgotten on the patio floor.

Brendan nodded.

I looked at Jamie. "Are you sure that's a good idea?" I couldn't tell what would be worse for him—finding his mother's body, desiccated and dried out, or not finding anything at all—and either way I wanted to spare him the pain of that.

"I want to know for sure that you're safe," Jamie replied, looking sheepish. He wasn't overprotective—not like how Brendan could be—but I could tell he was uneasy, and that this was important to him. He needed to know it was over. "Even though we're pretty sure she's gone...we also want to know what happened to her. If she's vanished or if...there's a body."

I could tell saying it had cost him something. His hands fisted and loosened at his sides and his shoulders were tight.

"What if it's dangerous for you?" I asked.

The naiad had been sick, and while her ravings made it seem like the dying land was the culprit, it could still be something passed from one being to another. She'd stopped him from coming closer in the cave, to prevent him from catching hold of the disease that was ravaging her. What if being near her body undid that one good deed? What if she'd released something into the air as she'd dissolved, like a poisonous spore?

"That's why I'll be going first," said Brendan. "And if you're up for it...we want you to come with us."

"Of course," I said without thinking. Anything they needed. Before I'd come into their lives, things for them had been almost normal, and though I knew it wasn't my fault they'd been dragged into this supernatural minefield, I had played a part. I needed the closure just as much as they did. I felt safer in this yard now, but *knowing* it, definitively, would be writing the last line to the story I'd been drafting in my head. This dangerous mystery that had held me in its grasp for too long would finally be finished.

They gave me a minute to change into more autumn-worthy clothing—adding a cardigan and heavy boots to my shirt and jeans ensemble—and then we were off.

Brendan and I took the lead, with Jamie following a dozen feet or so behind us in case we came across her body randomly in the woods. We figured she had been in no state to move, but she'd lasted for years in this dying land, and had the foresight to send her child away, so we didn't know how far she might have traveled before meeting her end, given her stamina.

My body started shaking as we walked further into the shade of the forest, and more than once I caught Brendan looking over to me, checking on me.

"If you need to turn back," he said, softly, "we would understand."

I shook my head. "I'm fine. It's just..." I trailed off, not sure how to articulate the strange sensation I had while inching closer and closer to the place I'd been dragged by the naiad. It was something like fear, but also sadness and anxiety and anticipation all in one.

"It's hard," Brendan summarized for me.

"Yeah."

He held a tree branch aside for me as the trail became narrow and then petered out to almost nothing. Already the quiet of the space was seeping into my bones, making me overly aware of every shuffle of leaves caused by an animal scurrying out of our path, and every moan of the trees as the wind picked up above us. The daylight had already started to wane.

I began to recognize the landscape, like it had been unconsciously mapped into my mind, but before we found the cave, we came upon her.

Her body was almost completely deteriorated into the ground, the leaves and grass growing over her soft-looking bones, as if she had been decomposing there for months instead of days. I gasped, standing back, and Brendan placed a reassuring hand on my shoulder.

I held a hand backward toward Jamie, stopping his progress. I didn't want him to see this.

The scraps of linen she'd worn were still discernible on her corpse, identifying her more substantively than her features; beyond the few strands of her dark red hair plastered to her skull and the long claws at her fingers, her flesh had been whittled away. There was no curve to her body, no eyes or lips to view. Something earthy had begun to sprout from her remains, dark green and mottled brown, like moss. I spotted a few mushrooms near her ribcage, growing in long, spindly rows. The land was taking her back, swallowing her into the dirt.

"It's her," Brendan breathed. His voice was astonished, like he couldn't quite believe it.

There was a dark stain on the floor beside her skull, and I wondered if she'd continued to vomit long after we left, my blood poisoning instead of curing her.

A sound like a sigh reached my ears and I turned to see Jamie, just a few feet behind us and off to the side. He could see the lump of her body, I realized, but not any details.

"We should..." Jamie started, and then took a shaking inhale. "Can we bury her?"

I nodded. "Brendan and I will do it." We couldn't be sure her body was safe for him to be near, even in death, and I would do everything in my power to spare him from such an unsure fate.

We stood there for a moment, unsure how to proceed, but eventually headed back to the yard. Brendan had thought to pack a shovel in the trunk of the Civic, taken from their basement, and Jamie's surprise was evident as his brother pulled it from the car and wordlessly started back to the spot where we'd found her.

"I can stay with you, if you'd like," I offered. Jamie hadn't moved from beside the Civic, as if stunned. I didn't blame him. All the questions he might want answered, all the history he'd never know...it would grate on me too. And it wasn't even my own life at stake.

He rubbed a hand over his beard, trying to look casual.

"It's fine," he said. "I'll be here when you get back."

"You're sure?" I felt horrible leaving him behind, as if this was robbing him of the chance to truly say goodbye.

"Just...mark it somehow? So I can come visit her." His eyes were watery when he turned his head away, and I wished he could be there, wished we felt safe enough to let him touch her body. She'd never talked to him, other than ordering him away in that cave, but there was love in that moment. She had protected him, going so far as to give him up to keep him safe. Suddenly, Brendan's protectiveness did not seem so extreme.

"I'll make sure you can find her," I promised.

With that, I darted into the house, grabbing a small gardening trowel I'd spotted in one of the lower kitchen cabinets, and a few other supplies, then rushed to follow Brendan's trail.

He must have been moving slowly, because I caught up with him only a moment later. Paused between two tall cedar trees, with the shovel slung over his shoulder, he watched me approach with a pensiveness that turned his mouth into a firm line.

"What is it?" I asked.

He shook his head. "Nothing, I...I'm just glad he has you right now. Through all this."

"You have me too," I reminded him.

The trees rustled around us, as if pressing us onward, and Brendan used the distraction to turn without responding to me. I let him, hoping he would eventually open up to me once more.

Despite the lack of path, Brendan expertly retraced our steps, with me following only a few feet behind. It was like her body was calling us forward, like a siren's song.

If possible, there were even more mushrooms along her corpse now, though we'd only been gone about thirty minutes. It was as if her flesh was being drawn back into the earth, sucked back into the muck before our very eyes.

"There's not much to bury," muttered Brendan, and I had to agree, but the idea of a grave that Jamie could visit was too important to ignore.

We started digging. I could only deepen the sides and widen the edges with my small trowel while Brendan did most of the work, but the ground was wet and easy to move. I wondered how the river could be so dry, and this area of the forest be so swampy, and made a mental note to focus more on the way a business might redirect water from a particular area, rather than the effects of pollution on water as a whole. My mind spun with possibilities as the grave grew under our hands.

Soon there was a cavernous hole in the ground, big enough for us to shift the naiad's corpse into. It was ungraceful work, both of us wary of touching her with anything but the metal of the shovel heads, but we were finally able to push her into the space we'd carved.

Once she was in the ground and we'd piled damp dirt on top of her, patting it down, I reached into my tote, pulling the rest of my materials free.

My collection of stones.

Jamie wanted an easy way to discern his mother's grave, but we had no tombstone or tree trunks to make a mark in. This seemed the easiest alternative. I reached for the mica and calcite and sandstone, placing each rock with care in a circle near where the naiad's head rested beneath the ground. The sun shifted above our heads, cascading through the heavy branches above to speckle the dirt at our feet with bursts of light. One beam grazed the calcite, making it glow.

I didn't need these reminders anymore. They were tokens of lives past; of places I'd breezed through with ease. But I had no intention of collecting a stone from Spindle River and moving on to another place. This was home now. This was where I belonged—with Jamie and Brendan and this land that needed my help.

"Can I have a minute?" I asked Brendan.

He paused, but then without a word he collected his shovel and headed back the way we'd come, stopping far enough away to give me privacy but near enough to keep me in his sights.

I turned to the grave, my chest tight with sorrow. Not for this creature, this woman who had tried to hurt me—kill me—but rather, for her son.

"I want you to know that I'm going to do everything in my power to keep him safe," I said to the circle of stones on the ground. "I'll find out what did this to Spindle River, what killed you, and I'll make it better. I swear to you, Jamie won't get sick like you did. I'll clean up the forests and the riverbed, I'll make sure the media gets wind of how this town is dying—whatever it takes. I'll make this a good home for him."

And for myself, I almost added, but given her last moments I wasn't sure she would appreciate that.

As I turned, walking away from the grave, I heard the susurration of wind through the trees, and a pattering of leaves falling to the ground like a beleaguered sigh. I imagined the sound was one of relief.

CHAPTER TWENTY-SEVEN

The night we went to Dio's for Shady Tree Lane's show was when I finally got my break in the Spindle River environment case. I felt like a real, intrepid reporter—not just doing quiet research in the library archives or scrolling through redacted reports on my laptop, but asking hard-hitting questions, connecting stories, and organizing the data into a whole, complete story. And it was all because of Jamie.

When we walked into the wine club, I was expecting rich leather sofas under soft pendant lights, and maybe a piano. But it was surprisingly casual, with wooden benches bracketing long tables that had been scuffed and stained from decades of use. The lights were a mismatched set of colored lamp stands with movable arms, like you might see in a college dorm, but they created fun orbs of blue and green light on the brick walls. Rock music from the '80s echoed through the space while Brendan and his band set up on the small stage at the back-right corner, only big enough for all of them to stand side by side. The dance floor in front of the stage was peppered with folding chairs and additional card tables.

Brendan glanced up as we walked in and I waved, grateful some of the awkwardness between our shifting relationships had begun to wane. He nodded, the hint of a smile causing one dimple to appear in the blue-tinted lighting by the stage.

Jamie and I took a seat close to the windows, the neon "Dio's" sign behind us stretching our shadows in pink along the floor.

"Jameson!"

An old man with a messy halo of white hair and ebony-dark skin padded over to us. He leaned one arm against the wooden table and smiled with a set of blindingly bright teeth that had to be dentures, and though he must have been in his seventies, his clothing was bright and youthful; he wore a mocha-colored suit that fit close to his body with a cobalt pocket square edged in gold.

He shook Jamie's hand. "Nice to see you! How's your mother doing?"

"She's doing good, Dio, thanks." Jamie put a comforting arm around my shoulder. "This is Sadie, my girlfriend."

Dio shook my hand as well, and his palm was warm and papery soft beneath my own. I was glad to have worn a nice dress for tonight—sapphire blue with a high neck and lace sleeves down to my wrists that hid the still-healing wounds on my skin. At least I looked presentable, even compared to Dio's impressive fashion sense.

The old man smiled at me. "Gorgeous! Good job, Jameson."

I adjusted my glasses, feeling a bit embarrassed, and was glad the pink sign probably hid my blush. Being presented as his girlfriend in that proud voice was making my heart flutter.

Jamie laughed. "Dio keeps track of everyone around here," he explained to me with a wink. "He knows everybody's secrets, since people love to get drunk here and tell him all their troubles."

"I also know everybody's favorite drink order," added Dio, pointing to Jamie. I noticed he didn't deny any of Jamie's claims. "Rum and coke?"

Jamie nodded.

"And you..." he turned to me with a discerning stare, and before I could open my mouth he said, "root beer?"

I gaped at him and then turned to Jamie. "You told him!"

He held up both hands. "I didn't! It's his superpower."

"Well, with that youthful little face I knew you were probably under-age," Dio said with a low, warm laugh. "It was just a good guess. I'll be right back with those."

He ambled back to the bar on the left side of the room as the sound of Frank pattering away at his drums signaled the show was getting ready to begin. I watched Brendan roll his broad shoulders, which were emphasized by his ripped T-shirt.

"Hey," I said, remembering something, "your brother—this is going to sound weird—but he's just as built as you are. How's that possible? I mean, now that I know it's not part of some..." I glanced around, to make sure no one was listening, and lowered my voice, "fae mimic ability." Jamie was the naiad after all, and not his brother.

"He works out," Jamie said with a wry smile.

I waited for more.

"You'd have to ask him," he added, raising one shoulder, "but I'm pretty sure he exercises in his room when he's stressed. Caught him doing push-ups more than once. Or could just be to look good for his groupies."

I nudged his shoulder with a laugh, taking another look around.

More people were pouring into the wine bar beside us, filling up the benches and chairs with an energy that was almost as raucous as the first Shady Tree Lane performance I'd seen, though I doubted this place would turn into a dance club. Not if all the extra chairs were any indication.

Lynne walked in with Casey at her side and when she spotted me, she not-so-subtly gestured to Jamie and pretended to fan herself. I made a mental reminder to thank her for listening to all my strange boy troubles, possibly even with a decent bottle of wine since I would be old enough to buy it legally in a few weeks. The girls weaved through the tables to find a seat close to the stage. I expected Lynne would soon be making goo-goo eyes at Brendan—she'd told me more than once that the idea of a twin was insanely hot—but the second she saw Frank's tattoo sleeves her attention was firmly locked on the drummer. I grinned to myself at her blatant interest, watching as Frank winked her way and spun his sticks, creating an impressive whirl of wood between his fingers.

"I wonder if other people in this town are secretly supernatural," I mused aloud, turning to watch Dio make our drinks with a flair that was impressive for his age.

"If that was the case, do you think that Fathom Biddies singer was a banshee?" Jamie asked.

I huffed a laugh. "They weren't *that* bad."

"We could ask Dio, he might know," he joked.

"Well...he doesn't know about you. Right?"

Jamie leaned back in his chair, tilting his head in contemplation. "If he did, I'd think he'd serve me something wilder than a rum and coke. But he does seem to have his finger on the pulse of the town. Who knows. He has a long history here—might even be a good source for your story on the river," he suggested.

The idea of someone who had been around for so long, watching the town grow and change around this little wine bar, suddenly seemed like the *perfect* source.

"Good idea," I said, giving him a soft kiss.

When Dio returned with our drinks, I crossed my arms on the wooden table and leaned toward him.

"Excuse me, I know you're busy, but when you have a minute could I ask you a couple questions about Spindle River history?" I asked. "I work for the university paper, the *Weekly Prowl*, and I'd love your take on a couple things."

"Sure thing, young lady, but only if you promise to keep this one in line. He could use some good influence." Dio nodded his head at Jamie, who I swore blushed under the rough stubble along his cheeks. I couldn't help but wonder if Jamie had spilled some secrets to this man after all.

Dio promised to stop by in a bit, so Jamie and I enjoyed our drinks while Shady Tree Lane finished warming up and introduced themselves. I noticed Andrea was a bit more smiley than I remembered; her strawberry-blonde hair was in high pigtails and her eyes were shining as they watched Brendan at the mic.

Brendan nodded to her as they started their first song of the set, a number they called "Alley Cat Strike." Her low, husky voice joined his in harmony while she tapped a high-tempo rhythm on her keyboard. The two of them sounded great together, both swaying their shoulders to the beat while they sang about screwing responsibility, having fun; being young and carefree for one night. I hoped Brendan would take his own words to heart.

Dio returned to our table after a couple songs, his weathered face glowing in the neon light as he sat across from us.

"Alright, what can I do for you, darling?" he asked me.

"I'm looking into the changes the river has gone through, and any potential connection it might have to the Santa Elena company."

"Santa Elena?" He leaned closer, having a hard time hearing me over the music.

I nodded and raised my voice. "It's the only connection I can find. It was right when they moved their shipping business here that the water levels started to recede. The local wildlife station said the water has been warming beyond natural means, but there are no other corporations near the water that I can find who have been in business the whole time."

Dio's bushy, white-tinted eyebrows lowered as he thought. "I don't know much about them, but you should talk to Miranda."

"Who's that?"

The old man turned in his seat and scanned through the crowds, looking for someone. "There she is," I heard him say.

Jamie and I exchanged a look, confused as Dio left his seat to approach a woman closer to the stage.

They were too far for me to hear their conversation, but then he was bringing her over. She looked to be in her late forties, with faded blonde hair and a brusque demeanor as she reluctantly followed him. Her expression was one of distrust as Dio gestured to us.

"Miranda, this is Jamie, one of Mia Barreto's boys. And this is Sadie, she writes for the SRU paper. Miranda worked for Santa Elena for how many years?"

"Too many," she answered, looking wary.

"Exactly. She can tell you about them if you like."

"Oh." I was taken aback, suddenly worried this woman was about to report me to some sketchy Santa Elena official for getting involved where I didn't belong. Would my investigation be over before it ever really began?

I cleared my throat. "That would be great, thanks."

"You looking for a job there?" Miranda asked, crossing her arms over her chest. "If so, I'd advise against it."

"No, nothing like that. I'm just doing a little digging about what chemicals they use..." I paused, unsure if I should continue, and then felt Jamie's hand move to my lower back, his thumb stroking in an encouraging circle. "I'm wondering if anything might have made its way into the river."

Dio motioned for Miranda to sit, and though I felt bad for making her miss some of the Shady Tree Lane set, this was my first actual Santa Elena source, and I couldn't let her get away. Ever since Ronald had mentioned the company, I couldn't get it out of my head that they were the most likely cause, but a hunch meant nothing without credible sources.

She didn't seem to mind though, and her wary expression turned more toward intrigue. I had the feeling there was no love lost between her and the company, and she was eager to air their dirty laundry if she could.

"S.E. doesn't use many chemicals," Miranda said, and then tilted her head as if trying to dredge up old memories. "They mostly organize and ship on behalf of other organizations. We never had a big spill or anything...though I guess the cleaning solutions we used on the metal went into drains."

"What kind of cleaning solutions?" I asked, taking out my phone to type notes.

She shrugged. "Nothing crazy, I don't think. Sodium-something, since it doesn't corrode the steel. The belts and conveyors are all metal, and we did a lot of work for meat shippers and laboratories in New York, so we would wash down all the steel with the stuff. Maybe…once or twice a week? I wasn't in charge of it, thankfully."

"Anything else you can remember? Was the stuff ever dumped outside or down drains?"

I was already typing "sodium" into Google, trying to determine what chemical was used.

"There were drains in the floor," she said. "But I don't know where they led. I only worked the floor for a couple years, and all I know is the guys who cleaned had to wear gloves."

She paused. "My friend Sam still works there. I can ask him for details on those chemicals if you want?"

"That would be amazing," I told her, my face sore from the wide grin pushing at my cheeks. I gave her my number and watched her put it in her phone.

She waited then, as if to be dismissed, just as the band finished up a slow, somber number.

"You've been really helpful," I said. "Thanks for your time. Do I have permission to quote you?"

"Am I getting a free drink for this?" she asked Dio, who'd remained close by.

He laughed, shifting out of her way as she stood to go. "One free glass of pinot gris, coming right up."

"Then okay, you can quote me," she answered.

I almost shimmied with glee in my seat.

After they left, Jamie watched over my shoulder as I continued to research. "You're going to miss the whole show," he teased, close to my ear. He pressed a kiss to my cheek, his nose brushing at the skin there. It gave me goosebumps.

Brendan started up another song then, one I recognized: "Smoke Signal."

I looked up, afraid he would be staring at me with those soulful eyes, intense and all-seeing, like he had that night at Caisse's, but his eyes were closed, his body inching back from the mic. I could see Andrea watching him with a tender expression. The memory of her cornering me and grabbing my arm flashed to the surface and I wondered if—given some time—she'd finally share her feelings with him. I'd like that for him, when he was ready. He deserved someone who thought the world of him and was willing to protect him. Someone who would never compare him to his brother. It was obvious she only had eyes for him.

"I'm watching," I said with a smile.

Jamie took me home from Dio's after the band was done performing, and I spent the entire car ride going over everything Miranda had said, and all the research I'd done on Spindle River and the surrounding lands. How it was becoming boggy in some places and dry in others. I could tell I was *so close* to a big reveal. If only I knew the specific chemicals they were dumping, I could prove it.

I worried Jamie might be annoyed by my babbling, but he had this amused grin on his face the entire drive, like he found my excitement adorable.

"Promise me you'll get *some* sleep," he said, as he pulled the Civic into my driveway.

"The news sleeps for no one," I responded, giving him a quick peck on the lips, ready to dash. "I need to research what this sodium cleaner might be."

"Hey," he whined, and I grinned, easing back into the car to give him one longer, lingering kiss.

He put one calloused hand on my neck, holding me close, and his tongue stroked over my lips, seeking entrance I couldn't deny.

I groaned after a few persistent, toe-curling kisses. "Stop it." Breathing against his mouth, I relished the coffee scent of him that somehow still lingered on his skin, familiar and exciting and addicting all at once. "I have evil to expose and rivers to save."

Jamie released me with a chuckle. "Always showing up the rest of us."

I waved to him over my shoulder, and he waited until I was safely inside before driving away.

It was time to put everything together.

CHAPTER TWENTY-EIGHT

Miranda called me the next morning, while I was finishing up my timeline of Santa Elena's warehouse construction. It was perfect timing—I'd gone through lists of industrial cleaners and how they might impact water temperatures, solubility, and ability to sustain life, and once I had confirmation from her, I had a feeling that everything was going to fall into place.

The sound of my phone ringing had my heart rate doubling, and I was close to trembling as I answered.

"Hey, Miranda!"

"Sadie? Hi. I just got those chemical listings from my old co-worker," she said, all business. "He said he doesn't want his name used in the article, but he works weekends and took a picture of one of the bottles this morning and sent it to me. Can you use that?"

"That's perfect!" I squealed.

Miranda drew in a loud breath, as if exasperated by my enthusiasm, but then I heard the chime of the photo coming through.

"Thanks again," I said, eager to end the call.

"Don't mention it." She paused. "Literally."

While I could tell Miranda and I would not hit it off as fast friends—that I didn't have that *spark* with her—I would still be thanking her in my memoirs for this incredible lead. She was a godsend.

The photo was crooked and a bit dark, but after some editing, I was able to transcribe all the chemicals present in the cleaner, and one of them caught my eye.

Sodium hydroxide was listed near the top as a main component. That had shown up in my research last night. I scrolled through my notes, trying to remember why that tugged at something in the recesses of my mind.

"Typical household cleaner," I muttered, reading through the endless doc where I'd been keeping my notes. "An inorganic compound, also known as lye..." I stopped. Lye.

Opening a new window, I typed "lye and water" into the search window, and the first thing to pop up was a video of a science experiment combining the two. I watched it, my fingers shaking over the keyboard with a mix of excitement and astonishment.

"Holy shit."

After a day at my computer, and about a hundred links later, I had the basis for a very convincing argument that Santa Elena, while only a shipping company and not directly producing chemical waste, was improperly disposing of their cleaning chemicals, which included sodium hydroxide.

Though commonly used in dyes, soaps, and petroleum products, when combined with water (such as being drained into waste systems that eventually lead into public rivers), it releases hydrogen gas and intense heat. While it appeared little of the chemical was actually making it to the river when their employees cleaned, it was clear it happened often enough that the subtle effects had begun compounding, burning through the aquatic life and leading to faster evaporation. This, in turn, was what caused the lowering water levels, which would only continue to worsen without intervention. It was also likely the reason water was seeping through now-porous hard ground and making its own warm, subterranean tunnels into tree-heavy areas, creating boggy marshes among the roots. Basically, the sodium hydroxide was dissolving the very foundations of the town.

At least, that was my working theory. I already had plans to call Ronald to guide me back into the forest along the river, so I might collect a sample close to the facilities. Then I'd bring it to Professor Jackson in the SRU Molecular Biology department to have it tested for traces of the substance. His profile on the university website spoke of his philanthropic work in the Philippines, and I hoped he'd be willing to sacrifice some personal time to run the tests. Sodium hydroxide wouldn't be a typical chemical that nature preservationists would think to test for, but since I had evidence that it was most likely involved, the examination would be quick, and the search for the culprit would become paramount.

If I was lucky, this story would break open in the best possible way and be picked up for a bigger publication before I had to get formal industries like MassDEP involved. That would keep things moving quickly.

And here I was, having hoped not to uncover any scandals in a rural college town. So much for that.

Either way, no matter the backlash, I wouldn't be leaving.

It was early morning the next day when I finished all my work and sent the draft to Kim and Professor Lewis so they would know how much space to allocate for printing once I had the definitive proof. I yawned, stretching my arms above my head to roll out the knots in my shoulders.

My phone chimed.

Jamie: *I kno its early but if I wanted to go to the grave...would u come with me?*

Now that the naiad was buried and it was safer for him to be around the corpse of his mother, I wasn't surprised he was eager to do so. He'd never really gotten a chance to meet her, and I couldn't imagine how unsettling or...*unfinished* that might leave a person feeling.

Me: *Of course.*

Me: *Plus, I have some exciting news.*

Jamie: *Be there soon*

I was exhausted, but there was still a buzz of energy beneath my skin as I freshened up and wrangling my hair into a bun.

When Jamie showed up carrying an insulated coffee cup, the morning sun haloed his ruffled brown hair, making him shine. He was back in that blue hoodie I'd first met him in, promoting what I could now see was Shady Tree Lane in a very ugly font, and dark jeans that hugged his muscular legs. They made him look strong and powerful, and as I took the cup from him and accepted a kiss, I thought I might just have the energy to climb him if he let me.

I took a sip of the drink as he came inside, closing the door behind him.

"Vanilla latte," I said, sighing in pleasure.

"You sure you're up for this? No offense, but you look a little tired."

I scoffed. "Offense taken. I'm radiant."

"You can be radiant *and* tired," he said, grinning wickedly, "but I guess I'll just carry you."

"Wha—" Before I could finish that question he bent and plucked me off the ground with the ease of picking a flower, one arm under my knees and the other at my back. His laugh was low as I squeaked.

"Is this really necessary?" I asked.

"Sip your latte," he ordered, though his lips were still ticked into a crooked smile.

I did as he said, very much planning some revenge climbing when we were back.

After some awkward fumbling at the patio doors and a few minutes in his capable arms, I finally wriggled my way back onto my feet just as we reached the edge of the forest. Jamie let me lead him through the uneven path, though I had the feeling he knew every step.

When I stopped in front of the grave, the circle of stones unmoved, Jamie's presence beside me became a tangible sensation, as if he was radiating something besides body heat.

"Can I...is it ok if I have a minute?" he asked. His voice was rough.

I nodded, giving his hand a squeeze before I backed away, just as Brendan had done for me. Giving him some privacy, I made sure to be far enough away not to hear him speaking. If it was some tearful goodbye or some damning critique, I'd never know. And that was okay with me. He had a right to whatever complicated emotions plagued him, and all I could do was be here when he was done.

I heard the call of some songbird in the trees and wondered if, once Santa Elena was exposed and actions were taken to improve the river, more wildlife would return to these woods. Maybe my backyard would soon be full of waterfowl drifting over from the esplanade. Maybe the grounds here would become dry enough for camping. I could imagine Jamie and I holed up in a nylon tent, basking in the sounds of crickets chirping and frogs croaking as we enjoyed a warm spring night.

Jamie straightened and turned from the grave after a few minutes, trudging back to me on wooden legs.

"You okay?" I asked.

He nodded, but I could see his fists clenched at his sides. The way he walked, shoulders stiff and face low, told me more about how he was feeling than he would probably let on.

"Hey," I took his hand as he got closer. I could see the anguish in his eyes, the sorrow at never really getting to know the woman who had birthed him, and the pain of never getting to learn more about who and what he was. "Whatever it is, whatever all this means, we'll figure it out," I told him. "I'm not going anywhere. And I have your name, locked up tight in here, just in case." Pointing to my temple with my free hand, I gave him a soft smile, which he attempted to return.

"I'm glad to hear it." His hand squeezed mine tighter, and then he sighed. "Sometimes I think it's insane how much things have changed since you bumped into me."

That moment was ingrained in my memory, sharp and clear as a photograph—the rainy morning in the hallway, the wink he aimed at me over his shoulder, the way my heart grew heavy in my chest.

"I'm sorry it couldn't all be good changes," I admitted after a moment.

He pulled me closer, the woods growing quiet around us. Or maybe it was that my entire focus narrowed, until all I knew was the strength of his body against me and the way those hazel eyes gazed into my own.

"I can handle it," he said, "knowing I have you to research my way out of trouble." And there was that smirk, that mischievous tilt I adored. Those dimples.

My arms tightened around his waist, holding us together. "I'm going to need that research to help you score the best professional hockey contract, aren't I?"

"I've always wanted a sexy agent representing me," he replied.

"Well, lucky you. And no matter where you travel, there will always be stories for me to tell. Investigations for me to solve." I licked my lips, bravery and hope filling my chest. "But this will always be home for me. With you."

He gasped in a small breath, as if stunned, and then he leaned down and kissed me. His lips were gentle and sweet on my own. I breathed him deep, my fingers clutching at the worn sweatshirt material beneath my hands. In his touch I could feel how elated he was at the idea of us moving into the future together, of making plans and keeping me close. I'd never felt so connected to another person in my entire life, and I meant every word. I even planned on buying some throw pillows, and furnishing my apartment with books and art. Thankfully, I already had an eclectic array of candles.

Jamie tilted his head, his mouth growing hotter, and my entire body started to tingle. Feeling dizzy with desire, and maybe a little fatigue, I pulled back.

"Too tired for research now, though," I murmured, holding back a yawn.

"Want me to carry you back?"

I nodded, grinning as he lifted me in one deep swing. A yelp escaped me as he settled me back into his arms.

"Let's get you home," Jamie said against my hair, pressing one last kiss onto my temple. I smiled, feeling sleepy and loved.

Home. It sounded so nice, in his voice. So inviting.

Home for me had changed hands as often as a card game, but I was stubborn, and this is what I had decided. For the first time, I knew where I belonged; I wasn't going anywhere, and neither was he—not if I had anything to say about it.

We would build and protect this home around us, the land he had been born from, and we would do so *together*.

THANK YOU
FOR READING!

If you enjoyed *The Autumn Effect*, please use the QR code below to leave a review – every comment counts!

And follow me on social media!

CassandraMortimer.com

and TikTok/Insta @cassandramortimerlit

ACKNOWLEDGEMENTS

Writing this acknowledgements page is hard. Part of me wants to be like Snoop Dog (or whatever his current name is) and thank myself, because publishing...is rough. I've written over ten manuscripts, sent a handful out on query, and received literally hundreds of rejections; no me gusta. The writing part is what I've always loved—the only thing I do where I don't feel like I should be doing something else—but publishing isn't writing. It's money, project management, research, design, marketing, and more. This is my first self-publishing pancake, and I wanted it to come out great, but it was a learning curve, and I'm sure I could have done some things better. Still, thanks to me for trying, again and again, to finally get one of my finished manuscripts in print, with a little ISBN and everything.

But of course, publishing means leaning on others, so I do have real people to thank: Danielle for her incalculable advice, expertise, and love of espresso martinis; my critique group who read this (and many other pieces) fresh out of the NaNoWriMo oven—Joe, Claire, Emily, Bethany, and David; my friends, who gave me their thoughts (always with the gentlest of touches) and encouraged me when I didn't think I was good enough—Chad (did you like that I named a restaurant after you?), Kat, Kaitlyn, Kelsi, Kelcey, Courtney, and Sarah—who not only championed and copyedited this ms like a fiend, but also graciously listened to me bemoan anything and everything while doing it; and Sophie, for adding another layer of polish to really make this story shine. A huge thanks to my mom, who put me through an expensive education so I could learn how to write words good, and hugged me every time the rejections stung a little too much. And finally, to my husband, who not only served as a rubber duck and sounding board, but also ordered me cookies when I was stressed, and reddited the hell out of various publishing processes so I wouldn't be going in blind. You're all so incredible, and this book wouldn't exist without you.

Here's hoping the next pancake is even more delicious.

Cassandra is a romance-obsessed individual with the memory of a goldfish and the purse of an eighty-year-old-woman. She once tricked her teenage crush into being her boyfriend, and then in true rom-com style, he married her. The two of them now live happily ever after near Boston, MA with their cat Pumpernickel and some very-packed bookshelves.

She graduated from Emerson College with a BFA in Writing, Literature, and Publishing (with a couple of very strange minors), and her short stories have been published in *Big Bad: An Anthology of Evil*, *Inwood Indiana Press*, "Rotten Leaves Magazine," and "the Emerson Review."